POWER UNDER PRESSURE

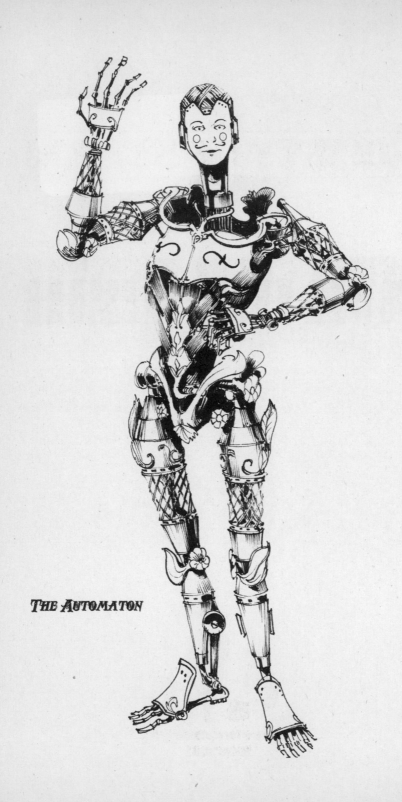

THE AUTOMATON

The
SOCIETY OF STEAM

BOOK THREE

POWER UNDER PRESSURE

ANDREW P. MAYER

an imprint of Prometheus Books
Amherst, NY

Published 2013 by Pyr®, an imprint of Prometheus Books

Cover illustration © Justin Gerard
Interior illustration by Nicholas Stohlman © Andrew P. Mayer
Cover design by Nicole Sommer-Lecht

Inquiries should be addressed to
Pyr
59 John Glenn Drive
Amherst, New York 14228-2119
VOICE: 716-691-0133 • FAX: 716-691-0137
WWW.PYRSF.COM

17 16 15 14 13 • 5 4 3 2 1

Library of Congress Cataloging-in-Publication Data

Mayer, Andrew P.
    Power under pressure : a novel / by Andrew P. Mayer.
        p. cm. — (The society of steam ; bk. 3)
    ISBN 978-1-61614-696-2 (pbk.)
    ISBN 978-1-61614-697-9 (ebook)
    1. Steampunk fiction. I. Title.

PS3613.A9548P69 2013
813'.6—dc23

                                                                    2012036324

Printed in the United States of America

For Jack Kirby,
who unleashed the Power Cosmic, and made heroes of us all

Contents

Chapter 1
Spiritus Sanctus

Emilio Armando pushed back his hat and mopped the sweat from his brow. While his workshop was a perfect place to work in the winter months, the change of seasons had transformed his beloved space into a sweatbox. May had been relatively gentle, but now the last vestiges of spring were disappearing and the sun was rising earlier and higher day by day, beating down longer on the wooden and iron train car that contained his steam-powered machines. Without some modifications, he'd be completely unable to work in the studio by day, and would instead be relegated to spending only the nights inside.

Hidden and gathering dust in a nearby cupboard drawer were the extensive plans he had put together to allow him to regulate the temperature all year round—with the obvious exception of the infernal temperatures that often arrived in late July and August. Any day when the mercury topped the 100-degree mark, the heat would be impossible to escape from.

And the arrival of a steam engine and other materials that he had liberated from the Theater Mechanique after the tragedy only added to the problem, although the main boiler was being kept outside. It would ultimately power an array of vents and fans that might allow him to work in an environment where the bulk of his day wasn't spent wringing out his handkerchief. So far, that hadn't happened.

Ever since he'd first seen Vincent's workshop out in the garden behind the theater, Emilio had harbored a secret dream of converting his own workplace into one of equal grandeur. Of course, he would have never imagined that it would be possible for him to afford the equipment. But, it had turned out that owning a junkyard had allowed him to gather up almost all the valuable material from the condemned building as scrap. Even the cost of hauling it back on the ferry had been such that he had been forced to sell some of it to simply pay for the transport costs.

Still, he was now in possession of not only a massively powerful steam engine, but lathes and drills that he could once have only dreamed of. And yet all the new equipment had left his once-perfect little workshop a shambles, and getting it back together was a project in itself. Like the old tale of the Monkey's Paw, having all your dreams come true was turning out to be far more of a curse than a blessing. The fact that it had all arisen from the same tragedy that had disfigured his sister only made the irony sharper. There had been such a cost in blood—the price paid by both Vincent and his sister.

Emilio squinted and shook his head with a single violent nod as he tried to break the connection between these machines and Viola's scarred face. It had been weeks since the accident, but when he closed his eyes he could still see her the way that she had been when the wounds had been fresh: the huge gashes in her flesh, like a piece of meat from the butcher. But finding some good in the bad did not make him a monster.

Letting out a sound that landed perfectly between a grunt and a sigh, he sat himself back down at his workbench and picked up one of the metal rings he had machined the previous night. He dropped it down over a set of metal pins sticking up from the object strapped to the table in front of him. There was no mistaking that it had been designed as a long metal limb, and the metal collar had been put into position where a human might have a shoulder.

It was a tight fit, but he had been very precise with his measurements, and with the application of a little oil he managed to shuffle it back and forth until it set firmly in place against the armature. When he was sure it was fully down he gave the ring another turn, looking to find where the catch was supposed to lock into the ring, and instead it slipped free.

"Dammit!" he said, surprising even himself with his choice to say the word in English. Frustrated by his stupidity, Emilio tried to wrestle the metal into place. When that didn't work, he pulled his hands away and let out a grunt.

He let out another, and then a third, before he finally pounded the palm of his hand against his forehead.

After a moment he took a deep breath and tried again to seat the ring. Taking more care this time, he finally found the catch and locked it into place. Reaching and taking another ring, he placed a second circlet on the outside. It caught the flanged edge of the inner circle. The steel armature gave a satisfying creak as it all pulled into place, the thread biting deeper and deeper into the brass plate with every turn. When he was done, Emilio gave the interior elements a spin, making sure that they hadn't pulled everything together so tightly that it could no longer move freely. Once he was sure that it was working properly, he strapped the entire armature into a brace on the side of the table using a few lengths of leather and some iron eyelets that had been built just for that purpose.

He took a moment to dab away more of the sweat from his eyes. As he let them close, his mind's eye resolved the other indelible image from that evening: the cold look he had seen in Sarah's eyes when she had been helping him with her sister. She had done all the right things, but there was something in her that had seemed less concerned with the human carnage, and more focused on revenge.

It was only later that she had told him that she had just discovered her father had died as well. He had been aware of the ability of New Yorkers to stuff down their passions, but until he'd seen it for himself it had seemed impossible that someone could go through so much suffering and barely shed a tear. There was a great deal of rage under the calm exterior, and it would have to come out eventually. Perhaps that's what it took to be a hero, but if it was, he didn't like it at all.

Grabbing some wire from a spool, Emilio threaded the metal through a small eyelet that he had drilled into one of the exposed pins. He wound it a few more times and then gave it a hard tug to make sure that it wouldn't pull free, then snipped it with a pair of pliers. Next he threaded it through a brass knurl at the elbow, and finished it off at the brass bolt at the wrist. Once that was done, he started back up the limb, reversing the weave and wrapping it back around the post exactly five times. He finished it off by placing a metal cap over the pin and tapped it down gently with a wooden mallet. He gave the wire a tug, and then let it go. It responded with a single musical note.

"Hmm." Emilio stared at his handiwork for a few more seconds. "The best I can do," he said as he rolled his eyes. He pulled out more wire, winding it into place with exactly the same movements as the first.

He did this six more times until the main bolt had been completely surrounded by the taut wires that spread out through it. As he ran his fingers across the strings, they all let out the same note. He had been working the entire day, and now late into the night, but it had been worth the effort.

The idea to use wire as a replacement for muscle had come to him when someone had brought a load of the fine-quality metal string to him at the junkyard. The distinctive script of the word *Steinway* had been burned into the top and bottom of the wooden spools. His English might have been limited, but Emilio didn't need to know how to read English to recognize the famous name. The world-famous piano factory was in Queens—only a few miles away—and it wasn't hard to imagine that the load had been "liberated" from a truck just before it made its way into the factory. Emilio had purchased it from a fellow named Willy. The man had owed him a favor ever since he'd constructed a metal replacement for his missing left leg, and told him that he might be able to make something better if he could get his hands on some high-quality steel string. The man had been very excited about having an even better model made for him from his ill-gotten gains.

Emilio frowned at the thought. Life came with more compromises than he cared to admit. He looked down at the arm in front of him. He was creating something that he would be proud of, but the Automaton he had met at the theater had been a monster. While it had intended to save Sarah, the machine had been more than willing to crush any other creature of flesh and bone that got in its way.

For weeks afterwards the newspaper headlines were filled with lurid stories of sightings of the mechanical man popping up all over New York. "The Mad Machine" had been given the blame for everything from murder and witchcraft to rape and impregnation—as highly unlikely as the possibility of *that* might have seemed. And the Automaton's innocence was guaranteed: Tom's metal heart had sat inert in a box in the corner of the room since that day, the Alpha Element removed and held safely around Sarah's neck.

The other bit of nonsense that the newspapers seemed to be unable to stop discussing was the possibility that Tom might have also been responsible for the damage to the Hall of Paragons and Alexander Stanton's murder. It was a theory that the Paragons' new leader, King Jupiter, had only been too happy to support, giving the reporters long quotes of how the Paragons had bravely driven the creature off when it had tried to somehow bond with the very structure of the building. It was a lie that served Lord Eschaton very well.

All the lurid headlines and ridiculous stories had driven Sarah to the brink of madness, although lately it seemed that her grief had begun to subside. Perhaps there was some power in denial, but her wounded feelings seemed to have left behind the same kind of ragged scars on her soul that had appeared on his sister's face. Both of the women in his life were forever altered.

It also seemed that since the incident Sarah's passions for him had cooled as well. He knew that she had lost so much, but after the events in the theater he had been determined to be there for her in whatever capacity she had desired. But despite his honorable intentions, when it turned out that she wanted nothing more than a protector and friend, he had discovered he was disappointed. The truth was that he wanted to be more, and having her so close, and yet no longer willing even to touch him, was both perplexing and frustrating. In his place she seemed to have instead developed a taste for vermouth, and she was no longer interested in the kisses that had followed it the first time she had drunk it.

Emilio tightened the straps, pinning the arm even more firmly into its vise, and then picked up the spanner again. There had been a time, not so long ago, when his attention to his work would have been so absolute that he would have been unable to hear a hammer blow, let alone the quiet whimper from the back of the room that distracted his attention. But his legendary concentration—like so many other things, seemed to have been left behind in the shattered rubble of the Theater Mechanique. "You can come out, Viola. I know you're there."

There was a moment of silence, broken by a quiet swear in a woman's voice. "I know you know," she said angrily. As she came out from hiding, Viola avoided the lights that blazed down from ceiling. Her face was almost invisible behind the dark cloak of shadows and hair. "I don't care. I just want to watch you work."

Emilio turned and sighed. "I can't concentrate when you're in the room."

"Why not? You never had a problem before."

Even if she was no longer quite the hellion she had once been, Emilio knew her well enough to recognize that her deeper nature was unchanged: Viola had always been a woman of strong desire, it was simply that her wants were deeper and darker than they had ever been before, and the anger that had once been directed at the world had turned inward. He could tell that she wanted *something*, but he could just no longer discern what it was. "Because things aren't the same as they were before, Viola. You know that."

His sister crept out from the darkness, and the arc light above his workbench illuminated the ruin of her face. Her fiery curls were straight and mousy brown, dirty from lack of washing. She had always been a woman of contrasts; smiles had risen and fallen across her features like a storm, each grin or smirk as much a threat as a reaction. Now the disparities were no longer simply a reflection of her inner emotions, but a permanent mask.

Sarah's doctor was clearly a talented man—he had done the best he could under the circumstances. But even with the surgeon's fine handiwork, the scars had pulled her lip up into a permanent sneer. Emilio had wanted to pretend that there was no irony to it, but the truth of it was that the damage had gone straight down to the ugliest part of Viola's soul and forced her to wear it as her face.

She turned and stepped over to the frame where the completed portions of Tom's new body had been bolted together in anticipation of his return to life. Viola caressed the brass and steel. His legs were done, but the arms were not attached and the head was only half-finished. Emilio had almost finished one arm, and its mirror twin would be done much more quickly. The Automaton's new body would be ready in a matter of days.

He had never seen Tom's original frame up close, although Sarah had described it to Emilio as best she could. From what he had seen and studied of Darby's work, the professor's machines had always been dependable and solid—devices designed to be long-lasting and bulletproof. That kind of stolid, reliable craftsmanship was a trademark of the old man, and Emilio would have tried to emulate it if he thought he could, but he was far more fascinated by creating things of beauty than sacrificing it for reliability.

And with no blueprints to work from except for the words he had dis-

covered etched into Tom's heart, Emilio had gone in a different direction—
one that expressed his own sensibilities. Inspired by Tom's previous appearance in the orchestra pit, he had given the new body the shape of an instrument, with the inner workings exposed and the structure of his body riddled
with rococo swirls that harkened back to the art of Emilio's ancestors in Italy.
It was more of a framework than the whole of a man, a handsome skeleton on
which Tom could, once he had returned to an animated existence, rebuild in
any way he chose.

Viola looked through the empty hole in the front of his head. For an
instant she began to frown, then winced from some pain the expression
caused her twisted features. She dropped back to a neutral expression. "You
haven't made him a face yet."

Emilio nodded. "Sarah wants a porcelain face, like the one he used to
wear. I'm having Alfonso make it."

As Viola contemplated his answer she ran her hands up a series of thicker
wires that rose up through a gimbal in Tom's neck, the twisted strings
sprouting out like a fountain of metal through the center, each one strung into
a separate slot around the circumference of his metal skull. The crown had been
bolted into the head through the center, locking the wires into place.

Emilio considered asking his sister to stop fondling the Automaton's lifeless body, but decided he didn't need to hear the argument she would make
defending her actions.

When she finally did speak Viola's tone of contempt punctuated the deri-
sion in her words, "Alfonso? That Venetian pig?" Ever since the incident
there was no one who was spared her wrath, but those she had known and
loved were always the fiercest targets of Viola's anger.

"He's a fine artist."

"He's a dog with paint-covered paws." She refused to look at Emilio
while she talked to him, instead choosing to concentrate on the details of the
new body that her brother was creating. "The only reason his art makes him
any money is he hires the models with the biggest chests he can find."

Emilio wanted to point out that his sister had once been one of those
models, and that any dog who could draw a decent picture of a woman with
a good-sized bust would find plenty of people who would gladly pay to see

it, no matter the shape of the hands that drew it. Instead he held his words. His sister's barbed tongue was sharper than it had ever been before, and he had no desire to be sliced apart by it yet again. "As you say, sister."

Her head tilted toward him, the anger clearly visible even in her half-formed expression. "I do say. Tell her to find someone else." She was also clearly eager to fight.

"Maybe you should tell Sarah that yourself."

"I will."

Emilio fought back an urge to laugh out loud. Sarah and his sister had hardly been on the best terms before the accident. Now neither woman seemed able to stand in the same room with the other for more than a few minutes without one of them doing or saying something that would send the other storming out the nearest door.

At least in Sarah's face he saw a dash of pity behind her anger. Although she seemed obsessed with determining how to battle the man who had murdered her father and Darby, she had some thought to the consequences of her actions. She still blamed herself for what had happened to Viola at the theater, and he hoped that Sarah had the good sense to see that revenge would only lead to greater sadness.

His sister, on the other hand, could not hide her almost-limitless contempt for everything she hated. Emilio supposed that to some degree she was of a mind with Sarah when it came to taking revenge on the Children of Eschaton, and their leader. But her anger was hardly limited to "justice" against him. Since the moment that Sarah Stanton girl had entered their life, it was his Voila who had paid the greatest price for their transgressions amongst the Paragons. He had tried to point out the risks she would take if she tried to involve herself even more deeply in the affairs of these gentlemen adventurers.

The Italian girl reached her hand through the empty face and began to pluck the wires inside Tom's head. The taut strings gave out a series of musical plinks. "We should give him a new face—something made of metal. *Una fronte infrangibile.*"

Resisting the urge to make her stop attacking his creation, Emilio let her continue to strum the wires and took the opportunity to look more closely at

Viola's damaged face. The wounds had healed cleanly, the scars pink and tight across her skin. It was as if the explosion had left behind a permanent impression in her flesh—a single instant of violence that would remain a part of her for the rest of her days. It was a tragedy, and yet everyone had agreed that her recovery was miraculous given the damage.

Viola flicked her eyes toward him, catching him in his fascination. Emilio looked away, but it was already too late. She swept back a curtain of limp hair to reveal her face more clearly. "Do you want to see more, brother? I'd be glad to show you."

"No," he said. He could feel his face flushing red, and turned his attention back to the arm. He locked the cap in place, and after giving each one of the strings a pull to make sure they were taut, he began to free up the straps.

"Are you sure? I want you to see what you've done to me."

He looked up at Viola with shock. What was it she had just said? "I didn't . . ." Did she really believe it was his fault?

She stared at him, unblinking and emotionless. It felt like an inquisition, and Emilio wanted to protest. And beyond his anger he wanted to reach out and offer his sister comfort, but she had never been that kind of a girl. Even if a part of her wanted affection, another part of her would judge him as weak for offering it. With Viola it was never possible to give her love until she asked for it, and right now it seemed she was only capable of giving and receiving pain. "You're distracting me, Viola. I need to finish this."

Viola nodded absentmindedly, ignoring his request. She dropped her hands down, letting her fingers stroke the machine's metal ribs. "Do you think he'll really come back?"

She reached into the chest cavity and ran the edge of her index finger around the empty space where his heart would go. A series of small gears hung in the empty air, waiting for the engine that would give them life. "Maybe he doesn't want to come back. Maybe he's had enough of a world filled with nothing but violence and hatred for a metal man." She let out a sharp laugh. "Let's rename him, brother—*L'Abominio*. What do you think?"

Before Sarah had started ignoring her, Viola had been constantly pointing out that the Automaton was gone when they needed him the most.

He knew that Viola must, on some level, blame Tom for what had happened to her, even if he was only the catalyst and not the bomb itself.

But Emilio had promised Sarah that he would help bring the metal man back. And, although it was hard to admit, it had been his failure to be able to repair the creature's heart properly that had forced him to bring it to Vincent, and that act had ultimately put them all in danger. This time he had the tools he needed, and he would do it right. "He'll come back, and I'm letting Sarah choose his face."

"Really?" She let out a short mocking laugh. "Doesn't the metal man get a say?"

Emilio nodded. "I suppose so, but he has to come back and say it."

After they had returned to the junkyard, they had tried placing him into a number of different machines, hoping to re-create the miracle of his rebirth. Sarah had hoped that simply having the Alpha Element would bring Tom back to life. But even with that it seemed that more was needed. Until they could figure out what it was, the Automaton would not return.

Emilio believed that although the Automaton was capable of transforming himself, in order to return to life the mechanical man needed to be given a familiar form to inhabit. Sarah was dubious that Tom was so bonded to the human form that he would be unable to return to life without it, but having no better theories to offer, she agreed that Emilio should construct a new body in the hopes that placing Tom's heart into the form of a man might convince him to return.

But whatever it was that had re-ignited the Automaton backstage at the theater, so far they had failed to re-create the conditions needed, and Emilio was beginning to doubt that this new body would be any better.

Viola's hands still played with the frame. "Can you talk to Alfonso for me, brother? I want a new face too." He knew she was testing him, trying to get him angry at her so they could have a reason to fight.

"If that's what you want."

"You've seen my face. Why *wouldn't* I want a new one?" She stopped playing with the Automaton's body and stepped around it to get closer to her brother. "Can I pick what I'm to look like, or are you going to let Sarah choose that too?" She began to laugh. The sound of it was low and mean, tinged with what Emilio was beginning to suspect might be a permanent touch of madness, although she clearly knew the pain that her words were causing him. "She's so good at getting you to do whatever she wants."

It was hard to tell whether the redness he could feel spreading across his face was the result of shame or anger. The two were so thoroughly mixed together that they felt like a single emotion. "If you really want a metal face, I'll build you one." Was she being serious, or would she mock him for offering?

"You would do that for me, wouldn't you?" She looked up at him and caught his eyes. For a moment he saw a flash of her old playful spirit sparkling within them. "I want my new face to be steel, and I want it to be covered in flowers." It faded away an instant later.

Emilio sighed. "You are my sister. I would do anything to make you whole again." He flexed the limb a few times, testing the gimbal he had created for it to move with. "I love you, Viola."

There was no reply. "Viola?" he said as he turned to look for her, but the girl had disappeared. Perhaps she was getting better, but he worried that she was healing like a badly set bone, forever changed and diminished by the experience.

He pulled the wires in the arm taut and the limb contracted, quickly at first, and then slowing as the metal strings found their natural tension. What he was creating was an odd mockery of genuine life, but that was his goal, wasn't it? Even if the Automaton would return to his animated state, he would still be a creature with a steel heart. Still, the thought of the metal man's return brought a smile to Emilio's lips. He had done a good job, and this would be his greatest triumph: a machine of far greater grace and complexity than the crude form of the Pneumatic Colossus. He would prove himself to Sarah and she would give him another chance.

Chapter 2

A Walk in the Park

N athaniel awoke to almost-total darkness, his head pounding—he'd been quite effectively blindfolded and only the smallest touch of light leaked into the edges of his vision. Although by its brightness it was clearly sunlight, the illumination told him nothing of his surroundings other than it was daytime. A piece of cloth had been stuffed into his mouth, and his tongue was dry. His ears, however, were not obstructed, and the chatter and clatter all around him led him to believe that he was still somewhere in the city.

Nathaniel was in a seated position, and yet when he tried to move his arms and legs he found that he had been tightly bound to his seat. Repeated efforts at struggling against his restraints only managed to shake the seat slightly, and there was a creaking and rattling from the chair he'd been strapped to.

He vaguely remembered being betrayed by another bottle of scotch, and as he squeezed his eyes and tried wishing the pain away, he once again came to the conclusion that he seriously needed to rethink his relationship with alcohol.

In the weeks since he had been placed into his cell, Eschaton had been, on occasion, drugging his liquor. What occurred during those periods of unconsciousness was still a mystery, but it had only been today that he had woken up outside the jail beneath the Hall of Paragons.

Every day since that cold February morning when Darby had died atop the Brooklyn Bridge—the very same day that his leg had been pierced by the Bomb Lance's steel shaft, it seemed as if every time he had taken a drink he had ended up in an increasingly bewildering set of circumstances, each time worse than the last.

After the Darby house had burned down around him, leaving him home-less and without almost any worldly belongings, he had asked some of his wealthier friends for help. Happy to assist a friend in need, they had allowed him to spend a few weeks in their "hideout." The building had appeared to be, from the outside at least, a nondescript East Side tenement. Not in the worst part of town, it was far from the best. But that was part of the building's appeal, as its doors concealed a well-appointed hideaway for the wealthy.

Although Nathaniel was a child of privilege he had a limited capacity for conspicuous display. Truth be told, although he could understand the intent, he had found the place disconcerting. Its ready access to so much freely flowing liquor also made it far too easy for him to drink to excess and indulge in activities that even he considered too debauched for his own good.

He was beginning to understand what it was that the people preaching about temperance had been prattling on about. Liquor might hide the pain, but it often left a bad situation worse—it was impossible to deny the fact that his consumption of the better part of a pint of bourbon before he had con-fronted the villains invading the Hall of Paragons had made it impossible for him to save his step-father's life.

But his guilt did not end there. His current situation was far more terri-fying than any that had come previously. And while it was true that drink wasn't *entirely* to blame, when Eschaton had drugged him it was Nathaniel's weakness for whisky that had been the villain's method of delivery. Even in his current predicament Nathaniel couldn't deny that what he wanted most in the world was a drink.

"Ah, so the dreamer finally arises." The voice was familiar, and Nathaniel tried to reply, but there was a rag stuffed into his mouth. The moist cloth made it impossible for him to respond in anything but a series of guttural grunts and coughs.

"Now, now," Eschaton continued, "there's no need for you to get upset so soon after waking up. The good Lord may have been angry at you," his captor said loudly, and in a manner clearly intended for public consumption, "but if you can find it in your heart to worship him fully, he will heal you. And he's about to bless you with gifts that you cannot begin to imagine."

Nathaniel tried to tell Eschaton to go to hell, but for all his effort the only sounds that came out of him were the muffled screams that reminded him of a particularly angry chimpanzee he'd seen at the Central Park zoo. At the time he'd found the creature's helpless cries amusing, but now he felt an odd kinship with the hairy monster.

"You have the Lord by your side," Eschaton continued, "and he believes that even a man struck dumb and blind may still improve his character if he is only given the right *sort* of help."

There were a million replies that came to mind, some of them so obscene they surprised even Nathaniel. But he was unable to put voice to any of them. It was only after another round of fruitless struggles and loud grunts that he finally settled down into his chair.

From somewhere nearby came the disapproving voice of a woman as she walked by, the leather of her heels tapping out her pace against the concrete. She was whispering loudly, and he heard her refer to "the poor spastic in the chair." It took Nathaniel a moment to realize that it was him she was referring to. Continuing in her shockingly loud whisper, she also expressed that perhaps it would be for the good of everyone if they simply kept him indoors.

Nathaniel dropped his head and huffed out a frustrated sigh through his nose. "And now you've settled down." Eschaton patted him on the shoulder. "That's very good. I know this may all seem quite disorienting, but I assure you that it's for your own benefit. All you need to do is simply relax and listen." From his last interaction with the gray man, Nathaniel already knew that he had a very broad definition of the word *benefit*.

"I'm sure you're wondering where you are."

Nathaniel nodded in response.

"You're currently sitting in Madison Park. It's a lovely spring day, the sun is shining, and we're surrounded by throngs of people out and about on their daily errands. It's a most wonderful and bucolic scene.

"I've brought you out here to this lovely park for a number of reasons. One is irony, but the most important one I will show you shortly. But we have a little time until my surprise is ready, so I thought I might entertain you with a bit of educational reading."

Nathaniel heard the sound of pages rustling before Eschaton continued. "When I was a younger man—far more naive than I am today—I had a strong philanthropic bent. I spent a great deal of my time helping those I believed to be less fortunate than myself." His voice had dropped from its usual rumble, and seemed almost kindly in tone. Nathaniel found it both terrifying and cloying. He wondered if this had been how the man had spoken when he had been more . . . human? "And as I grew older and wiser I began to realize that no amount of fortune would change the human condition, and that word *unfortunate* was a label that could be applied to almost everyone in the world."

Nathaniel grunted out a "damn you" that he thought might be sufficiently formed to be understood, although if Eschaton comprehended it, he chose to ignore it.

"One of my favorite hobbies before the accident was reading to the blind. It was quite popular at that time, and I always thought of it as mutually beneficial for all involved: I would get to re-acquaint myself with the classics, and some poor person bereft of sight would have a chance to hear the words of Plato, Shakespeare, or Kant. As you are currently blind, at least temporarily, I thought I might read to you while we wait and see if you enjoyed it as much as I do."

Nathaniel wondered what they were waiting for. He had spent long days locked in a cell underneath the Hall. If this was to be his execution, a part of him would be relieved.

"But today, as a treat, I've decided to read to you from some of my own writings."

Nathaniel let out a moan.

"Oh, I'm quite aware that it's a terrible indulgence to read my own words," Eschaton said, "but I've been most curious to hear how my words sound when read out to an audience, and none of my Children have your considerable education in the classics. I'm hoping you'll indulge me."

"But where to begin?" He heard more rustling pages. "Or, perhaps it would be best to just start at the beginning, since this will be the first time that you have heard it." There was a long pause, then an audibly dramatic intake of breath. "The gospel of Eschaton. Book one: *Regenesis*." He took a dramatic pause, and when he started again his voice had dropped an octave. "There was, of course, no one there at the beginning, nor will there be at the end. And there can be only now. But humanity persists in telling its stories of what was, and what will be." His voice was a monotone, mumbling growl, and Nathaniel felt an instant of pity for those poor, blind folks. "It is an unhappy and unfortunate artifact of human language that we are doomed to try to define the past and control our future."

Nathaniel, already tired of this ridiculous sermon, tried to let out another yell, but all that came out was a muffled moan. He struggled harder against his bonds, hoping to discover a flaw in the ropes, but they had been tied with expertise. His most strident efforts only managed to cause more creaks and rattles from his chair.

"There can truly be only the eternal now," the gray man continued. "The Buddhists say we must live in the moment, but I believe that enlightenment comes from reaching toward a goal that we will never attain. For it is only through constant striving that we can continue to survive in the hellish fire of this eternal moment."

Nathaniel began to twitch his shoulder and head, and found that after a few shakes he had gathered enough momentum to begin to rock the chair he was sitting in. After a few moments he had it rocking back and forth, the metal pins and wooden joints clearly stressed by his actions. Perhaps if he could tip over his chair he might be able to gain the attention of a passerby with more sympathy than the woman from before.

As the chair rocked he heard Eschaton sigh, and a moment later there was a sharp slap across his face. The open palm hit him like a thunderbolt, both literally and figuratively, sending a surprising jolt of electric energy through his body. Every muscle in his back, already in pain from his bondage, spasmed simultaneously, and when the twitch released him he hung limp in the chair. "Not a supporter? I suppose I should have known better than to try to educate you."

There was a long quiet moment, and Nathaniel began to regain some sense of equilibrium. He prayed somebody would notice his plight and rescue him from this madman. Where had he been taken that nobody would notice someone striking a man who had been bound and gagged? "Since you obviously aren't interested in hearing my story, how about I tell you what is about to happen to *you* instead?"

Nathaniel was tempted to try screaming again, but he knew it was hopeless. He was in the villain's clutches, and he was better off simply sitting quietly and seeing what the madman had to say.

There were two metallic snaps on either side of him, then a lurch, and Nathaniel was moving again. He had been tied to a wheelchair! No doubt the passersby thought he was some kind of idiot, incapable of speech, or any movement beyond his jerks. No one would come to the aid of a moaning invalid no matter what kind of action he took. He wondered how Eschaton had dressed himself to hide his strange appearance.

The wheels bounced and creaked as he was rolled across the cobblestones. "I want you to know, before I show you your destiny, that there is nothing you could have done to stop this. Not Darby, Stanton, or any of the Paragons would have been able to fight what is coming. Your only misfortune is that you were fighting the inevitable fate of humanity. But knowing that you could never win, you should feel honored that you have survived to be such an integral part of it."

As they rolled quietly along the path, Nathaniel listened intently to the voices all around him. Most people seemed to be engrossed in conversations about nothing important. They spoke of family, food, and how pleased they were that there had been the sudden arrival of a warm spring day. No one seemed the least bit interested in anything of import.

He wondered if the rest of the world knew that Alexander Stanton was dead. He supposed that Eschaton would keep it secret for as long as possible.

The wheelchair lurched to a stop. "Now, before I remove your blindfold and show you your surprise, there is one more bit of preparation that we need to take care of."

The sound of Eschaton's voice moved behind him. "Since you are to be my only controlled subject in this experiment, I've decided to attempt something a little more radical with you." There was a slight pressure on his arm, then a single point of terrible pain as a metal needle entered Nathaniel's flesh. The cool liquid it contained left a trail of agony as it spidered out into his arm.

"I'd tell you not to worry, but the material I've just injected into you is, in fact, quite toxic, and most assuredly fatal. It's a concoction of my own invention: a blend of my fortified smoke in a mercury base. Based on my experimentation with animal subjects I can assure you that if left untreated it would lead to a most excruciating death.

"But," the gray man said with a chuckle, "I can promise you that one way or the other, this poison won't be what kills you."

He felt a pair of hands fiddling behind his head, and suddenly his mask was lifted away. Nathaniel blinked a few times as his eyes adjusted to the blinding afternoon sun. But they seemed unable to focus, and whatever it was that Eschaton had put into him was already making him feel dizzy and confused. After a moment, he saw a large green arm in front of him, a torch of brass and glass held in its hand. "Do you like opera, Nathaniel?"

Nathaniel seemed barely able to move his head, let alone answer the question. He wanted to scream and shout, but the poison had hit his organs, and they were rebelling most painfully.

"No matter," Eschaton replied. "I definitely do. Another indulgence of mine. It's all ridiculous melodrama with larger-than-life characters in outlandish costumes. . . . But there's a sense of truth revealed by all that spectacle. I'm particularly struck with Mozart's *Don Giovanni*. Have you seen it?"

Nathaniel tried to shake his head, but it refused to move. Mozart had always struck him as terribly old-fashioned. He liked contemporary music, like Strauss—not something that sounded mired in the past.

"No matter. The story is simple enough: it's about an unstoppable man who refuses to repent for any of his crimes. He sees himself as a superior to those around him, but in the end he is dragged down to hell, destroyed by a specter of his past.

"Many men have found the story puzzling, or confusing, but it has always spoken to me as a prescient tale that perfectly encapsulates our mad century."

There was a sudden sharp pain in his chest, and his heart began to pound. Nathaniel gasped through the cloth stuck in his mouth, but no air seemed to reach his lungs. "Ah, I see that the poison is starting to do its work."

Eschaton walked toward the arm, stopping at a large wooden box in front of it. Nathaniel could barely make him out, but he seemed to be wearing a suit.

The box was about the size of a large coffin, lacquered black, and he made out the white Omega symbol painted on the front of it. The gray man undid a latch and slid open a panel on the side of the box. "I wish you luck, Nathaniel. No matter what happens next, you are about to embark on a journey to a place where no living human has ever gone before."

There was a metallic "clunk" as the switch was thrown, and from somewhere deep inside there was the chugging sound of machinery springing to life. A few seconds later a puff of black smoke spewed out from the side of the box, and the cloud began to grow. "Either way, if you want to have any chance of surviving the poison in your veins, I'd suggest that you start by breathing deeply . . ."

Eschaton leaned down and gave Nathaniel a kiss on his forehead as the smoke began to swirl around them. The electric jolt that came from the gray giant's lips threw him back into full consciousness for an instant. He could see the cloud in front of him growing, and the concerned looks from the parkgoers nearby as it rolled toward them. "I'd wish you good luck if I believed there was any intelligence in the universe."

The black smoke enveloped him, and Nathaniel could feel it burning his skin as if he were being rubbed with liquid fire. Although he was still gagged and unable to scream himself, it didn't take long before he could hear the shouting of people nearby.

Chapter 3
In Gratitude

Jenny Farrows hopped off the carriage and looked up at the one-eyed driver's haggard and dark-skinned face. "Thank you, Mr. Niles." He wore a patch over the missing eye, and despite a tiny bit of curiosity about the scars that peeked out underneath its edges, she had no real wish to see what his eye looked like uncovered.

Despite her staring, the man looked down from the cart and gave her a warm, lopsided smile. "You can call me Willy if you like, Mrs. Farrows." He winked at her with his remaining eye.

Jenny only nodded in response. When his grin faded away she realized that he had expected a smile in return and not the emotionless mask she had cultivated through a lifetime of devotion.

Digging deep she conjured up an expression that she hoped was suitable for the situation. At the same time, she was a married woman, and the idea of becoming so familiar with a man she hardly knew . . . She was certain that her husband would not approve.

Still, the man and his old mare were kindly enough, and they had driven her out along the desolate dirt road that led to the junkyard from the train car. "Thank you, Willy," she replied, hoping her distress at the uncomfortable level of familiarity was not too obvious on her face.

From what little she knew of him, she liked the man, and to her mind the Negroes had been treated poorly from the start. With the end of the war, and with it the end of slavery, things could only improve for everyone.

It had taken her a few trips before she had coaxed Mr. Niles's particular story out of him, and despite it being a true tale of mystery and adventure, the old man seemed almost embarrassed by his past. Jenny had found it very interesting; the man had escaped from servitude on a cotton plantation, arriving in New York just in time to be drafted, and then lost his left eye as a soldier for the Union in the Great War. It was the kind of bravery she felt the world could use more of.

The old Negro grabbed her bag and jumped out of the car, running around the back end of the cart to reach her before she could even begin to step down.

The back was half-filled with junk—Willy being one of the few men who still both brought and took away odds and ends from the rusting piles of metal in the junkyard. He held out his hand to help her down. "Take care, Mrs. Farrows. I'll be back 'round this way tomorrow morning. I'll check by and see if you need a ride to the city."

Jenny was shocked to find herself needing to take a moment before grasping the brown fingers in her own, but when she finally reached out she grabbed his calloused hand firmly. "You're too kind, Mr. Niles."

"Willy."

"Thanks very much, Willy." She gave him only a wave as he jumped back up onto the wagon, and then turned toward the junkyard. Behind her she heard Willy shake the reins, and the muffled clip-clop of the old mare's hooves as it started down the road.

She had only taken a few steps when she saw another Negro running directly toward her. He was a much younger man, and far more whole and handsome. As he came toward her, he was waving his right hand frantically in the air.

She thought he had been trying to get her attention, but just as Jenny opened her mouth to ask what the man wanted, he sprinted past her. He moved with grace and speed, far more like a dancer than she would have expected for a man of his stature. His features were sharp and striking, and his skin as dark as any man she had ever seen. His clothes were worn, but the creases were sharp, his pants held up by a pair of black leather suspenders with brass buckles so well-shined and crafted that they somehow seemed out of place with the rest of his clothing.

His black bowler was tilted loosely back.

"Willy!" the man shouted, and the wagon slowed almost instantly. "You got room for me up there?" the man asked.

Willy lit up with a smile that seemed a bit wider than it had for her. "Sure do, Abraham. Come on up!"

The other man hopped up off the ground and straight into the car in a way that seemed to defy the bounds of earth, landing directly in the passenger's seat.

"So long, Mrs. Farrows!" Willy said with another wink. Jenny was shocked to realize that she had been staring at the two men the whole time, and she felt her fair skin flush red with shame, but it seemed that Willy and Abraham had a great deal to discuss, and neither of them were paying any attention to her.

Jenny grabbed her suitcase and clomped toward the house across the stony, rutted mud. The fence around the main building was a motley collection of clashing cast-iron gates that had been lashed together with bailing wire. The hodgepodge wall of spears ran along the entire outer edge of the yard. Most were plain and simple, with straight metal bars, but others were adorned with fleur-de-lys, or metal roses.

The piece above the entryway was the most ornate of all. It was a full gateway, and it was covered with tiny cast-iron grotesques. Each cherubic demon had the same pair of bat wings and a toothy grin, and the first time she had walked through the door she found the little creatures quite shocking, but over the course of her visits to the Armandos' home she had begun to warm to their cheeky smiles, and now she found them almost endearing. She reached out and patted one of them gently with two fingers.

For all its patchwork qualities, the fence that surrounded the junkyard seemed to give the place a genuine sense of security, and it was a stark contrast to the feeling of barely contained formality that the walls in Manhattan always seemed to project.

As Jenny slipped open the main gate, it squealed loudly on rusty hinges. If there had been a dog living there Jenny was sure it would have come out bounding and barking—intent on discovering what the commotion was, while causing one of its own. But it seemed that this particular junkyard was the only one in all of Brooklyn that didn't have a canine guardian. She had been barked at dozens of times on the way here from the train station.

The sprawling compound made Brooklyn seem exotic and very far away from the cramped hustle bustle of New York. Jenny tried to keep a smile on her face and not let it lapse into a disapproving frown as she walked the twenty yards from the gate to the front door of the house. When she had first come to visit, the thing that had shocked her most was just how much the sprawling junkyard had matched the image in her imagination.

But what did surprise her was the ramshackle palace that Emilio and Viola had built in the center of it. It was hardly a mansion—as she knew from experience—and yet it was so much more . . . *Italian* than she could have ever believed possible. She knew that the races of Latin descent were by and large an ostentatious people—they had been the founders of the Roman empire, after all—but it was strange to see just how much gaudy ornamentation the Armandos had crammed into every nook and cranny of their home. It was a spectacular feat to be ostentatious in an age as gilded as this one. For years, every time she picked up the feather duster she had found herself muttering a small prayer of gratitude that Mr. Stanton was not addicted to the accumulation of ridiculous knick-knacks that many of the other wealthy families had encrusted their homes with. She wondered how the servants could ever manage to keep them free of the ever-present scourge of dust.

As she thought about the mansion, a sudden wave of sadness washed over her. Both of Sarah's parents were gone now; both victims of the terrible curse of heroism. It was a disease that had brought tragedy to the family time and time again, and now Sarah seemed determined to make sure that particular sickness would be the death of her as well.

The front door was wide open, and before she walked through the doorway Jenny yelled out Sarah's name. When there was no reply she tried shouting out after Emilio, but the response was equally absent.

"Lord preserve me," she said, and crossed herself before heading in. As she passed the living room she poked her head past the gauzy curtains to peek inside. Sitting on a low table was a bottle of vermouth. It had been tipped over on its side, although even from here she could see that it still contained a swallow or two of drink. Standing next to it was a glass stained with the sticky residue from someone's adventures with the alcohol the night before. She hoped that Sarah hadn't taken up consumption of the liquor. A girl her age already had enough to worry about in life without adding intemperance to her problems.

And she knew where it could lead . . . Jenny knew that there was some kind of romance between Sarah and Emilio, although whether they had consummated that relationship was a question she wasn't sure she actually wanted the answer to.

Walking around a threadbare couch covered in crumpled blankets, Jenny picked up the bottle, intent on righting it. Instead, after taking a quick look around, she finished up the remains, the flowery taste warming her body as it slid down her throat. She placed the empty bottle back on the table, telling herself that she was protecting Sarah from temptation as she headed back into the hallway.

The house was surprisingly sturdy for its ramshackle nature. The place had been built like a maze, with each "wing" of the house sprawling out from this main room. Jenny pushed back a heavy Persian rug. The thick piece of carpet acted as a doorway into the section that Viola had claimed for herself.

The hallway that led down to her bedroom was dark and cramped, lit only by the tiny slices of daylight that had managed to creep in through the cracks in the walls. When she had first seen the light leaking in, Jenny had suggested to Emilio that he might want to consider sealing the cracks, but he had only laughed and informed her that this was exactly the way his sister wanted it to be.

She trailed her hand along the wall to guide her way as she walked down the black corridor. She had been down this hall before, and was well aware of the sharp angle at the end that marked the entrance to the girl's bedroom. The first time she had discovered it, it had connected directly with her nose, leading to shouts and blood.

The main space was better lit, with a cloth-covered window in the roof letting in enough gloom that she could make out that there was someone in the bed, snoring solidly.

Seeing a cracked chimney lamp on a cracked marble table, Jenny picked it up, lifted the glass, and lit the wick from a match that she pulled out of her skirts.

The yellow light smoked viciously as she adjusted it, but once she had it set right, it provided a cheerful glow to the otherwise-dreary scene. The room had a musty, unhealthy smell, and she had to tamp down an overpowering urge to rip everything down and start cleaning.

Viola's tastes had run toward the dark even before the accident. Since then, it seemed that she had banished anything that wasn't red or black in color. The black taffeta that hung along the walls had been ripped from the skirts of mourning dresses, and gave the whole place a sad demeanor.

Moving the light closer, Jenny Farrows looked down at the sleeping girl and frowned. Viola wriggled in response to the illumination, and for a second it appeared as if she might awake. Jenny tugged back the light, and after a moment the snoring began again, although this time Viola was on her back.

Raising the lamp, she examined Viola's face. They had waited so long for her to heal after what had happened to her at the theater. After the stitches, there had been weeks of pain, and now that the scabs were finally beginning to fall away Jenny found herself still wondering if the girl might not have been better off if she had simply never woken up from the explosion at all.

Jenny scowled and chastised herself for having such thoughts, and then took another look. The expression on Viola's face wasn't exactly peaceful, but at least she was at rest. The wounds had taken weeks to heal, and for a short time an infection had taken hold, threatening to melt away the rest of her skin. It had been the girl's brother who had come to the rescue, finding an old Italian woman who had a way with herbs that put a halt to the creeping damage.

After Sarah and Emilio had taken the girl to the doctor, it had been Jenny who had been pressed into service to care for her. At first she had resisted, but the entire mansion had been thrown into disarray after the news of Alexander Stanton's death.

What had previously been a stately home was now filled with lawyers and accountants, busily tearing open drawer and safe in search of the details of the family fortune, clearly intent on cutting through the legal morass that kept them from getting their hands on the money.

O'Rourke, the old butler, had taken to wandering the mansion aimlessly for hours at a time, the dementia that had been held at bay by his work suddenly overwhelming him in a single wave. Jenny imagined that perhaps losing his mind was a better way for the old man to stave off his grief.

Jenny had begged Sarah to end her exile and return to the real world, but so far she had steadfastly refused.

Sarah believed that the same evil forces that had sent the Ruffian to her apartment were still intent on doing her harm. Jenny had considered going to the authorities about it herself, but it was impossible to live as a member of the Stanton household and not recognize that some problems were simply beyond the usual defenders of society.

And then there was the matter of the mechanical man. Jenny had to admit that she found the very idea of a mechanical creature that could mimic a living, breathing human disturbing and unsettling on both emotional and spiritual grounds. Surely even the idea of such a thing was an affront to God? But it was equally clear that Sir Dennis Darby had a very different view of the way that the universe worked.

Jenny had only ever actually met Tom once, and her encounter with the machine had done nothing to alleviate her concerns. That said, she also strongly trusted Sarah's instincts, and her forthright devotion to the Automaton meant that Jenny was willing to keep an open mind when it came to the true motivations of the mechanical man.

But hearing about the events at the theater, it was clear that things had changed. Emilio was working to bring Tom back to life, but she could tell by the tone in Sarah's voice that she was no longer sure that what they were attempting to reanimate was still the same being she had known. In Jenny's opinion, destroying what remained of Darby's work would not only put a stop to the danger to Sarah, but quite possibly it could halt whatever mad plan Lord Eschaton had in mind, as well.

On the bed, Viola let out a grunt and twisted under the sheets, turning her face away from the light.

Jenny had been standing by Viola's bedside when she had first woken up. The girl had been rightfully angry when she discovered what had happened to her, although she had never before seen a woman so willing to express her unhappiness through physical violence.

Jenny had hoped that time would have caused some sort of revelation inside the girl as well, but if anything, her broken beauty had only managed to increase Viola's anger, and after barely surviving the infection Viola had begun to retreat from the world. She had also taken to smashing things around the house whenever the mood took her. Most of her wrath was focused on any inanimate object with a face or capable of displaying one, and almost every mirror in the house was now smashed or splintered.

For a moment she considered waking Viola. It was already midmorning, and it would certainly do the girl no favors to simply let her sleep the day away. If there was one thing that Jenny had learned during her thirty-odd years, it was that life and progress marched on, no matter how great the tragedy. In fact, she was coming to believe that tragedy was a driving force that made the world go around.

There would come a day—and she had to imagine that it would be soon—where Viola would need to be forced back out into the world: scars and all. Jenny let out a quiet sigh. Whatever Viola Armando's ultimate fate would be, today would not be that day.

Deciding that she would let the girl sleep, she backed out of the space and into the dark corridor. The journey back through the hallway was easier now, her eyes having adjusted to the gloom, although she was slightly blinded as she headed into the parlor.

Jenny grabbed a pillow from the pile on the couch, and then let out a shocked yelp when the pile of sheets began to move.

"Is she?" Jenny heard a familiar voice asking her. She blinked away the sunlight as best she could, and saw Sarah Stanton rising up from underneath the mismatched mass of cloth and cushions.

Jenny felt herself blush. Had Sarah seen her pick up the bottle? "I'm sorry, Sarah. I called out when I came in, but there wasn't any reply."

"What?" Sarah said, then let out a laugh when she comprehended that Jenny was attempting to apologize. "Oh, don't be ridiculous. We hardly stand on ceremony around here." Sarah looked over at the table, and then waved her hand back and forth, as if she were searching for something that wasn't there. "Having you around can only improve the place."

"True enough." Jenny frowned. There was a casualness in Sarah's demeanor that she hadn't noticed before. Something about it reminded Jenny more of an upstart street urchin than a Stanton. "Are you trying to find something?"

Sarah shook her head and crashed back into the couch. "I guess not."

Jenny bustled her way toward the couch and pulled up one of the sheets.

She could see it letting off a cloud of dust in the beams of morning light. "I think I'm going to start cleaning up this place whether you like it or not."

Sarah rolled her eyes. "Go ahead, Jenny. But once you pull all the junk out of a junkyard, then you just have a yard."

"Are you giving me sass, Miss Stanton?" said Jenny, giving Sarah a disapproving look she usually held for the household staff. She frowned more deeply when Sarah pulled back the rest of the covers and revealed her choice of nightclothes. "What is that you're wearing?"

Sarah stopped and looked down at her garment. "This thing?"

"My sentiments exactly." Sarah was in a man's robe. It had been belted tightly around her, and though the material was thick enough that it didn't show her figure in excruciating detail, what it did reveal was shameful enough.

She wanted to scream at Sarah, but she knew that would only make things worse. "It's not ladylike," was all she could muster with civility.

"What *should* I be wearing, Jenny? Are you suggesting that I wake up every day and put on corsets and crinoline so I can play the most upper-class girl in the junkyard?"

"Now you sound like Viola." Her tone turned cold. "You're a lady, and you have duties."

"To whom?" Sarah replied, her tone rising. "My father? Sir Darby?"

Jenny could see that the conversation was going nowhere. If there was one thing she had learned over years of teaching and training willful women, sometimes the best way to explore a subject more deeply was to simply change the subject. "There was a Negro man here earlier, I saw."

Sarah looked shocked, and then sighed and shook her head. "What does that have do with the price of tea in China?"

"Who was he?"

Sarah's lips curled up in a smile as she stared down at the floor. "The things you don't know, Jenny Farrows." It seemed almost startlingly adult, and Jenny didn't like it.

Then Sarah looked up her, a flash of anger in her eyes. "But you're right. I'm supposed to be responsible. That's how I was raised. That's how my mother raised me, then my father, and then Darby. But they're all gone now. So the question that I keep asking myself is, who is left alive that I'm supposed to be a lady *for*? Nathaniel? He seems to have found happiness being a lackey for the man who murdered his step-father."

She took a step forward. "Besides, what has being a lady ever actually done for me, Jenny?" Sarah took a second step, and her next question was louder. "Whose life has it saved?" And then she did it with a yell, "I want you to tell me!"

The housemaid's open hand lashed out and struck Sarah hard across the face. For an instant there was a look of grim anger that she had never seen on Sarah's face before, and yet Jenny almost smiled when she recognized it. Sarah Stanton was, it turned out, still her father's daughter. "I'm sorry," Jenny said, "I shouldn't have."

"Sorry for what?" She spoke in a low tone without looking up. "It's not your fault. You just think that somehow I'm supposed to go out and get my life back, but it's gone." Sarah turned away in a flurry of red hair and threw herself on the couch. The robe fell apart, revealing a more-than-shocking portion of Sarah's leg. She did nothing to cover it. Jenny took a step closer, but she could see Sarah visibly stiffen.

"The mansion is still there."

"And will the walls of the mansion protect us when the Children of Eschaton come for me?" She was shouting again. "They broke through solid granite. Do you think wood shingles will stop them?"

Jenny shook her head. "Then what are you planning?" The girl had been living with this nonsense for so long that it had already consumed her. "You can't just hide here forever, Sarah. This junkyard isn't a world for you."

"While the man who murdered my father is ruling the Paragons, there is no world for me."

Jenny knew that Sarah was wrong, but there was no way to avoid the fact that if there were villains intent on taking her life, staying in this ridiculous place might actually be best for her. "Then what are you going to do?"

Sarah shook her head. "I don't know. I've been trying to answer that question for weeks. It always seemed so easy for Darby and my father. Whenever things got too hard for them, they'd just invent another machine, or hit something." Jenny snickered at that. "But I can't do either of those things. I can't even bring Tom back."

"Then come home. We'll tell the papers."

Sarah looked up at her friend, and Jenny felt a tightening in her heart. "I can't do that either." There were clearly tears in her eyes, but somehow they refused to break free and roll down the girl's face. "I won't expose you and the others to that danger!"

"Sarah, if you *don't* come home soon, they're going to take the house away. The lawyers said . . ."

Jenny jumped back as Sarah jumped up, but the girl was too fast, and she crushed Jenny into a hug. "Then it'll be over and you'll be safe, Jenny."

Jenny looked down into Sarah's eyes. "Don't be ridiculous, girl."

Sarah curled her lips up into a smile. "They say you hurt the ones you love."

"If you're so sure that that dreadful man wants the heart, then why not just give him what he wants? If that's all it takes, you have to end this. It's madness."

"Jenny, before you saw that brute in my apartment, had you ever seen any of the villains that the Paragons fight? I mean, in person?"

Jenny thought it over. Over the years she felt as if she must have. In the early days there had seemed to be a constant parade of men in costumes around the house. And Jenny had followed the Industrialist's exploits in the paper. There was a time when it seemed like there was a new villain appearing every day—not just the ones she'd read about, but the stories she'd heard through half-opened doors. "Met them . . . no, I haven't."

Sarah shook her head and stared down at her feet. "Did I ever tell you what my father told me after my mother died? The words he said to me right after he killed the man who had murdered her?"

Jenny felt a wave of compassion strike her heart. Sarah had been so young when that had happened. No one had ever discussed the details of that day around the house. She supposed there was a time when she could have asked, but Jenny had still been quite young when it had happened. And when she did say something, it was far more important that she tell Alexander Stanton to go and talk to his daughter about her mother's death than it was to find out the details of a most gruesome incident. A quiet "No," was the only reply that she could muster.

"I hadn't even let myself think about it since that day." She smiled as she ran her fingers down the tattered lapels of the robe. "I suppose that's part of what comes with being a lady."

"You were so young. Maybe it was better if . . ."

Sarah laughed, and then looked up with such sadness in her eyes. The tightness in Jenny's chest became an ache as she realized that the final remnants of the little girl that she had loved for so long had almost entirely disappeared. Now there was a woman in her place. "In retrospect," Sarah continued, "the Crucible was a ridiculous villain. Truly, he would have been pathetic if he hadn't been so deadly. Later we found out he'd been a wrestler . . . a former circus performer who had lost one of his arms to a torturer when he'd tried to turn against the Russian royalty. Somehow he replaced it with one that spewed fire. The Czars had burned his face terribly, so he wore a mask as well. You would have pitied the man if he hadn't been a ruthless murderer.

"He'd hoped to hold my mother hostage so that he could get enough money to return home and take vengeance on those who hurt him."

Jenny wondered if Sarah could see the irony in that. "No one ever seems to be able to let go of their past . . ."

"No, we don't. But most men don't put on a hood and attach a fire-spewing device to the end of their stump, either. Those who do seem a bit more . . . dedicated than most."

Sarah looked into the distance. It almost seemed to Jenny as if she were peering into the past. "He wasn't really much of a villain at all, compared to some, but his torturers must have driven him insane. What they left behind was very strong and utterly ruthless. He'd already burned Mother and Nathaniel's parents to death when he came for me. He told me that they had been cleansed."

Jenny felt a stab of horror. "You didn't see . . . Not in front of you."

Sarah shook her head and looked up at her. "No. Even he wasn't that mad. But I could *smell* what he'd done. And just as he was about to send me off to join them, my father came bursting in, with Darby and Tom by his side." A single tear slipped free. "If he'd come ten minutes earlier . . . But, of course, it was the discovery of my father's impending arrival that had sent him into a murderous frenzy. He had always known that he would never survive a direct confrontation with the Paragons. He just wanted to make them pay."

Did Sarah blame her father? There were so many questions, but would having answers make any difference?

"The actual battle was short. He foolishly thought he could burn the Automaton. I still remember Tom disappearing underneath the flames. When he stepped out of them, his clothes had almost burned away. But he was different back then. Far more of a machine than a man."

Sarah faltered slightly, and Jenny stepped forward to give her support. "Are you all right?"

"That day at the Darby mansion . . . I thought it was embarrassment, but . . ." Sarah shook her head and stood up. "I'm all right Jenny. Really."

Somehow she doubted Sarah's words, but she had to admit that she was desperately curious to hear the rest. "All right then, go on."

"Tom grabbed the Crucible's weapon and tore it from his arm. The scream the man made when the limb ripped free was terrifying. But it was short. When my father saw me standing there, he shot him in the head."

"He just executed him?"

"'Don't anger the Industrialist,' people used to say. A reputation that I think was well earned."

Sarah leaned back. "And then suddenly he was my father again. Even though he was still wearing that black leather suit of his that always terrified me as a child—all full of bullets and buckles—I don't remember being scared when he held me then. He folded his arms around me and told me that it wasn't my fault. Although I think it clearly was."

This part of the story Jenny was intimately familiar with: it had been Sarah who had revealed the Industrialist's true identity to the world, and that had made the Stanton family a target for the villain. "Sarah, you were so young."

"That's an excuse. Maybe even a good one . . ." She turned to Jenny and took her hand. "But it doesn't wipe away the truth."

"You're wrong."

Sarah ignored her and continued. "I asked my father why he killed him.

I suppose that at the time I didn't fully understand what was happening. I couldn't comprehend that the Crucible had killed my mother, although I must have known he'd done something terrible. Or maybe I was just too young to understand just how broken and wrong some men could be."

There was a cruel bravery in what Alexander Stanton had done. Compassion, on the other hand, had never been one of his strengths. "What did your father say?"

"He told me that there were people with terrible powers who had forgotten that there was justice in the world, and that it was up to him to stop them."

She doubted those words would provide much comfort to a child who had just lost her mother, then or now. "Sarah, I'm so sorry."

"You need to stop apologizing, Jenny. It doesn't become you."

"You're probably right." Jenny sat down on the couch and patted the seat next to her. "Can you come sit next to me?"

Sarah looked down at her for a moment. "You've always been there for me. I know it can't have always been easy."

"Stop being so sentimental, Miss Stanton, and take a seat."

"All right, Mrs. Farrows." Sarah sat, and the mood seemed to change almost instantly.

Jenny grasped Sarah's hands in her own and realized they weren't nearly as soft as they had been before. "You've always been a good girl, Sarah: smart, trustworthy, and forthright, if a little bit too curious for your own good. And no matter what happens, I'll stay with you. But you can't blame yourself for what happened to you mother."

Sarah nodded. "Darby once told me that even though God loves us, he wouldn't—or couldn't—save us. Instead he gave *us* the power to do it for ourselves. He told me that men of justice always had to fight alone, and if they didn't remember that, there was always a price to pay." Jenny could feel Sarah's grip tighten around her hand. "*That's* why my mother died." She took a deep breath. "And then *I* chose to fight, and now that monster has killed two men that meant more to me than anything in the world, leaving me to fight alone."

"They were both men of honor, but what can you do?"

She looked up and smiled. "I'm not sure yet, but I'm trying to figure it out. I know it starts with Tom."

"The mechanical man? You know the papers say that he killed your father."

"That's a lie!" Sarah said, and snatched back her hand. "I'm going to bring him back. I have to! And once I do, I'll show the Children of Eschaton that there is still justice in the world."

For a moment Jenny wondered if the girl had gone mad, but there was something in her bearing that seemed to deny it, and when she looked up into her eyes, she realized that Sarah Stanton was her mother's daughter as well. "I'm going to need your help, Jenny."

"All right, Sarah." She reached over and gave the girl a hug. She still missed being able to wrap her arms around her. "But be careful. I couldn't stand it if you got hurt."

Jenny could feel Sarah's face nodding against hers. "I'll do my best, Mrs. Farrows."

They hugged each other tightly, and Jenny felt better, if only a little bit. She couldn't say why, and darker emotions seemed to be swirling inside of Sarah, waiting to break free.

And when she let go, Jenny looked up. Her eyes caught on something in the darkness. It took a few moments for her to realize that it was Viola—hiding in the shadows, staring at them both through angry eyes.

Chapter 4

Under a Dark Cloud

There was, Anubis had determined, little work done in the factories of New York that couldn't be described as punishing. Although much of the construction and manufacturing that had once been located on the island had begun moving to the nearby cities of Queens and Brooklyn, there were still plenty of machines that clattered, rattled, and chugged during the day. Their smokestacks, although diminished in number, continued to belch gray clouds of smoke across the city's sky, choking the people below. But though the products of this endless industry allowed fewer men to create far more, they still could not work without human hands to direct them.

In the years following the war, more and more machines were being used to stamp, bend, and mold objects in massive numbers. While it seemed as if people should have been satisfied with this sudden explosion of things, the opposite seemed to be true: people's appetite for manufactured goods had started to grow and grow. And although one might have thought that men who owned these mighty factories might share their good fortune with the workers who had made it possible, it seemed that the opposite was true: there was a sense of entitlement that had come over the ruling class of the city: anyone who wished for a share in their success was a parasite. Life in the factories was growing crueler, and all the legal and social engines seemed only to churn out wealth for the rich, and punishment for the poor.

Not that, as far as Anubis could tell, there was a time where things had ever been easy for those members of society whose role in life it was to take orders from others. But in the last decade, with the heavy costs incurred by a country battling against itself still unpaid, it seemed as if the wealthy and powerful were, as always, happy to heap as much of the responsibility and suffering as they could onto the backs of the least fortunate.

Despite all his skills he was still just a worker, of that there was no doubt, but he had been lucky enough to avoid the worst of it. He had some genuine skill, and his prowess with a spanner and screwdriver had allowed him to put together his staff and costume. It also made him handy at fixing sewing machines and power-looms, so that when he wasn't covered head to toe in black leather he was eminently employable.

And the machines, no matter how miraculous they might appear, were complicated and prone to breaking under the best of circumstances. But in his time working on them, Anubis had discovered that, as often as not, what caused a machine to fail was not a mechanical flaw or fatigued metal, but an act of human carelessness with catastrophic consequences. He had retrieved more severed fingers from between the shifting wires of the looms than he cared to think about.

Because he was often indispensable, the men in charge at the factories seemed to live for the opportunity to point out a flaw in his work, or berate him for laziness. And although they were often obviously attempting to find a way to feed their egos at his expense, their complaints weren't *always* without merit.

His activities as Anubis were mostly nocturnal, and they conflicted with his ability to do his job effectively. Not only did he spend many days on the verge of unconsciousness from sheer exhaustion, but the fact was that physically he was already paying a toll for pursuing an activity that often ended in violence.

The battle at the Theater Mechanique had left him in such a state that over the next few weekends he could do nothing but recuperate. Taking multiple blows to his head had left him bedridden for days, and paying for the services of a doctor willing to ask no questions had put a large dent into the money he had earned with the Children of Eschaton. His intent for that money had been far nobler than using it on himself; he had been saving it to make a large charitable donation. But that source of income was closed to him now.

By helping Sarah he had finally revealed where his true loyalties lay, and there was no turning back. Jack and the other boys would be looking for him, and Anubis had decided it would be better for him to lay low while the man behind the mask returned to more mundane work. He hadn't worn the costume since that day, and truth be told, it felt like a kind of torture. There wasn't a single night that had passed since then where he hadn't been wishing he could still leap across the rooftops . . .

It was, he reflected, somewhat ironic that he had been biding his time by working with the Children of Eschaton, and now that he had finally revealed his true intentions, he was waiting once again. But this time he had put his fate into the hands of a nineteen-year-old girl.

If no longer being a costumed hero had its downsides, there were at least a few good things to brighten his day. He had managed to find time to train, and being back at work he rediscovered some genuine satisfaction in coaxing broken machines back to life. Compared to men like Darby and the Italian boy, his skills may not have seemed like much, but it had been too long since he had used his hands for more than punching, and his current employer ran a number of different factories where his help was actually needed. And while he couldn't call the man he worked for "honorable," he was less than cruel, and the work was far from the worst thing he had ever been forced to do.

He was even able to get out and about and enjoy the spring air for at least a few minutes each day as he travelled from one factory building to the next. The entire route took him only a few square blocks, but Anubis imagined that there were few people who were more aware of just how much could go on in such a small patch of New York. And even if it all had been nothing more than empty lots, even a few minutes in the outdoors was better than spending each and every day boxed up inside the brick walls of a factory.

Perhaps those walks wouldn't be something he would be so fond of once the summer turned to fall, or when the rains came, but hopefully by then he would be able to put on his mask once again, and on this fine, late summer day in the year of 1880 there was nowhere he could imagine he'd rather be than walking the streets of New York.

Realizing that he should enjoy the moment—something that his old fighting teacher had constantly told him was equally as important as practicing his skills—he stopped and took a deep breath. Closing his eyes, he concentrated on the warmth of the sunlight on his skin, focusing the faculties of his mind.

He still missed the old monk in moments like these. He had been more than just a teacher, he had been a true friend.

A simple act of kindness had brought them together, and he had been amply rewarded for the bruises he had received when he'd helped the old man fend off the gang that was attempting to rob him of his last few dollars. Much more difficult had been helping him break free from a long dependency on opium. His first lessons in fighting had been stopping the old man from trying to escape.

Anubis's moment of recollection was shattered by an explosion that came rattling down between the buildings. It sounded like a clap of thunder, but had been preceded by the sharp report that was the distinct signature of a man-made ignition. "Dynamite, probably," Anubis muttered out loud to himself.

New York was constantly full of the incredibly loud bangs and bumps that came plowing under the past to grow taller every day. But even those demolitions were usually not as loud as this one.

He looked up to the sky but could see nothing. Instead he surveyed the faces of the afternoon crowd. Everyone had frozen after the report—and now their heads were craning around. He expected that he'd discover the answer he was looking for more quickly by watching them.

It only took a few seconds for the answer to appear. First one, then every-one, looked toward the sky. A black mushroom cloud roiled as it rose up above the tops of the buildings, looking like an ebony rip in the bright blue sky. There was a collective gasp as the greasy vapor rose up. Within its surface Anubis could see flashes of lightning, as if a tiny thunder cloud had formed over the city. He could figure the general direction, but where *exactly* was it coming from?

Now he turned his thoughts inward, to his internal map of the city. "Madison Square Park," he mumbled to himself, and with that realization his mood took a sour turn.

He had seen the results of dynamite explosions before, having spent some time working for the railroads, not to mention having been exposed to Doctor Dynamite's handiwork on more than one occasion. But TNT had never looked like this. There was something ominous and unnatural about the cloud. Rather than simply rising and dissipating, the hanging smoke seemed to almost seethe and contract in the sky, as if it were a living thing.

He closed his eyes for a moment, ignoring the murmuring chaos around him. It was a technique he had been taught as part of his training in the oriental fighting arts, and his teacher had impressed on him the importance of recognizing that *every* decision made before an action was taken was the most important, whether the result was to fight or to run.

A part of him practically screamed for him to move toward the danger, but at the moment he was dressed as a technician, not a leather-clad adventurer. And even though they might not notice his absence immediately, technically he was still at work and his destination was only a few blocks away. And this was New York: disaster or not, they would expect him to arrive at the next factory within the next ten minutes.

He told himself that there was a real life to be led. "And real money to be made." His alter ego couldn't have all of his time. A man needed to make money, and he needed to eat.

A feeling of inevitability rose up, and he sighed as he looked down at the toolbox in his hand. If he was going to check out the explosion as Anubis, he would need to find a safe place to hide the box before he put on his costume.

The costume was hidden nearby. He'd taken to stashing the outfit in its hiding place every morning before work. So far no one had uncovered it, but it hadn't stopped him from breathing a sigh of relief every evening when he returned to retrieve it. Sadly, the hole wasn't the right size for his tools, and if they were stolen he'd be unemployed in an instant.

People gasped, and he followed their gaze back up into the sky. The roiling cloud seemed to suddenly tire of floating, and was in the process of crashing back to earth in a dark rain. After a few seconds there was only a gray smudge where the blackness had been just moments before.

Something about the way it twisted and moved in the sky had struck him as familiar, and as it fell the truth became obvious. "Fortified smoke . . ." he whispered to himself. "It must be."

The last remaining pangs of guilt about abandoning work vanished underneath a sense of urgency, and Anubis ran as fast as he could toward the alley where his costume was hidden, the toolbox in his hand letting out a loud "clunk" with each step.

He had only ever seen Lord Eschaton's magical gas in its natural form once, back when he had spent a week guarding the factory on the West Side where Lord Eschaton had been manufacturing the substance. The man who had run the place had been a young engineer named Eli.

Before working with that man, Anubis had known nothing about the Jews beyond the usual broad generalizations he'd heard from friends, and the occasional professional interaction. But he also knew better than to let the reputation that came with a race of men effect his actual opinion of an individual. Eli had been a challenging man to get to know, at first, but over the course of that week he had come to find out that Eli was truly fascinating. Although he was a man of many contradictions there was no doubt of his genius, and he was also devoted to Eschaton's ideals beyond reason. Eli had been born into the world with one arm missing, and he was not willing to trust that world to give him anything that he wasn't willing to take, nor was he willing to accept his limitations within it.

The fortified smoke manufactured at the warehouse had been kept in a large iron boiler in the middle of the room. The white Omega painted onto the pitch-covered metal clearly marked it as an important part of Eschaton's plans.

On the last day, Anubis had followed Eli up the wooden ladder to the top of the iron boiler. Pulling open the brass hatch, the one-armed engineer had used a set of mechanical tools attached to the stump of his missing arm to decant some of the material into a glass bottle. The material was like nothing he'd ever seen before. It moved almost like a living thing; a cloud one second, a greasy liquid sliding down the side of the bottle the next. Every time Eli would give the container a shake it would roil up again like a miniature storm, tiny sparks of electricity flashing inside of it. "This, my friend," Eli had told him, "is the very stuff that made Eschaton the man he is today. And tomorrow?" He had leaned in very close to Anubis's leather-covered ear to whisper the future into it. "This is going to change the world. And you, me, and him . . . we'll all be better than we are today."

Even at the time Anubis hadn't been able to hold back his doubts that the black gas would be the savior of the human race. "And what about everyone else?"

Eli smiled and twisted open the bottle. "They'll have to take their chances." The smoke inside seemed to almost sense its freedom, and wriggled up and out of the container into the fresh air. "Some win, some lose—just like always."

But, having escaped from its glass prison, the smoke began to lose cohesion, and after a few moments it fell to the wood below in a wet stain. A moment later a thick white cloud rose up from the ground where it landed, and an acrid smell invaded his nostrils. "Very dangerous, this stuff," Eli had told him. "You wouldn't want it on your skin, that I can promise." According to what Jack had told him, in the end the engineer had died underneath a blanket of the magical smoke. Eli, it turned out, had been one of the losers.

And now, Lord Eschaton had unleashed a cloud of fortified smoke into the park. Clearly this was part of his plan, although Anubis couldn't imagine that this was even a fraction of the gray madman's ultimate goal. It would certainly spread fear and confusion into the world, and there was no telling what damage it would do to the poor souls caught in the explosion.

He reached the alley he had been searching for. At the end of it was a tall wooden building that looked, from this side at least, in serious danger of collapsing from rot and neglect. He lifted up some of the loose shingles and stuck his hand into the hole. Groping his hand up along the wall, he found the end of a rope; giving it a tug, he pulled down a dirty leather satchel that contained his costume.

Anubis looked around for a useful place to hide the toolbox. When he'd picked this location he'd chosen it to be near to his work, and because it was out of the way, but it hadn't occurred to him that he might need to be hiding a three-foot-long box of tools, as well.

He hastily shoved the tools under a dirty sheet of canvas and shoved the whole thing into a pile of shattered junk. The pile was constructed mostly of broken wagon wheels, their iron rims twisted and rusting. For a moment he wondered who might have put them there, or if someone intended to take them back. But asking where things came from and went to in New York was a game that could occupy every second of the day. He'd have to trust his luck.

Taking a quick look in either direction to make sure he was unnoticed, Anubis slung the satchel over his back, then took a few running steps and flung himself at the wall of the building, his hands finding purchase on the high brick sashes of the ground-floor windows. He scurried up toward the roof, his fingers grasping for the protruding edges that stuck out of the sheer brick face.

It was at moments like this that he most missed having his staff. The new version was in his bag, but using it now might put his identity at risk. At the same time, a man who didn't know how to climb up a building bare-handed had no business trying to do the same with a rope. Safety was an illusion most of the time, and it always paid to have a backup plan in place for the moment when things inevitably failed.

Still, climbing without it was slow work, and it took him almost half a minute to reach the roof. By the time he had travelled halfway up the brick facade sweat was already trickling down from his hair and across his face. He barely noticed it except for a subtle feeling of happiness that settled over him. Sweating was a feeling that he had gotten used to after spending so much time sealed into a leather suit. What differed from his expectations was that by the time he pulled himself up onto the rooftop he was breathing heavily. He was paying the price for his new line of work. He'd made the effort to exercise, and he had convinced himself that he had maintained his fitness, but clearly practicing to be a hero didn't keep a man in the same shape as actually being one.

Now that he was up above the city he had a clearer view of the location of the incident, although he wasn't close enough to see the park. Anubis thought he could hear the distant screams, and it spurred him to put on the costume as quickly as he could, his fingers almost trembling from the excitement of pulling on his chestplate and tightening the buckles that held it in place.

He screwed together his staff and gave the completed device a spin. It felt good to hold it in his hand again. There was, he had to admit, a sense of power that came with the costume, and even though his vision was slightly blurred by the taut fabric that hid his eyes from the world, it felt good. He liked to believe that he was the same man in or out of the mask, but it was hard to deny that he was different when he wore the costume. He and Anubis weren't *exactly* one and the same.

He fell into a run and threw himself across the rooftops. As his feet left the building he could feel himself rising just a hair less high than he had before. He doubted it was something that anyone else would notice, but his edge was missing. He'd need to remember that when he came into contact with someone dangerous.

As he reached the next rooftop and leapt into the air he couldn't deny the warmth rising in his body. He was a hero again! Moreover, he was free from the clutches of the Children, no longer a morally compromised man, although his mission to destroy them from within had failed utterly.

As he got nearer to the park things quickly became more serious, and the scene that unfolded in front of him was one of unbound terror and carnage. Wisps of the black smoke still crawled around the grounds of the park, burning and blackening the grass that it touched. The trees were stripped of their leaves, the bark burnt and black. Most of the people who had been caught in the cloud were already dead, their bodies tight like coiled springs, their hands and legs pulled in and backs bent. Some of them seemed to have almost become wrapped around themselves.

A few unlucky survivors wandered in a daze, their clothes mostly gone, their skin blackened. Or perhaps they were just . . . smoked? And one man stood in the center of the park. All that had survived from the explosion and the corrosive gas were rags, and a cloth wrapped around his waist—but rather than black, his body had been turned to purest white by the exposure to the deadly gas. "Eschaton," Anubis whispered in recognition. Sitting in front of him was a man in a wheelchair. He was writhing in the chair, his wrists and arms clearly bound.

Anubis lodged the head of the staff into a nearby smokestack and jumped off of the roof, letting the unreeling wire break his fall. The moment he reached the ground he retracted the spines and retrieved the tip of it, and sprinted toward the park. Survivors begged for help as he ran past.

As he got closer, he was almost blinded by the brightness that surrounded the huge figure of Eschaton, white lightning flashing underneath his skin. "Anubis! Of course you came!" The white man's voice seemed amplified somehow, the sound of it ringing off the walls of the buildings nearby.

Perhaps this was the fruition of Eschaton's mad plans. Had he come too late? "What have you done?"

Either Anubis's eyes were adjusting, or he had become more accustomed to the villain's dazzling light. "I'm so glad it was you, Anubis. Who better to be witness to the first dazzling rays of the new dawn."

"You're a twisted murderer!"

Eschaton shook his head. "You can no longer judge me! I am your superior now, Jackal! Look at me and rejoice, for I am your Ra! I am the god of a new day, the bringer of light for all mankind!" He swept his hand around him. "And these are my subjects." As Eschaton laughed, Anubis felt a wave of sickness rising up in him.

He took a breath to steady himself, and realized that there was something familiar in the sharp chemical odor of the smoke. He had smelled the same strange scent when Prescott had burned to death in front of him. The stink of Eschaton's corruption truly was everywhere.

The man in the wheelchair let out a moan. Now that he was closer, Anubis could see that there was something terribly wrong with him. His skin was a sickly white, as if his flesh had been transformed into living alabaster. Flickers of silver raced up and down his exposed flesh, like tiny fish swimming in his veins.

Eschaton noticed. "What do you think of my latest creation?"

"It's an abomination," he replied, "like everything else you create."

Eschaton let out a laugh. "Do you hear that, Nathaniel? This man thinks you're a monster."

"That's Nathaniel Winthorp?" It was only half a question, and as he realized that it was true, recognition still fought with disbelief that the boy could have been so utterly transformed.

"Indeed," Eschaton replied as he reached down and ran his hand almost lovingly across Nathaniel's shoulder. "An experiment of mine . . ." The bright glow around Eschaton was definitely fading, but it was still powerful enough that creeping bolts and electric arcs travelled across the flesh of the bound man as he caressed him, making him twitch. "Whether I can control not only the frequency of successful transformation, but the method of it."

Anubis had harbored his suspicions previously, but surely there had to be more to it than this. "And this is your plan? To smother the entire world in your deadly smoke?"

"And you call me a maniac! The world is, sadly, out of my reach, so currently I am only concerned with the population of this city. But once I have transformed New York, then my new brothers and I will set our sights on the other great cities. Paris next, I think."

"Your brothers?" He stared at Eschaton, his eyes wide with shock. "You want to create an army of men like yourself?"

Eschaton nodded vigorously. "Men, women, children, dogs, cats . . . A new race: a true ruling class. One born of technology, and not of the pathetic whims of biology."

"A race of monsters."

"The first step toward godhood."

Anubis looked around him. For every one moaning survivor there were a dozen or more of the silent dead. "You'll kill hundreds." Somewhere in the distance he could hear the shrill melodic trilling of police whistles.

If Eschaton had heard them, he was completely unconcerned by the imminent arrival of the authorities. "And now you're thinking too small. Thousands will perish—millions, if I have my way." He placed his palm on Nathaniel's head. What remained of the boy's hair came away under his hand. "But they would all die anyway. Their lives would have been meaningless, but now they can be the first martyrs of a new and better world."

"That's what you want to believe, but all I see here is murder."

The glow around him had almost vanished now, and the figure of Eschaton was becoming less blurred all the time. A dark hue was beginning to return to the giant's skin.

Eschaton slid his hand down toward Nathaniel's mouth and slipped his fingers into it. "Tell him Nathaniel. Let him hear the words of the first true child of Eschaton." Lifting up his glowing arm, he pulled a scrap of charred cloth out of the writhing figure's mouth.

Nathaniel let out a sound that was halfway between a shout and a whimper. "Help me! For the love of God, please help me."

Eschaton chuckled. "Your God clearly doesn't love you the way that I do."

Anubis felt the anger rising in him. He took a single step forward, and then charged toward the figure, raising his staff and firing the tip of it at Eschaton as he ran.

The ankh slammed into the gray man's hard flesh and bounced away, almost without effect. Anubis followed a second later, dropping low and slamming himself into the towering figure's legs.

A normal man would have toppled under the assault, but crashing into Eschaton was like slamming into a brick wall, and Anubis fell to the ground instead, all the air expelled from his lungs. He could feel the tingling electric energy coming off of Eschaton's skin even through his costume.

Taking a moment to shake off the pain, he twirled his staff, managing to drop a loop of the wire around Eschaton's neck.

Rather than staying within the gray giant's grasp, he ran off toward the iron fence. If he could reach it, he could find enough purchase to topple Eschaton.

Only a few feet from his destination, the wire pulled taut. As he fumbled for the catch that would allow him to reel out a bit more cable, Anubis had an instant of hope. Perhaps he could gain enough of an advantage to at least grab Nathaniel—not that he'd have any idea what to do with the boy once he had him. So far Eschaton had won every battle. Even a desperate victory was a victory.

Just as he was about to string the wire through the iron fence, he felt a tug against the staff in his hands strong enough that it almost threw him off of his feet. Instead it spun him around completely so that he was suddenly facing Eschaton. The gray man was holding the wire between his massive hands and smiling at him. He reached out with his other hand, grabbing the taut end and tugging it toward him. Anubis tried to hold his ground, but it was useless. His boots slid across the concrete as easily as if he were standing on ice.

"You are already most admirable as a man, Anubis." Eschaton yanked again, closing the distance between them by a few more feet. "I can only imagine how much more spectacular you'll be once I've purified you."

For a moment Anubis considered throwing down the staff and running away. Despite any wounds his pride might take, at least he'd survive his encounter to fight another day. But what did that mean, really? Would he go back into hiding? Pick up his tools and head back to the factory?

And then what would he do next? Simply wait until the next cloud of gas rose over the city?

Anubis had had enough of that. And the casualties of his cowardice, no matter how tactically sensible it was, were all around him.

The next yank brought them within a few yards of each other, and the grin on Eschaton's face was clearly growing. "What element would you like me to inject you with when I expose you to my smoke? Silver perhaps, or maybe gold, like that ankh on your chest."

As the giant pulled again, Anubis let himself go with the momentum. As he flew across the distance that separated them, he reared back with the staff, and then cracked it across Eschaton's head.

The gray man did at least have the courtesy to flinch from the impact of the metal rod against his face, and the annoying smile disappeared. But if the attack had been a minor annoyance, it was clearly not much more than that.

Then Anubis felt his staff ripped from his hands, and before he could respond it was being turned against him, crashing into his chest. Unlike the villain he was facing, Anubis was neither towering nor unstoppable, and the impact of the attack drove him to the ground.

Perhaps, he thought, now would be the time to escape. But as he struggled to catch a breath, Eschaton's hand reached down and grasped Anubis by his chestplate. A moment later he felt himself being lifted directly up into the air. He felt like a child's toy as he was spun around, and suddenly he was staring directly at Eschaton's terrifying gaze.

The gray man could hold him up with a single arm, and he took his free hand and wrapped it around Anubis's head. There was a familiar tugging sensation as his mask began to slip free. His lungs had gasped in enough air for him to choke out a single word . . . "No."

Eschaton shook his head. "Don't worry, Anubis. I already know your secret. Jack saw your skin weeks ago, after you killed that boy." He pulled off the mask completely, revealing Anubis's true face underneath. "But it had never really been hard for me to guess why you might want to hide your identity. No white man would willingly accept a Negro's help, or consider you anything but a criminal, really. But wearing a mask could allow you to pretend to be a hero in an ungrateful world."

"Didn't kill . . ." Anubis tried to choke out, but the words wouldn't come.

Eschaton tilted him toward Nathaniel. "What do you think Mr. Winthorp? Is this the savior you expected?"

The boy looked away. The expression on the young man's face said everything Anubis needed to know about his opinion of being saved by a man with brown skin. But Anubis had never let that stop him. He was the same man, with or without the mask.

Still, for a moment, Anubis wanted to rage and scream. Then the moment passed, and he suddenly felt at peace.

He let himself relax in the gray man's electric grip. Eschaton lifted him higher and studied his face. "I'm surprised at you, Anubis. How sad it must have been for you to hide your true face from me all this time."

"*My* secrets . . ." he choked out.

"In my new world, you won't need them. We will all be new colors: black, white, gray! Our new hues will reveal our power, and we will all be equals in each other's eyes!"

From the corner of his eye, Anubis saw Jack running toward them. The thin man was smiling. "Hello, Anubis. It's good to see you and our lord together again. We were getting afraid that you'd never come back to us."

"What's going on, Jack?" Eschaton asked.

"Me and the boys got the coppers on the run, for now. But it won't be for long. We need to get out of here."

Eschaton nodded. "Round up any of the survivors you can, and put them in the wagon." He lowered Anubis to the ground. "Take him, as well. I'll use him for the next experiment. I've never exposed a Negro to the formula before. Perhaps his dark skin will give us an . . . interesting reaction." Then he turned to Nathaniel. "Although it would have to be spectacular to be more interesting than you, my boy. And we're not done with you yet."

Anubis prepared himself to attack the moment he was let go. It might be that he couldn't fight this monster directly, but he could certainly escape Jack Knife and a few of his thugs.

Eschaton's arm went white, and Anubis suddenly felt every muscle in his body contract and shake. It was as if his entire self had been stolen by some mysterious demon, grabbing him and shaking him from within like a gibbering puppet. When Eschaton let go, Anubis crumpled to the ground, every muscle exhausted. He found himself staring into his own discarded mask—the face of Anubis. He had been judged, and was found wanting.

As he lay there, helpless and unmoving, he watched Eschaton turn and walk away. White lines crackled across the giant's bare flesh, and Anubis could feel the ground shuddering slightly with each step the man took. It was hard to deny that whatever Eschaton had become, he was certainly no longer human. But what did that make him? A god? Eschaton would have certainly claimed the title, or at least used it as an excuse to mock the deity he had fashioned himself after.

He could feel Jack's hands on him, rolling him over. He tried to will himself to lash out, but there was no fight left in him. "Come on, Anubis," the tall man said, lifting up the limp man's legs and tucking one boot under each arm to drag him away. "We're heading to the Hall of Paragons. You'll love what we've done with the place."

Chapter 5

The Body of a Man

"I'll do my best, Mrs. Farrows."

Sarah hugged Jenny tightly, her eyes squeezed shut. She could feel emotions pounding through her in waves: relief, fear, sadness, love . . .

For as long as she could remember, growing up meant watching the world take away everything she had ever known or loved: her mother, her father, Darby, Tom . . . But Jennifer Farrows was still here, and still alive. For now that would have to be enough.

As Sarah opened her eyes and blinked back the haze of tears, she was startled to see something staring back at her from the shadows in the corner of the room. It was a dark, angry gaze that compelled her to look away. She fought off the instinct and simply stared, the power of her embrace with Jenny only moments before now almost utterly forgotten. The conflicting feelings still swirled around inside of her, but the intensity seemed to be have been dwarfed by the sudden quiet battle of wills with the wild, damaged creature that she shared the house with.

She knew that if she turned away even for an instant she would never find the courage to be able to look Viola Armando in the eyes again. Instead she stared directly at the girl, trying not to focus on the dark wounds on her face. Instead, she stared directly into her soul.

Viola had always been uncivilized—there was no denying that to a greater degree her wild, exotic nature was a part of her charm. Sarah had admired Viola's ability to move through the world unencumbered by the rules of society. In many ways the short time they had spent together as friends (or something close to that) had increased Sarah's desire to throw caution to the wind and live the life that she wanted in her heart, instead of the one that her sex and position demanded of her.

Looking back at her life, it seemed that all of Sarah's greatest moments of happiness had come during those times when she was breaking the rules, whether it was playing in the secret passageways of the Hall of Paragons or being taught forbidden subjects by Darby.

But that kind of freedom also came with a heavy cost. As she widened her eyes and stared intently into the angry visage of Viola Armando, she realized that being outside of society also meant that when the world began to collapse around you there was nothing to hang on to. If you ran away from the world that supported you, there was no foundation on which to rebuild your life. Yet that was exactly what she had chosen to do the night she had run away from her father in the park.

At least Sarah had known what it was that she was giving up. In Viola's case, she had never been given a choice. Her anger was a survival mechanism, and even so, the world had reached out and punished her for it. Thinking about Viola's plight made Sarah's hard stare soften with pity. The returning gaze narrowed angrily in reply—clearly enraged that anyone would dare to feel sorry for her.

But everyone faced challenges in their lives, big or small. When she had first met Tom, Sarah had asked why Darby had made his body so round, rather than making him more human in shape. "We are all birthed in the shape of our creator's intentions," he had replied to her, "but we die in the form given to us by our actions."

Whatever the intentions, whether they were good or bad, Viola had arrived here defined by the actions that she had chosen to take. When she was beautiful she had tried to make everyone in the world feel nothing for her but envy. Now that Viola's beauty had been ruined, no one would give her even that. It was only her brother who seemed unable to see just how broken his sister had become.

Sarah began to feel Jenny's grip around her loosening. Sarah stiffened, locking her friend into the hug for just a moment longer, and then quietly, and with some exaggeration, mouthed the words "I'm sorry," to Viola.

Jenny pulled back, breaking out of Sarah's grasp with some awkwardness. Sarah quickly caught her friend's eyes and she smiled at her. Then, her eyes twitched, looking back into the corner, unsure whether the Italian girl had seen what she had done. But the shadows were empty now. Viola had scampered away into the curtains and the darkness.

"You saw Viola," Jenny said matter-of-factly.

"I'm sorry," Sarah said, and she meant it. It seemed that Viola had an uncanny knack for twisting moments of closeness into uncomfortable encounters. "She's lost her mind, I think."

"Maybe more than that." Jenny turned to look in the direction where she had run off and frowned. "It's a shame. You and she are more alike than either of you would ever be able to admit." Her words trailed off at the end, almost as if she was simply reciting an old saying.

Sarah furrowed her brow. "Do you think I'm mad, as well?"

"What?" The maid replied almost dreamily. Then, in an instant, she snapped back to reality. Jenny looked at Sarah sternly and waved a dismissive hand at her. "Don't be so sensitive, girl. One minute you're perfectly happy to consider yourself free of your responsibilities to anyone else in the world, and the next you're complaining that I might compare you to someone who has managed to build a life where she doesn't have any responsibility for anything."

Sarah could feel herself being put back on the defensive. Jenny's crushing descriptions were legendary amongst the staff of the Stanton mansion, and only Mr. O'Rourke seemed to always have a ready retort for her sly barbs. Having grown up around intelligent women for most of her life had given her a few tricks of her own. "All right, Mrs. Farrows. So maybe you don't think I'm a madwoman, but I think it's safe to say that Viola and I have parted ways at this point."

"Oh, you're both definitely mad," Jenny replied with a devilish smile. "You're also both stubborn, willful, and so cocksure and full of pride that neither of you can recognize that the moment when you feel the most alone is also the moment that you most need to rely on others."

Sarah tried to reply, but instead found herself looking sheepishly down at her shoes. Perhaps the maid had a point.

Sarah looked up at her and smiled. "Thank you, Jenny. Because if I'm going to fight this madman, I'll need my good friends by my side." She'd closed the trap. "I'm glad to know you'll be there with me."

Jenny frowned. "All right, Sarah. You know I'm not going to abandon you. But I'd like us all to come out of this alive."

Sarah nodded, and then felt a sudden pressure of a different kind. "Thanks, Jenny."

"Now," Jenny said, rising up, "I need to go out to the privy." After a few steps away she stopped and turned back to face Sarah. "But I still haven't promised to join you on your crusade." Just before she reached the curtains in front of the exit, she stopped again. "And if you're going to try recruiting people for your mad schemes, you may need to consider wearing something more than a housecoat."

After a few more steps she stopped and turned around for a third time, cutting off Sarah just before she started to reply. "And while you're considering what you're going to do, there are plenty of chores around this house. That'll keep you busy while your Italian friend tries to put Humpty Dumpty back together again."

Sarah opened her mouth to tell Jenny off, but then simply let out an exasperated sigh as the maid danced out the door. She wondered why it was that her father had wanted so badly to become the leader of the Paragons if this was how everyone acted when you asked for their help? "Maybe he didn't bother trying to lead maids and madmen," she muttered as she flopped back onto the couch. But it was a question Sarah would need to answer properly if she was going to face Lord Eschaton.

What was it that allowed some people to lead while others followed? And worse still, what if that particular instinct, whatever it was, was something she didn't have?

Sarah sighed again, a bit more theatrically this time, stood up, and then grabbed a wrinkled dress that she had pulled out of a closet and then thrown over the back of one of the nearby chairs. It was cut from heavy black cloth, and she was convinced that the previous owner of the shapeless and dusty thing had once been a nun. Still, it was clothing. Sarah heard the sound of feet running back toward the room.

Sarah had managed to wriggle herself far enough through the dress that she could poke her head out through the top of it by the time Jenny returned.

Something had given the maid quite a fright. Sarah had only ever seen her so flustered once before, and that had been over a precious vase that Nathaniel had managed to knock down when roughhousing with another boy. "What is it Jenny?"

"Please. You need to come see this," Jenny said in a discomfortingly serious tone. Jenny snatched up her hand and began to drag her outdoors. "There's something very bad happening in Manhattan."

As she parsed the words, Sarah let her resistance give way and allowed Jenny to pull her out into the daylight. Even before Sarah's eyes could finish adjusting it was obvious what had frightened her friend: a heavy black cloud hung menacingly above the empty blue city sky. Even from this distance she could see that it was roiling in a most unnatural way.

"You see? It looks almost like one of those horrible sea beasties that your father liked to eat." Years ago Alexander Stanton had once consumed octopus for dinner. The unfortunate monster had been a gift from an Asian dignitary who had visited their home. It was the only time that Sarah could remember her father eating any kind of seafood that didn't have a tail. It had also, apparently, scarred Jenny for life. "What do you think it could be?"

Sarah studied the roiling black cloud for a moment longer. Although she had never seen such a thing before, it still seemed somehow familiar. She was unsure whether or not she should say her conclusions out loud. "I think," Sarah said with a degree of certainty in her voice that was shocking even to her, "that Lord Eschaton has just shown us the next step in his plan." And as she said the words the cloud seemed to collapse, almost as if it could hear her and was trying to escape. It dropped out of the sky, falling onto the city as a sudden black rain.

"What should we do?"

For a moment Sarah wondered whether it wasn't already too late. If this *was* the first step in Eschaton's plan then their best action might be to run away from the city as fast and as far as they could. "Emilio should be in his lab. Go tell him what's going on."

"What are you going to do?" Jenny asked her.

Stantons didn't run, especially from villains. Sarah would face down her fate with her fists swinging. And, if she could help it, she wouldn't do it alone. "I need to get something first." Sarah followed the maid back into the house, taking a right turn when Jenny turned left toward the workshop.

Although she mostly slept on the parlor couch, there was still another room in the house that was considered hers. It was the same one in which she woke after she and Emilio had fallen out of the sky from le Voyageur's balloon.

For the first few weeks she had thoroughly enjoyed having such a spacious, open room in this ridiculous ramshackle house. It was a far cry from the cramped urban spaces of the family mansion, and she had been ecstatic to live someplace where she could leave a few things around without them immediately being pounced on by an endless parade of overeager, disapproving servants. But once it began to settle in that this house was now her new *home*, the excitement had quickly soured. Sarah would wake up in the morning finding herself feeling lost and lonely. And in the dark the broken statues and hanging curtains had seemed to take on a life of their own.

The main room was larger, but less cluttered. It also seemed more friendly and open. She trusted Emilio, if not Viola. It hadn't been her intention to make the sofa her new bed; the first few times she had fallen asleep on the overstuffed settee, she had woken up after a few hours and dragged herself back to her room, chastising herself for dozing off in such a vulnerable position. But after a time she realized that no one really cared where she slept, nor did they have any desire to disturb her slumber in the parlor. It wasn't long before Sarah let herself spend the entire night there. Other than Jenny's disapproval this morning, there had been no consequences.

Still, even after she had stopped using "her room" as a bedroom, Sarah found that there were some advantages to having one's own private space, no matter where she actually slept. Crossing over to the large bed, Sarah dropped to the floor and reached down to retrieve her battered leather suitcase from underneath the mattress. She pulled it out and landed it on the bed in a single smooth motion, then flipped open the cover to reveal what was inside.

Unlike when she'd lived in her small apartment in Manhattan, Tom's metal heart was no longer wrapped in paper. Instead she had been able to find a long bolt of dark purple velvet that she had fashioned into swaddling to protect the device.

Emilio asked her for use of the heart from time to time as he attempted to reanimate the mechanical man. Sarah was always happy to let him take it for experimentation as long as she was present. But after nearly losing the heart permanently after the incident at the theater, she was no longer comfortable letting anyone take it completely out of her hands. Instead she would stand there with him while Emilio tried to bring it—and Tom—back to life. She needed to be sure that this time there would be no disasters or mistakes.

But, far from another disaster, so far none of Emilio's experiments had managed to show any signs that he could conjure the mechanical man back to life. She flipped the lid closed and said a silent prayer. Sarah wasn't sure that God would be interested in the fate of a mechanical man, but if Sarah had a single powerful belief when it came to spiritual matters, it was that it could never hurt to ask for divine inspiration in moments of need. Eschaton was on the move, and their time was running out. If God wasn't on her side, there were much bigger problems with the universe than she thought.

Sarah wedged the case awkwardly under one arm. Looking around the floor, she spotted a pair of sturdy, well-worn red slippers. She slipped her feet into them and headed for the workshop on the other side of the house. When she walked through the door into the ramshackle space, the light inside was blindingly bright. As her eyes adjusted to the glare, she could see that Emilio had thrown open the door of the old train car to let in the sun. He was staring out the door through a large spyglass that he had focused squarely on the city. "Are you sure of what you saw, Mrs. Farrows?" Emilio said. "A black cloud?"

"She's quite sure," Sarah said, and walked up to an empty space on one of the workbenches. She placed the suitcase on it with a heavy thump.

"Hello . . ." Emilio said cautiously. Sarah frowned. In the weeks since the incident, her once-dashing Italian suitor had seemed to retreat inside of himself. Between what had happened to Viola and his obvious lack of interest, Sarah felt unsure what her current feelings were toward the man. Where once he seemed unstoppable and exotic, now he was quiet and staid, like a nervous boy at a ball. He almost entirely refused to make eye contact with her.

As first she thought that perhaps he had simply grown shy, but remembering his performance with the vermouth, Sarah harbored a suspicion that when it came to matters of the heart, Emilio's true nature was far more that of a libertine than a retiring gentlemen. And since the theater he had managed to keep any inappropriate urges so deeply under wraps that another woman might have doubted he had ever had them to begin with. Truth be told, if it hadn't been for the evidence of the kisses they had shared, she would have never known just how much he was attracted to her. She had begun to suspect that Emilio blamed her for the damage that had been done to his sister. And who was to say that it wasn't her fault?

As Sarah flipped open the lid, she turned to her right and saw what looked like a half-completed manikin on the stand next to her. "Is this Tom's new body?"

Jenny turned to look at it as well, and scrunched up her face. "It looks more like a harp with delusions of grandeur." If there was one thing that Sarah could rely on from her friend, it was a dismissive attitude when it came to anything mechanical or technological. Jenny didn't mind machines, but she had a habit of seeing them as a one might a feral cat or untrained dog— always ready to strike when least expected.

From the darkness there was a hiss, and Viola melted out of the shadows. The girl dragged closed the squealing train car door, shutting out much of the daylight with a painful crash. She turned around with a menacing look in her eyes, and somehow seemed to be glaring at both Sarah and Jenny simultaneously. "Don't make fun of him. I think he's beautiful." Viola marched over, wrapped her hands around the inanimate thing's neck, and gave it an almost-lustful hug. "He's my favorite man."

Sarah tried to ignore Viola's disturbing display and took a closer look at Tom's body. As her eyes traced out its form, Sarah realized that this time the mad girl was right: what Emilio had created was beautiful. There was also something strangely familiar about it, although it took her a moment to place it. "Why does this make me think of the Frenchman's balloon?"

Emilio smiled and nodded as he came up to her, his eyes finally meeting hers, if only for a fraction of an instant. "Ah, yes!" he said with a tone of slight embarrassment. "You noticed!" His last few words even seemed to have a hint of the old Emilio's intensity. "I borrowed some of his techniques. At first I thought they were ridiculous, but then . . ."

"I'm not a complete fool," Sarah said, cutting him off. "But le Voyageur was a dangerous madman. Is it safe to give Tom a body designed after him, especially given what happened last time?"

Viola lifted up her head and smiled a grim smile. The scars pulled tight;

a vivid reminder of the consequences of awakening Tom in the wrong body. "Poor little rich girl . . . I think that maybe *all* the men in your world have been mad for a very long time and now you're just starting to notice." The Italian girl plucked one of the wires in the manikin's shoulder, and it let out a clear musical tone.

Sarah felt her face flush. Once again the Italian girl had managed to wind her up, but she was not about to get into another argument about men, mad or otherwise, with Viola Armando. Their fights had been troubling enough before the girl had lost her mind. There seemed to be no possible benefit in trying to convince her of anything now. "And it isn't over yet," Sarah said.

Emilio shook his head. "No, not yet—but very close. Another few days."

"*You* didn't see what was up in the sky, but *I* did," Sarah pulled the mechanical heart closer to her chest. "We're out of time, Emilio. If Eschaton feels that he can attack in broad daylight, then he must be very close to completing his plan."

"Maybe it was an accident. . . . Maybe it was not him." Emilio paused and stared straight at the heart in her hands. "Is New York. Things happen all the time."

Sarah brushed her hand along the manikin's metal frame. It was almost shockingly smooth and cool under her fingertips. Perhaps waiting for Emilio to finish *was* the right thing to do. "It was him. I know it," she said. The words were as much for her own benefit as they were for anyone else's.

But the body didn't even have a new face yet. . . . Could they bring him back without one? It wasn't like Tom had ever actually *needed* eyes to see, or even a mouth to speak. . . . But time didn't seem to be a luxury they had anymore. "I've spent my entire life around adventurers and villains. I can tell when they're doing their work."

Emilio rubbed his hands together. "We tried before, Sarah. It was no good. What do I do differently now?"

Sarah thought of Darby's failed experiments with the Alpha Element, and held the heart out toward Emilio. "Try it now."

Jenny looked shocked. "Sarah, he's already told you that he needs more time."

"I heard him, Jenny, but we're running out of options and time. He just needs to try."

Emilio looked up at her, but made no movement in her direction. She tried to look into his eyes, but all she saw in the small glimpse she could get was the same dark cloud of retreat that had been smothering him ever since that night his sister had been hurt. If they were going to change their luck, she would have to be the one to do it. "Emilio . . . you have to."

"I don't have to do anything."

Sarah was shocked. Was she the only one here with any spirit left? But before she could reply, Emilio spoke again. "All right. We try," he said with a weary nod. "So everyone move out of the way!"

The women stepped away from the manikin. Emilio popped open a latch on the metal frame, then grabbed the top of the machine's rib cage and pulled. The front of the metal chest swung open as a single piece, revealing the mechanical workings within. The steel had all been polished to a silvery gleam, the light reflecting off of every edge. What Emilio did next almost made Sarah gasp out loud: reaching into the cavity, he pulled on the ring that he had designed to hold the heart in place. Where Tom's heart had previously been locked deep into the cavity of his body, for his new incarnation Emilio had created an ingenious swinging armature that slid smoothly out from the center of the mechanical man's chest and locked into place with a satisfying click once it was fully extended.

"All right, now his heart." Sarah held it out, and Emilio took it delicately from her hands and placed it into the platform. Whereas in Darby's version, Tom's heart had been locked into position with numerous screws, this new device was more of a harness with a series of spring-loaded clamps that held the metal sphere in place gently but firmly. Once Emilio had finished placing it into position, the metal sphere seemed to be almost floating in the air. Sarah felt a warm tingle of emotion that ran through her from head to toe.

Looking at Emilio she recognized that it was a feeling of attraction for the man that she hadn't had in a long time. There was, she had to admit, something about him that she found undeniably compelling—so similar to Darby in his skills, and yet so different in his approach. Less skilled, but more wild and alluring.

As Emilio swung the heart back into the body, Sarah had a shocking realization—she had never known the professor as anything but an old man.

Who was to say that he hadn't been similar when he was Emilio's age? The Darby she had known was a man nearing the end of his years; full of the kind of calm confidence and stories that could only come with years of work. But what failures had occurred before he could reach that place? It would have been a question to ask Peter Wickham, or her father. But now all those men were gone, taking with them the answers to the mysteries of the past. Perhaps that was part of the price of progress. She was sure that Lord Eschaton would agree with her.

It took Emilio a moment to fully lock the chestplate back into place. Even half-finished, what he had managed to accomplish with the tools he had "liberated" from the Theater Mechanique was astounding. "Amazing," she said out loud.

"Now what do we do?" Viola asked with an undisguised tone of scorn. "Because I don't think he's simply going to come back all by himself."

Sarah felt her heart sink. She had half hoped for a miracle—that Tom would simply decide to reanimate once the heart had been placed back into his body, the same way he had at the theater. That was clearly not going to happen today. They would need to try something else—anything else. "Are the boilers up?" Sarah asked, nodding out toward the yard.

"Is up," Emilio said, and reached out for one of the long hoses that hung from a wire along the back wall. He grabbed it from the valve on the top and pulled downwards, the slack spring that had held it out of the way unwinding with a series of throaty "boings" as it fought in vain to reel the rubber tube back.

When he had pulled it down far enough to reach the mechanical man, Emilio attached it to a nozzle sticking out from the manikin's (no, not Tom's . . . yet) back. Emilio had clearly figured out what it was that Sarah was intending, and as he stuck it into place, he let out a weary sigh. "We try this before. It doesn't work."

"Please try again, Emilio." She tried to sound commanding as she spoke the words. It would be better than pleading. She was unsure if he would continue to humor her if he knew that she was simply guessing desperately. From the look on Viola's face, she had no faith in Sarah at all.

Jenny was hanging back, slightly curious as to all the goings on, but clearly nervous. Sarah wondered if her friend would be terrified if this faceless, half-finished creature actually did spring to life.

"You ready?" Emilio asked, his hand resting on the wheel that would unleash the pressurized vapor into the tube.

Sarah nodded, and after a moment he began to turn the valve. As steam poured into the manikin it began to twitch and jerk. The taut wire strings hummed as it moved, playing a tuneless song. Peering into the chest, Sarah could see that the reverse power was causing the heart to spin. Moisture dripped off of the frame where the steam poured out, and it splashed against the floor in sloppy dark drops. "Turn it off now," she said.

As the valve squeaked closed the whole device once again fell limp. Sarah peered into the chest, hoping (praying?) for a sign that they might be at least headed in the right direction. But whether Tom's previous animated state had been true life or simply a crude approximation, one thing that it shared with the genuine article was that it was either all or nothing: something was either dead or alive, and there was no space in between.

Feeling a sense of rising desperation, Sarah told herself not to panic. "That was just a test," she said out loud.

"Of what?" Viola said with a mocking sharpness in her tone. "Shove a steam-hose up my backside and I'll jump, too."

"Hush now, you rude thing," Jenny said sharply. Her rebuke came so quickly that it was practically a reflex.

Closing her eyes for a moment, Sarah tried to relive the moment of Tom's return to life back in the theater. It all seemed like a blur now. She had been afraid for her life, desperate to find a way to hide the Automaton's heart from the Children of Eschaton. Shoving it up into the body of the Colossus had been an act of desperation, and yet it seemed to be the only sensible act at the time. She could remember how it felt as she had pushed it in, her arm scraping against the side of the hatch, the brass organ catching against the gears once she had shoved it in as far as it could go. Then she had pulled out her arm, covered in muck from the inner workings of the machine. "Maybe it was the grease?" she asked out loud.

Emilio shook his head. "Plenty already, Sarah." He looked unhappy. "Maybe we should stop. I finish him tomorrow and we try again."

His hand had already reached out to undo the latch on the cheastplate when Sarah's fingers landed on top of his. "Please Emilio," she said. This time the pleading in her voice was obvious, and his hands tensed almost as if her flesh had wandered too near to a fire. "I know we can figure this out. I *know* you can do it!" She moved her head around, trying to catch his eyes with hers, but he was better at looking away.

From somewhere behind her, she heard Viola's shrill laughter. "You think you can just make him come back to life because you want to?" The mocking sounds sent a chill up her spine. The feeling was halfway between anger and dread. "Stupid rich girl, nothing can bring back the dead."

Reaching her limit of frustration, Sarah reached out and placed two fingers against Emilio's chin. He resisted only slightly as she pushed his face around until he was looking directly into her eyes. She spoke her next words as simply and clearly as she could muster. "I can't fail this time, Emilio. *Not again.*"

"Not again," Emilio repeated. For a moment she thought that she was seeing the clouds clear, and then his eyes glanced over to his sister. "No, not again," he repeated, but this time she could hear that the tone in his voice had changed.

"Damn you, Emilio Armando," she shouted at him, "I know you can be better than this. Where is your fire? What happened to the man I was falling in love with?"

"*You* did, rich girl," said Viola without missing a beat. "You and your heroes happened to *all* of us."

"It's time for you to shut up, Viola," Sarah said, her anger obliterating any remaining sympathy she had for the girl. "I'm done with your guilt. What happened wasn't just my fault."

"Sarah!" Jenny was shocked. "No matter what you want, the poor girl *has* suffered. Don't be cruel."

Looking at Viola, Sarah saw that the girl was smirking, clearly pleased that she had managed to garner genuine sympathy from Jenny. Sarah walked over and stared hard at the scars with an impassive scowl. "You think you know me well, don't you? *Rich girl. Rich girl.* But you have no idea what that even means. If I was the spoiled child of privilege you think I am, would I have come anywhere near a fallen guttersnipe like you?"

Viola moved away from her. It was only the smallest flinch, but it was enough for her to gain purchase, like finding an unexpected crack on a sheer cliff face. Sarah was determined to climb it. "You should be happy that you're still alive, grateful that you can go on living. But that's not possible for a mean-spirited, horrible creature like you. You cling to life out of spite, making the lives of everyone around you into a misery. I've seen so many better people lose their lives . . ." Sarah let out a barking laugh that washed away her feelings of sadness. "There's no more fitting mark of the unfairness of your continued existence than what happened to your face, and I refuse to let you torture me with it anymore."

Viola turned away, her hands over her eyes as if she had been struck. It had taken a long time, but Sarah had finally made the girl react. She knew she might regret it later, but just for this one moment, it felt good.

"Sarah, please . . ." Emilio pleaded. "Stop."

"No," she said primly as she turned to face him. "You can't ask me to stop. Not if you won't be by my side when I need you." Taking a step closer, she gave him the same intense glare she had just given his sister. "I'm afraid that's not one of the options I have available for you. But here is what I can offer: you can help me, or you can get out of the way."

Sarah pushed Emilio aside, revealing the faceless visage of Tom behind him. "And you!" Sarah pushed the metal body, sending it rocking on the metal stand that held it up. "You were supposed to be my *friend*!" Sarah wanted to stop. She knew it was ridiculous to be chastising a lifeless manikin. But a curtain of red had descended over her world, and she realized that it felt *good* to finally tell the truth for a change.

Besides, the fact that Tom's lifeless frame couldn't fight back made him the perfect target for her rage. "What's the matter with you? You promised me! *You promised!*" She was shrieking now, and she shoved the half-finished manikin body back into the workbench. Somewhere on the tables something shattered, and there was a hiss as one of the burners belched a ball of flame.

Sarah hadn't felt that kind of heat since the day Darby's house had burned down, and she brought her hands up over her face to protect herself, but the heat had already vanished. There was the familiar scent of singed hair, and it brought back the memories of being in Tom's arms. "I'm sorry," she said as the tears rolled down her face. But truth be told, the only thing she truly felt sorry for was herself.

Emilio ran around her, scrambling to get the damage she had caused under control. Maybe the whole place would burn down . . . maybe that was what they all deserved.

He pushed the scorched frame aside, and it began to slide sideways. Sarah grabbed it, trying to stop it from falling, but she underestimated its weight, and instead it took her down with it. She and the metal body crashed to the ground together in a cacophony of snapping strings and broken notes. She turned her head to look at the faceless thing—another dead friend. "Another failure."

"No . . ." said Emilio, from somewhere up above. She felt the weight coming off of her as Emilio pulled Tom's body away. "I think I know." His tone sounded different.

"Now stand up, Sarah," Emilio said, taking her hand. "I think you will want to see this."

She let herself rise up, and wiped away the tears from her eyes. "What is it?"

"To invent the impossible, imagine the improbable," Emilio recited. Sarah recognized the words—they had been inscribed inside the walls of Tom's heart.

The stand had been bent slightly in the fall, leaving the body hanging at a slightly odd angle. Behind it the wooden surface of the workbench was still smoldering.

Emilio took a few minutes to straighten up as best he could. Once he had things fairly stable, he reattached the tube, and then re-opened the steam valve. Once again the mechanical man started to jump and shiver. Emilio pulled out a wooden match from a small paper packet and struck it against the table. It flared to life, and he used it to light a shard of wood he grabbed from the floor. After it was burning merrily he waved the stick out, and held the smoking ember underneath the steaming organ.

"You must will your success into being," he continued. Sarah was impressed with how clear Emilio's English was when he was quoting Darby. "I say, *live*, Automaton!"

Sarah felt herself flush with embarrassment. Tom hadn't returned to life because she'd shouted at him.

The smoke rising up from the smoldering stick mixed with steam, surrounding the heart in a gray glow. "Live," Emilio said again, more loudly this time, and grabbed Sarah's hand. "Say it with me!"

Sarah frowned, but Emilio was not willing to take no for an answer. "If you need him, he will come back to you, Sarah." This was ridiculous. "Say it!" he said.

She had tried everything else—maybe it *could* work. "Live!" she said, but even she couldn't hear the meek words over the clattering metal and the hissing steam. She said it again, this time yelling as loud as she could. "Live, Tom!"

Then she began to chant the words over and over again, a tiny flicker of hope rising up inside. But nothing seemed to be happening to Tom except for the same twitching that had come from the steam.

As Sarah felt her feelings of hope turn to despair, the shivering stopped entirely. Emilio had obviously shut off the steam again—hadn't he? But his hands hadn't moved and the hissing continued.

When she looked up, there was a smile on Emilio's face. He reached out and closed the steam valve. The hissing died away, except for a small, steady beat that came from the heart, small wisps of white vapor rising out from it in regular beats. "It's working," he said.

Tom's working arm rose up, and Sarah held back a gasp as he began to speak. "I am . . . here." The voice was different than it had been before. Instead of the previous throaty whistle, the sound was a glissando from twisting strings—far more musical, but somehow unearthly, like an angry choir of angels singing together to form a single voice. "But . . . where am I?"

The arm groped around blindly, clearly trying to discover more about the world. Sarah reached out and took his hand, grasping it in hers. As his fingers closed around hers, the grip was tight, almost painful, but not more than she could stand. "I missed you, Tom. I missed you so much."

"Sarah . . ."

She could feel the hot tears rolling down her cheeks, and flinging sensibility to the wind she wrapped her arms around his shoulders. The metal was cold and unyielding, but it felt somehow different knowing that Tom was animated. "Thank God," was all she could think to say. "I didn't know what to do without you."

"I am sorry . . . Sarah."

She pulled away, but kept his hand in hers. "Sorry? Whatever are you sorry for?"

But before Tom could reply, she heard Viola's voice from over her shoulder. "He's sorry that he came back." Once again she heard the sharp sound of the Italian girl's mocking laughter tearing apart her joy. "You're sorry that your rich girl didn't let you stay dead."

Sarah felt the anger rush up into her. "You couldn't know. You don't remember. He wanted me to save him. He wanted to live! He said so!"

Then she felt Tom's metal hand on her shoulder and she turned around to stare into his faceless visage. "I am sorry I . . . left you. I am sorry I . . . hurt you."

She stared into the emptiness, trying to remember the face he had worn before. Those eyes had seemed kind, but they had been painted that way. It had never been possible to know what it was that truly lay behind them. And now there was this new Tom. Was he the Automaton she had known, or the colossus that they had faced in the theater?

Every time her metal friend had saved her, it had come at a cost to the people around her. "Stop! You weren't in control of yourself, but you are better now." If Tom was a weapon, at least he was her weapon.

"I think that your . . . friend may be . . . right."

"No. She's not." Sarah could hear the anger in her voice, but she didn't care. She had been given a miracle, and Viola wouldn't ruin it. "We *need* you Tom. I'm so glad you came back to us."

Sarah looked to Emilio, hoping to find some support in his eyes, but his gaze was locked on the Automaton. He had been the one who had truly believed, and now he seemed astounded by what he was seeing.

"Hello, Tom. I am Emilio."

Tom's voice dropped lower, and it came booming out of him angrily. "I . . . REMEMBER YOU." His hand pulled free of Sarah's and rose up threateningly.

Emilio stumbled back, and Sarah gasped.

"Tom," Viola said, and stepped in between the automaton and Emilio. "This is my brother. He's your friend. He rebuilt you!"

"YES! He . . . I . . . understand. I AM . . . sorry." The hand lowered, and then extended in a far more friendly gesture.

Emilio took it with a surprising lack of hesitation. "I am pleased to meet you."

But Sarah could think of nothing to say. The idea of Tom returning to life had seemed ridiculous, and yet that had been her dream. Now it was shattered by the realization that the monster she had met at the theater was still there, hidden somewhere inside of him. The thought was dizzying—or, perhaps, Sarah was simply becoming dizzy. She certainly could feel the walls closing in around her. She had been waiting for this moment for so long, it had come at such a cost; and even now there was still more to be done.

Trying to maintain her composure, she stood up and took a few unsteady steps. From behind her she heard Viola's mocking tones. "Is this what you wanted, rich girl? Is this what you *wanted*?"

She opened her mouth to reply, but she had nothing to say. Instead she heard Tom's voice. "You brought me . . . back. I came back for . . . you."

She looked at the metal man in front of her, and wondered if she had made a terrible mistake. Before she could stop herself, her feet were carrying her out the door.

Chapter 6

The Transformation of Fear

When Jordan Clements first saw the truth that lay behind Anubis's mask, he realized that he'd known the truth all along. In retrospect, it had been staring him in the face every time the jackal had turned toward him and he could see nothing behind his hidden eyes. "As simple as black and white," the White Knight muttered to himself, and then stifled a laugh.

As he walked down the granite halls and down the stairs to the cells, he marveled again at just how grand the Hall of Paragons was. There was little of the usual opulent collections of artifacts and paintings that stuffed wealthy homes of the city—Darby would have never allowed that. What little ornamentation there was had been mostly destroyed after Hughes had been swallowed into the belly of the building. But despite the lack of all of that, it was still impossible not to be impressed by the sheer size of the structure, and all the different rooms they had hidden inside it.

One of Clements's first acts after moving into the headquarters as a Paragon had been to claim the Industrialist's old office as his own. The quake that had proceeded Hughes's rebirth as the Shell had almost emptied the shelves of Stanton's dusty collection of books. Jordan had taken them all and piled them high into a corner, waiting for one of the servants to collect them and throw them out. So far, no one had come. Most of the servants had fled the building during the shaking and had never come back; the ones that remained were employed in doing Eschaton's bidding.

In the end, the abandoned books had been a blessing in disguise. Clements had burned many of them in the fireplace, using the blackening pages to warm his hands during the cold nights.

He had considered keeping a few of the fancier books, since people in the north often assumed he was stupid or uneducated simply because of his accent. But Clements wasn't really much of a reader, and most of the books that Stanton had been interested in seemed to be concerned with philosophy and justice, two subjects that Jordan always felt were most often used to try to explain why all the bad things that happened in life weren't actually bad— or how, if you just looked at them right, they'd one day turn out to have actually been good for you after all. Worst of all were the ones that explained why the bad things that happened *to* you weren't really bad for anyone else *but* you. There was a simple truth about life which Clements had figured out after the Union had burned down his family's home: it was all bull. There were no excuses for all the terrible things that happened in the world. Good things were good, bad were bad, and that was the way the world worked. Everyone wanted more of the good things, but you had to fight to get them.

It seemed like a harsh way to live, but it was reality. And once you figured *that* out, you could stop pretending that when people pissed on you, it was actually rain.

When Clements had turned ten—just old enough for him to truly understand what was happening—war had come to their bucolic plantation. It had taken only a matter of hours: bullets and bombs had reduced his home from a triumph of Southern finery to a shattered ruin. He'd watched brave Confederate soldiers die in front of him, and his mother had been gravely wounded. But in the end, with the help of his father and the other men, they had driven back the Northern aggressors.

Over the next few years he watched his mother fade away, leaving him in the rough hands of his remaining parent. His father had often told him that fighting any worthwhile battle, whether against man or animal, would always come at a great cost. But if you destroyed your enemy and survived, you must never forget what you lost—you needed to keep a trophy. That prize, he had told Jordan, was not only an important part of keeping your sanity in the madness of war, it was also a reminder that you remained in this world and they did not, and that one day, no matter how hard you struggled, your time would come as well.

To this day, Clements still had the hat he had taken off the dead Yankee soldier before they buried him. After he had killed Stanton, he had wanted to keep the Industrialist's gun, perhaps to even use it for himself, but Eschaton had decided he needed to study it, and had taken it away. He was still a bit angry about that, truth be told. If he had been brandishing that man's weapon in the theater when that machine had come back to life, things might have gone very differently. Instead he had kept Stanton's ridiculous red-white-and-blue top hat. It still sat on one of the empty shelves in the office.

Clements smiled a tight little grin as he remembered the look on Stanton's face when his fist had crashed into it. That was the moment the Industrialist had discovered that the White Knight wasn't actually the fat, hapless bumpkin that he'd been expecting—he was a man with power. Stanton had offered to let him beat him to death, and he had almost been able to take him up on it. Then Nathaniel Winthorp had interfered. If the boy hadn't surprised him, if his powers hadn't failed him at just that moment, he would have taken him, too.

But when Clements had taken Stanton's life, the boy had been watching him. And now Nathaniel had become one of the more freakish examples of Eschaton's purified humans. Surviving was winning. That was the best kind of justice. And maybe Eschaton would let him take Anubis's mask to add to his collection of "scalps."

He reached the jail cells and found the entrance guarded by one of Jack Knife's flunkies. The man was built like a fortress: so many muscles on muscles that it almost made him look fat. His tweed jacket was ill-fitting, shabby, and worn. He also stank a bit—although less than Clements would have expected of one of Jack's pieces of street trash.

Since they'd ousted the original Paragons, the men in tweed jackets were all over the Hall. They were mostly working to keep the building secure. Eschaton had brought in a large number of men to become his "Paragon Militia," but Jack's "Blades" were considered the most trustworthy despite their lowly origins.

Clements didn't like the idea of having all these uniforms around. It made him nervous, and reminded him too much of the war. Still, they were useful, he supposed. And they *were* docile enough, although if you stared at them directly they always had a look in their eyes as if they were planning something.

"Open the gate," he snapped at the guard, jerking his head in the direction of the door. The big fellow pulled a key out of his pocket and slipped it into the lock. Jordan took the opportunity to study the man a bit more: he had a thick red beard that covered most of his face—obviously Irish. Clements didn't really have anything against the potato eaters—although he didn't have anything *for* them either. There had been a lot of Irish soldiers fighting for the Yankees in the war. And if they were going to be a problem, it was one that belonged to New York and Boston. When Clements finally did leave this wretched city to go back home, he would leave them behind as well.

As soon as the door had been unlocked and opened enough to permit him access he shoved past the Blade, managing to "accidentally" land an elbow in the man's stomach on the way through. Clements felt the shock of fear as he wondered how the man might respond, but all the bearded gorilla did was let out a grunt. He hadn't risen to the challenge. These men were nothing to be scared of!

The cells were a row of small square caves carved directly into the building's stone foundations. Each one was set behind an iron door and contained a wooden bench, a mattress, a blanket, and a bucket. Although the accommodations might be simple, during the war he'd seen men held in far worse holes. After the attack on his home there had been dozens of captured Union soldiers who had simply been placed into dirt pits to wait for justice. More often than not it had come from the end of a rifle, although his father had told him those men were lucky. Yankees, he said, would sometimes bury men alive. That had never seemed like much of a problem to Clements—the object of war was to always make sure that there were more dead men on the other side than there were on yours. Winning was surviving, and history never seemed to care much for *how* people lost.

These prison cells were certainly far too good for the prisoner they held now. He stared at the man sitting on the cot inside the cell, hoping to catch his eye. The Negro's head was bowed, and if he noticed Clements, he refused to acknowledge him. "Hey boy!" Clements yelled as he walked up to the cell and rattled the iron bars. There was no response. "Can you hear me, boy?" he asked, dropping his tone on the last word.

"I can hear you," the prisoner replied. His tone was flat and grim—the same deep voice that had come from the jackal mask, but it was much less terrifying from human lips. With his mask ripped away, Anubis had become simply another pathetic Negro with delusions of grandeur.

"Then answer me when I talk to you."

The man looked at his hands and slowly clenched them up into fists. "You can go to hell."

Jordan felt something rising up in his stomach, and he swallowed it down. He knew there was nothing to be afraid of: the metal bars between them protected him completely. And the time for this man was coming very soon. One way or another he'd get his due. Justice was everywhere in the Hall of Paragons.

If Eschaton had let him have the Industrialist's gun, he'd have been here as an executioner, but the gray man had warned Clements that he wasn't allowed to harm this man before they had conducted their trial. Once he had been found guilty of treason against the Children, Eschaton would take him for his experiments. "When that's done," he had told him, "you're free to execute him." But first Eschaton was going to try to turn Anubis into one of his purified humans. Clements had seen what had become of Nathaniel, and he had been glad that his own results hadn't been nearly as traumatic.

Early on, when he had first been brought into the Children of Eschaton, the gray man had told him that if Clements was willing to be a part of Eschaton's experiments he could become something more than "just" a man. "There is a new race of men coming, Jordan," he had told him, "and this is your chance to be one of them."

Eschaton made no secret of the fact that the procedure was risky, and left it up to Clements to decide exactly how much risk he was willing to take. It had taken Jordan a few days to work up the courage to accept the offer.

The procedure itself had been very simple. He had been given an injection, then put in a smoky room with a mask over his face. Three hours later when he came out, his skin was raw and burning. He had spent the next week in his bed, overcoming the terrifying symptoms of bathing in the strange vapor.

At first it had colored his skin with a strange, dark pallor and he had been terrified that his flesh might turn black, as Eschaton's had. Instead it had simply vanished, leaving him even more pink and pale than he had been before. And for a while he thought it had done nothing to him at all besides making him ever so slightly more impervious to damage—hardly worth the pain and suffering he had gone through.

It wasn't until the fight with Stanton in the courtyard that Clements had begun to understand the full extent of his transformation. It had turned the tide of the fight, but he knew that there was more under the surface. He had only begun to discover the full force of his new powers.

But when Eschaton told him that he planned to give the same treatment to the Negro, Clements had asked him if it even could affect a man with black skin.

Eschaton had laughed at him for that, and told him that the color of the flesh made no difference to its composition. "Skin is skin."

Jordan found that hard to believe. It didn't take much time in a city like New York to see that the superiority of one race over another was more than just about color. It wasn't how people looked, but their very actions and thoughts that set one race apart from another. It was no accident that the residents of the mansions of New York were every bit as white as the plantation owners of the South.

And if Eschaton was right, and he did manage to give this Negro powers beyond those of the average man, what then? Clements had watched men try to domesticate wild animals for his entire childhood. If he had learned one thing from all those years on the plantation it was that just because you put a collar around a creature's neck, it wasn't suddenly your pet.

"What's your name, boy?"

"Anubis." The Negro still hadn't looked him in the eye. He supposed that was better, in a way. At least some part of the man knew his place, even if his mouth didn't.

"Not that fake name, your real one." He wouldn't call him Anubis ever again. The idea that he had ever managed to fool any of them with his secret identity now seemed ridiculous. It was like one of the monkeys at a circus claiming to be the ringmaster simply because it knew how to carry a whip.

The man's head raised until Clements could see the whites of his eyes. He was staring at him now, and the look he gave him was shockingly hard and angry. Jordan's stomach did another little flip. "My name is Abraham," he finally replied.

It was odd seeing those eyes. Anubis had been one of Eschaton's Children for far longer than Clements had, and during that time he had somehow managed to keep his face completely hidden. He supposed that he knew the shame of his race.

Clements felt nothing but pride in his heritage. Even under the hood of the White Knight he had always made sure to reveal a little bit of his white skin. He had sometimes imagined that Anubis's eyes would be squinted or slanted, like a demon or a Chinaman. But now that they were finally revealed, Abraham's eyes were wide and green, surrounded by the purest white. It was an unusual color for a Negro, and one that he couldn't remember seeing on any of the slaves that had been on his plantation.

He wanted to ask the Negro for his surname as well, but when he took another glance at the angry stare he felt the bile in his belly start to rise, and he looked away. It didn't matter much anyway. If this man had been born into slavery it would just be the name of his first master, or something they made up.

Jordan Clements had been a nervous child, clinging to his mother's skirts until he had been almost ten years old. It was a shameful memory, but in the end it had been his father who had broken him away from his cowardly ways and taught him how to be the kind of man who might one day properly run the family's plantation.

His father was a quiet man who rarely showed any emotion at all, neither smiling nor scowling. Jordan's greatest memory of him was the whip he wore at his belt. The old man had always been handy with a lash, and was quick to use it when someone needed a reminder of authority.

He still bore the scars from the times his father had felt the need to teach his son those lessons. The muscles in his back and legs stiffened from the memory, and there was a tightness where he had been marked by the lash. It had been a hard way to learn, but he would also never forget what he had been taught. When he had been given the "treatment" by Eschaton, it had been those old scars that had caused him the greatest pain and discomfort.

Jordan expected the Negro to still be glaring at him, but he'd dropped his head back down. He stared for a moment, hoping to catch his eyes and prove to him who was the better man, but Anubis—Abraham—refused to look up again. "Where'd you come from?"

"What do you mean?" the Negro replied.

"You an escaped slave?"

The Negro shook his head as if he couldn't believe the question he was being asked. "I don't know if anyone told you, but there aren't any slaves anymore."

"But they weren't all *born* free. And I don't think you were, either." Hiding his identity under a mask was exactly the kind of thing an escaped slave *would* do. This was a man who was clearly ashamed of what he had been, and who he was.

"No. They weren't." Abraham took a deep breath and continued. "You're right, I *was* born on a plantation. When I was eight my parents and I escaped. We reached New York, and I wasn't a slave anymore." Clements could see a flicker of something on Anubis's—Abraham's—face. He'd struck a nerve.

Clements took a step toward the bars. "Whose were you?"

A dark look came over the Negro's face. "I wasn't yours, don't worry."

If his father had been in the room, the lash would already be out. "How do you know?"

"Because I know who you are." Abraham rolled up his head and stared at him once more. "And because I *am* Anubis," he said in rumbling tones. "I know what weighs on the hearts of men, and yours, Jordan Clements, is very heavy and very dark."

"You—you're nothing!" Clements was shouting. "Nothing but a Negro who doesn't know his place!" But Clements could feel himself staggering backwards, his legs betraying him, revealing the fear that now seemed to be spreading through his entire body. The room was small, and it took only a few steps before he could feel the wall digging into his back, thankfully preventing him from running any farther. Before he could bolt for the door he swallowed again, the sour taste of bile rising up from his stomach.

But why was he so scared? He was no longer that child. He had power now! He could hear his father's voice in his ear: "Jordan, you are a craven, cowardly boy! But I'm going to show you how to be a man!"

Doing his best to gather his wits, Clements stepped forward again. The sad black creature in front of him was helpless—an animal locked behind the bars at the zoo. There was nothing to be scared of. "You don't know me!"

Anubis smiled at him. The grin was lean and cruel, and Jordan realized that it made the Negro look a bit like a jackal even without the mask. "Your family plantation," he said, "it wasn't far away from where I grew up. And sometimes, when your family came to visit, they'd bring a few slaves, and we'd talk. They'd tell us how your father was a cruel, sad man who beat his slaves for the slightest insult. He was weak and afraid, so he took out his fear on others. And they also told us that his son was a scared, weak little child." He had slurred the words, letting just a touch of a Southern accent come through.

"That's a lie!" But Clements could feel his hands trembling and his stomach tightening. As a child he had often been sick—every part of his body clenching and shaking until he ended up on the floor, retching and coughing. But he was more than that now: he had become one of Eschaton's purified humans. He was better than this piece of black filth!

Waiting a moment for the sickness to subside, he turned and yelled toward the door. "You! Irishman! Get in here!"

When he turned back to look at the Negro, he saw that Abraham was staring at him again, but the grin was gone. "Stop looking at me, boy," Clements said. "I'm about to teach you a lesson."

Anubis—Abraham—the man, didn't flinch or look away. Instead his gaze only seemed to grow more intense. "Anubis has judged you, Jordan Clements, and I have found your heart heavy, filled with sadness, anger, and greed." He leaned forward, and Clements felt his hands beginning to tremble once again. "And very soon I'm going to send you straight to hell."

Jordan reached up toward his neck, expecting to find the cold comfort of the wire noose he wore, but there was nothing there. He hadn't considered coming dressed as the White Knight to visit an unarmed man in a cell, but now he wished that he had.

"What do you want?" The gruff voice startled Clements. He whipped his head around to see the red-bearded Irish guard peering at him from the end of the hall.

"Open the cell door."

"No," the Irishmen said, shaking his head. "I'm not supposed to do that."

"I'm not asking you, boy. I'm telling you."

The Irishman pursed his lips together for a moment, as if trying to decide whether or not he had been insulted, and then tilted his head. "If you say so." He pulled a heavy ring of keys off his belt and walked up to the iron door. "But it's on your head."

As he slipped his key into the lock Anubis lifted himself up off the bench. "I know you," the Negro said to the red-bearded man. The Irishman seemed unimpressed by his recognition, but said nothing. "You were one of the boys fighting Jack in the square," he continued. "You threw a knife at his head."

"Yeah, and you saved him," the Irishman finally replied. "You saved him, and now I'm working *for* him. Funny how things work out." He turned the key in the lock with a sharp click.

Clements grabbed the bars, more eager than ever to enter the cell. The red-bearded guard swung open the door. It was almost silent on its hinges. Once it was open the guard turned and pointed. "I'm not responsible if you get into trouble."

Clements nodded. He was tired of being treated like that scared, helpless child. He'd prove to the world that pathetic little boy was dead and gone. And to do it he would have to act *now*—fighting the fear before it could take him. "All right, all right."

The Irishman stepped back, and Jordan entered the cell. "Okay, Mick, you can leave now." He didn't bother looking at the guard to see how he had taken the insult. He knew the man wasn't looking for a fight. After a few seconds he heard footsteps diminishing behind him.

Clements turned to look at the black man. It was cramped inside the cell, and as he stepped in, the stone room seemed somehow both hotter and damper than the hall. He wondered if it was some kind of effect from the walls, or perhaps it was simply his close proximity to the Negro that was making him so warm. It had been years since he stood so close to an African—perhaps not since he had left the plantation. He'd forgotten what it was like to be so near to something that looked almost like a human, but was so different in so many ways.

"You don't really need my judgment, do you, Clements?"

He hated the way the Negro talked. It was all riddles and questions, as if he somehow was better than everyone around him, when he was better than no one at all. "What do you mean, boy?"

"In all my life," Anubis said, narrowing his eyes, "I've never, *ever* seen a man so afraid of what's in his own heart."

Clements's hand shot out, striking Abraham in the face. He had underestimated the strength of his blow, and both his fingers and Anubis's jaw smashed into the cell bars. They let out a simultaneous yelp.

The pain was intense, but clearly not nearly as bad it had been for the Negro. Clements felt a thrill as Abraham collapsed to his knees, and seeing the Negro on the ground in front of him put a smile on his face. "See, boy? You needed that, because I just asked for a little bit of respect."

Anubis took a moment, then grabbed the edge of the bench and pulled himself up off of the floor. He had clearly been hurt, and Clements could see that the wound to his head was already starting to ooze blood. "I . . ." he started, and then coughed heavily, wiping away his ability to say anything else.

The smile grew on the White Knight's face. What was it that he had been so afraid of? A pathetic Negro with a growl in his voice? "What were you trying to say to me, boy?"

Clements felt something strike the edges of his shins, hard, knocking his feet out from underneath him and wiping the smile off of his face. His hands instinctively reached up to grab the bars, but his momentum was too strong, denying him any purchase. Instead, the stone floor rushed up to meet him, and in his head there was a sound almost like a hurricane. The air was forced out from his lungs as he hit the earth, followed by an uncanny silence.

For just a moment Jordan's world was free of pain and fear, although he could feel a kind of fuzzy tingle in the fingers of his left hand where they scraped hard against the rough iron bars on his way down.

Then he could hear Anubis's voice coming from somewhere up above him. Amplified by the stone walls, it rumbled almost like thunder: "I have judged you, and found you wanting." He felt the pressure of a foot on his back, and as he gasped for air the fear came rushing back, pushing past the pain and filling him like some terrible liquid that had been injected into his body.

Clements's jaw clenched tight. He needed to push his fear back down, but there was no place in his mind that would give him purchase to fight back. The world was fighting his attempts to escape as well, and as he pushed against the floor, desperately trying to rise up, he could feel Anubis's heel grinding against his spine and pain beginning to blossom in his hand. His fingers were wet from blood, and his hands slipped against the floor when he tried to rise.

Helpless and desperate, Clements's fear began to shift to terror. A rumbling voice commanded him to "stay down!" but it might as well have been a million miles away. The fear had filled him completely now, until he felt like he might be ready to burst. His throat was on fire from the acid that clawed its way up his throat from his stomach. He was helpless, at the mercy of an angry Negro—a man clearly intent on killing him if he didn't *do something*!

And then, like waking up from dream, the fear inside of him began to transform from a cold dark terror to warm power flowing through his veins. It was the same alchemy he had felt before, when he had been fighting the Industrialist in the courtyard: the terror inside him was melting away, replaced by a rush of energy that flowed through his veins like sunshine. Muscles that had been trembling and weak only a moment before were suddenly solid and strong. Clements pushed upwards, easily dislodging the man from his back.

He rose, smiling. He could actually feel his muscles pressing tightly against his clothes where they had expanded in size. He glanced down at his hands and saw that his skin was practically glowing. Not quite as powerfully as the gray man's, but with more purity. "A true white knight," he whispered to himself.

This was his power, the gift Eschaton had given him that turned him from just a man into a purified human. It was all he had wished for and more. It was only a shame to have to go through so much fear to arrive at the place where he could finally be the man he always wanted to be. His heart was pounding in his chest like a mallet smashing against stone. He could hear the sound of his blood roaring through his ears, drowning out all other sounds from the world around him. His vision was tinted red, pulsing in time with the beat of his heart.

He saw Abraham lying against the wall. He hadn't been badly hurt, and the Negro was trying to right himself and make another attack. Watching him now, it seemed to Jordan as if the man were moving in slow motion.

The White Knight's thick hand wove through the meager defenses that Anubis tried to put up, and his fist landed hard against Anubis's face. The brown skin rippled and shivered from the force of the impact, and as his hand rolled away Clements could see the imprint that his fingers had left on Anubis's face.

As his enemy reeled from the blow, Clements reached out and wrapped his hands around the black man's neck. His fingers dug deeply into the soft flesh and his grip was already more than tight enough to choke the other man, but not quite enough to snap his neck—yet. As he considered his next move, Anubis's hands beat hard against Clements's arms. The attacks would leave bruises, but none of that mattered for now. He had this animal underneath his hands, ready for slaughter. If he squeezed just a bit harder, the problem would be gone forever. He would win again. He could keep the head as a trophy and place it up on a shelf in his office. Maybe he'd make it wear Stanton's hat.

Anubis's blows slowed, and Clements could see that Abraham was quickly losing consciousness. Those green eyes that had been so terrifying before had begun to roll up into his head. Clements's fingers twitched. It would be so easy to finish what he started, to do what he hadn't been able to do before. Surely Eschaton couldn't need him *that* badly. There were so many other men in the world. And what if Anubis somehow actually was able to become purified? What if he became too strong to stop? The risk was too great—the Negro had to die.

Clements felt another tug on his arms: another pair of hands trying to pull his fingers from Anubis's throat. The interloper wasn't nearly strong enough to break his grip, but it was annoying nonetheless. He turned to see that it was the Irishman. The man was screaming "stop" at him, barely loud enough for him to hear it above the roaring of the blood in his head.

He nodded and released one hand, cradling Abraham's limp head with his other. He turned and faced the red-bearded man with a smile. Without warning he lashed out, his fist catching the other man full in the chest. Caught by surprise, the Irishman reeled back, landing hard against the stone wall before sliding down to the ground.

Clements looked at his hand and marveled at the power it suddenly contained. He was so much stronger than he'd been before. Perhaps his powers would continue to grow. Maybe he would be able to control them without the fear. Maybe he'd soon be stronger than Eschaton himself!

But just as he thought he could feel his power growing to new proportions, it began to drain away. The strength was rushing out of him like hot air from a torn balloon, vanishing back to whatever unknown place it had come from. Last time, Nathaniel had managed to surprise him, attacking him before he could complete his fight with the Industrialist. He wouldn't make that mistake again.

He turned his eyes back to the Negro. When he looked down at the unconscious man's face it was Lord Eschaton's angry features that he seemed to be holding in his hands . . . the smooth gray flesh . . . the lightning bolts that he could throw at command. No matter how much power he might have when he needed it, Clements was still not nearly close enough to having the strength and skills he would need to stop Eschaton when he was angry.

He felt his fear growing. The body of Anubis—which had seemed almost weightless in his hands—now slipped heavily through Clements's bleeding fingers, crashing back into the hard straw mattress.

His heart hammered in his chest, and Clements gasped for breath. He shivered at the sight of the two men's limp bodies on either side of him. He sat down, onto the edge of the bed frame, rocking as he moaned quietly to himself. "What have I done?" he repeated to himself over and over again. It seemed that an eternity passed before he could manage to gather together enough of his wits to answer his own question by checking on the conditions of the men.

Anubis was unconscious but still clearly alive, his chest still rising and falling, if only slightly. The other man was utterly still, a pool of blood growing around him from the place where his head had smashed against the wall. If he was still alive, then it was just barely. He pulled the keys out of the man's hand and noticed that his fingers were still warm. Not proof of life, but a chance at it. Then again, the fool shouldn't have tried to stop him.

Clements dragged himself out of the cell and closed the door behind him. It took him multiple attempts with the keys before he managed to slip the right one into the lock and throw the bolt closed.

Utterly drained, he collapsed onto the wooden stool that the Irishman had been using just outside the door and fell into a deep, hard slumber. He had no idea how long he had been asleep when Jack found him.

Chapter 7

The Heart Should Be Home

Emilio found himself with nothing to say to the Automaton, even as he sat at the table and worked to attach Tom's last remaining limb to his body.

At some point they would need to converse, but he wasn't the only one having difficulty finding something to say to the reincarnated creature. In the two days since the return of the metal man, Sarah had refused to come see him. What had clearly been intended as a grand reunion had instead been a sad revelation.

Viola, on the other hand, had discovered a kindred spirit. She had taken to spending almost every waking moment with Tom, only leaving when Emilio came into the room to work toward his completion.

He had tried to listen in on the conversations between his sister and the Automaton, but so far Emilio had only heard whispered mutterings and the twanging of the Automaton's piano strings.

But for all his trepidation about having this dangerous machine in his lab, he had to admit to himself that so far Tom had shown nothing that hinted he might once again lose control the way he had before. And he was relieved at that. For better or worse, he was the man responsible for bringing this creature back into the world.

And now, under orders from Sarah, he was giving the Automaton back his ability to walk and fight. He wondered how Darby had lived for all those years knowing that no matter how miraculous his wonderful inventions might be for humanity, there was also the possibility of death and destruction in every creation.

It was Emilio's greatest fear as an inventor. Mankind could find endless ways to hurt each other. It was no wonder that the old inventor had been such a philosopher: every creation of genius came with so many *consequences*. It

made sense that some sense of direction must be provided in each act of creation, just as God had given man the Bible after he had created the Earth.

What had always puzzled Emilio, and what he most wished he could have
asked Darby before he died, was whether he had ever regretted playing in the
garden of life—creating something that mocked the ultimate domain of God
himself. And by reanimating the creature, had Emilio aided in that heresy?

The mechanical man sat patient and unmoving as Emilio loosened the
bolts in his shoulder. The legs were already in place, and he only needed to
mount a final limb before the Automaton would be complete. Glancing over
at Tom's painted face, Emilio realized for the hundredth time that the expression that Tom wore would provide him with no clues to his true intentions,
although even a bolted-on smile made him seem far more human.

Alfonso had shown up with the new face soon after the Automaton had returned to life. Viola had pounced on the portly Venetian the moment he had
walked through the door, demanding that he make her a mask. She had unleashed reserves of charm that she had not shown to anyone since the accident.
Emilio doubted that the man would have denied her a chance to cover her
damaged features under any circumstance, but it had been enough to convince
the "Talentless Pig" to paint her a new face of her own to match that of the
Automaton. He had fitted her that day, and come back the next morning with
a half-metal plate that she now wore constantly to cover her ruined flesh.

It was, despite it being a lie, also an improvement. The molded steel
worked well with her unique looks, and only a tiny view of the scars around
her eye were visible through the hole in the mask, making her more mysterious than monstrous.

The image that had been painted onto Viola's mask was intended to be
more than the simple mockery of humanity that Tom wore. From a distance
it seemed to be a re-creation of her lost features, but up close it was almost a
work of art: a finely detailed bouquet of rose blooms that came together to
form her eyebrow, the thorny stems reaching down to outline her eye itself.
It made her appear even more exotic than she had been before.

It was a stark contrast to Tom's new features. His face was far more similar to that of the Pneumatic Colossus than to the images Emilio had seen of
the original Automaton's soft smile. He had rosy dots on both cheeks and a

painted mustache that completely obscured the line of his mouth. The effect was as if someone had attempted to make a china doll of a proper gentleman.

Emilio jumped when the Automaton spoke to him. "Why are you . . . smiling?"

"Ehh?" he said, trying to regain his composure, but instead simply ended up feeling slightly foolish for trying to hide his thoughts from a machine. If there was a single advantage to metal over flesh, it was that it had little concern for the rules of society. "I think of you in a top hat and a proper coat."

"I like wearing . . . clothes."

Emilio nodded. This wasn't the first time the Automaton had spoken to him directly, but it seemed that it was going to be their first conversation. "But you don't need to."

"No. But I . . . like them. It makes me . . . comfortable around others."

"And how did you know I was smiling? You can't see!"

"These . . . wires," Tom said, and sent of a trill of musical notes through the piano strings running across his body, "have made me far more . . . sensitive than I was before."

Emilio considered asking the mechanical man for more details, but resisted the temptation. He had held the creature's heart in his hands and constructed the body he wore, and yet the fact the creature lived and talked was still nothing less than a miracle. No amount of questions would ever allow him to completely understand the transformation that brought this creature to life.

And yet, for Darby, the creation of this creature hadn't been an accident. Creating Tom had been his *intention*. *"Meraviglioso."*

The head turned to face him. "I'm . . . glad you think so." The tone was a flat and definitive statement. If Tom was truly pleased, it was still a very different kind of happiness than was felt by creatures of flesh and blood.

Even if the Automaton was no longer the dangerous monster he had become that day in the theater, there was also no doubt that whatever or whomever this new version of the mechanical man was, he was not the same Tom that Darby had originally created, or that Sarah had known before.

He was cold and considered, and perhaps it was that very lack of humanity which seemed to have created an almost instant bond between the mechanical man and Viola.

Before the creature had returned to life, he had assumed that Viola would detest the metal man. While it was possible to argue that the Automaton wasn't *directly* responsible for the damage to her face, it would be equally impossible to avoid the fact that if Tom had not gone mad in his new body, the events in the theater might have had a very different outcome.

And yet, his sister was now determined to make the machine her friend; and Tom, for all his inhumanity, seemed to be responding positively to her attempts to reach out to him.

When they stood together, the mechanical man looked more closely related to his sister than Emilio did. Tom's painted features allowed him to pretend to be something he had never been, and Viola's mask let her pretend to have regained something she had lost forever. Perhaps her new face was the only way that she could reveal the insanity inside her head. But the Automaton's intentions toward his sister were still a riddle to him.

He grabbed the ends of the wires coming out from Tom's shoulder and began to slide them into the arm. He wound the end of the wire around a clamp, then crimped on a metal bead before dropping them into place and screwing down the bolts that would hold the wires in tension. "I have a question for you, metal man."

"Please feel . . . free to ask whatever questions you would like, Mister . . . Armando."

"Why do you need me to do this for you? I saw how you can remake yourself, in the theater. Why not fix yourself?"

"I thought you wanted to . . . finish me. This body is your . . . creation, and your vision."

Emilio nodded, and then felt foolish for thinking of the Automaton as a creature of flesh and bone while simultaneously reattaching his arm. "Because I thought that giving you the right body would bring you back to life."

"And it did. It allowed you to . . . discover the method of my . . . reincarnation."

He felt as if they were going around in circles. "So why can't you finish it?"

"I cannot . . . reconstruct myself. My . . . abilities are only for . . . repair."

Emilio shook his head. "But at the theater, I saw you—"

"No," Tom said, cutting him off, almost as if what Emilio was about to say had made him angry or upset. His tone was as smooth and cool as ever. "I do not remember much of what happened at the theater. That . . . body was not meant for me . . ."

"But it *was* you. Angry and out of control, but still you."

The mechanical man gave no response. It was odd how similar in attitude he could be to Sarah, or perhaps her current unimpassioned attitude was something she had learned from her metal friend.

Emilio lifted up the arm. It was heavier than he had originally intended it to be, but even with his new tools, he had still found it necessary to make the metal bones that ran down the center of it thick enough to allow Tom to effectively use them without having them snap or break during the moment of greatest stress. "Why don't you try to finish yourself?"

"After last time, I think I will become . . . what you make me."

"But what do you want to be?" Even as he finished asking the question, he wondered if he would regret it.

There was a long silence before Tom lifted up his arm. "If you were to . . . lose an arm, or your . . . leg, would you still consider yourself to be the man you were before?"

Emilio took a moment to consider the question. He had seen numerous men over the years with missing limbs. Many of them claimed to be veterans of one war or another. And whether that was true or not, whatever life they had lived as whole men had been stripped away from them. He peered down at his own hands and tried to imagine what he would do if even one of them were lost.

With a missing leg he still might be able to work as he had before. He might even be able to build a mechanical replacement that would let him walk again. But if he were to lose so much as a finger, his world would be changed forever. Tom's question made him feel uncomfortable, and that made the answer clear. "No . . ."

"This," the mechanical man said, waving his hand in front of his torso, "is my third . . . body. Even if my . . . heart were to have remained entirely intact, I would still be . . . different than I was before."

"None of us choose who we are when we are born."

"I've been . . . born three times. I never . . . chose."

"I think every man would wish for that kind of immortality, if they could have it."

"I do not. I am what I am . . . made to be."

"By who?"

"By . . . Darby. By . . . you."

That might be at least a partial explanation for why the Automaton had suddenly shown an affinity for his sister. And perhaps also why things had gone so wrong at the Theater Mechanique . . . "Was that why you lost control," Emilio asked with rising excitement in his voice. "Because you became something you were not supposed to be?"

"I do not know."

"Tom, if I commanded you, would you finish your arm for me?"

"This . . . body is new. I want to feel what it will be when it is . . . complete before I . . . modify it."

For a moment Emilio considered holding his tongue, but once again his curiosity had overcome his fear. "Tom, if men could repair their bodies, they wouldn't just become what they were before. Do you see?"

"I do not."

"They would make themselves better, or at least they would try."

"You think I can be . . . better?"

Emilio nodded. "Hold on for a minute." He walked a few feet, then rolled out the large spool of piano wire from where it sat in a corner of the room. "You want to be solid, I know. But if you could rebuild yourself in a new way, you could become your own man."

"I could . . . try. Darby created my original form with the ability to . . . modify itself as part of the . . . design. But your new . . . frame is more . . . ethereal." He reached up with his working arm and took a pair of pliers from the workbench. "Perhaps if I became more . . . substantial. Perhaps if you would give me some . . . steel and . . . brass rods I could . . ."

"You would *try*."

"Yes."

Emilio grunted as he slid the spool up and onto a slanted pipe. What he was proposing to Tom was clearly far beyond Darby's original vision for the machine. But what would he have thought if he had lived long enough to discover that Tom could do more than just repair himself? What would the old inventor have wished for if he had discovered that Tom was capable of re-creating himself as well?

He thought of the words he had seen etched onto the heart: "Human ingenuity is the art of seeing, and then making. It will never be enough to simply copy something. You must will your success into being." He wondered if that had ever been something he might have considered his creation capable of.

"Here, Tom," Emilio said, holding out the end of the piano wire. "See what you can do with this." He fed the wire into Tom's chest until he could feel it make contact with the gears inside.

"I don't understand."

"Finish yourself. Re-create yourself."

"I will . . . try."

The wire began to reel off of the spool, slowly at first, and then faster and faster as Tom pulled more and more of it inside of him.

For almost half a minute the material seemed to be going nowhere, simply disappearing into Tom's body. He could see it moving through him, and there was a musical hum, and as it grew louder Emilio saw that every wire that he had used to build the structure of the Automaton's body was now vibrating simultaneously. "What are you doing?" he asked.

The humming stopped. "I am . . . discovering myself."

Emilio laughed at that. "And what have you found out?"

"I hope that you will not be . . . offended."

"By what?"

"My . . . improvements."

The humming started up again, louder this time. As it reached a crescendo, there was a single "plink" from inside of him, as if someone were plucking hard on the Automaton's strings. A second later Emilio saw one of the metal wires snap free, the end of the broken wire curling up into the air. Then another break, and then another. After a few minutes almost all his meticulous work had been snapped apart. "What are you doing?" Emilio asked, trying to hide his concern.

Tom's body hung limply in the frame, but his head turned to face Emilio, the blank, eternally staring eyes pointing his way. "What you . . . suggested," replied the Automaton, his voice quiet and thin, vibrating softly through the few wires that remained. Then the last of the strings broke with a sharp "plink" and the mechanical man's head slung forward, supported only by his frame.

For a moment there was no movement at all, and Emilio began to wonder with terror what he would tell Sarah if Tom had once again gone away.

Emilio leaned closer, moving his ear toward Tom's chest, then jumped back when he felt something slim and cold strike his face. Jumping backward, he thought for a moment that he might have been cut, and rubbed his hand against his cheek, but nothing was wrong. Looking down at the metal body, he saw loops of piano wire growing from all over Tom's limp body. They shimmered and twisted, like a thousand shiny metal worms growing out from inside him. The loops moved in a precise and regulated way, managing to fold over each other, and then around and back into his body.

As the wires grew taut, Tom's hands sprang to life. Fingers twitched and grabbed the strands of wire that peeked out from underneath his torso. His arms began to move, weaving the metal strands down into his legs. After a moment the growing hum began again, and the wire began to sprout out from the mechanical man's feet.

The newly reanimated legs pushed up against the floor and Tom rose up. The stand that had held him was stuck for a moment, and then crashed to the ground. Emilio was smiling now as he realized that the mechanical man was using the tension of the strings against his frame in way that allowed them to respond almost like human muscle. "Amazing!" said Emilio, and clapped his hands.

Reaching up, the Automaton unscrewed the plate on the top of his head. Wires grew up and out from the holes, criss-crossing back and forth inside the skull. Emilio couldn't help but notice the beauty of the pattern that was forming. And it wasn't just his head: Tom's entire body was now criss-crossed with patterns that made him appear as if a talented spider had spun steel inside him.

Tom pushed the skull-cap back into place around the threads, gave it a twist, and the head lifted itself back up again. The movement was still inhuman, but almost shockingly fluid when compared to the jerky twitching motions of the Pneumatic Colossus.

Tom reached out his right arm toward Emilio. The Italian stared at it for a moment, so entranced by the details of what the Automaton had done to himself, he was almost unable to notice that the mechanical man was offering to shake his hand.

Tom's arm shot out to meet his, and metal fingers tightened around the flesh of his hand. As their limbs moved up and down Emilio could feel the wires twisting and snaking across the metal palm. It was a shocking feeling, not only because of the cold unreality of the metal against his skin, but the realization that the frame underneath the sliding steel was his own creation. And rising up from the fear was a sense of pride. This was his creation, but it was only the seed of what the Automaton himself had created! Life had moved forward!

"You are *magnifico*!" His earlier doubts were gone completely now. This was what Darby had seen in his science—the idea that knowledge *itself* could push the future forward. Emilio felt tears stinging his eyes.

"You . . . inspired me."

Emilio laughed at that and pulled his hand free. "How do you feel, to be truly yourself?"

Tom lifted up his arms and began to run his hands over his flesh. "The wire, is so . . . sensitive! I feel . . . everything!"

Emilio clapped his hands together and ran toward the door. "I go!"

Tom's head turned. "Where?"

He turned back to look at the mechanical man. "I go to tell Sarah that you are ready to see her now."

Chapter 8

Manifesting the Unwanted

After the attack in the park, Nathaniel had been forced to watch helplessly as Eschaton had slaughtered innocent civilians. He had also been witness to the capture of Anubis, along with the unmasking of his would-be savior.

Eschaton had handed Anubis off to his men, who had wheeled Nathaniel into the back of a carriage and driven him back to the Hall of Paragons through the devastated streets.

On the way back, the gray man had lectured him further, telling him that he was a lucky man; the first of a new generation of humanity, poised to be greater than his creator. "But you are not," the gray man had said ominously, "quite finished yet."

After they returned from the park, he had been brought down to what had formerly been Darby's laboratory underneath the Hall of Paragons. The large space had been almost unrecognizable except for the obvious perversion of the technology and experiments that it contained. Most ominous of all the new additions was a large chamber that stood next to a massive metal cylinder. Both of them had been covered with layer upon layer of black pitch.

Darby would have been distraught to see what had become of his laboratory, but he would have been sickened by the monstrosity that Eschaton called "the Shell."

When the broken creature rolled into the light on a pair of twisted wheels, Nathaniel recoiled in a moment of genuine terror.

"Don't you recognize your old friend?" Eschaton asked him.

He did recognize the creature. It was the same monster he had seen in the meeting room when Stanton had died, although it had obviously been somewhat repaired.

At first he thought that what he was seeing was simply another parody of humanity; a mechanical man designed to look human the way Tom had been. But as he looked closer, peering beneath the metal exterior, Nathaniel realized this was something far worse: hidden just underneath the metal was black and ulcerous flesh. He was glad he had been spared seeing the face hidden underneath the metal mask.

Nathaniel was still reeling, but why had Eschaton called the thing his old friend? As he looked at the metal shell and broken legs, it all came together. "Is that . . . Hughes?" The man had been turned into a sad parody of the Iron-Clad. To think that the most powerful of them had been reduced to this. "He's a monster."

Eschaton nodded. "For a moment I thought you didn't recognize your fellow Paragon. After he managed to stop you from trying to escape, I saved what remained of him by using the same application of fortified smoke and steam that I used on you, Nathaniel. Of course, I was only able to save some of him." The gray man pointed to the wheels that Hughes had been attached to with tight iron bands. They had once been part of the miraculous self-powered chair that Darby had created. Somehow they had been attached to him in a way that allowed the wheels to simply follow his will.

Eschaton gave a tight grin that revealed at least a touch of sadness at Hughes. "There's not much of his humanity left, I'm afraid. Whatever process it was that Darby had intended, it clearly wasn't meant for human flesh. It's truly a testament to the power of this living metal that even these tiny remains of him survived."

He gave the pathetic creature a condescending pat, much like a man might give to an old dog. "But I do think he's happier now than he was before. He wanted to walk so badly, and now he still can. Isn't that right, Shell?"

The creature whimpered slightly, the pathetic noise amplified by its metal casing.

What at first seemed to be rising sickness and nausea flooded over Nathaniel like a wave. A moment later he felt seizures running through him, pulling his arms up tight against his bonds. Pain flooded through him as the ropes cut into his limbs, and for those long moments he had little or no control over his own body.

"Are you all right, Nathaniel?" Eschaton maintained the same tone he had with Hughes.

"I have no idea. You did this to me." Nathaniel wondered how long he could continue to live in his current state. There had been no doubt in his mind that whatever Eschaton had done to him, the outcome would ultimately be fatal.

He could feel that the specter of death was hovering nearby since the Darby house had burned to the ground. Now he had been poisoned by a madman, and any claims that he would somehow be "purified" by what had been done to him were directly contradicted by the terrifying pain and nausea that travelled up, down, and through him.

But if he was going to die soon, it also wouldn't be quite yet. As the last of the spasms subsided, Nathaniel felt a terrible thirst come upon him. "Water," he cried out. It came out more desperately than he had intended it to.

"I'm sorry, Nathaniel, but my experiments may have rendered your physiology incompatible with Adam's ale, and you're certainly in no state to test it out."

"Bourbon, then . . . something for the pain," he begged.

Eschaton laughed. "Your commitment to liquor is admirable, Nathaniel." The gray giant leaned in to take a closer look. "I'd be curious to see what effect it might have on you . . . and I *can* see the suffering in your eyes, my boy. But if you can be patient for a little longer, you may discover your desire for drink replaced by other concerns."

Once again Nathaniel felt a wave of nausea rip through him, but this time instead of a tremor he felt what seemed to be a sudden surge of strength.

Using its power, he struggled against his bonds, tightening his hand into a fist.

Eschaton stood back. "You see? It does take a while for the full effects to become apparent."

As Nathaniel pulled harder, a metallic smell reached his nose. It was strong enough to penetrate the thick chemical stink of fortified smoke that still clung to every inch of his skin, and not entirely unpleasant.

He and Eschaton both were simultaneously entranced and terrified as metallic strands coalesced underneath his skin and turned his wrists to a shimmering silver. Nathaniel could tell that there was tremendous heat coming off of his flesh, but it didn't burn him at all. The ropes that bound him were not immune, however, and they flared up and burned away.

The gray giant had stepped backwards, but Nathaniel leaned up from the chair and grasped Eschaton's neck. He could feel the hard flesh underneath his fingers, but his hands were still weak from being tied up for so long. He wasn't strong enough to even make a dent in the stony skin.

"I'm sorry, my boy," Eschaton said, "but you're not powerful enough to kill me yet. And when you are, you may no longer want . . ." The gray man's look of smug assurance literally melted away as the hand around his neck turned hot.

Eschaton pulled away, clearly shocked. In the instant before he put his hand up to his throat, Nathaniel saw that he had left a black smudge on the villain's neck. It was a minor victory, but after what seemed to be an eternity of being at everyone else's mercy, it was good to know that he could still be a threat.

"Shell," Eschaton barked at the remains of Hughes. "Take him into the chamber."

The mechanical monstrosity grabbed Nathaniel around his neck, holding him down hard against the back of the chair.

There would have been a point in the recent past when Nathaniel would have thought it impossible for such a damaged creature, no matter what it was constructed of, to overpower him, but the Shell had far more strength than first appeared. He attempted to use the heat of his arms to burn the creature, but the silver threads had dissipated back into his body.

Unable to escape, he was rolled into the chamber and manhandled onto the metal table inside. Despite his every effort to escape, he shortly found himself chained down and once again unable to move.

After that the door had been sealed, trapping him in darkness, and more of the same acrid smoke from the park had been pumped into the chamber.

When he had first breathed it in, it felt like he was drowning and burning simultaneously. Nathaniel tried to yell out, but was unable to make a sound while his lungs were full of the thick black gas. But he wasn't dying—not yet.

He remained in that dark room for what he believed had been a day or more. And although he was exhausted, both physically and mentally, he had been unable to sleep. Instead he hallucinated, his vision appearing in the pitch black, playing out over and over again all the terrible things that had happened to him since the day that Darby had died on the bridge.

After spending endless hours burning in the smoke-filled hell of the chamber, Nathaniel had almost forgotten how to hope for the torture to end. There had been no sound other than the hiss and endless rumbling of the fan as fresh helpings of black smoke churned into the room.

And then, finally, something changed. There was a rattle as the fan slowed, and silence descended onto him.

It was broken by a heavy clanking of chain, then the obvious sound of metal against brick as something inside the chamber opened, letting a tiny shaft of light pierce the hazy darkness. He felt a cool breeze against his skin, the smallest bit of relief from the pure black smoke—and yet one that he seemed to have spent a lifetime praying for.

The rumble of the fan started up again, but this time it was drawing the black gas up and out of the room, and his lungs labored to try and draw in more of the pure air that he had craved. It had been so long since he had last tasted it that it seemed as though he had almost forgotten how to breathe anything but the dark poison. Now that his lungs were exposed to even a tiny bit of pure, clean air, they rebelled.

Nathaniel gasped and coughed, expelling more of the smoke. He could see it coming out of him now in a gray cloud.

His hands and feet were still chained to the metal table, and he didn't have the strength to move them. Instead he listened quietly and waited for someone to open the door, waiting to see which one of the villains would come for him.

When seconds turned to minutes he couldn't wait any longer. "Help me!" he shouted. "Help me, damn you!" There was a moment of terror as he realized that the sound of his own voice was so altered that he could barely recognize it. There was no use denying that whatever it was that Eschaton had done to him, it had transformed him profoundly.

How rapidly the world had fallen apart now that the old man was no longer. Nathaniel was beginning to realize just how important Darby had been, not only to the Paragons, but to all the people he had left behind. He had not just been the inventor of dreams, he had been the protector of them from men like Lord Eschaton.

And now, Nathaniel had been brought down into this hell and forced to endure a nightmare that had been crafted out of an old man's dreams.

With Sarah and Alexander Stanton both gone, he was completely at the madman's mercy: there was no one to save him, and worse . . . there was no one left to care.

His short reprieve was interrupted by the return of the dreaded hissing sound. Nathaniel felt himself tremble. But this time the gas that poured out was white, and the smell that reached his nose wasn't the acrid stink of the smoke, but instead the clean, familiar tang of Darby's fortified steam.

His skin still stung where the gas touched him, but the mild pain he felt was a far cry from the endless burning that had come from contact with the smoke. Then his muscles began to twitch and contract uncontrollably as the moisture settled into his skin. His body slammed him hard against the metal table over and over again. It had exhausted him in an instant, but he kept on twitching. It seemed that whatever effect the steam was having on him, it had no care for his own desires.

Eventually the jumping slowed, and all his muscles simply seized into a constant state of tension, leaving him frozen like a statue on the tabletop.

Nathaniel had fully expected for this second bath to last as long as the first, and he was wondering if he would be able to survive the experience without the onset of madness. Or, perhaps he was mad already, and another day pinned to the table would send him into new depths of insanity.

Just as he began to ponder the ramifications of the question, the hissing stopped and the rattling of the fan began again.

This time, once the gas had cleared, the iron door to the chamber opened with a scrape and a clang. Lord Eschaton stepped into the room, ducking under the low mantel of the door. "Did you survive, Nathaniel?"

"Yes, damn your hide!" His voice was rough and gravelly now, like one of those old sailors who had spent years on the high seas surviving on nothing but tobacco and rum, but at least he could speak.

"Well then, let's have a look at you." Eschaton loomed over him, examining his handiwork. "If I'm right, you're going to end up being something quite marvelous, but I suppose, having just lived through it, you don't care to hear more about it right now."

Nathaniel felt the anger roll through him. It was better than having to endure any more pain. "I've had a belly full of your pontificating, you sick monster."

Eschaton smiled, revealing his shining white teeth. "It's good to see that your transformation seems to have left you with your passions intact."

"You murdered all those innocent people!" He thought of them, choking to death on the fumes, and realized he truly did feel compassion for them. The sickness and lethargy that had plagued him ever since his initial experience with the smoke seemed to have left him now. If anything he felt stronger than he had before, as if he could take on an army single-handedly. "Unchain me from this table and I'll show you just how passionate I can be!"

Eschaton nodded. "I will give you that chance, but if only you could see yourself . . ." The gray giant studied him for a moment. "Yes, yes," he muttered to himself, and then smiled. "Shell, come in here."

The machine-man rolled into the room. "Put him onto the cart and bring him out into the light. I want to take a closer look at him, and I'm sure the boy is curious to see his new appearance."

Once again Nathaniel found himself being manhandled by the monstrosity that had once been Hughes. The creature pulled the tabletop off of whatever it had been standing on, and transferred it to the top of a two-wheeled cart.

As he struggled, he could feel the metal flexing beneath him, and after a moment he managed to tear his right hand entirely free, ripping the chain out of the steel.

The Shell attempted to grab the escaped limb, but Nathaniel slipped his arm out from the creature's grasp. He was almost shocked to realize that he'd regained dominion over his own arm, and lacking the time to formulate a better plan, he rammed his fist into the creature's face, leaving behind a dent in the already-mangled steel.

The Shell let out a pathetic howl, as if somehow the metal flesh could feel. Ignoring the cry, Nathaniel pulled back to strike again, and then paused with a shocking realization: when they had placed him into the chamber, his flesh had been alabaster white, with silver flashes running under his skin. But he had undergone yet another transformation: the milky color had vanished, and his skin had taken on a glassy translucence. He could see the outlines of his bones and muscles underneath, although they too were faded enough so that he could practically see right through them.

Eschaton's experiments had turned him into a man of glass! And it seemed that the resemblance to crystal was more than just an appearance: the impact of his fist into the metal monster's face had caused a series of cracks to spider out across his hand.

The creature pulled him off the tabletop and strapped him down to the top of a flat metal cart. But this time, as he struggled he could see that the machine was having more difficulty holding him down. Was his own strength greater, or had the abominable man-machine grown weaker?

Nathaniel kept staring at his shattered flesh, distracted from his fight against the straps. He watched in fascinated horror as a tide of silver swam underneath his skin, settling into the spider-webbed cracks in his hand until it was covered in the silver. What was this? His blood? His essence? Perhaps Eschaton would know how to correctly describe it, but he refused to consider asking. He felt no pain, and if anything his hand seemed almost more flexible than it had before.

As the silver continued to collect underneath his flesh, there was once again the strange scent. Once again he could feel the heat coming off of his skin.

He watched his flesh slowly melt back together, cracks vanishing as the heat sealed up his skin. Could he simply will himself to burn hot enough to melt his way free? But before he could try, the silver drained away from his fingers and back into his body. He flexed his digits and realized that his shattered flesh was whole once more.

"Out of the way, Shell," Eschaton said. As the two of them switched places, the Shell bumped roughly into the cart, almost toppling him over.

"Watch out, you awkward beast," Eschaton snapped, and gave him a shove.

The creature let out another whimper, backing out of the way clumsily on its wobbling wheels.

Nathaniel felt another tinge of pity. How was it possible that this pathetic creature had ever been the Iron-Clad? Where Hughes had been a proud fighter, the Shell seemed more like the remains of a whipped dog than a man.

And yet pain turned almost every man into a frightened beast. Had he been any different when the Bomb Lance's spear had pierced his thigh on the top of the bridge? He had begged Sarah to help him while Darby lay dying only a few feet away. And at every turn since then, when the world had challenged him, he had turned to the bottle for comfort, preferring to dull his pain rather than face it head on.

Eschaton rolled the cart forward. "Where are we going?" Nathaniel asked. "You won't get me up those stairs."

"That's not the only way out of this chamber." He pushed the chair onto a platform and waited for the Shell to join them before throwing a handle that stuck straight up from the floor.

Even through the cart he could feel the thrum underneath the earth as the subterranean machinery started up. Steam began to rise up from the cracks in the square metal plate under them. Finally there was a jerk as the platform began to rise, taking all of them toward the ceiling. "What are you planning to do with me?"

Eschaton smiled. "There are a number of men who are considering my offer to let them become my Children. I want to show them what a successful transformation looks like, and that it is far better to become a purified human through controlled experimentation."

"And how many of those people in the park survived the attack?"

Eschaton turned his eyes away. "Five."

"Of how many?"

"Hundreds." It actually seemed that the madman had a touch of regret in his voice. "More than I expected, although I doubt they'll last more than a day." Eschaton threw a second lever, and the ceiling above them began to open. "You may be my only survivor."

"And now you're the murderer you've always dreamed of becoming. How does it feel? Are you still proud of what you've done?"

"Humanity will continue to suffer with or without me. What I'm offering is a better tomorrow for our entire species." He could feel Eschaton's hands tightening on the grips of the chair as he turned his white-eyed gaze back toward Nathaniel.

Daylight washed down on them from the opening roof up above. "And what about the ones who die?"

"They are sacrificed for the greater good; spared from more of the endless pain that all humanity must endure. It is the living who continue to suffer." He paused for a moment, and Nathaniel wondered if even Eschaton believed his words. "I'd think you, of anyone, would sympathize with ending their pain."

He shook his head. There was no point in arguing ethics with a madman, even less so with one who had been steeling himself for genocide for years. He was sure that Darby or even Sarah *would* continue the conversation, pitting their philosophy against Eschaton's until one or the other of them ran out of breath to fight. But Nathaniel had never been one to waste his words on fools, and in his current condition he thought it better to avoid pricking the madman's wrath any further.

It seemed that, although he was now a circus freak, his survival meant that Eschaton valued him. His own life had already been irrevocably shattered, but perhaps, if the opportunity presented itself, he could do right by the spirits of the dead.

The platform finished its journey, pushing them up through the opening and stopping with a harsh jerk once it was level with the ground. The Shell seemed about to lose his balance, and let out another pathetic noise as he tilted wildly back and forth.

Eschaton let out a deep laugh at the creature's expense. Nathaniel supposed that he had been wrong to try and appeal to the villain's humanity, and yet there *had* been a moment that he could only interpret as genuine regret. . . . Not enough to stop his plan, but perhaps Nathaniel could create another opportunity.

Nathaniel barely recognized the chamber; it had once been the main courtyard. The old benches and the dying bushes had all been stripped away. Nearby a large platform had been constructed, and a series of machines had been placed along the wall.

He couldn't begin to imagine their purpose, but it was easy enough to tell that whatever it was, it wouldn't be good.

The Shell led the way, opening the doors into the building, and Eschaton pushed him through. Nathaniel recognized where they were going, and as they headed inside he began to see more and more people in the halls. But these rough-looking men were not Paragons, nor were they fit to be part of the building's staff. They were clearly gang members and other ruffians whom Eschaton was using to staff the Hall.

"This is appalling," Nathaniel said out loud. "You've filled the Hall with thugs."

"All men are created equal, or so the founding fathers believed," Eschaton replied.

"But they don't stay that way," Nathaniel quipped back. The phrase had been a favorite of his—one he had often quoted during drunken nights without a second though   t. Even as he spoke the words, he wished that he could take them back.

"No," said Eschaton, "they don't." He smiled down at him, but didn't slow down as he pushed the rumbling cart down the corridor. "You're living proof of that. But as you pointed out, some of us are born to lead."

As he considered the villain's words, he felt an emptiness gnawing inside of him. It was, unlike almost everything else he had felt today, a familiar sensation. "You said you'd get me a drink if I still wanted one after the treatment."

"Did I?" Eschaton snapped his fingers, sending out a bolt of electricity that gathered the attention of some of the men in the room. One of them ran toward him. He was a young man, but his face was an appalling mess of scars and broken teeth. "How can I help you, my lord?"

"Donny . . . It's good to see you up and around. How are you doing?"

"My boneth ith healed, mothtly. I thtill have some acheth and painth my Lord, but onthe you purify me I'm thure I'll . . ."

Eschaton reached out and ran his hand though the boy's hair. "Just a little bit more patience, Donny." He glanced down in Nathaniel's direction. "As you can see, I'm getting closer all the time."

Donny's eyes widened as he took in Nathaniel's visage. "Look at him! Who'th he, then?"

"Why don't you introduce yourself?"

For an instant Nathaniel considered refusing, but was in no position to be petulant. "I'm Nathaniel Winthorp."

It seemed impossible, but Donny's eyes grew even wider. "One of uth now, eh?" There was a tremor in his voice that said he was slightly unsure whether he wanted to be transformed into the creature he saw before him.

"What do you have to say to the boy?"

A biting reply jumped into Nathaniel's head. The very idea that this broken boy would consider him a colleague was insulting, but he held his tongue. He had been utterly transformed by Eschaton's purification process, and it would do him no good to offend the only people who understood his condition. For better or worse he had been purified, and he would have to figure out how he would make the best of it in short order.

"Our Donny wants so much to become one of us," the gray man said, "I can't make him wait for much longer."

"Pleathe, thir . . ."

"I do have some wonderful plans in mind for you. . . . Let's see how things go today. Perhaps we can get started very soon!"

The boy smiled nervously, revealing even more of the shattered enamel in his mouth. He was obviously pleased at the attention he was receiving, but was clearly not entirely sure about impending transformation from human to freak. "But first," Eschaton continued, finally getting to the heart of the matter, "I need to know if you have a flask on you."

"I . . ." The boy seemed startled by the question. His face hardened as he tried to determine the right answer.

Eschaton spoke with a tone of tenderness that still seemed to carry with it an undercurrent of menace. "Come on, now . . ."

"Yeth, thir," Donny said, and dug out a good-sized container from his pocket. It had been made from silver and leather, and from what Nathaniel could see of the engraving, it was clearly something the boy had appropriated from a far wealthier man.

Eschaton plucked it from his hand and unscrewed the lid. He held the flask over Nathaniel's face, tilting it slowly forward. Opening his mouth, Nathaniel accepted the stream of brown liquid that began burbling down from it.

There was an unusual sensation of pain as it touched his tongue, and although the thickness of the liquor was familiar, the flavor was almost entirely unlike any spirit he had ever tasted before. As he swallowed, a sensation of coolness ran through him and it felt as if he had just consumed a cold glass of water on a hot summer's day.

Rather than stopping to let Nathaniel take a breath, Eschaton continued to pour the liquid down his throat. The villain laughed as Nathaniel sputtered and gasped, but just as it seemed like he might actually drown in bourbon, the last dregs drained out of the bottle and into his mouth.

Nathaniel coughed. Despite the fact that he was no longer drinking, the sensation of coldness continued to spread through his entire body, and he shivered as it reached down into his legs.

"Was it good?" Eschaton said as he tipped the bottle back up. "It seems that your body is still capable of consuming liquor, although I can't imagine the full effect it will have on you."

The boy was still staring at him—even more intently than before, if that was possible. Nathaniel could see in Donny's eyes that something was occurring underneath his transparent skin.

"What was that?" Nathaniel said, breaking the boy's concentration.

For all his gawking, Donny refused to look him in the eyes. "Good Kentucky Whithky," replied Donny, clearly unhappy that he hadn't been the one drinking it.

"Thank you, Donny," Eschaton said, slipping the bottle into his robe. The boy looked up at the gray man with a look of disappointment that he assumed was only matched by his own. "Now you can do me another favor and start to gather the men together. It's time to call the council."

"When, my lord?"

"Right now."

Eschaton craned his neck, looking through the crowd. "And where's Clements? He was supposed to bring Anubis. It's time for his trial."

"Jack went down to the cellth to feth him!"

"Hopefully he won't be long . . ."

"No, thir."

Eschaton stared over at the broken remains of Hughes. "Shell, go down and help Jack bring up Anubis. Can you do that?"

The machine let out a pitiable moan, and began to roll away.

Eschaton looked down and shook his head at the sight. "I suppose at some point I'll have to put that creature out of its misery."

"Haven't you already hurt him enough?"

"The quality of mercy," Eschaton said, wagging his finger for effect, "is clearly one of many places where you and I differ." The gray giant turned around. "All right, Donny, call the men in."

The boy nodded enthusiastically, and then ran out of the room, shouting as he went. "Counthel in the meeting hall! Counthel in the meeting hall!"

Eschaton raised a hand and yelled after him. "And bring me a mirror. The largest one!"

The Hall had suddenly burst into activity, almost every person springing to life from Donny's simple proclamation. Nathaniel felt a distant ache. He had once wished for the power to make men do his bidding, but that was less likely now than it had ever been.

After a moment they began to scatter in all directions—some of them running into the main room, others heading off into corridors and side halls. Many of them had picked up Donny's message, and were repeating it over and over again. Nathaniel had never seen the once-quiet halls filled with so many shouting men.

His surprise was doubled as Eschaton wheeled Nathaniel into the main conference room. As he was tilted forward and rolled down the ramp, what he saw made him gasp with shock. The space had been utterly transformed from the shattered ruin it had been the last time he had seen it, and it was nothing like the once-stately meeting room it had once been. The gaping hole in the floor had been patched with concrete, and work was almost complete on the complicated mosaic that was being laid across it. Enough of the design was finished that Nathaniel could make out its intended final form: a massive Greek letter Omega: the symbol of Eschaton.

But it wasn't only the floor that had been rebuilt; the rest of the room had been changed, as well. Rows of wooden benches had been built down to the floor, creating a hexagonal theater around the center of the space. Men of all shapes and sizes were already filing into these dark pews, and Nathaniel couldn't help but notice that some of them were wearing costumes and masks, clearly intent on seeing themselves as Paragons.

He felt the urge to cry. The villain had torn down the old Hall and replaced it with this mad senate. "What have you done?"

Most of the work had been done since he had been taken into captivity more than a month ago. There was clearly no shortage of industry inside these walls.

But exactly what was it that the outside world imagined was now occurring behind the brass doors? Certainly there must at least be some suspicions. Could anyone possibly begin to guess what had become of the Turbine?

He supposed the world at large must still think that the Society of Paragons was an organization of honorable men, and not what they truly had become: a parade of monsters, rabble, and criminals.

Eschaton laughed as the cart bumped roughly down the wooden ramp that led down to the center of the floor. "Does it shock you to see your precious Hall turned into a place where men of all backgrounds can come together as equals? This is the first step to my better world—no longer is the Hall of Paragons an ode to Darby's vision of false charity, but a place where men of strong will can come together to decide not only their own future, but that of all mankind."

Nathaniel found himself shocked by the insinuation. "We helped so many people!"

"You helped yourselves, you mean." Somewhere above them there was a buzzing sound, and Nathaniel saw a glow rise up in the room. The gaslights had been replaced by electric bulbs. Their glow was harsh—still, their brilliance would have been marvelous if they hadn't been revealing a monster.

The look on Eschaton's face was grim as he leaned down over Nathaniel. "You and the others handed out false justice. You supported a broken philosophy while you perpetuated the very destruction you thought you were so nobly fighting against."

With the artificial illumination he could now see the objects surrounding him as clear as day—clearer, if truth be told, although with harsher shadows.

At the bottom of the ramp was a box-shaped object hidden under an expanse of black cloth. Just behind it, where Darby's magnificent wooden chair had once sat high atop a pedestal, there now loomed above them a towering structure. A set of spiral stairs wrapped around it.

The new structure was similar to the pulpit in a cathedral. It made him feel the same cynicism as when he entered a church. He had always been of the opinion that all the religious pomp and circumstance would be unnecessary if the men who relied on it were truly able to call up the power of the divine.

In the case of Eschaton, however, it was clear that the villain was able to manifest abilities beyond those of mortal men. The gray man tilted the cart so that Nathaniel was essentially standing upright.

He watched as the gray man walked up the steps, the wood creaking as they accepted his prodigious weight. "It saddens me that you don't, as of yet, fully appreciate what my purification will bring to the world." After a few steps Nathaniel could no longer see him, but he could hear his voice. "You are already my greatest creation. I'd hoped the process of your transformation would have cleared away some of your sad misconceptions."

Up near the ceiling another Omega symbol hung down where a cross might have been placed in a church. "I think I understand well enough," Nathaniel replied. "You think you're some kind of god."

Eschaton's shining head appeared at the top of the pulpit and looked down. "Perhaps I am. I am certainly your creator. But unlike the Christian God, I am willing to share my deification. I don't need to tower above a race of broken creatures just to prove my superiority."

"And what happens if all the purified humans don't agree with your dream?" Nathaniel shouted up.

"I suppose there will be fighting for a time, as we discover what it means to re-imagine society in a world of superior beings. But that is the way of the world."

Eschaton raised his hands upward and a rousing cheer came up from the stands around them. Nathaniel had been so busy arguing with the man that he hadn't even realized that the council was now in session.

"Gentlemen! Thank you so much for attending this council. My Children, we have work to do tonight."

The crowd once again roared in response, and then they began to chant Eschaton's name over and over again. Nathaniel could feel despair settling into whatever remained of his bones. It seemed too late to stop whatever awful plan this villain had in store. The Paragons were gone—there was no one left to stop him.

As the cheers died down, he heard a single voice from the entranceway. "Here you are, my lord! I've brought the mirror you athked for!" Nathaniel recognized the massive looking glass immediately as the one that had once stood in Peter Wickham's chambers. It was tilted upward, and it glowed brightly from the electric lights in the ceiling, almost as if the surface of it had been lit on fire.

"Bring it here . . ." Eschaton said, motioning toward the boy hidden behind it.

"Yeth, lord!"

Without being asked, a number of men hopped from their seats to help carry it down the ramp.

As it grew closer, Nathaniel thought that the image it displayed had somehow been distorted, the glass melted or scratched in such a way that it was hazy, or unreal.

It was only when he realized that the reflection in the mirror was truly his own, that Nathaniel began to scream.

Chapter 9

The Mechanics of Emotion

Two full days had passed since Tom had returned, and yet Sarah was still avoiding him. She knew she couldn't delay long. Wasn't she the one who had warned them that inaction only brought Eschaton's plans closer to completion? And that was hardly the only reason that she had to go and see her friend.

Ever since the day Sarah had seen Lord Eschaton smash Tom to pieces with his own arm, she had dreamed of the day that he would return to her—not as the gigantic monster he became in the theater, but as the Automaton who had saved her life that day in February. As the metal man who had run her through the streets of New York to get her to a doctor after she had been injured in the fire. And now he had returned and Sarah was still terrified, afraid that this still wasn't the same Tom she'd lost, but something else that merely looked and spoke like her old friend.

And according to Emilio, he was more alive now than he had ever been. He told Sarah how Tom had rebuilt himself, using the piano wire to weave wire flesh on top of his new frame. Was this the Tom she knew? Would he have abandoned Darby's designs so easily for his own desires?

But no matter how else he might have changed, the heart that beat inside of him, the one she had fought so hard to protect, was still the same.

"Or is it?" she mumbled to herself, letting her hand fall to the place on her chest where she had worn Darby's Alpha Element, the one that now gave Tom life.

She thought back to the promise she had made to Darby just before his death. He had asked her to help Tom discover what he was capable of. But what if that was not what *she* wanted? What if he became capable of terrible things?

The thought filled her heart with terror, but also a tiny thrill. The choice between the great and the terrible was one that every living being had to make. Whether she was ready for it or not, the moment she had waited for, for so long, was finally here.

And Sarah had, so far, been unable to bring herself to actually go and face whatever the Automaton had become. Instead she found herself walking down by the East River, watching the boats go by.

Whoever had owned the junkyard before the Armandos had constructed a large wooden dock that hung out over the edge of the river. It was dilapidated, but still serviceable.

Emilio had told Sarah that there were still occasionally barges loaded with junk that would come down the river and tie up to the dock to try to sell scrap to the junkyard. Once they realized that Emilio only dealt in metal and machinery, fewer and fewer of them had come calling.

Still, keeping river access was worth the effort to Emilio, especially when it had become necessary to use the dock to get the machines he wanted from the theater back to the yard. Emilio had even hired on a few hands, and repairing the structure had been a way to free himself from worrying about his sister.

Sarah had never been fond of the water as a child, but as the spring rains had given way to the summer sunshine, she found the idea of the river that ran along the western edge of the junkyard to be more and more alluring.

When she stepped out onto the dock for the first time, Sarah had only been able to stand out on the wooden slats for a few minutes before the mere thought of the river rushing under her feet had driven her to the safety of the muddy shore.

But by the end of a week she was no longer afraid, able to trust the floats and wood that kept the dock afloat. She soon discovered that there was something deeply soothing about simply standing out on the dock and watching the world go by. And as her fear vanished the river had become a revelation: a living painting filled with boats of all sizes and shapes, backed by the rough mystery of the city of Manhattan outlined behind it.

It was only over the last few days that she no longer wanted to stare out at that particular view, concerned that she might see another black cloud rising up above the city—proof that they had waited too long.

Instead she stared down into the rushing waters of the East River, contemplating the possible ways she might still put a stop to Eschaton, occasionally glancing away as some poor creature or horrifying lump drifted by the shore. She had yet to see anything that she could clearly identify as a *human* body, although she was sure it was only a matter of time.

The sun was rising high into the sky now. She had spent the morning wandering along the waterfront, but she would go to speak to Tom this afternoon. She had to!

But as she rounded the remains of a rusting boiler that time and tide had firmly planted into the muddy shore, Sarah saw that the moment she had feared had come to her.

Standing in front of her, only a few short yards away, were Tom and Viola. The two of them were facing each other, and Sarah saw them only for an instant before hiding herself inside the rusting chunk of metal.

At the angle they were standing, she was sure they must have seen her. For a moment she held her breath, waiting for the inevitable confrontation. But as their muffled conversation continued, it became obvious that neither was aware of her. She exhaled softly, thankful that the breeze that carried their voices in her direction also made it more difficult for Tom's incredible hearing to detect her.

Viola's voice was her usual shrill staccato, although the tones were far softer than they might have been if she had been directing them at Sarah. Tom's voice was totally different—musical notes instead of the familiar whistling tones.

His words now came out in an almost-angelic harmonic trill. The sound made Sarah think of a choir of singers, each one of whom had been given the task of producing a single syllable before letting the next one talk. She found it both entrancing and alien at the same time.

Pulling together her confidence, Sarah peered out around the edge of the metal slab. Viola was closer to her, and turned slightly away. Despite that, she most likely would have seen Sarah if her vision hadn't been obscured by the edge of her mask. The metal face-covering was new and completely different than the porcelain one she had seen the Italian girl wearing previously. It came only halfway down her face, but covered both of her eyes . . . looking far more like a theatrical mask than her previous one had.

The hammered brass gleamed in the sunlight, the shape of it sensual. The curve of it around her face and nose gave it a soft shape somewhere between a butterfly and Viola's own lips.

But her mouth itself was not obscured: hanging down from the bottom curve of the metal mask was a lacy veil that obscured the lower half of her face without hiding it completely. The entire effect was clearly intended to be alluring, and Sarah thought it did an effective job.

"Has anyone ever told you that you are," Viola said to Tom loudly, the sound of her voice almost a growl, "an absolutely gorgeous creature?"

Sarah realized now that what the Italian girl was wearing was most decidedly a *costume*, although it was one that would have never been allowed inside the Hall of Paragons. Viola seemed unconcerned with the scandalous nature of the outfit. She approached Tom, not so much walking as swaggering. As she moved, her dress parted near her hemline in a way so far beyond scandalous that it seemed almost ridiculous. Each step revealed a flash of leg covered in a pair of long leather boots laced so tightly that they almost appeared to be nothing more than another layer of particularly darkened skin.

The material of the dress was surprisingly simple and elegant, and it only took Sarah another instant to realize that it had once been hers. "My last good dress," she whispered to herself. The girl had stolen it from her!

The metal man turned, and Sarah could see Tom's eyes clearly. The way the painted eyes were facing it appeared as if he was leering directly at Viola's scandalous outfit. But the eyes saw nothing—they were simply a painted reminder of something he did not actually have. "I appreciate your . . . opinion," the mechanical man said to Viola, "but I have no need for any . . . compliments."

Viola laughed and ran a finger down the side of his mask. "You are such an innocent, Tom. Like a child."

"I am . . . older than you are, I think."

"No. You were born yesterday. I saw it."

"Reborn. But I have existed in many . . . bodies since the professor first . . . created me."

Realizing that being caught eavesdropping by Tom or Viola would be far worse than the embarrassment of simply interrupting, Sarah had every intention of moving forward and revealing herself, but just as she was about to step out from behind the old boiler, the sun broke through the clouds. The light struck Tom's rebuilt body, and she was once again transfixed.

The mechanical man glittered in the sunlight, the wire wrapping him reflecting it in waves. Even from this distance she could make out places where whirls and patterns lay trapped underneath the weaving of metal that crossed him. In some places he seemed positively ethereal, the wire shimmering as he moved. It gave the suggestion of being some kind of living flesh while at the same time being nothing of the sort.

She began to take another step forward, but then witnessed something so shocking that she found herself once again frozen in place.

"You should see yourself, metal man," Viola said, "you're an angel." She stretched out her arms in a languid, almost-sensual manner, and draped them at either side of Tom's neck. After a moment she brought them together behind his head, her wrists loosely piled on top of one another. They hung limply, in a way that any woman of candor and class would have considered lurid intent. It was wanton, and—in a word that leapt unbidden and unwanted from Sarah's subconscious—*whorish*. "You may be the most perfect man I've ever seen."

As she stood there, her shock mounting, Sarah realized that she was failing spectacularly at not being an eavesdropper. Still, she decided once again to interrupt the conversation.

But as Sarah shifted her weight to take a step in their direction, Viola moved as well, pressing her rouged lips fully against Tom's own painted mouth.

Sarah felt shocked, despite the fact that she knew it was quite impossible for Tom to respond to the girl's amorous advances. And yet, what did she really know about this new Tom's feelings? He wasn't human to begin with, and Viola's kiss would have seemed shocking no matter *where* it was planted. Could it stir the feelings of a machine, as well?

Sarah knew she should have felt nothing but pity for the girl—Viola was clearly a madwoman. But to see an act performed with such licentiousness, and to see it practiced on Tom, shot a bolt of . . . what? Anger? It ran from her heart straight down to her knees.

Whatever the feeling was, it caused Sarah to clench her right hand into a fist. Closing her eyes had been her *intention*, but Sarah found herself taking in every moment of the sordid scene before her.

The wind shifted slightly, carrying Viola's voice directly to Sarah's ears, along with the scent of the river. Her nose wrinkled from them both. "Did you like that?"

"It was . . . warm." Tom sat unmoving as Viola planted a second kiss on his face, leaving another smudge of red face paint below his right eye. "I know that . . . people can find such . . . activities . . . pleasant."

Was he stuttering more than usual?

"But that's other people. It wasn't you."

"This is . . . true."

Viola interlaced her fingers and leaned backwards, using Tom's neck for support. "You have the heart of an artist."

"I have the heart of a . . . machine."

"I've held your heart in my hand."

Sarah felt a wave of nausea as she heard those words. She had clutched Tom's heart to her chest for months. Viola knew nothing of Tom's heart! Part of her wanted to scream at the top of her lungs just to put a stop to this insipid conversation.

"How did it . . . feel?" Tom asked.

"Magical," Viola purred in reply. "Like holding a miracle."

"It does not feel like . . . magic, inside of me."

They were both silent for a moment, and Viola took the opportunity to kiss him again, although this time with less fervor. "Why do you talk like that?"

Tom's head tilted slightly to the left. "Talk like . . . what?"

Viola laughed. "Talk like . . ." she let the pause linger. "This," she finished, in a slightly mocking mimicry of Tom's musical monotone.

Underneath Sarah's anger—it was most definitely anger now—Sarah found herself marveling at the girl's ability to turn the smallest phrase into a bold seduction.

"No one has ever . . . asked me that . . . before."

"Well," she said, placing her hands against his chest, "I'm asking you now."

There was a pause. "It is not . . . intentional. If I could I would . . . speak like you. But sometimes it takes . . . time for the words to . . . form."

"I don't understand."

"I will try to . . . explain." Tom's right hand rose to Viola's head. "Your words come from . . . here."

Viola nodded. "So they tell me."

He took Viola's fingers into his own. Bringing her arm down, he pressed her hand against his chest. Whether Sarah wanted to admit it or not, and she most certainly did not, there was no denying that what she was feeling now was worse than anger. It was jealousy, and it felt hot and deep. "My words come from my . . . heart."

"All men say that, but they're usually about two feet too high." Viola gave a noise that was almost a giggle. "But in your case, I suppose I can believe you."

Tom ignored the crude innuendo. "But my . . . heart must also . . . beat, so sometimes when I am trying to . . . remember something, or say something in . . . particular, the words take . . . longer to come."

Sarah wondered why it was that *she* had never thought about Tom's pauses. She supposed that it was because she had never wanted to think of Tom as any more inhuman than she had to. She had never wanted Tom to *know* that she considered him *different*.

What Sarah had avoided out of fear, Viola, true to her nature, had simply done without hesitation. Sarah had never considered herself to be a jealous person, but perhaps that was only because up until now she had never truly had anyone to be jealous *of*. For an instant Sarah again considered charging forward, but she knew that the opportunity to reveal her presence without embarrassment had passed.

Instead she began backing away silently, hoping that she might escape unseen. She craned her head to see where she could safely place her next step, and iron and bone collided, sending up a loud ringing that was impossible to ignore. She had been undone the moment she had attempted to be stealthy . . .

Viola turned to her, eyes staring out from underneath the metal mask. Now that she could see it fully, Sarah realized that the Italian girl had been right in covering her face. With the damage concealed under metal and paint, Viola had regained much of the exotic beauty that had been stolen away by the scars.

But, having discovered Sarah watching, the Italian girl didn't move her hand, or back away from Tom in any way. Instead she simply smiled, with a look that hinted that perhaps she had known that Sarah had been there all along. Either way, the look of satisfaction gave Sarah a powerful urge to walk up and smack Viola's horrible mask completely away.

She was halfway to unleashing that attack when she heard Tom speak. "Sarah?" Tom didn't turn to face her.

Once again Viola spoke before Sarah could, "Yes, Tom, it's her. How long were you spying on us, rich girl?" She finally pulled her hand off of Tom's bare chest and took a step back from the metal man.

Sarah felt the heat of an involuntary blush coming down over her cheeks, but she forged ahead, ignoring Viola's taunts. "It's me, Tom. How are you?"

"I am . . . well. I am . . . glad you have come to see me."

"It took you long enough," Viola said with a sneer.

"Please . . . Viola," Tom said. "Sarah is my . . . friend."

Sarah stepped forward to take a closer look at this new Automaton. Almost everything about him was different than the last time that she had seen him, and yet somehow she knew with certainty that this was Tom—or mostly Tom.

The last time she had seen him in a truly human form—unbeaten, unbroken, and fully formed—had been after his battle with Nathaniel at the Darby house. Even then he had been badly scorched, his face shattered. But he had still seemed repairable—hurt, but not destroyed. Then Eschaton had torn him to pieces.

It all seemed long ago now. It had taken so much to bring him back. If Tom wasn't entirely the same being he had been then, Sarah could safely say the same was true for her, as well.

Sarah desperately wanted to take another step forward, this time to embrace her friend, but Viola was again standing in the way.

Almost as if sensing her distress, Tom moved toward her, forcing the Italian girl to get out of the way. Sarah smiled as she wrapped her arms around his metal body, expecting to feel the solid weight of him, the same way she had when she had said good-bye to him on the doctor's doorstep that cold winter's morning. But he was different now; taller and more ethereal than he had been before. The taut wire that he had wrapped around himself gave slightly under her embrace. As he lifted his arms to hug her she realized that his new form wasn't just an illusion. There was something more truly *living* about him than there had been before.

"It is good to see you again, Tom. I . . ." She felt the walls she had worked so hard to build up inside of herself fall away in the moment she said his name. Just for an instant she felt as if she was once again the naive girl that she had been before all of *this* had begun. Sarah felt the stinging pressure of tears in her eyes, threatening to drag her down into another torrent of emotion. But she would not let herself fall that far so easily, especially in front of Emilio's sister.

"I am . . . glad you are here," Tom said. "Viola had said that you were . . . worried about me."

"I'm sure she said a *lot* of things about me."

Viola's voice didn't hide her anger, "You wrong me, rich girl. I am not here to steal your metal man away from you."

"You'll just kiss him and steal my clothes."

She could see Viola's smile through her veil. "You've borrowed so many of our things: my brother, my home," the Italian girl said, frowning. "I figured you wouldn't mind so much if I borrow something of yours."

"And now you want to be a Paragon as well?" Sarah snapped.

"Not a Paragon. Nothing like you, rich girl," she said with derisive snort of a laugh. "Do you know the Commedia dell'Arte?"

Sarah shook her head. The term sounded vaguely familiar, but if she had previously been familiar with it, she no longer remembered the lesson.

"It is the characters of Italian theater. La Signora is the concubine—the Harlot. I call myself that. It's very good, I think, but it is no Paragon."

Sarah couldn't deny that there was some poetry to the girl giving herself an identity pulled from the stage, and it explained the outlandish rouge on her lips.

At the same time, the whole notion of Viola as any kind of costumed heroine was utterly ridiculous. The last time she had been face-to-face with

Eschaton's henchmen the Italian girl had barely managed to escape with her life, and now she wanted to be an adventurer.

And yet Viola was now as much of a veteran as Sarah was: not only battle-scarred, but willing and eager to throw herself back into the fight. "It's ridiculous," she muttered, forcing herself to stop entertaining the idea that this mad girl might somehow be helpful to her cause.

"You think so?" Viola said, pulling out an object from her belt. "But you still haven't seen the best part." She flicked it open with a metallic snap: an oversized hand-fan.

As it caught the sunlight, the device revealed itself to be made entirely of metal. The leaves clanked as they fluttered, but it seemed to be doing an effective job of blowing air into her face, and the lacy veil fluttered seductively enough.

Sarah let out a sigh. "Are you planning to allure your enemies to death?"

"No. It's much better than that." Viola spun her hand around, and Sarah heard the telltale sound of fortified steam being released.

From the tips of each rib popped out a small blade, each one an inch long. They were small, but menacing enough that Sarah took an unconscious step back. "Impressive, no?" the girl said, waving the deadly device in front of her face.

Sarah wanted to say no, but in her retreat she had already given herself away. "I suppose it is . . ."

"Now look." Viola flipped her hand over again, holding the fan in front of her. She snapped her wrist and something escaped from the fan in a blur. It let out a sharp "tank" as it slammed into the old boiler that Sarah had used to hide behind. The projectile pierced the rusting iron, leaving behind a small hole that daylight poured through.

In the revealing glow, Sarah could see now that another blade was already rising up to take its place, fed by a line that was attached to her arm. The design of it was like a lady's version of the weapon that had been wielded by her father—or, now that she thought of it, the Bomb Lance.

Sarah tried to control her temper as she spoke. It would certainly do no good to shout at a woman wielding a self-reloading blade gun, no matter how it had been dressed up. "You didn't make this, did you, Viola?"

"I . . . created it," Tom said, taking a step forward.

"Based on my idea," Viola said, clearly impressed with her own ingenuity.

"Tom, what were you thinking?"

"If we are going to stop . . . Eschaton, we will need . . . allies. And they will need to be . . . armed."

From the few times she had heard her father discussing tactics (for the benefit of Nathaniel), he had defined an ally as someone who you could trust not to intentionally put a bullet into your back. Sadly, Sarah had a hard time believing that she wouldn't find herself on the receiving end of an "accident" from Viola's new weapon. "You should have come to me before . . ."

Snapping her fan shut, Viola stepped forward. "And who says you run anything, rich girl?"

"Back to this again?" But Sarah had to admit that for all her concerns it was good to see that reinventing herself as a heroine had restored the Italian girl's confidence. "I didn't know you fancied yourself as the leader, Viola?"

The girl pondered that for a moment. As one second stretched into several, Sarah considered trying to disarm the girl of her deadly weapon. She hoped that Tom might help her as well, although there was no way to be sure, especially since he had helped to create it in the first place. If there was any hope of rectifying their relationship she would have to find a better way of working things out with Viola than fighting with her.

It was Tom's voice that cut through the silence, "Sarah is the . . . daughter of a . . . Paragon. She is the leader . . . of the . . . Society of Steam."

Sarah could see the faint outline of Viola's lips pursing under her veil. "Did you come up with that name, rich girl?"

Sarah nodded. Up until now it had been half a joke—something to talk about until she could come up with a real name. But having heard Tom say it, perhaps it wasn't such a bad name after all.

"It's ridiculous," Viola said, snapping her fan back open. "It sounds like a group of old ladies making tea."

"Well, if you don't have a better one . . ."

"The People's Guardians," the Italian girl said firmly.

Sarah barked out a laugh, and then covered her mouth. She could only imagine the look on her father's face if he had lived to hear that her daughter was leading a group of adventurers describing themselves as communists. Although it probably wasn't too far off from what he had thought of her, anyway.

Viola rolled her eyes under the mask. "I knew the rich girl wouldn't like it."

"I'm sorry Viola, but our job is to save the world from villains, not to change the world to make it the way we think it should be."

"And who chooses the people who we are supposed to shoot with our fancy guns?"

"We shoot the people trying to hurt other people," Sarah said, although she wasn't sure that was *exactly* right.

"Darby," Tom said, "always told me that the . . . villains were the ones who thought that . . . murder was . . . justified to get their way."

"Then maybe we go after the government, and stop the wars . . ." The sarcasm in her tone had reached new levels.

"'The new world,'" Tom suddenly chimed in, speaking without his usual stutter, "'will no longer be built on fear and war, or any of the products of man's hatred and the rising tide of humanity. It is a world that will be built on nobler pursuits.'"

"That's right, Tom." Viola said. "You see, rich girl? Not everyone thinks I am so foolish."

"Who said that, Tom?" Sarah asked him.

"It was something Lord . . . Eschaton told me, just before he smashed me to . . . pieces."

Viola stood silently for a second, her hands clenched tightly at her sides. When she spoke again her voice was raised to a shout. "You Paragons are all idiots! All the power you have and all the pain you cause, and you use it all to fight your rich-man wars." She pointed her fan accusingly—threateningly—toward Sarah's face. "What is the good of having all this power if we don't *do* anything with it?"

Sarah felt her righteous anger melt away—the question was one she had once asked her father. Asking those questions had been what led her to meet Sir Dennis Darby in the first place.

While Alexander Stanton had little patience for an endless barrage of childish questions, Darby had been glad to talk to her for as long as she wanted.

And once her father had been willing to leave the old man and the child alone together, she could remember talking to Darby for hours while he worked on one project after another, patiently answering question after question.

Not only had he responded to them completely and thoughtfully, he'd done so without hesitation or censorship. Far from finding such interrogation annoying, the old professor had seemed to revel in the challenge of facing off against the infinite innocent curiosity of a child.

And if she didn't understand one of his answers, or if Darby referenced something she had never heard of, Sarah could simply ask him to explain, and he would, in detail, describe whatever it was she didn't yet know until he was sure she did. It had been an education like no other, and it had made her the woman she was today. Sadly, Sarah didn't think she had anywhere near the old man's endless patience, especially where Viola was concerned.

"We can," Sarah said, choosing her words carefully, and trying as much as possible to channel the spirit of her mentor, "simply do the best we know how."

"More drivel," Viola said. "If we have the power to make the world better, then we should use that power."

"I haven't had your life, Viola, and I never will. And I know you've suffered, but none of us can change the world alone. And it matters *who* you do it with."

"I expect childishness from you. All of your class think that you have something to offer the poor besides pain, but you can't ever see yourselves as the cause of the sorrow you pretend to cure. But you, Tom, I think you *do* understand."

"But I will not . . . kill to get what I . . . want."

"But you will kill," Viola said, and Tom gave no reply.

"It's still a *game* for both of you, but it has never been one for me. It has not been one for Emilio since he lost his family." Viola pulled off her mask, revealing the scars underneath. "You spent your life around machines," she said to Sarah, "so you think you know so much about the way things work, but you know nothing about the heart and the soul. You don't know what makes men and women do the things they do when they are hungry, or desperate."

Viola looked up at the metal man, and ran her hand across his mask. "Thank you for this, Tom, but I won't use it to fight in your rich-man's wars. I have already hurt enough."

"Then who will you fight for, Viola?" Sarah truly felt sorry for her. She was no fool, but the girl was also treading into dangerous waters. "You need to trust someone." She held out her hand. Perhaps if she gave her a gesture of friendship . . . She needed more heroes on her side. There was no way that she could fight Eschaton alone.

"I do. But not you," Viola said, replacing her mask. "You have your world, and I have mine. And in between them all we share is my brother. I'm sure you will get him to fight in your wars: he is a dreamer, and I think he loves you very much." The sadness Sarah saw in Viola's eyes was heartbreaking. "You will get Emilio, but not me." Sarah's hand lingered for a moment. She took it back, untouched.

"I think," Sarah said, looking at the costume, "that given time, you would be a great hero."

Viola smiled her twisted grin. "That is not what these costumes are about, and that is something *you* still need to learn. It is all a lie. It is something we all hide the truth behind." It seemed as if the Italian girl's madness had subsided for the moment. But Sarah wasn't completely sure she was comfortable with the woman Viola had become. "And I will let you have Tom as well."

The red marks she had smeared across Tom's face told a different story. "As if you could take him," Sarah said angrily, wishing that she could recall the words after she had said them.

Viola's tone remained surprisingly calm. "He is more of a real man than you give him credit for."

Sarah glanced up at Tom for an instant and tried to hide her scowl. There was no doubt if she kept trying to play these jealous games with Viola she was going to lose, as she always did.

Instead she let her fingers clutch at the rough fabric of her dress. "I'd like to talk to Tom alone now, if you don't mind."

Viola laughed. "So, I'm not the only who's curious just how much of a man he might be."

"Don't be vulgar," Sarah said, blushing. "In fact, don't be here at all."

"This is still my home!" Viola said, the calm veneer of her cool finally cracking slightly, revealing the madwoman still hidden beneath the mask.

"Please . . . Viola," Tom said. Sarah could literally hear a note of concern in his voice that echoed through his strings. "Sarah and I have not . . . spoken in a long time."

The metal mask on her face shifted as the Italian girl pursed her lips together. "All right." She pointed a finger at Tom. "I do this for you," she said, and then swung the accusing digit toward Sarah, "but not for you."

Sarah nodded. "Fine."

Viola turned and ran back toward the house. Sarah found that she was still staring after her when Tom spoke again. "You don't need to be . . . angry at Viola."

"I know." Sarah felt a flush coming over her cheeks. It had been ridiculous for her to be jealous of the Italian girl. "She's in pain."

"And it is my . . . fault."

"No. Tom, what happened in the theater . . . That wasn't really you."

Tom paused for a long moment, and Sarah was about to try and tell him again when he interrupted her, "I am . . . sorry that I scared you . . . Sarah."

"Don't be foolish, Tom." She turned back to him and tried to raise up a smile. "That's all over now. You're here, and you're safe."

"No," he said, shaking his head. "This is only just . . . beginning, I am afraid."

She couldn't tell what he was afraid of. "What happened in the theater was an accident, you were confused . . ."

"I am . . . changed. The Tom you knew . . . before is gone. I am something . . . different. And I am not yet . . . sure if that is . . . better, or worse."

Sarah wanted to block out his words and pretend she hadn't heard them. This was everything she had been afraid to hear—the reason she had avoided talking to him. But *she* had been responsible for bringing him back, whatever he was. "In the theater, you told me you wanted to live."

"I did and I . . . do. But being alive is not . . . the same . . . as being . . . good. The heart of the . . . Pneumatic Colossus is still the same as the one that beats inside of me now."

"But you're different now. You're Tom again."

Tom stepped away from her. As he moved, Sarah could see how true his words were: he was different. "You are . . . right, to some . . . degree." Where his original body had been deliberate and mechanical, there was now a liveliness in his actions. "My new . . . form is a part of . . . who I am." Previously he had been urging himself into motion, and now it appeared it took all his will for him to *stop*. "It was . . . Emilio who suggested that I try to truly . . . re-create myself, rather than simply . . . rebuilding who I was."

She marveled again at the intricate weave of wire that covered his body. "You did a marvelous job." Tom may have rewoven the wire to take ownership of the frame that Emilio had given him, but Sarah wanted to believe that some of Emilio's goodness had come through in that new body as well. "I can't imagine that anything dangerous could come from the person who had saved my life."

"Sir Dennis once . . . told me that any man could choose to wield a . . . paintbrush or a . . . gun with equal . . . dexterity."

"'And it is only their will that sets them apart,'" Sarah said, completing the saying. It was a phrase he had been fond of repeating to her when she was a young girl. But there had come a point when he had stopped saying it. She wondered what had changed his view of the world.

"Both . . . Viola and you think I am a man because that is the shape that . . . Sir Dennis gave me."

"I believe you have a soul, Tom."

The metal man stepped closer to Sarah, and she found herself slightly breathless. It came not only from his gleaming attractiveness, but also from the shape of his new body. Now that she had a chance to fully take him in, Sarah realized he was slim and tall, with an attractive curve that travelled down his spine. The tension in the wires that wrapped his frame made them vibrate with every move, giving him a hint of a predator about to strike. She tried not to let her fear show as he closed the space between them. "I have a . . . heart. Anything more than that is . . . conjecture."

Sarah looked up at him and put her hand against his chest, exactly the way Viola had. "I know better." The metal was warm from the sunshine, and she could feel his heart beating beneath it.

After a moment she reached into the pocket of her skirt and pulled out a handkerchief. Standing up on her toes, she began to wipe the red smudges of paint off his face. "Thank you . . . Sarah."

"Someone needs to take care of you." Most of the smudges were coming away, but even after repeated tries there was still an aura of Viola's lips that remained. She had marked him.

Tom nodded. "I meant . . . thank you for bringing me back."

Sarah smiled and kept cleaning. "I still need your help."

"To stop Lord Eschaton."

"He's still looking for you." The wind suddenly kicked up, and Sarah could feel dirt and sand swirling around her ankles. There was a time, not too long ago, when any breeze that could have penetrated her petticoats would have been shocking; now she was surprised she even noticed that her ankles were bare. "He still wants your heart."

"I believe that he needs it to create more . . . fortified steam."

"But he already has his smoke. Isn't that what he needs to bring about his evil plan?"

"He does not simply want to . . . destroy the world, he wants to . . . transform it."

Sarah had removed as much of the remnants of Viola's kisses as she could without damaging the features underneath. Tom still looked as if he'd been attacked by a painted whore or an actress, but only slightly. "I'm afraid I don't understand."

"Eschaton was . . . transformed by the smoke and steam. Now he wants to rebuild . . . the world so that there are . . . thousands more, just like . . . him."

"And to do that, he needs your heart."

"It is the only . . . source. But he could make more, given time."

"You don't think that . . ."

"I am a machine . . . Sarah. What has been . . . created, can be . . . re-created. He will find a way."

Sarah wanted to argue with him, but she was tired of disagreeing with everyone. "We're running out of time. I need to stop him."

"No, Sarah, you need to be safe. I will go to the . . . Paragons. I will convince them to . . . help."

She laughed bitterly. "Of course. You were gone. How could you know?"

Tom cocked his head to the side. She wasn't sure whether she found his oddly human gestures charming or condescending. "What has . . . happened?"

"Eschaton has infiltrated the Paragons. They're gone."

"Surely your . . . father . . ."

Sarah felt an ache across her heart. "My father is dead."

"And . . . Nathaniel?"

"Missing for months. If he's still alive, that villain has him."

Sarah waited for Tom to reply, but he simply stood there, unmoving.

"Are you all right, Tom?"

"I will go and . . . fight him." He rose up taller, as if preparing for battle.

"Last time you tried he tore you to pieces. And everyone in the city thinks you were behind my father's murder."

Tom slumped forward, his posture of defeat almost comical. "I must . . . protect you, Sarah."

"No, Tom. It's not about me anymore. We must do what Darby created the Paragons to do . . ."

"To protect those who cannot protect themselves." He said it cleanly and perfectly, as if it had been burned into him. Thinking about Darby's handwriting, etched into the walls of Tom's heart, she wondered if it wasn't.

A new thought popped into Sarah's head. "But now I know we have something that Eschaton doesn't."

"Fortified steam."

"Exactly."

"So, we will re-create the . . . Paragons?"

Sarah thought about it for a moment. It was tempting to think that they could do what Darby had done. But it seemed as if every time they had tried to rebuild the past it had simply crumbled away. She could no longer stand in the shadow of Darby or her father. Win or fail, there was no turning back. "No."

"Then we are . . . the Society of Steam?"

"Yes." When she had been a child, pretending to be a hero like her father, she had never wanted to be anything more than a Paragon. But at a young age she had known in her heart that they would never accept a woman in their midst. So instead she had imagined a team of her own; one that wouldn't turn away girls with an indomitable spirit, or anyone who truly dreamed of being a hero. "And whatever Eschaton's plans are, we will put an end to them!"

"It is a good name . . . Sarah."

"Of course *you'd* like it," she said, slightly embarrassed at indulging her own childish whim.

The wind blew stronger now, and Sarah could feel dust stinging her eyes. She slipped her arm through Tom's and pulled him toward her. The limb gave slightly, strings yielding to the pressure she had put on them. "Come on, then, let's go back to the house. Whoever, or whatever, you are, I need your help, and there's a great deal of planning to do."

Chapter 10
Up the River

"Come up hewe Gwüssew. I want you to see ze night, she is so bewutifuw, and it is about to be ze dawn." The old man's commanding voice echoed down from above, his particularly nasal tone ringing off the ship's hull.

The Submersible's craft sat low in the water as they chugged along the East River, puffs of steam and smoke coming out from the tall tubes at its tail.

Grüsser grabbed the rungs of the ladder and hauled himself up and out of the boat, crawling through the hatch to reach the main deck. He felt slightly dizzy, his breathing heavy as he pulled in a breath through the tight collar of his Chronal Suit.

The old man didn't bother to extend a hand to help him as he pulled himself up through the hatch. The first rays of dawn were streaking through the sky. It wouldn't be long before the sun broke over the horizon. "It is very gut."

"But youw ship, my fat fweind, she is not vewy good."

"Zen ist gut that der ship ist nicht mine, now," Grüsser mumbled to himself as he got to his feet. The insane Frenchman had stolen it away from him, and then, adding insult to injury, Grüsser had been forced to assist le Voyageur in turning it into something else.

"You awe aways compwainig, awen't you, weetle pig?" The Frenchman looked over his shoulder at him, squinting in the way that he always did when he was looking for something else to criticize Grüsser for.

And recently the old man had plenty of time to needle him. They had spent the last few days driving the boat up and down the coastline looking for the rumored junkyard hideout of the man who had been with Sarah Stanton when the Automaton had made its deadly reappearance at the theater.

Grüsser had been shocked to learn not only that Alexander Stanton's daughter was still alive, but that she had managed to successfully bring the metal Paragon back to life.

He had seen the shredded remains of metal man's body in the park, and he would have thought any kind of restoration of the Automaton was impossible, but if there was a single trait that had defined both Sarah and her father, it was tenacity.

Grüsser certainly wouldn't have suspected that a society girl would be able to survive and *thrive* in the streets of New York. Even so, the rumors were that she had taken up with a man, so it was likely that her honor was no longer intact. He supposed that was the price that a woman paid for trying to ignore her duty.

But she was Stanton's girl, and he was sworn to protect her from threats such as the Children of Eschaton, and here he was hunting her down. He could only marvel at how quickly he had fallen so low, and yet his capacity for self-loathing had yet to be satiated. And that made him sicker still.

"Is thewe a pwobwem?"

"*Nein.*" Grüsser shook his head and swallowed his pride.

"Good, my soft Pwussian." The Frenchman's tone was utterly patronizing. "We have much work weft to do."

Le Voyageur gave the metal wheel a hard spin to the right, and the engine's roar rose in pitch as the ship steered toward the other side of the river, navigating around a steamship anchored in the harbor.

"Not bad, eh? This wittle ship is now so much more nimbew than it was when it had simpwy been Dawby's cwunky invention." Grüsser couldn't disagree more. The Submersible had been an elegant ship, capable of sliding beneath the water with only a ripple on the surface above. Darby had even equipped the latest iteration to travel without any external oxygen for an hour or more.

The old engineer had sacrificed all of that for an "improvement" in speed and handling that was hardly worth the effort. Now the ship was a disaster—filled with machinery he barely understood—a victim of le Voyageur's endless quest for power and speed. What had once been spacious and simple was now a spider web of pumps and pistons. It was Grüsser's firm belief that the Frenchman's most basic goal had been to deface Darby's work.

"And we wiww make it bettew stiwe." As if in protest to le Voyageur's boast, there was a loud bang, and flame spat out from the pipe in the rear of the boat. A second later the engine groaned, and dark smoke began to leak out from a tube at the back of the ship.

Le Voyageur turned to him and scowled, looking at the German as if the misfire might have somehow been his fault. "*Merde*! Zis wotten tub will be ze death of me! Go downstairs and fix zis!"

Grüsser started back down the ladder.

Darby and he had originally built the boat together, and while it might not have been perfect in every way, it was still a thing of beauty. And when he had captained it, Grüsser had felt special: for just a moment he had been a man capable of something that no other living human had mastered.

He looked around at the mess of the engine, seeking the source of the malfunction, but there was nothing apparent.

"What awe you doing down zere, Prussian? Do I have to wet you choke to death befowe I can get wowk out of you?" It *was* well past time to wind the suit again, but he knew better than to ask the old man to do it. The last time he had actually mentioned it to the Frenchman, the old man had waited until the last possible moment, waiting until Grüsser was lying on the ground, half-unconscious and gasping like a fish.

In the endless weeks since he had been handed over to the Frenchman to act as his—what exactly? Henchman? Lackey?—Grüsser had come to understand that the man was incapable of issuing any type of motivation but punishment. He had come to accept that as enough—not that he had any choice in the matter. "*Ich bin*—"

"*Angwaise, angwaise!*" the old man shouted at him from up above and slapped his hand against the wheel to emphasize the point. "You know I cannot understand your Gewman gwunting!"

Grüsser shouted upward, "I am tryink, *trying*, to make zis ship do vhat you vant, Herr Voyageur, but ist nicht . . . *not* . . . doing it." Taking another look, he finally saw something that looked like it might be a broken device, although with the Frenchman's mad designs it was often hard to tell.

Meanwhile, the tighter the collar grew, the more confused he became. How the old man expected him to do such delicate work while he was half-strangled was a mystery to him.

"Let me see, let me see," the old man said, and slid down the ladder, landing against the wooden floorboards with a thunk.

Stomping in with his usual twisted walk, he practically shoved Grüsser out of the way so that he could peer down into the mechanism. "What have you done? It is a mess in hewe." He leaned forward to look more closely at one of the devices, his head practically disappearing into the machinery.

If Grüsser had been a braver man he would have taken the opportunity to grab le Voyageur and throw him headfirst into the engine. But then what? Wait while the Chronal Suit finished its work of snapping off his head, or— worse yet—drown in what had once been his own vehicle?

What other men thought of as cowardice Grüsser thought of as simple self-preservation. Once again he wondered if simple survival was worth all the sacrifices he had made. And yet, here he was, still alive to contemplate it.

"So . . ." the old man said, his voice amplified by the space where he had stuck his head. "You wiww be pweased to know that this is not youw fawlt." A hand popped up from the chugging machine, holding a thick brass gear. It had been scored and scorched, clearly not up to the task for which it had been pressed into service.

The Prussian obediently took it from the old man's clutches, pinching the object firmly between his fingers before lifting it away. "Ten millimeter Jaw," the Frenchman said with clear conviction.

Grüsser found the toolbox, opened it, and looked for the wrench. When he spotted it, he lifted it up and spun it around so that the working end was facing away from him. With a firm but steady grip he laid it against the old man's withered claw, holding it with firm pressure until the ancient fingers had wrapped themselves around the spanner and taken it away.

It had taken him weeks to learn precisely how the Frenchman had wanted objects given to him and how he wanted them removed. The lessons had been hard won, with every failure earning him a stinging whack from the old man's cane.

Grüsser was certain that it had been a task he had been intended to fail, and he took some pride in the fact that he had earned some grudging respect. He had always been handy with tools, even as a child, and for all his failings at sport and learning that had so devastated his parents, it had been his fascination with machines that had not only given him an edge over other students, but allowed him to rise so quickly within the military.

He had little of the true genius that Darby had, but not every man needed to be a virtuoso to play the violin, and in a world where technology was changing so quickly, being very good was more than good enough.

More than that, his unique moral failings put him into conflict with society as a whole. As a young man he had held very little interest for what the world wanted him to do. He was always happiest when tinkering with his machines. But unlike Darby and the other tinkerers he had met, he had little or no interest in actually *making* anything. Simply being around machines had been enough for him.

But as he grew older and rose up the chain, he found that even his interest in mechanics had begun to wane. And in the world of Teutonic values, Grüsser had been labeled as a practitioner of the greatest Prussian sin: laziness.

He had been saved by war. As Chancellor Bismarck's victories grew and his armies marched across Europe, Grüsser quickly found that virtues and vices meant less and less. The only things that were important on the battlefield were devotion and victory.

Grüsser had dreaded the idea of combat, but he had been thrown into war and discovered—much to his own surprise—that he was a man who felt at home on a battlefield. Where most men seemed to be concerned with nothing but their own mortality, it was in a world of death that he often felt the most alive. Even though his skills were not usually ones that might put a man onto the front lines, he had taken every opportunity to stay within the line of fire. And his self-destructive urge had given him a reputation for bravery that he knew he did not deserve.

Not that he didn't deserve to die. His desires were monstrous, even to him. But they were also uncontrollable. And in the end it had been his penchant for young women (and men) that had finally put an end to his (at least to him) meteoric career. The fact was, no one had even seemed to mind his moral peccadilloes very much—at first. There were certainly worse perversions to be witnessed in war. But then one of his superior's daughters had made an accusation, and he suddenly found himself branded with every evil imaginable. The fact that her charges were true only pushed Grüsser further into despair.

And for all his supposed heroism on the field of battle, when he was off it, his first (and only) instinct when faced with danger was simply to run. Grüsser knew that he should have felt more chastened, both by what had occurred, and by his decision to flee from justice to America.

But new beginnings were what this country had always been about, and weren't all men guilty of something, in the end?

The Frenchman popped his head up from the machine and stared at him. "What awe you doing, you wazy oaf?"

"Vaiting for you."

The Frenchman frowned, but was too far away to do anything. "This could have been vewwy bad, and it would have been youw fauwt." He rapped the machinery lightly with the wrench and it responded with an ominous ticking sound. "But I think I have fixed it fow now—if you wiww just tighten this."

Grüsser nodded. After weeks of working side by side with the Frenchman he had learned that le Voyageur was not only a mad visionary, he was also hopeless without a second pair of hands.

Every bolt on every engine needed Grüsser to tighten it. Every screw on every drive shaft needed his eyes to make sure that they were true.

Without that effort, nothing the Frenchman created could actually *work*, and despite the fact that Grüsser's days in the Chronal Suit were torture, he had managed to find a sense of accomplishment in succeeding as the old man's assistant. It was a feeling that he hadn't had for a very long time.

"Take a wook at my wowk, Pwussian," the old man said, waving his hand vaguely at the mechanics he had just been messing with. Handing Grüsser the wrench, he turned and grabbed the ladder. "You might weawn somezing." Le Voyageur pulled himself out of the machinery, giving Grüsser the chance to step in.

Leaning down, the Prussian looked into the device and nodded. Once again the old man had indeed managed to find the problem, but his attempt to "fix" it had left things in worse condition than when he started.

He ducked down and began tightening bolts with the wrench.

148

"What awe you doing down thewe?" came the voice from up above. "Don't damage anything, you oaf!" He knew that the Frenchman wanted to get moving again, but despite his taunts the man was no fool.

Moving the ship without Grüsser's okay would be very dangerous, even if his method of obtaining that assent was through bullying and criticism.

The Prussian was about to speak when he felt the tick of the Chronal Suit. The collar around his neck tightened, and the only sound that escaped from his throat was a gasping croak.

The Frenchman shoved his head down through hatch. "Gwüssew! I asked you what awe you up to?"

"I . . ." he gulped, his Adam's apple rasping against the metal band at his throat. "I am trying."

"Perhawps you need a winding?" From any other man it would have sounded like concern, but le Voyageur was incapable of it.

Grüsser knew better than to respond with any kind of agreement, even if it was only a squeak, or a choked nod. Asking the Frenchman for help would only reduce his chances of receiving some relief before he (once again) fell to the ground. Even then, the old man was as likely to accuse him of playing for his sympathies as he was to actually help in any way.

One of the first things he had learned over the last few months with le Voyageur was that if the old man had ever had any pity in him at all, age had robbed him of it.

Grüsser stood stone-faced, starting up at le Voyageur, breathing heavily through his nose as he tried to draw in enough air to stay standing. It would be a few minutes now before the suit clicked over to the next notch. When that happened, he knew, he would truly begin to choke.

He tried not to panic, but in spite of his efforts his mind played out the events that were about to occur. Starved of oxygen, he would drop to the floor, helpless, gasping for breath like a fish out of water. That was no small irony for a man who had called himself the Submersible.

But the Chronal Suit was hardly his first brush with suffocation. He had come close to drowning a number of times: first when his enemies had managed to pierce his ship; a second time when one of the rubber seals had given way from the shock of a nearby explosion, and the sub had begun to fill with the foul liquid of the Hudson River. Darby and he had installed a pump after that, although after le Voyageur's modifications he was no longer certain that it would work if tested again.

Unlike many other forms of fear, it seemed that exposure to drowning did not lessen over time. In fact, Grüsser found that after each event he was a little *more* sensitive to it than he had been before, although so far he had always managed to overcome his terror and return to the water.

But the inevitable attacks of Eschaton's sadistic device had made everything far worse. Not only was he constantly under threat of choking, but the key to his continued existence now rested in the hands of a madman who actually enjoyed watching him suffer as he clutched at his collar, gasping for another desperate breath.

But if the old man had almost no compassion, at least he was not murderous. Although Grüsser had fallen unconscious numerous times, at least the Frenchman had returned him to consciousness after every event.

But constantly living in the shadow of another round of life or death was wearing on Grüsser rapidly. The Prussian was beginning to wonder if he might not be better off if le Voyageur simply let the suit finish carrying out its work, allowing him to drift off to whatever afterworld the devil had constructed for lazy, broken Prussians.

He continued to stare at the twisted old man, waiting for him to respond to his distress. It was a game they played daily, and Grüsser's only chance at winning an early reprieve was to keep his face a calm mask devoid of emotion.

Luckily such skills had always been a necessary part of his life back in Prussia, although he'd never been particularly adept. Even at his most stern, his parents had always been able to read him like a book.

Mercifully, le Voyageur had no such ability. The utter inability of the French to hide their passions had always been their greatest weakness. To think that Napoleon had managed to defeat the Austrian army on multiple occasions! Clearly Corsicans were of a different breed.

Le Voyageur lifted one of his wild, furry eyebrows, the tangle of white fuzz arching. "Well Gwüssew," he said matter-of-factly, "once again you will see zat I am not all anger and evil. Wet us wewind youw suit."

A sense of relief descended over Grüsser as the old man began to stomp down the ladder. He hadn't been looking forward to the next click.

Pulling out his keys with one hand, le Voyageur gestured with the fingers of his other. "Awight then, tuwn awound."

Grüsser spun obediently in place, pulling down his jacket as he did so. Had it been so long ago that he had been a free man? Now his life ran to the tune of clockwork gears in a box on his back, each tick bringing him one small step closer to death.

He felt the metal object sliding in against his back and locking into place.

He waited as patiently as he could, the device ticking away as the old man slowly twisted the key around and around.

In Grüsser's estimation, the cruelest aspect of Eschaton's invention was how slowly it released its grip on the victim as it was rewound. He supposed that in the gray man's mind that was part of the charm of its time-bending properties, and sitting here, waiting for the key to release him as the suit clicked away, he had to admit that it did feel like an eternity.

But this time, before the procedure could be completed, something hard slammed against the side of the ship, toppling both men to their knees.

As they fell to the ground he heard the old man curse through the roaring sound of something scraping up against the ship. The collar seemed to grab him even tighter as he crashed down into the floorboards, forcing him to cough and sputter through the band around his neck.

For a moment the world seemed to swim, and the ship tilted at a sharp angle, sliding both men down against the wall. Le Voyageur tumbled down onto him, sending fresh waves of pain out from where the device's shackles bit into his skin. The Frenchman stank of perfume and age, like some old parchment found in a long-forgotten attic.

"*Sacwe Dieu!*" the Frenchman cried out, an edge of suffering in his voice that Grüsser found himself pleased to hear.

"Get off of me," Grüsser choked, and heaved upward, tipping the old man onto the floor. As soon as he'd done it he knew he would regret it, but his panic had gotten the better of him.

The boat freed itself and bobbed back to center, throwing them both back down toward the center of the floor.

Grüsser fell to his knees as the old man scrambled back up the ladder to see what had happened.

"Help me," he shouted after the Frenchman.

"Hewp yousewf, you ungwateful monstewe."

The Frenchman put a single foot on the rung and turned back to look. Grüsser rolled upwards. He was already feeling winded, and as he gasped for breath he regretted every sausage that he had not been strong enough to say no to. He looked into the old man's eyes.

"Don't wook at me wike that! I dwopped the key somewhewe in this sewer." What he saw reflected behind the old man's glasses was not pity, but need. "Find it, bwing it to me, and I wiww wind you up."

Grüsser nodded and rolled himself over. Despite the small arc lights that Darby had rigged up to provide lighting inside the confined space, Grüsser couldn't see the key anywhere. He crawled across the floor, sweeping his hands back and forth.

As he did so, he prayed that it had not fallen through a gap in the floor and dropped down into the bowels of the ship. What lay underneath was a maze of pipes and machinery, the already-complicated array made even more so by the Frenchman's attempts at "fixing" Darby's work.

Grüsser craned his neck, attempting to find some small bit of room beneath his Adam's apple. But the suit had, as he feared, come close to reaching the level at which his exertions would drive him to unconsciousness. His vision was already swimming, blackness forming around the edges. It wouldn't be long now before he would simply drop to the ground.

As he slid forward, trying to find a position that might at least be some- what comfortable to die in, his leg brushed against the key.

He reached down and picked it up. As he held it, Grüsser realized that he had never actually seen the key before—it had always been held in someone else's hands, and used only behind his back.

Looking at it face on, he saw that from the front it made the shape of a small clock, the hands inside set at fifteen minutes to midnight.

The object of his salvation in hand, Grüsser dragged himself over to the foot of the ladder. The world was still hazy, but he seemed to have settled into some form of stable consciousness.

Despite his incapacitated state, he pulled himself up the rungs, one at a time. As he rose he found his thoughts becoming clearer, as if they were purified through his desperation and pain.

He would rather die than live his life on the edge of suffocation, working with his enemies to bring about the very apocalypse that he and the others had so long fought against.

In some ways he had always been the least of the Paragons, but now he was also the last of them, and if he was going to die, he would make sure that he didn't die alone.

As he pulled himself up through the hatch he saw le Voyageur staring out at the horizon, a set of opera glasses pressed up against the old man's eyes, allowing him to look more closely at whatever it was that had captured his attention on the Brooklyn shore.

"Help me," Grüsser croaked out, his hand lifting up the key and holding it out in front of him. He could only imagine what a pathetic sight he must have been, begging for his survival.

Le Voyageur pulled his eyes from the spectacles and turned to look at him. The sneer on his face confirmed Grüsser's suspicions about his state. "You found it. I'm so gwad."

Grüsser dropped his face to the cold iron of the main air tube. He could barely feel anything as the old man plucked the key out of his hand and began to wind the Chronal Suit once again. "Thank you," he croaked out.

"Nowmawwy I wouldn't cawe about youw fate one way ow anothew, but it seems that ouw cowwission with that ship did us both a favow."

On the fifth wind Grüsser could feel the mechanism catch. Somewhere inside the clockwork box on his back a spring began to turn, slowly releasing the collar around his throat. He sputtered and coughed, his body trying to expel the spit in his throat even as he desperately tried to draw more air in. "It seems," le Voyageur continued, "that we have found the object of our jouwney, and I would hate to have to twy and fiwe the ship's guns without youw help."

"Our mission?" He had almost forgotten the reason he and the Frenchman had been sent out in the first place. "Du hast found Sarah Stanton."

"It seems," he said with a cackle, "zat she is wiving in a junkpiwe aftew aww."

He held out the glasses. "Take a wook fow youwsewf."

Grüsser was still dizzy but already recovering from his most recent brush with death. Grabbing the edge of the steel box he pulled himself to his feet and pulled the glasses out of the old man's hands. The brass binoculars were heavy, both from the metal and the glass prisms they contained inside. For an instant he saw himself taking them and smashing them hard into the old man's skull. But despite the resolve he had when he was dancing on death's door, the sudden return of blood to his brain seemed to have melted away his need for escape.

Killing the Frenchman would only solve his problems in the short term. He would need to find a more permanent solution. As he pressed the glasses up to his face he saw clearly what had made the old Frenchman so sure that they had found the right location. Glinting in the moonlight was a metal statue in the shape of a man.

For a moment Grüsser thought it might simply be a sculpture. "*Unmöglich*," he said when it turned and began to walk away from the beach.

"Ze Automaton," le Voyageur said.

Grüsser's next actions were beyond his own comprehension, but something about seeing the machine had given him hope. Taking a few quick steps, he leapt off the platform and into the air.

There was a cold shock as the water of the East River enveloped him, and he realized that it was already too late to worry about what would happen to him if the device on his back got wet.

But as he began to swim to shore he realized that he no longer cared. Whether he lived or died, he would find salvation soon.

Chapter 11
Iron and Glass

Anubis awoke to the sound of yelling, and found himself gasping for air. For a man who spent his days in a leather mask, the feeling of suffocation wasn't an entirely unfamiliar one, but when he reached up to pull off his mask he realized that it was already gone. Instead he felt a sharp shock of pain from his jaw, and as he coughed he could feel an ache in his neck where the White Knight had almost squeezed the life out of him. It almost made him forget about the pounding in his head.

Something trickled down his throat, and he began to cough. The yelling voices paused, and after a moment he could taste the blood in his mouth. He spat it out on the floor and coughed again.

"At least you didn't kill him." He recognized the atrocious, broken English accent immediately, and opened his eyes.

"Ja—" Anubis could only get out the single sound before he began to cough again. This time he could feel his entire body spasming as his lungs tried to expel an object from his throat that didn't exist. It took an incredible force of will to make it stop. "Jack," he rasped out, "I didn't know that . . . you cared for my well-being."

"I don't, really. But Lord Eschaton would have had my hide if he didn't get his hands on you first."

"See there, Jack," said Clements, clearly nervous. "There was nothing to worry about—he'll be fine."

Jack spun around on his heels. He walked quickly out of the cage and delivered a sharp blow to Clements's stomach with the head of his cane. "You ridiculous clown!" As the White Knight bent over from the attack he revealed his backside, and Jack struck again, slamming his stick hard against the Southerner's posterior. Abraham couldn't help but marvel at the calm efficiency with which Jack delivered his blows. "You've killed that boy, one of *my* men, and Anubis is only alive because you're too pathetic to be able to kill anyone except by accident. If Eschaton doesn't snap both our necks it won't be for your lack of trying! You're a sad sack of meat and potatoes, and there's no denying it!"

Clements opened his mouth as if to protest, but when Jack raised up his cane he quickly closed it again. "Now stay there and be quiet until I speak to you."

The White Knight simply nodded his reply, but even from across the room Anubis could see a narrowing of his piggish eyes. He was clearly scheming for revenge. If Jack had noticed, he didn't show it. Instead he crossed back across the floor in a few smooth steps.

Anubis forced himself to smile even though it sent a fresh wave of pain up through his face. How was it that every blow he had taken over the last few months seemed to be aimed directly at his head? "How do I look?" At least all his teeth seemed to still be intact . . .

"You mean other than the fact that you're a Negro?" Jack said smiling back.

"I already knew that," Abraham replied.

"Well, I wish you had told me." Jack leaned over to peer directly at his face. "You're starting to look like a rotten apple that's been left in the sun all day long."

Anubis laughed. It was odd to think of it now, but if he had ever been forced to reveal his true identity to someone, he always thought that Jack would be the most obvious candidate. He seemed to hate everyone equally, and despite his aristocratic heritage, his time on the streets seemed to have given him far better tools to judge the value of a man than simply the color of his skin. "I appreciate your honesty."

"Don't thank me just yet. I'm bringing you upstairs for your trial, and I don't suppose it's going to go well for you." He prodded Anubis gently with his cane. "Can you walk?"

Nodding before he was sure the answer was yes, he pulled himself up to his feet and took a halting step to the door. There was no doubt that he was still feeling the effects of the attack. It had taken weeks for him to recover, and from the moment he'd decided to wear the suit again, he'd been attacked again. Taking a single step back, he sank onto the cot. "Maybe, although I could make good use of your cane."

Jack looked down at the wooden stick in his hand and then back at Anubis. "I'm sure you could."

Anubis had liked the cane better when it had belonged to the Sleuth. The fact that it now sat in Jack's hand was a reminder of the fact that Anubis had been partially responsible for the old man's death—he had given him a clue to help him uncover Eschaton's plans.

At the time, he had assumed the Paragons capable of stopping Eschaton. In retrospect, the true depth of his failure to understand the situation had been stunning, and it had been one of the Sleuth's own teammates—William Hughes—who had cut him down.

From somewhere outside of the room there came a moan. Jack and Clements both seemed to recognize it. "Come in, Shell," Jack said.

What came through the door sent a chill straight through Anubis. He had seen ruined men before—the last war had left behind thousands of men with missing limbs, and burned and scarred flesh—but he had never seen a living creature quite as horrific as this. Covered in twisted metal, the abomination teetered into the room on a pair of equally-twisted wheels.

"What is that?" At first Abraham had thought that it might be some kind of monstrous clockwork, but as it moved closer there was an undeniable stench of rotting flesh, although it was covered by a thick scent of oil that suppressed his need to gag.

Jack smiled. "You remember Mr. Hughes, don't you?"

Anubis nodded, speechless.

"That's the Iron-Clad?" Anubis had never actually seen the man in the flesh, but it seemed that he had claimed some kind of twisted justice for the murder of his fellow Paragon.

Up until his disappearance, Hughes's declining health had been a topic of hot debate in the papers. But his legendary armor had always made him, physically at least, one of the Paragons' most powerful members. "What happened to him?"

Clements snorted. "Darby had a plan to turn the entire building into one of his mechanical men. Unfortunately, Hughes got caught in the gears."

Abraham frowned. Since the events in the theater, he'd had more than enough of intelligent machines and madmen willing to play with the fundamentals of human existence. But even after its rampage, the Automaton had been able to convince him that it was ultimately a creature worth saving, and Sarah had even asked him to come to the junkyard to help in its resurrection. In this case, on the other hand, life was clearly a curse rather than a gift. "How did he survive? Is he one of Eschaton's purified humans?"

"A poor copy," Clements said with a laugh. "But he still came out better-looking than a monkey like you. Although if it turns your skin white, I suppose that's a start."

Jack flicked out his hand, the metal tip of the cane banging hard against the cell's metal bars. "That's enough." The Southerner visibly flinched in response.

"Anubis, it's time to get going." Jack held out his hand, and Abraham took it. As he rose to his feet he felt a sickening rush of dizziness, but managed to maintain his balance.

"Shell," Jack said, "our friend here needs some assistance."

The machine-creature wobbled closer, letting out a shrill whine when it came to a stop.

Anubis placed his arm over the thing's shoulders. The metal was disturbingly warm, the temperature of human flesh, but without the yielding comfort of skin.

The Shell wobbled slightly on its wheels as Abraham lent it his weight. The putrefying odor was stronger in such close proximity. Still, he was glad for the assistance. "Thank you, Hughes," he told it as it wrapped one of its metal arms around his back. But if the creature was aware of his gratitude or even its own name, it didn't respond. Instead it began to move slowly forward, and Anubis limped out of the cage.

"The two of you make a mighty fine pair," Clements said as he passed him by. "You'd do well to remember that I *let* you live, boy. Lord Eschaton told me that I can have you as soon as he's done with you, and I won't make the same mistake agai—ooow!"

Jack had jabbed him with his cane, this time thrusting the knob-end straight into his stomach. "You'd do best to keep your mouth shut."

"Don't underestimate me, sir," Clements said. Anubis wondered if the White Knight would be able to manifest his supernatural strength again so soon, although he supposed that Jack would be at least somewhat aware of the White Knight's powers.

But before he had transformed, Clements's skin had first flushed a deep red. This time it remained the same pasty white color that nature had saddled him with.

"I'm not a sir, and he's not your boy," Jack answered.

For all the bickering that Anubis and Jack had done during the time that they had spent together, they had come to communicate pretty well, despite Jack's homicidal tendencies. His philosophy was everything that Anubis's wasn't: the man cared little or nothing for anyone else but himself and his boys, and he had no real regard for human life.

Certainly there were reasons for that. Jack's atrocious accent spoke to a past that was complicated and tragic. But the number of people living in New York who grew up without tragedy could probably be counted on Abraham's fingers. It wasn't what happened to a man that defined him, it was how he chose to respond. Jack had decided to take a very dark path.

But Jack Knife also had instincts and insight that were hard to ignore. Of all the Children, he was the one who had been the most vocal about his distrust of Anubis, while being the closest thing he had to a friend. And there was a purity to the man's philosophy, one that made him unafraid to stand up to bullies like the White Knight.

Clements and Jack continued to glower at each other until the Shell let out a gurgling whine and moved forward, dragging Abraham out of the room and into the hallway.

Standing up and moving was obviously doing Anubis some good, and he quickly found himself taking surer steps as they travelled along. Before they reached the end of the corridor, Jack had caught up with them, his long legs easily matching the pace of the wounded man and the monster as they wobbled together down the corridor.

"I'm sorry about what happened back there," Jack said.

"That's the first time I've ever heard you be sorry about anything. Usually you're too busy sticking a knife into things to care."

Jack smiled his usual wolf's grin. "You can't blame a man for liking what he's good at." There was a moment's pause before he continued. "But I don't take pleasure in tormenting the weak."

Anubis considered that for a moment. If he'd been forced to judge Jack, would he truly have found him wanting? It had been the job of Anubis to judge the full worthiness of a man, not his philosophy. While he was utterly at odds with Jack's motivations, he couldn't deny that the villain practiced them in a most exemplary way. "Clements hates me because of the color of my skin."

Jack chuckled. "Oh no, friend, I think there's far more to it than just that. He hates *everyone* who he thinks might be better than him in some way. It doesn't leave him with many friends."

"And what about you?" Anubis asked him.

"We had this discussion last time we met, didn't we? I don't have many friends either, but I have enough. It comes from being such a busy man with so many responsibilities."

They had reached the stairs at the end of the corridor. "I'm afraid, Anubis," Jack told him, "that this creature won't be able to help you up the stairs."

The Shell rolled to a stop and let out a whine. Anubis let go of it to stand, weakly, on his own two feet.

Freed of its burden, the Shell tilted forward on its wheels, falling to the ground with a ringing thud.

Using its metal hands it began to drag itself up the steps. Anubis stared at the metal claws. There was no flesh there, but simply chunks of iron that had been cut into rough approximations of fingers, with hinges connecting them and rods that pulled them open and closed. The digits scraped against the stone to find purchase, and when they did the arms heaved the body up the steps, lugging the twisted wheels up behind it. It was a pitiable sight.

Jack offered Anubis his arm as a replacement.

Even if he was still a bit dizzy, Anubis felt more able to walk than he had been a few minutes before. Once again, he found himself trying to sort out which of his recent injuries were temporary, versus those that would take days, weeks, or even months to heal. He was sure there were already bruises

160

forming on either side of his throat where Clements had dug his thumbs into his flesh.

Anubis slung his right arm over Jack's shoulders. The villain was shockingly slim under his coat, and yet he seemed to have the strength needed to take Anubis's weight. It was yet another contradiction in a person who seemed to be almost entirely constructed of them. "Jack, you can call me Abraham, if you'd like."

"So we're trading names now? I'm still Jack, either way."

"You got lucky with that name." They took the steps slowly, but they managed to move up them faster than the Shell.

"Or I'm just clever. But I'll admit that Abraham doesn't seem to lend itself to much in the way of titles. Now where were we?"

Anubis saw Jack glancing backwards over his shoulder. Clements was clearly somewhere behind them, just out of sight. Given the choice, Anubis wouldn't have let the man out of his vision for a second, but Jack seemed convinced that he would still be able to react if the White Knight took the opportunity to try and backstab them. Or maybe he was confident that he'd try to kill the Negro first. "I wanted to know what you thought when you found out the true color of my skin."

"Do you think a man who lives on the street and surrounds himself with gutter trash cares that much about what color his enemies are?"

"I've seen all kinds of men in all kinds of places, but I noticed you didn't have any Negroes in the Blades."

Jack chuckled. "Fair enough. Though I suppose that's because none have asked."

"Maybe they thought you'd say no."

"The boys might balk, but I'd set 'em straight. But I'm afraid it's a little too late for you to join now, if that's what you asking."

Anubis smiled at that. There was no doubt that Jack was always good for a quick turn of phrase. "And I gather you weren't interested in my other offer . . ."

It took Jack a second to register his meaning before he replied. "Ah . . . the 'alliance' you offered me back in the alley. I supposed I might have considered it if things had turned out differently, but I'm not looking to put my future into the hands of a battered Negro on his way to the gallows."

"That's a shame. I'm sure you and Clements can work something out."

Now it was Jack's turn to smile. "I still have more people on my side than you do. Or did you finally manage to make some friends of your own?"

"I found one."

"That's good for you. No man should go to his death with only enemies to mourn him."

"You won't be sad to see me go?"

"It'll certainly make the world a little less interesting, although once I knew what you were hiding under that mask, most of the mystery was gone."

"So, how did you discover my secret?"

"You had a tear in your suit after you burned the Hydraulic Man."

That wasn't what had happened, but Anubis didn't bother trying to set Jack straight.

When they reached the top of the stairs, Anubis assumed that Jack would hand him back to the machine. Instead he continued to support him as they walked through the granite-walled halls. The Shell, now back on its wheels, wobbled past them, rolling down the corridor.

Looking back over his shoulder, Anubis saw Clements rising up the steps behind them. His hands were balled into angry fists, his eyes were squinting with rage and locked so intensely onto Jack that Anubis thought he was trying to simply will the man to die.

When the White Knight's stare flicked over to his own eyes for just a moment, Abraham found himself looking away. Whatever else had happened back in the cell, the villain had almost killed him with his bare hands, literally expanding in size and strength as his anger grew.

Abraham believed it was his compassion and aversion to killing that separated him from men like Jack, but it was clear that if he ever was given the opportunity to stop Clements, he would need to take it without hesitation.

The Shell had disappeared in front of them, and a few seconds later a roaring noise came echoing down the corridor. After a moment, Anubis recognized it as a chorus of shouts and cheers. He could hear bloodlust and rage in the hollering. He'd heard it many times as a boy when one of the slaves was going to be punished. Now it was his turn. "Are you sure I have nothing to offer you that might convince you to let me go?"

Jack tightened his grip on his arm. "Steel yourself, Anubis, and there's a chance that you might survive this."

Anubis's thoughts turned to Shell. "As what?"

Jack shook his head. "I have no idea, but if it makes you feel any better, he plans to do it to all of us."

"And is that what you want?"

"You don't get what you want in life. You just have to take the best alternative."

Anubis didn't agree, but he didn't feel like arguing.

As they turned a corner up ahead, he could see a group of men crowded around an open doorway. When they saw Jack and Anubis the yelling grew louder, igniting the unseen crowd in the room beyond.

Abraham took a deep breath and pulled himself free of Jack. He closed his eyes for a moment and tried to evoke the spirit of the ancient god he'd named himself after. In his thoughts he imagined putting on his mask, hiding his true visage from the world. He would be Anubis in spirit only, but it would have to be enough.

Some of the men jeered at him as he reached the door, screaming slurs at him that he hadn't heard in years, and others he had only heard in whispers on the streets. He felt hands pawing at him, attacking him as if he were a monster and not a man.

"Keep your hands to yourself, you unruly bastards!" Jack swatted at them with his cane.

The men pulled back, but it took only a single glance at Jack's face to realize that he was enjoying this as much as they were. The man had always thrived on chaos and violence; even now, hidden under his coat, were the rows of gleaming blades that he was eager to throw into human flesh at a moment's notice.

To think that he could have somehow convinced this homicidal villain to help him only served to prove how truly desperate a man he had become.

As they entered the Hall, the already-deafening cheers grew louder still. A wave of dizziness swept over Anubis as he tried to take in the entirety of the scene around him. In the pews that lined the Hall were dozens of men, most of them clearly common folk. It stung him to think that the people who were now cheering for his blood were much the same men whom he had fought in the streets to protect.

Dotted amongst the crowd were men in a variety of different costumes. Most of them were the crudest approximation of an adventurer's colors: a single piece of colorful clothing with a mask or hood; a couple with outlandish hats or a fancy coat.

A few of the would-be villains were clearly more well-off, and had paid someone to construct them an impractical and ridiculous costume intended to approximate the Paragons, but they all fell far short.

Anubis had seen their type before: their outfits were devoid of any trace of practicality, and, if they had succeeded in becoming adventurers, would have probably found their only true act of bravery to be catching a bullet to the chest. It was exactly the type of man Chadwick Prescott had been before his own costume had betrayed him, covering him in the deadly mix of acid and fuel that had burned the poor fool to death before Abraham's very eyes.

If the intention of this motley gallery was to create a new Society of Paragons, it was already a failure. Instead, what Eschaton had gathered together was a room full of mismatched, misbegotten ne'er-do-wells dancing on the graves of better men.

"Welcome, Anubis," said Lord Eschaton, his thundering voice coming from the back of the room. The villain towered above everyone else in a grand pulpit that rose twenty feet above the floor on a spiral staircase. There was a large Greek letter Omega painted in white across the front of it, shining in the electric light.

Standing beneath the gray man, in front of a black curtain on the back wall, were the Shell and another man who had been bound by chains onto a sheet of metal.

The remains of Hughes rolled around in a short figure eight, pacing beneath Eschaton like an anxious but faithful dog.

There was something deeply wrong with the other man on the impromptu stage. Even staring straight at him, it was almost impossible to make sense of him. His skin was transparent, giving him more the appearance of a blurry outline than a full human. Underneath his glassy flesh, silver bolts flickered through his body like a school of fish, running from head to toe and back again.

But there was something else in the room as well, and seeing it instantly filled his heart with both longing and dread. Propped up on a table by the wall were the mask and chestplate of Anubis. It had, up until that moment, been easy to pretend that he was wearing his costume. But now that his other identity was staring at him—judging *him*—it was hard to keep a hold on the part of him that was more hero than man.

Next to his suit was another costume. It was made of metal with a large metal wing across the back of it. The steel was etched with fine lines that danced and shimmered in the electric lights. He had never seen this exact costume before, but it was safe to assume that this belonged to Turbine, put up as another scalp next to his own.

Standing next to them was the familiar red, white, and blue of the Industrialist's hat. "Trophies of the dead . . ." Perhaps he'd soon be joining them.

Clements drawled angrily in his ear a moment before he was roughly shoved forwards. "Less talking, more walking. I'm tired of waiting to get my hands on you."

Thrown slightly off-balance, Abraham stumbled down the ramp. The men in the pews jeered, and as he got closer to where Lord Eschaton was standing he noticed the Bomb Lance seated in the row nearest to the front, behind a short wooden wall.

Coming closer to the transparent man on the stage, Anubis could now see that he was straining against his bonds. This man was clearly one of Eschaton's experiments—another in a seeming parade of freaks that the gray man was threatening to turn Anubis into.

The metal sheet he had been bound to was on top of a cart, and the wheels rattled as he struggled. "Are you all right?" he asked. Anubis was as curious to hear the man speak as he was to find out the answer to his question.

"I don't think I should have had that drink," the bound figure replied in a familiar voice.

As he looked closer at the transparent man, the silver streaks travelled through the man's face, and as his features flickered into full view, he realized that he had seen this man before: this was Nathaniel Winthorp. The last time Anubis had seen him had been in the park, moments before Jack had captured him.

At that time, the Paragon's skin had been a chalky white. Now he had undergone another metamorphosis, and it had left him looking even more wretched now than he had been back then.

Clements gave him another shove. "Stand here," he said, placing him directly in front of the black curtain. This close he could see now that it was made from silk. At first Abraham thought that it was intended to be a backdrop, but now he could see that it concealed something the shape and size of a large box.

As he turned to face the audience, a jeer rose from the crowd, and he ducked as a few bottles and other objects were thrown in his direction from the unruly mob.

As he tried to comprehend the whole horrifying tableau, it struck Anubis as being almost infinitely strange. He had finally reached the Hall of Paragons, but under circumstances he could have never imagined possible.

When Abraham had first put on the mask of Anubis, he had entertained fantasies of meeting the Paragons. He had imagined his heroic actions would catch their notice, and although cautious at first, they would invite him into the Hall, to consider asking him to join their group.

In his daydream they would demand that he reveal his identity to them before he could become a member. He would refuse, of course, telling them that they would never be able to accept him if they saw what was under the mask.

Unable to accept his terms, the Paragons would send him back into the world, having forged a grudging respect between lone wolf and gentlemen that would one day . . . lead to the death of the Sleuth.

Even without these fools and ruffians that currently inhabited them, these granite walls and gleaming brass doors had always been the symbols of everything that he detested. The fact that Eschaton had been able to install his terrifying carnival into what had once been the stronghold of the most respected men in the world was not only proof of the weakness of proud men, but proof that it had been his own pride that had kept him from putting a stop to Eschaton when he'd had the chance.

Slowly the lights in the room began to go out, first on the left, then on the right. In a few seconds the only illumination that remained was a strip of lights that ran down the ramp, and the bright beam of an arc lamp that shone down on Eschaton from above.

"Thank you, my Children, for coming tonight." The applause started up again, but Eschaton started to shout over them, cutting it off before it could reach the fever pitch again.

"I know many of you have eagerly, but patiently, been waiting for the time when my plans will be complete and you will be able to step up to the next level of human evolution. I know that it has been a frustrating wait. But your patience will pay off!"

There was more applause and some cheers, although Anubis wondered if perhaps there wasn't some fear as well. "Tonight, for the first time, I can tell you that there is a truly uplifted human in our presence." Nathaniel was tipped upwards on his cart by the Shell, and the spotlight turned on him, washing out his body with its harsh glow. "I wish to introduce to you the newest of our Children, and the future of all humanity—the Mercurial Man!"

He existed only as the faintest outline as the sparkling of the silver bolts swam underneath his skin, and rather than the sudden thunder of applause that Anubis had expected, there was a long pause. Clearly whatever the crowd had been expecting to see it was not a transparent man strapped to a metal table. But after a moment's hesitation, and with the Bomb Lance and the White Knight leading the way, the clapping began, and it took only a moment to reach an almost-respectable level.

Nathaniel struggled against his bonds, but didn't say a word. Anubis wondered if the boy was drunk, or simply beyond caring.

"Now, on to other business . . ." If Eschaton was disappointed in the reception his creation had received from the crowd, he wasn't letting it slow him down. "Below me stands Anubis," the gray villain said loudly, letting the sound of his voice hush the mumbling crowd. "Formerly one of us, now revealed to be a traitor." He wore a wide grin on his face as he raised up his arms. "We welcome home this wayward Child." There was a cool threat contained in his words, and the crowd reacted to it, letting out a chorus of jeers.

Abraham half expected to be pelted with rotting vegetables, but it seemed that some small shred of decorum still remained in the Hall.

"Shell," Eschaton said from above, "bring the prisoner forward."

The horrible creature wobbled toward him and grabbed his arm. Once again, Anubis was reminded that no matter how twisted Hughes had become, the monster had still been blessed with exceptional strength. The metal hand pulled him up along the ramp until he was able to face Eschaton directly.

He could see the faces staring at him with anger, ready to tear him apart, but the crowd remained hushed, clearly waiting for the cue from their leader to tell them when to react. "As you can see, our ranks have swelled since you left us," Eschaton said, retaining a conversational tone. "Many of the men you see here today have joined us only recently, and they may not know you, but we are all glad to finally have the chance to see what a traitor looks like face-to-face." Eschaton raised his arm. The arc light dimmed, and his flesh turned white, crackling and glowing with a white light that came from within. It was an impressive trick, and one that Anubis had never seen him perform before.

The audience gasped and clapped. It was clear they had never seen it before, either. As the arm returned to its normal gray, he lowered it down, pointing his finger directly at Abraham. "Anubis, do you know why you are here?"

Of course he did. It had been obvious from the moment he'd woken in the cell. "I'm here to be judged." He remembered that his face was now visible, and he smiled through his pain.

"Exactly right!" Eschaton thundered back. "You are here, amongst your peers, so that they might learn of both the righteous fury and infinite mercy that comes to those who would betray the Children of Eschaton."

"Mercy?" he asked with surprise. "Why would I expect any mercy from a murderer like you?"

"You'll need to speak up, Anubis. You're speaking for the edification of everyone, remember."

"Is that your mercy? To be judged by my peers?"

"To be judged by these men, you would need to be one of them. Are you telling me you want to rejoin the Children?"

Anubis remained quiet for a second, considering what to say next. It would do him no good to anger Eschaton, but at the same time, he expected no real mercy either way.

Abraham reached down into himself to bring out his own thundering tones—the ones he had used as Anubis. "You put on a good show, Eschaton, but I have never truly been a part of your group of maniacs and murderers."

Eschaton shook his head and looked out at the crowd. His performance was ridiculous and theatrical, and yet the crowd was clearly entranced by his dramatics. "We spent so much time together, and yet you still think of me in terms of black and white, good and evil. But I am so much more. Those who follow me have a chance for a new life!" He raised up his arm, and the crowd once again let out a deafening cheer.

It was easy to see what it was that the gray man had to offer. In a world filled with despair, his desire to remake the world was a sliver of hope. More than that, it was proof that their miserable lives had meaning, and that it had been the world that was wrong in misunderstanding them. Eschaton offered them more than hope, he gave them justification for their failed lives.

But it was still all a dream. Why would a world of freaks be *better* than the one that they inhabited now? Would new powers improve their souls? And if everyone was a superman, then no one truly was. Was he the only person here who hadn't been corrupted by Eschaton's ridiculous dream?

He looked around the room, and noticed Jack, standing next to Clements and the Bomb Lance. The thin man's hands were still at his sides, and he seemed to be taking the whole thing in with his usual expression of amused detachment. Perhaps Anubis wasn't alone . . .

"Let's get this over with," Anubis said, shouting through the applause.

Eschaton put his hand up and hushed the crowd. "What did you say?"

"I said, if you're going to kill me, or whatever you have planned, then let's get on with it." He spoke calmly. There was a certain kind of confidence, he was discovering, that came when you realized you were the only sane man in hell.

"I won't *kill* you," Eschaton said, drawing out the word so far that it would have embarrassed an actress. "I told you that I would be merciful." He waved his gray hand at the stage below him. "Shell, if you would be so kind. Show this man his fate."

The arc light turned downwards to illuminate the cloth-covered box. The creature rolled toward it and grabbed the sheet.

He pulled it free, revealing the box beneath it to be a chamber of iron bars fitted with glass plates. In the center was a large open grating in the floor. Black smoke swirled out of it, licking against the glass in waves like something halfway between a liquid and a gas.

Also inside was a steel chair fitted with shackles. It had clearly been designed to hold an unwilling occupant in the chamber.

"Behold, the Uplift Chamber!" shouted Eschaton. With that, the crowd went wild. Anubis saw Donny leaning forward with such eager anticipation that he was in danger of falling over the stand.

The air around Anubis suddenly seemed warmer, as if someone had lit a fire. Heat normally didn't bother him, but this was more than just a flash of warmth.

There was a thumping and screaming that pierced the silence, and he turned to see Nathaniel shouting and struggling against his bonds.

Anubis frowned, feeling pity for the boy. "It's all right."

"Look what he's done to me!" Nathaniel replied. "He's stolen away my life."

Anubis couldn't help but notice that there seemed to be more of the silver slivers swimming through the boy's skin than there had been before. He stared into Nathaniel's eyes, realizing that unlike when he was wearing the mask, the boy could stare back into his. "You haven't lost all of your life yet." If there was any hope that they would be able to escape from here with their lives, he needed the boy calm.

Anubis gestured toward the box. It had always been foolish to believe that he could spend so much time with these maniacs and not be dragged into their insanity. "What do you want from me?" he asked the gray man. Some part of him had known that this moment would come, sooner or later.

"I don't *want* anything from you, Anubis, that I cannot take. I already have everything I need." Eschaton started down the spiral staircase, the light following him. "I have the Hall of Paragons, and I have Darby's laboratory."

"You don't have the Automaton's heart."

Eschaton seemed shocked at that, pausing for just an instant before he continued to the bottom of the steps. "No . . . not yet. But there is more than enough fortified steam contained in this building for me to continue my experiments until I get it."

Anubis forced himself to remain calm. "You have enough for your experiments, but you can't change the world." It had not occurred to him before just how badly Eschaton needed what Sarah Stanton had. And that meant that Abraham had a secret that he knew and the villain didn't. He wondered if the Children had already known of the limited reserve of fortified steam.

"Enough!" Eschaton shouted. "We'll find the girl soon enough. The Stanton child has enough of her father in her, I think, that she won't be able to sit idly by while the man who murdered him simply takes over the world." He walked over to the crowd, where a tall boy held out a case toward him. The gray man lifted a large glass tube out of the open case, a thick cork stuck fast in the open end. Illuminated by the spotlight, the liquid inside of it glittered and shone like gold. Once again Anubis could feel the heat rising in the room.

"Meanwhile, there is more than enough steam to make you one of my purified humans."

Immediately a chorus of howls and boos rose up from the crowd. There were also shouted slurs and epithets, along with demands that he simply be killed outright. He glanced over to Clements and saw that the man was enthusiastically joining in, his hand cupped against his face as he screamed for Abraham's execution.

"Quiet!" Eschaton shouted, and once again the gallery obeyed, except for Nathaniel.

"You're a monster! I want my life back!" The boy's chains rattled as he struggled against them.

"There is no turning back for you . . . or for me," Eschaton informed him. "But you've made a great sacrifice and proven that my transformation was no accident. Now Anubis can become something even better than you, my pathetic boy." Eschaton held out the vial toward Anubis, offering it to him. The liquid inside swirled and churned. "I gave him Mercury, but I'm offering you gold."

"And what am I supposed to do with this . . . gift?"

"You're supposed to drink it," Eschaton said, and pulled the stopper free.

He took it from the gray man's hand, a short shock travelling into his fingers as they brushed Eschaton's. "What is it?"

"The engine of your rebirth: a pure element," he announced loudly, "along with a few . . . other things."

Anubis sniffed it, his nose wrinkling at the strong chemical smell. "And if I choose not to?"

Eschaton shook his head. "Either way, you're going into the chamber, so you can die in the smoke . . . or you consume my elixir and discover with me what will happen to a man who is infused with gold." Eschaton walked over and unlatched the chamber's door. "Your fate is, within reason, entirely up to you. But I'll warn you that what this contains is poison. Once you've consumed it, your only salvation is in the smoke."

Anubis nodded. "Then I suppose I'll take my chances." As he prepared himself to consume the golden liquid, another scent rose up, far stronger than the sulfurous odor from the vial. It was the smell of burning leather . . .

A moment later a shout rose up from the crowd and Anubis felt a wave of heat roll toward him. The air suddenly became scorching hot and difficult to breathe, as if he were standing too near to a vat of molten iron. The sensation was followed by a bright light, as bright as a flare, that appeared to be growing behind Eschaton's shoulder. After a few moments it had become so bright that it eclipsed the arc light and cast hard shadows across the entire room. Some of the shouts in the audience were turning nervous.

A figure rose up from behind Anubis, glowing with such intensity that it was almost impossible to look at him directly. It took a moment to realize that this was Nathaniel, transformed again. No longer translucent, he was now burning with a white flame that seemed to consume his entire body.

"That's enough!" the glowing boy shouted. "This has to end!" There was still the sound of desperation in his voice, but it was no longer helpless.

For better or worse, the opportunity to escape that Anubis thought might never come had finally arrived, and he yelled out Eschaton's name. When they gray man turned toward him, he threw the golden contents of the vial straight into the villain's face.

The gray giant stumbled backward into the smoke-filled chamber, his hand shattering one of the thick glass windows. Black gas crawled out into the room.

Chapter 12
Roundheels

Emilio had been hopeful that the return of the Automaton would bring things back to "normal" around the house, but it seemed as if they were anything but.

Both Sarah and Viola seemed enamored with the metal man, and both of them had spent the last few days with their attention entirely fixated on Tom.

At first Emilio had considered that to be a good thing and thought he would be able to get back to work on his spinning shield, but every time he heard Tom's heavy metal footsteps on the stairs, he found his usually-focused thoughts instead trying to figure out which of the two women he was supposed to be siding with: his sister, or the woman that he was beginning to suspect that he loved, despite his own best intentions.

Sarah had spent most of the night talking with Tom, reading through the newspaper accounts of the "massacre in the park," as the headlines had called it. The two of them had still been up when Emilio had gone to work; and she had fallen asleep sprawled out on the couch.

He felt a tinge of guilt at entering the living room, but it wasn't as if Sarah had ever asked for permission to take over the main room of the house as her personal sleeping area. Her tendency to take other people's permission for granted was something else she and Viola had in common.

Sarah had been keeping the articles together inside the pages of a Bible, but now they were spread out across the floor, arcing out from the couch like dingy fireworks.

He carefully bent over and tried to read some of the tiny type on one of the smaller articles. It told the story of a man who had survived the explosion. He had actually claimed that his eyesight had improved, and that he felt invigorated by the incident.

Nearby was another article discussing how the man had been discovered a few days later with a knife in his neck. Sarah had written the word "*Eschaton*!" over the article.

Did Sarah think that the villain was murdering the survivors of his experiment? And to what end?

Weary of trying to guess the answers to his questions, Emilio walked up to a gaudy, chipped cabinet, and opened the doors. Inside was their last bottle of vermouth, part of their dwindling supply of food and drink. Looking back he saw that there were already two glasses on the table. They were dirty but serviceable, and he'd already found himself washing the dishes far too many times in the recent past.

Breaking the wax, Emilio sat down next to Sarah on the couch. She grumbled slightly as he leaned back into the plush velour.

It wasn't until he began to pour the liquor that she finally managed to pull herself out of her slumber and look up at him.

"What are you doing?" she asked sleepily.

"Drinking," he said, only barely managing to hold back a sigh.

"So late at night?" she said, slowly pulling herself upwards.

"It's before dawn."

"In the morning?" she asked.

"Yes," he replied, and poured a second glass for her. "You, too."

It had been a long time since they had last had a drink on the couch together. He still had hopes that perhaps he could discover whether the girl who had overwhelmed him with emotion on that ferry boat a few months ago was still somewhere inside this angry woman.

"We make a toast," he said, and handed her the glass. It was slightly sticky and clouded. "To Tom!" He raised up his own flute.

Sarah nodded and clinked her glass against his.

"You're happy your friend is back?" he asked her.

"Yes," she replied, but there was something missing in her tone.

"Then why do you seem so sad?"

Sarah shook her head. "Morning or night, I've still just woken up. I need some time to . . ."

Emilio frowned. "When will that be, Sarah? How long will I have to wait?"

174

She let out her breath in a huff and put the glass up to her lips. Sarah took a longer sip this time, and if Emilio hadn't known that she had taken her very first taste of alcohol on this same couch only a few months before, he would have thought she'd been drinking for years. "You really want to go through this, Emilio?"

He nodded. "For better or for worse. I do so much to bring him back, now tell me why."

Sarah nodded. "He's different now. Something happened to him in the theater."

"We're all different since then." Emilio was surprised to find himself feeling defensive of the metal man. "And we're also still the same. Perhaps he just needs you to tell him you are his friend."

"I have," Sarah said with a sigh. "But everything he's gone through . . . the new body . . . It's all damaged him in some way."

"Then I can fix him for you." It sounded good. But after letting Tom rebuild his body to his own specifications, Emilio was immediately doubtful that "fixing" Tom was actually something still within reach of his skills.

At least his offer had managed to raise a genuine smile on her face. "Thank you, Emilio, but I don't think even you are able to repair someone's feelings, whether they're made of metal or flesh."

"I don't know," he said, reaching out and taking her hand. "Maybe people need to give me the chance."

Sarah's smile widened, and only for an instant he felt as if perhaps he had broken through. Then the look faded, and she pulled her hand away from his. "I want you to know that I appreciate all that you've done for me here; taking me into your home, fixing Tom."

He had hoped that by being bold he might just get the smallest glimpse of what was going on inside her head. It had always worked with his wife, but Sarah was a very different woman. "Tell me, Sarah, do you think anyone stays the same? You want him to be alive, but you don't want him to change . . ."

She turned her head slightly to the side. "I want to *trust* him, Emilio. Just like I wanted to trust you."

He was about to push her again, but it seemed as if some kind of shutter had fallen into place. It was almost as if she were becoming more like the Automaton, except he couldn't see the tiny gears turning behind her eyes.

Wasn't it the men in this country who were supposed to hide their emotions? What was she trying to do? "This isn't about Tom at all!" he said with a sudden realization. "You want to be your father."

"That's not . . ."

He wrapped his fingers around her free hand. "He was a good man, but you will not win this by becoming him."

She looked away from him, and he knew he was right.

She didn't pull her hand away, but she didn't react, either. She simply kept her head down, breathing deeply.

"I know you are young, Sarah, but not so much more than me."

She stared at him, and the lost look on her face made him sadder than he could remember being in a long time. "Whom can I trust, Emilio? Everyone I love is dead."

He smiled back at her and stroked her hand lightly. "Then you need to love more people. You can't do this on your own."

She pulled her fingers away once again. "No. I can't. Not until we put an end to this."

"Why?"

"I have to be strong."

"Loving people isn't weak." Did she think she was the only person to lose someone they loved? "Everyone we love dies, eventually."

"But they weren't all murdered by the same man."

"Eschaton," Emilio said. "You *still* want to fight him? He has the Paragons now. How could we ever win?"

"You're wrong," she said, and a pained look came over her face. "We *can* win—now that we have Tom."

In that moment he looked out over the clippings and notes she had written, and began to see the shape of her obsession. It was ridiculous to think that the two of them—even with a miraculous mechanical man—could take on a villain with the power of Eschaton. And yet Sarah was clearly drawn to it, like a moth blinded by the light before being consumed by the fire. "We aren't strong enough. We aren't heroes."

Sarah sat up. "No one ever wins without trying, Emilio. Darby, the Sleuth, my father—they all spent their lives being better than what was supposed to be possible."

He shook his head. "And *now* you sound like your father."

"It was something he used to say."

"Look where you are, Sarah," He waved his arm at the room. "This isn't your Hall or your home. You and I aren't real heroes or adventurers. But maybe we can escape—leave New York and head West. This madness wouldn't follow us."

Before she even opened her mouth he could see that she would never follow his plan. "You're wrong, Emilio. Madness grows. If Eschaton destroys New York, who would stop him then? None of us would be safe."

"This isn't our responsibility, Sarah. We don't have to save the world."

"Somebody has to."

"But not us! We could be together."

"The world won't be right until we've put a stop to him." Sarah picked up one of the clippings from the table. The headline shouted out its message in bold black type: DOZENS DEAD IN PARK MASSACRE! "This is what happened while we waited. There's no one else left to stop him but us. We have to fight."

Emilio drew in a breath, preparing to argue with her. But maybe there was no other choice. The attack on the park had made it clear that Eschaton was willing to sacrifice all of New York to feed his ambitions. There was no safety for any of them until the villain was gone. "But why does it have to be us?"

"There's no one else," Sarah said, and gave a nod of conviction. "You didn't have to build that shield, and you didn't have to come to my rescue."

"I thought you were beautiful." Just a moment ago they had been talking about her. When had this become about him?

She gave his fingers a solid squeeze. "And you're a good person. I wouldn't have made it this far without you." Her eyes caught his, and for a single moment he could see a flash of the Sarah he had first met peeking out at him. There was something beneath the sadness. "And you're right, I need to trust you."

It wasn't what he wanted to hear, and it wasn't what he wanted her to want from him. But somehow she had managed to turn the conversation her way, and suddenly he found himself on the defensive. "Even if we fight, how could we possibly win?" he said, still trying to protest. But it was a weak argument, and he knew it.

"If you can help me with Tom, then more will come. He can become the most powerful thing in the world. And you are the one who proved it to him."

"What do you want me to do?"

"I want you to help him understand his power to fuse with machines."

Emilio frowned. That was a miracle and mystery. And it was also terrifying. If Tom could take control of any machine, and infuse it with his consciousness, who was to say that he wouldn't be more of a monster than Eschaton could ever be?

Sarah had already been corrupted by the promise of power. He wanted her to turn back into the shy but steadfast girl he'd fallen in love with, but it seemed that girl had become another casualty of that night at the theater. Instead, this hard woman had taken her place, and he wasn't sure that this was someone he could ever feel the same emotions for. "And what about you and me?"

"I'm sorry, Emilio. This has to come first. And then, maybe . . ."

Emilio took back her hand into his and squeezed it tightly. "You are strong. I know this very well. You don't have to fight against *everything*."

She gave him the slightest squeeze in return. "I'm not, Emilio."

He laughed at that. "No? Are you sure? Then tell me what it is you are fighting *for*."

"I'm fighting to save the world from a madman," she said, with a definitive nod at the end to punctuate her words.

"No," he said, shaking his head, "That's no real reason," Emilio told her. "You would give up everything for that? Are you the savior? Do you love the entire world? Does the world love you?"

Sarah flinched, her face twitching almost as if she'd been struck. "It isn't about that."

"Nobody fights for the world: it's a dream—a fantasy. We fight for the things we love . . ."

A sour look came over Sarah's face. "All right, then. I'm fighting for the things I love *in* the world."

"And what are those?"

"Are we playing a game now?" She glared at him.

"No," he told her. "But if you do this, if *we* do this, all of us, together, then there needs to be a reason. There will be bad times for us soon."

"Bad times have already come, Emilio."

He wasn't surprised by her response. "My uncle used to say that things that begin badly always end in worse."

"So you want me to stay here and be your pretty little junkyard housewife?"

He felt an ache when she said that, as if she'd uncovered a hole in his heart that he didn't even know he'd had. But he couldn't say yes to that. "You want revenge, but you don't admit it. Things that start in revenge, they can end very, very bad. You and Eschaton both do this for revenge: him against the world, and you for your father."

He waited a moment for Sarah to deny the reality of it. When she made no attempt to, Emilio continued, "I know we can't make it stop, but when these things come . . . these very bad things, you have to have a *reason* why you are fighting. Because you may lose all the things you love, and when you make hard choices, you should be making them *for* the things you love." Emilio tried to not think of his wife and children, but their faces flickered in front of him, and he could feel the loss again.

Sarah sat quietly for a moment, and then her eyes hardened. She turned her gaze away from his and pulled back her hand, using it to pick up her glass and take another long sip. "Thank you, Emilio." Sarah contemplated her glass, swirling the liquor that remained at the bottom. Then she placed the glass onto the table and stood up. "I'll think about what you're saying."

She swayed slightly as she rose. He was glad to see that there had been *some* visible effect on her from the alcohol.

"I'm sorry, Sarah. I care for you."

"I know you do, Emilio." Sarah turned to him and stared for a moment, as if she were making a decision. Then she grabbed his hand and pulled him up from his seat. "I have a suggestion. Let's get out of this ridiculous room."

Emilio, surprised by her sudden burst of energy, let himself be dragged forward.

Emilio unlatched the large door on the side of the car. Just outside the door was the concrete terrace that he and Tom had poured out over the last few days. As soon as it had finished curing they would drag the machines onto it and construct a tarp to protect them from the rain, at least temporarily.

Looking up at the sky, he could see the first long tendrils of daylight already beginning to reach across the sky. "I have an idea!"

He closed his eyes for a moment, letting his plans—as exciting as they were—drain out of his head. He was a fool around women, he knew, but not so much of one that he didn't know enough to remember that the key to success with them was to pay genuine attention from time to time.

He jumped down from the open door onto the bare slab, holding out his hand to help Sarah down, although she barely needed it. She no longer wore anything like traditional women's clothes. In the last few weeks, Sarah had completely changed her wardrobe, choosing simple skirts and blouses that she found around the house.

It was odd to see her wearing some of the same simple clothes as his sister, although somehow she wore them with far more modesty.

"What do you have in mind, Emilio?" Her mood had shifted with the location, and the smile on her face was warm and inviting—so much so that he felt tempted to kiss her right then. It would not, he remembered with a warm thrill, be the first time—or even the second. But it could be the first in quite a while.

But he had other plans, and instead he pointed up at the iron rungs that ran up the side of the rail car. "Are you okay to climb?"

Sarah nodded eagerly and hopped up onto the ladder. Her shoes, although not as fancy as the boots she had worn when she arrived, were still made more for showing off than for climbing, and Emilio couldn't help but laugh to himself as she awkwardly made her way up to the roof, each iron rail ringing as she jammed the leather sole of her boot against it.

He jumped up behind her, trying not to notice (too much, at least) the view of her exposed legs as she hoisted herself up onto the top of the car.

"It's dirty up here." Sarah yelled. A moment later she peered back down at him. "And a bit cool."

Emilio frowned. Growing up in a circus seemed to have left him poorly equipped for anticipating the needs of a New York society girl. "I go back down and get a blanket."

She laughed and waved her hand in an upward motion. "I'm not that delicate—not anymore, anyway. And it's beautiful up here."

Emilio took her at her word and bounded up the ladder. As he reached the top, he stood and turned to face Brooklyn.

There was still some time left before the sun rose, but the rolling hills and tall buildings of the growing city were outlined in the rising light.

Turning around, he looked out at Manhattan, but in the dim glow of earliest morning the details were lost. He could make out only the hazy outlines of the high roofs and the flickering pinpoints of the street lamps. The river, on the other hand, was glowing beautifully, appearing far more serene and beautiful in the morning light than it would under a harsh daytime sun.

Emilio sat down next to Sarah, testing that the pitch was dry before he committed to resting his bottom on it. The gravel bit into him, and he realized that upper-class or not, he should have brought a blanket with him.

He could practically hear Viola mocking him for being such a fool—but the gentler loving sister was gone now, replaced by the mad, bitter creature she had become. He was beginning to doubt that the kind-hearted Viola would ever return.

"What are you thinking about?" Sarah asked him.

He blushed, realizing that despite his best intentions he had been ignoring her, lost in his own thoughts. He stretched out a hand at the view. "Is beautiful, no?"

Sarah turned her head and smiled. "It will be a lovely place to watch the dawn. I don't think I've ever seen the city quite like this before. Do you come up here often?"

Emilio nodded. "I used to come up often. But lately, not so much."

"It's been a busy few months." The look on her face was still serious, but he thought that perhaps it was not as sad, lost, or angry as it had been back in the living room.

"Yes." He nodded again, but when he tried to find more words to follow the first, it seemed he had nothing to say. In the past when the two of them had been alone together, there was always something else happening at the same time. Villains, dirigibles, mechanical men . . . "It seems as if there is only romance for us when something terrible is over our heads," he said. Perhaps what they needed now was a large cloud of black smoke to appear in the sky.

When Emilio turned toward Sarah, he could see that she was looking at him. With most women, he would have expected them to be smiling in spite of themselves, but there was an earnest look on her face, as if she was studying him, trying to uncover his secrets. The light gave her face a golden glow, and he had to admit that he found her scrutiny attractive. "You're smiling at that, Emilio. I suppose you think that's funny?"

"No. Not funny." He moved closer to her. His face was close to hers, and she didn't pull away, although her expression changed somewhat. "But true." As he leaned forward her lips parted, and he kissed her.

Unlike their previous short attempts at intimacy, this was fueled by neither liquor nor adrenaline, and yet neither of them seemed interested in slowing things down.

Emilio lifted his hand and put it behind her neck. The feel of her skin was soft and smooth. He felt his heart skip a beat as the thrill of it ran through him.

After a long embrace, Sarah finally pulled away and gasped for breath.

"Is okay?" Emilio asked, worried that he had once again broken some kind of unwritten rule, although he supposed that in America the rules against men and women kissing were probably written down in any number of places, and then reprinted in all the newspapers every day.

"It's very nice," she replied.

There was a long pause before she tilted her head and spoke again. "Do you love me, Emilio?"

The boldness of the question shocked him. The very idea of answering it made him want to jump down from the roof and run away, but Sarah's eyes were focused on his, and Emilio could tell that she was intent on reading any truth in them that she could find.

He opened his mouth to answer, but then realized he had no idea what to tell her. Simply saying "yes" would be what most women would have wanted to hear, but Sarah was hardly most women, and things with her were rarely that simple. Hadn't they just been arguing a few minutes ago?

It wasn't the first time someone had asked him that question, but it was only the second time in his life that he had genuinely cared for anyone with such intensity.

And he did love her. She wasn't simply a conquest to tell the other boys about, although there had been a few of those back in his circus days. He had thought his wife was one of those girls at first, and she had turned out to be anything but.

Sarah was so completely unlike his wife in a million ways, but somehow he had again found himself with a woman who demanded more of him than he felt comfortable giving.

"Emilio, are you okay?"

Emilio reached out and took Sarah's hand. A few bits of stone had freed themselves from the pitch and were still pressed into her skin. He brushed them away and covered her fingers with his. "Is been a long time since anyone wanted to know the answer to that question."

She nodded. "I understand." Her hand suddenly was gripping his very tightly. "But I need to know, because I think I do love you, Emilio. I've certainly never felt the way I feel with you with *anyone* before. And I'm sorry if I'm being difficult, but you have more experience than I do with these things." The words were rushing out of her, and he realized just how innocent and lost she was.

"Is never easy."

"I know you think I've gone mad, and that I'm taking on the world, but I need to know that I can trust you, and that I can rely on you."

"You have Tom."

She nodded. "I do, and I love him, but what I need right now is a man made of flesh and blood. Maybe I don't have to fight against *everything*." She took a deep breath. "I may regret it tomorrow, but to be honest," she said, her face colored red with a deep blush, "I'm ready for some regrets that are my decision, rather than someone else's."

Once again he found himself astounded by her bravery and determination. Her whole world had collapsed, and yet she was still looking to take responsibility for her own actions. It was a rare quality in anyone, and for an instant he felt sad that he would never meet the man who had created this girl and brought her up in the world, although he could only imagine that Alexander Stanton would think an Italian boy was an utterly unworthy match for his daughter.

Emilio inhaled deeply. "I love you too, Sarah." If she was willing to take the risk, then so was he.

Sarah kissed him again, this time with a passion and intensity beyond anything he had thought her capable of. Her arms wrapped tightly around his neck, pulling him closer to her and locking them together.

And for just an instant, before he allowed himself to become completely lost in his passion, he wondered what he had just gotten himself into.

Chapter 13
Mistrials and Tribulations

While Eschaton lectured Anubis on the stage, Jack peered around the conference room.

This Hall of Paragons was essentially his home now, and even after spending a few weeks inside these thick granite walls, he had to admit that he still felt less comfortable inside their cold shelter than he had when he arrived.

Soon after the events in the theater, Eschaton had called him up to the Hall of Paragons, telling him that his Blades would now be the main security force for the building. It would be their job to keep the peace as more and more would-be heroes (and villains) began to arrive.

Once he might have argued, but this wasn't the time for that. He had taken over the Sleuth's old quarters and turned them into something that approximated a home.

The old man had seriously eclectic tastes, but Jack could read, and he found himself whiling away the long, boring hours reading a large number of books.

Some were titles that he was vaguely familiar with, including many translated classics from across the spectrum of history. It had been a long time since he had opened a copy of *The Odyssey*, and the first time he had ever considered it as an adult. He had also consumed a number of old Wilkie Collins novels, which he was surprised to discover on the dead Englishman's shelves.

It had taken him a good deal of time to get used to reading fiction again, and the made-up tales interested him even less now than they had when he was a boy. At least back then his head had been full of noble dreams, and the only men he had ever murdered were painted metal soldiers. Now that his experience of dying men was no longer an abstract idea, the battles that Homer described had taken on a very different tone.

But fiction was not his only area of study. He had also taken to reading the old man's journals, many of which the Sleuth had put together into edited volumes. They were typeset and bound—clearly intended for eventual publication after a retirement that would now never come.

They were well written, if obviously embellished (and whitewashed). While Jack had only ever met the Sleuth face-to-face the once, during his time in the underworld he had heard enough stories of the Paragons to know that the Sleuth's version of events often made the heroes appear far more reserved and honorable than any man actually could have been.

Still, seeing the events of the man's life committed to the written word made him wish that Hughes hadn't done in the old duffer before he'd had a chance to have written about his exploits with Jack and the Blades. He certainly would have liked to have discovered exactly how the old man had escaped through the labyrinth, although in retrospect it was clear that he'd had Anubis's help.

He was rather wishing that he could be reading one of those journals now, instead of being forced to watch yet another round of Eschaton's theatrics.

Despite the gray man's attempts, there was no real drama in what was happening on the stage in front of him. The entire event was nothing more than an execution, although one that might yield some mildly amusing results.

But even with the transformation of the Industrialist's ward into a man of glass, it was obvious that Eschaton hadn't quite honed his transformation techniques—although he was clearly getting closer with each trial.

If it wasn't for the amount of fortified steam he needed, there would be nothing stopping him from turning any number of the eager idiots in the Hall into any variety of monsters and obscenities. But until they recovered the Automaton's heart, Eschaton's ability to start changing people wholesale was going to be limited by the dwindling reserves of steam hidden in the building.

And that served Jack fine. Truth be told, he wasn't eager to undergo Eschaton's process any time soon. He rather liked just being an ordinary person, and with his finely honed marksmanship already giving him a defin-

itive advantage over the average idiot, he couldn't imagine what being purified would provide for him.

The audience began to applaud and Jack turned back to look at
Clements. The man was standing up and clapping like a giddy child. He had
tried to hold back his contempt for the Southerner, but he was vile beyond
imagining—motivated purely by fear and anger.

He thought about the red-bearded boy that Clements had murdered, his
body still cooling in the basement. He had been named Dirk, which Jack had
enjoyed to no end.

It had taken a better part of the week for the boy's spirit to break. Every
day, Jack had pulled him out of the little shack they had kept him in at the
back of their cul-de-sac, and let Dirk try to attack him. Every day the boy lost.

Jack proved over and over again that strength wasn't the only attribute
that mattered in a fight.

Finally, after a week of their one-sided battles, Dirk had relented, and
Jack had thrashed him anyway—an object lesson in the unfairness of life, and
that he fully expected his men to win instead of playing by the rules.

Once that was over, he'd trained him to be a Blade: hard, sharp, and
deadly. The training he had given the boy was beginning to pay off. As he
had expected, not only was Dirk loyal, he was stronger than the Ruffian, and
as smart as a whip. If there had ever been a man he might have considered
handing the gang over to, it would have been him.

Now Dirk was gone: another victim of Clements's uncontrollable nature.
Jack didn't consider himself a man of much sentiment, but he was beginning
to think that it wouldn't be long before he'd need to find an excuse to deal
with the issue of the White Knight in a more permanent way.

The Shell . . . now, he was living proof of what worried Jack most.
Eschaton constantly told the others that a world of purified men (and hopefully women, as well) would be one where everyone was equal. Jack had more
than his fair share of doubts that would actually be the case. And was it even
necessary?

Despite the fact that the world was a mess, Jack had come to like it that
way. He even liked his place in the pecking order: high enough on the scale
of things to be living in comfort, but not so high that he needed to watch his

back at every turn. What he didn't like was the way Lord Eschaton's philosophy seemed to be constantly intruding on what was quite a fine deal.

And whether the plan succeeded or failed, at some point it would all come crashing down. Everything always did—eventually. That was the way of the world. Until then, Jack was more than content to enjoy his position on top of the world without the addition of fortified smoke.

Jack was suddenly struck by a heavy wave of heat. For a moment he wondered if he was suddenly getting sick, but looking at the men around him, he could see that he wasn't the only one who felt as if he'd be been placed in front of an open oven door.

Nearby, the Bomb Lance pulled a threadbare handkerchief from his pocket and held it up against his thinning hair. It was hard not to notice how much Murphy seemed to have aged in the last few months. Perhaps they all had.

Having descended to the stage, Eschaton had once again begun to pontificate, lecturing Anubis about his grand plans, and doing it in a way that was clearly designed as much for the audience's understanding as it had been for his victim.

Since coming to live in the Hall, Jack had more than enough time to hear Eschaton discuss his plans to fix the world in excruciating detail. He'd heard it often enough that by now it was all running together, although there were plenty of men who couldn't seem to get enough of it.

Jack found himself ignoring the speech, and instead trying to figure out what Anubis would do with his fate staring him straight in his unmasked face. Even before he knew his secret, Jack had always thought of Anubis as a man who played at being noble, far more than someone with actual nobility in him. But he still found himself impressed by the black man's calm demeanor.

He turned to peer past Clements, at the eager face of the Bomb Lance. Ever since Jack had first held a weapon, people had referred to him as a maniac, but it was a title that fit Murphy far better. The Bomb Lance had once been a family man: hardworking, married, with a brood of children. But rather than a single disaster, his world had been torn away from the Irishman one relative at a time. War, disease, and misfortune had slowly destroyed his world, leaving behind this angry, vengeful creature.

Jack might smile when he killed a man, but he didn't consider it to be an act of revenge against humanity as a whole.

Jack hadn't ever thought of his own misfortune as something to be thankful for, but looking at Murphy he saw the advantage of having been thrust into misery at an early age. Facing sudden tragedy was, he had to imagine, far better than having your life ripped away from you piece by piece.

The Irishman was leaning forward. He was clearly looking forward to seeing Anubis thrown in the chamber. His eyes were wide, and a small stream of spittle ran from the corner of his mouth.

It was clear why the Bomb Lance was Eschaton's favorite. The Irishman didn't just have a penchant for violence, he loved the madness of it as well— the gadgets, jim-crackery and ridiculous knickknacks that bored Jack half to tears. Even now, Jack could see the silver glint of some ridiculous machinery hidden under the Irishman's coat.

When he had first joined the Children, Eschaton had offered Jack some gadgets as well: folding blades, knife shooters, and other nonsense. He had tried a few to humor his new mentor, but in the end what he liked best was a large supply of well-balanced blades. A good, sharp knife was something a man could rely on in any circumstance, and Eschaton had given him his jacket in response.

The crowd around them started to holler, pulling his attention back to the stage. Eschaton had come down from his pulpit, a golden vial in his hand, and Jack felt another wave of heat roll toward him. It now seemed obvious, to him at least, that Nathaniel was causing the temperature in the room to rise.

For a moment he thought he might say something, but Eschaton shouted out "Quiet!" and the entire audience went silent.

"You're a monster!" Nathaniel shouted at Eschaton. "I want my life back!"

The boy was becoming frantic, and sensing a rising moment of danger Jack slipped a finger into the buttons of his coat and let it drop open slightly, putting his knives in easy reach. He considered the idea of throwing a few blades at the boy simply to see if he might put an end to the danger early, but Eschaton still seemed unconcerned.

The gray man had to realize that Nathaniel was becoming a genuine threat—didn't he? After all, he had been the one responsible for creating him. Maybe he was curious, or perhaps this reaction was the one the gray man wanted. But if it was drama that Lord Eschaton intended, it could still quickly grow out of control.

Either way Jack decided that a front-row seat might not be the best vantage point for a brawl involving purified humans.

While he was perfectly willing to engage in hand-to-cane combat when the situation called for it, Jack was always at his best advantage with a little distance between himself and his target. Slipping out from his chair, he stepped quietly into the aisle and started to move toward the back of the room.

He had only gotten halfway up the aisle before he felt a rough hand wrap around his wrist. "Going somewhere, son?"

The voice was gruff and familiar, and Jack looked down into the shattered face of Doctor Dynamite. The man had been badly hurt in his fight against the Automaton, and while he had spent the last few weeks recuperating, he clearly wasn't all the way there—and might never be.

The cowboy still had one arm in a splint, but there was some strength left in the remaining limb. While most of the crowd was already on their feet, he remained seated. He could walk only with the use of a cane now, although Jack wondered if the Doctor's aim was still able to rival his own.

More than once, Jack had suppressed the urge to challenge the flamboyant cowboy to duel, to find out which one of them was the better marksman. If the gunslinger ever fully recovered from his injuries, Jack thought he still might.

"I—" It was the only word Jack got out before a stronger wave of heat enveloped him. This time it was followed by an intense blast of light, and when he turned to look down at the stage he needed to shield his eyes. He could make out a figure on the stage, lit up like the sun. Eschaton's purified human had, it seemed, come into his own.

"Dammit," Jack said, yanking his hand free from the surprised Texan. Reaching into his coat with both hands, he pulled out a pair of blades.

Shielding his eyes, he could dimly make out Anubis on the stage, throwing some kind of liquid directly at Eschaton's face.

For the first time since he had met the man, he watched the gray giant stumble backwards, clearly affected by the concoction.

Eschaton reached out his hand to stabilize himself and touched one of the thick, square windows that made up the Uplift Chamber. The instant his fingers brushed the frame there was a discharge of crackling electricity from his arm that shattered the glass. The smoke, now free from its cage, poured into the room.

With all the experiments that had been going on inside the Hall, it was well-known that exposure to the smoke was very dangerous without proper preparation.

A collective shout rose up from the audience, and the gathered Children of Eschaton seemed to react almost with a single mind. The combination of heat, light, smoke, and the collapse of their leader had sent them into a panic.

Jack suddenly found himself swimming against the tide in a sea of desperate would-be heroes and villains, all of them rushing toward the door. Doc Dynamite was thrown to the floor, and Jack realized that if he didn't do something, the man was going to be trampled to death.

That wasn't any of his business, really, and there was no way to know if Doc Dynamite would have done the same for him if their positions had been reversed. Given what he'd seen of the man's attitude, he highly doubted it. But it was a trampling that had turned him into an orphan, and it was no fit way for a man to die—not to mention that his coat was probably full of explosives.

Jack thrust his fist into the solar plexus of one of the men desperately rushing out of the pew. The man fell back with a shout, breaking the balance of the nearby crowd and slowing their momentum.

He reached down for Doc Dynamite's working arm and dragged him up to his feet. The cowboy looked shaken, but somehow, even in the confusion, the man had still managed to keep his ten-gallon hat on his head. "Thanks pardner, I owe you one."

Jack nodded. He knew that most men had a sense of pride, and they needed to be taken seriously. It wasn't a condition he was personally afflicted with, and the last thing he really wanted was to be owed a favor by a man with a fetish for dynamite. "If you want to pay me back, you can hobble your broken arse out of here before the fighting starts."

He could see the cowboy's hand twitch, considering, just for an instant, responding to him by reaching for his gun. Jack clutched the blade hidden in his palm. This wasn't how he wanted to face the cowboy, but if push came to shove, he'd do his best to be the one who came out alive.

The cowboy looked into his eye and winked. Relaxing his hand, he turned and walked away through the panicked crowd.

No longer concerned with Doc Dynamite's fate, Jack turned to face the stage and scowled at what he saw there. Nathaniel was still transformed from translucence into a silvery glow, although not as bright as before. Standing around the shining man were Eschaton, the White Knight, Murphy, and the Shell. They were ready to fight, but clearly being held back by the heat the man was generating. A few of the braver Children—men he didn't recognize—were standing a bit farther back.

Anubis had used the confusion as an opportunity to grab his breastplate and begin strapping it on. The man was no fool—Jack had to give him credit for that. Although, had he been in the jackal's position, he would have joined the other men in running out the door.

By that measure, he should have been doing just that at this very moment, and for some reason he was being brave instead. Jack decided to chalk it up to morbid curiosity, and walked back down the ramp.

The heat was intense, and if he didn't know better he would think that he was about to be burned alive. Eschaton and the Shell had some immunity, no doubt, but he wondered if the Southerner and the Irishman might not regret standing so close.

"Stay away from me, you monsters!" Nathaniel yelled at them, waving an arm around. Whether or not the boy fully understood his new powers, his time as a Paragon had clearly made him quickly adaptable to any situation where villains were involved. "I'll burn all of you to death."

"Don't be a foolish boy, Nathaniel," Eschaton said in low tones, "I don't want to have to destroy you, but I will." Jack had been around the gray man long enough to know that the more threatening his tone, the more afraid he actually was. In this case, he must have been fairly terrified under all the bluster.

As he neared the stage, Jack turned left and walked over to Anubis. The man was sweating profusely, and there was a desperate look in his eye. Jack wondered if his inability to hide his emotions was one of the reasons he liked to conceal his face. "It's nice to see you back in costume . . . or at least a shred of it."

Abraham slipped his black hood over his face. It took him a moment to adjust it so that he could see out of the eyeholes, and Jack considered using his blindness as an opportunity to attack. He felt conflicted for a moment— the thought of attacking him seemed unfair.

As Anubis finished adjusting his mask, Jack berated himself. He had never considered himself a sporting man, and the idea of fighting fairly was something that he considered to be a weakness in other men, and yet here he was.

"You could have attacked me just then," Anubis said, pulling on the outer mask that hid his eyes and gave him the visage of the Egyptian god. Still, the jackal was only half the hero he once had been, his leather leggings and cloth skirt nowhere to be seen.

"And I didn't." Jack peered over his left shoulder. The standoff happening on the stage hadn't erupted into fighting yet. "I'm not here to fight with you, unless you plan to take on *all* these men."

Anubis nodded. "Then why didn't you run away with the rest of the Children?"

"Why didn't *you* escape in the confusion? That's what I would have done if I were you."

"You're not me," he replied enigmatically. "So why *are* you here?"

Jack smiled in response. "Let's call it misplaced loyalty."

"To whom?" Anubis replied, his voice slipping even deeper into his enigmatic rumble. Jack had never seen a man who was more clearly comfortable in his secret identity. "Not to *me* . . ." he said with a note of surprise.

"You have quite the opinion of yourself," Jack said with a laugh. "I was thinking you might want to try and 'judge' Eschaton while his back is turned."

"It crossed my mind."

There was another blistering wave of heat, and Jack turned just in time to see Murphy scream and stagger back, batting his arm against a smoking patch on his coat in the shape of a hand. Clearly he had been touched by the silver man.

"I'm beginning to think I made a mistake when I gave you so much power," Eschaton said. Jack could see that his face had turned from gray to yellow where the liquid had touched it. The white lines running through his gray skin stopped on the edges of the stained flesh, framing it with an electric glow. Its effect on him was not a good one.

Nathaniel scowled at the gray man. "The mistake you made was killing my father." The boy was angry, confused, and ready to die for his revenge.

Jack clutched his hand tightly around the knife he held. He was ready to throw it, although he doubted he could use it to do any real damage.

"You're not an ordinary man anymore, Nathaniel. You've become the first truly purified human. Surely you can see that you're beyond the need for petty acts, such as revenge."

Eschaton took a step toward the silver man, and Nathaniel lifted up his glowing arms in a threatening gesture. Silver flickered across his palms. "You've turned me into a monster! Now I want you to *change me back*!" The mercury under his skin flared white, and more heat poured out of him. It was blistering, but either the boy was weakening, or—more disturbingly—he was beginning to learn to control his newfound powers.

"Let's kill him," the White Knight said, but Jack noticed that he wasn't doing more than talking.

"No, Jordan. This isn't a fight . . . or at least it doesn't have to be," Eschaton turned slightly, giving the Southerner a stern glare.

Anubis took a step forward. Jack slipped out the blade he'd kept hidden in his hand—just far enough that the metal edge was visible, and stretched his arm out, barring Anubis's way. "Let's you and I not get involved just yet. I want to give it a moment to see how it plays out."

Ever since Eschaton had started this experiment, a question had been running around in the back of Jack's head: what if Eschaton's process worked *better* than he expected and he managed to create a being more powerful than himself? Why was he so convinced that such a creature would have any interest in being his underling?

The gray man did have genuine charisma, and an innate skill for manipulation. All it took was a look at the surprising number of men that he had managed to bring into the Children for Jack to appreciate those skills. The fact that he had managed to involve a man as cynical and obsessed with self-preservation as Jack himself was a testament to just how persuasive Lord Eschaton could be.

"I just need you to relax, Nathaniel," Eschaton said. "I know it's hard for you to accept, but you're one of us now. Perhaps the most powerful of us all."

The gray man held out his arm in a gesture of friendship. "Take my hand. If you come with me we'll discover your true potential." As he reached out to Nathaniel, the intense heat caused Eschaton's skin to glow and crackle.

For an instant it seemed as if he would accept, the glowing arm lifting tentatively. "No!" he shouted, "I won't accept you! You're the monster that destroyed everything I've ever loved." Instead of taking the offered hand, Nathaniel grabbed Eschaton's arm, and there was an explosion of dazzling white light that obliterated not only the already-harsh glare of the electric bulbs, but the rest of Jack's vision as well. As he turned away to shield his eyes he could barely make out the other men doing the same. There was some heat as well, but not the skin-searing blast he had expected.

It took Jack too long to blink away the blindness, and for an instant he began to panic, wondering whether his vision was permanently damaged.

He stared at the men through squinting eyes, but what he saw as the initial flash faded was almost impossible to comprehend. Nathaniel and Eschaton were clasping each other's hands, fingers intertwined as they wrestled in a fantastic tug of war. Eschaton's electric white battled against the other man's mercurial glow.

If the battle was purely to determine who could martial more of the power within them, it seemed that Nathaniel was already winning. The silver inside him had filled his arms, stretching up past his shoulders and down into the flesh of his back. Eschaton's silver had filled to just past his elbows.

But the gray man clearly didn't agree with Jack's assessment. "You'll never win this, Nathaniel! I gave you these powers, and I know how they work far better than you ever will."

Nathaniel let out a laugh that sounded halfway between mockery and a mad cackle. "Who's been the hero longer?" He heaved against Eschaton, and the gray man sank just a little bit. "I may be a drunkard and a fool, but I was Alexander Stanton's son." Heat flared off of Nathaniel, and this time it was clear that Eschaton felt it. "And I'm the last damn Paragon!"

There was another blinding flash, not as bright as the first, but with his eyes already burning Jack couldn't help but turn away once again. As he tried to blink his sight back he heard the growling voice of Anubis coming from the other side of him. The man had clearly gotten past his miserable defenses. "Lord Eschaton, you and your men have been judged and found wanting."

The shouts and grunts that came next were clearly from Murphy and Clements. He assumed that they had been similarly incapacitated by the light, perhaps even more than he had been, and when Jack finally was able to clear his vision he saw the Irishman slumped down against the side of the pews.

"You killed my father, you killed Sir Dennis. Now it's my turn." Eschaton was down on his knees, his massive gray head held between Nathaniel's glowing hands.

As the glow became brighter it was clear what Nathaniel intended. For a moment he considered letting the boy carry out his plans. Eschaton was a madman, and Jack truly had no desire to become a purified anything. But despite his conflicted emotions, Eschaton had saved him—pulling him out of a life of violent poverty and giving him the chance to prove himself. He certainly couldn't let that savior die in front of him without a fight.

He prepared a handful of knives to release toward Nathaniel. Jack was hit hard, his entire body thrown sideways as Anubis crashed into him. But the jackal's attack had come too late, and the daggers struck home.

Pierced five times, Nathaniel screamed and let go of Eschaton. The gray man, no longer conscious (and quite possibly no longer alive) crumpled down to the floor like a sack of rocks.

For a moment Jack was hopeful he might have genuinely hurt the boy. He had thrown his knives with all the deadly accuracy he could muster, and they had struck Nathaniel along his entire left side: three of them piercing his arm, one in his shoulder, and one in his head. But Jack's moment of triumph was short-lived when he saw their minimal effect. The blades had managed to pierce the transparent man's skin, but only barely. Around each of them was a small spider web of cracks, as if his body had been made from pure glass.

Nathaniel plucked them out of his skin one by one and threw them to the floor. "Who are *you*?" Nathaniel asked. The high-pitched terror in his voice had disappeared completely now, and Jack felt a cold chill go up his spine as he realized the question was being directed at him.

"My name is Jack Knife."

"And you're one of the Children?"

Jack only nodded in response. There was no point in hiding it.

"I'd run if I were you," Nathaniel said coolly, "because once I've finished burning out Eschaton's brains I'm going to kill you next." The silver, although not as bright as it had been, was still moving underneath his skin, swirling around the cracks in the boy's flesh and repairing the small amount of damage that Jack had managed to do.

Jack had been threatened before, and was tempted to stand his ground. But he had never been bullied by a monster like this.

If he had felt any unease about the world that Eschaton wanted to create before, he was even more terrified by it now. He couldn't fight the transparent man, but he knew someone who could at least slow him down. "Shell!" Jack shouted, "Stop him!"

Jack hadn't actually seen the broken creature since the events had begun on the stage, but he prayed that the abomination was somewhere nearby.

Just as Jack began to wonder if the creature would obey his orders even if he *could* hear him, the broken man-machine trundled forward, its twisted metal hands balled into fists, the wheels underneath it wobbling furiously.

Nathaniel seemed unimpressed. "You're a pathet—" but whatever insult the boy had in mind for the Shell was wiped away as a metal-covered fist cracked hard against his jaw. The impact of it was powerful enough to shatter the side of his head, the splintering spider webs spreading upward through his translucent flesh and into his eyes.

The attack dazed Nathaniel, and while he reeled the machine took the opportunity to strike again, this time coming up from underneath his jaw. The second blow was hard enough that this time some of the shattered flesh actually fell away.

Transparent or not, somewhere inside that head was a brain. If they could shatter it, he doubted even the boy's silver blood would be able to repair him.

Jack reached into his jacket to pull out another handful of knives, and as his eyes narrowed to take aim, he felt a hand grip his arm. "Anubis," he said, without looking up. "Haven't you already caused me enough regret today?"

"Eschaton needs to die," he growled. "I think you know that."

The jackal clearly thought that Jack had some hidden good inside him—something worth saving. He knew better, so why was he helping Anubis? What was in it for *him*? This altruism was dangerous nonsense for both of them. "He's the man I work for."

Jack twisted out of Anubis's grip and swept out his arm. He could feel the blade grazing the jackal's skin, although he was unsure if he'd managed to cut more than leather.

He should have pushed harder, but it was obvious that despite his brain knowing better he still didn't have it in his heart to kill the man.

Anubis's punch connected hard, followed quickly by a second blow. Before there could be a third, Jack spun around and threw out his elbow, catching his opponent on the jaw, although not with the solidity he would have preferred. Finishing his turn, he hit Anubis again, sending him crashing into the pews. He almost felt bad as the jackal lost his balance and sank to the floor.

Jack considered running, and then turned to see the unconscious form of Eschaton. He frowned as he stepped forward: self-sacrifice wasn't his style, but it seemed that his newly formed conscience was keeping hard at work trying to get him killed.

Jack put his hands on the gray man's shoulders and looked up. The Shell had his hands wrapped tightly around Nathaniel's neck, choking the life out of him.

Or attempting to. The boy made a fighting move Jack had never seen before, slipping his arms inside of the Shell's and pushing outwards. Having freed himself from the machine's deadly grasp, Nathaniel followed the graceful movement with a desperate one, shoving the metal man away from him with both hands.

They stumbled in opposite directions—the mechanical man teetering backwards on his wheels until he banged against the first row of pews where Murphy was already managing to regain some semblance of consciousness.

Nathaniel fell hard against the remains of the glass and metal cage. Most of the smoke it contained had already floated up toward the ceiling or had been burned away, but enough remained to allow for a steady stream of the black gas to trickle out and onto the floor.

It quickly flowed around both the transparent boy and the metal man, and where it touched Nathaniel's skin it caused it to turn back to the alabaster color it had been when Jack had seen him in the park.

Jack yelled at Murphy. "Get over here and help me, you pathetic potato eater."

The Irishman stumbled toward him, still a little bit groggy from the last attack, but not too much the worse for wear. "What's going on?"

"Eschaton's purified pet was about to burn us all to death."

Murphy looked down at the unconscious figure of the gray man. Jack could practically see the calculations going on inside the Bomb Lance's head. They were undoubtedly the same ones running through his: live or die, save their leader or run.

They were both men of expediency, but Jack once again found his conscience winning out. "We *need* to do this, Murphy. Now grab on, and let's get him out of here."

Eschaton's flesh was even more rock-like than Jack remembered, and he seemed as heavy as a boulder, as well. Even with both men tugging as hard as they could, he seemed to barely budge.

For a moment Jack considered trying to drag Eschaton through the back door and out into the courtyard.

It was certainly closer, although there was no way to know if there was any safety to be had out there. He knew le Voyageur had taken over the space to build one of Eschaton's other experiments, but he had no idea if he'd be working there now.

Worse still, Nathaniel and the Shell were in their way, and it was getting hotter by the second. He looked up to see that the boy had risen up, and now had the metal monster's head between his hands. With no one to save it, the Shell was letting out a pathetic noise that landed somewhere between a whine and a scream.

Jack tugged at Eschaton's frame with renewed urgency. They'd have to get him up the ramp and out the door. "Pull, damn you," he yelled at Murphy.

The Irishman sneered and grunted, but the yelling seemed to have some effect. Eschaton began sliding across the floor. Soon they had him moving up the ramp that led toward the exit.

Hearing the Shell's whining growing louder, Jack looked up to see that things were not going well for the metal-covered man.

"I'm sorry, Hughes," Nathaniel said with what sounded like a genuine note of regret, "but this madness has gone more than far enough." The boy's arms were fully silver now, and their heat was travelling straight through the metal. A terrible charnel-house smell invaded Jack's nostrils: the scent of cooked meat and rotting flesh.

It only took a few more seconds for the screaming to stop, but it still managed to seem endless.

And then something inside of the Shell ruptured with a crack. The metal on its chest burst open, spattering Nathaniel with a dark liquid that might have once been blood.

Whatever sad force had been keeping it in its terrifying state of half-life was now gone, and the creature toppled to the floor.

Jack realized that he and Murphy had both been standing mesmerized by the scene in front of them, and it wasn't until Nathaniel began to turn toward him that he remembered the boy's promise to do him in. It was well past time to go.

As Jack let go of Eschaton he felt slightly cheered by the fact that he seemed to have overcome his current bout of conscience. He was sure that, all things considered, Nathaniel would much rather have Murphy than him, and he turned to run from the room, leaving the Irishman behind as a sacrifice.

But just as he began his pirouette, it was interrupted by a familiar pair of hands that roughly grabbed his wrists and pinned them behind his back.

The scent of leather and sweat clearly marked his captor as Anubis, as did the voice in his ear. "You're not getting away that easily."

"Run, Murphy," Jack said, resigning himself to his fate.

Chapter 14

All Turns to Ruin

A smile crossed Sarah's sleeping face as she slowly came back to consciousness. Her first thoughts were of being with Emilio on the roof as the sun had risen. The kissing, the touching, and the desire.

She could still feel the scrapes across her skin that had finally led her to suggest that they head back into the house, and into her bed.

And as she recalled the rest, another feeling overtook her, blowing across her thoughts like a dark storm. "What have I done?" Sarah said, whispering to herself.

There was no denying it or turning back—Sarah was a ruined woman now. For years she had been told by everyone important in her life—with the notable exception of Sir Dennis (who had strenuously avoided any mention of sex)—that anyone who ever committed the sinful act outside of the sanctity of the marriage bed, as she just had, would surely find the full wrath of God coming down on their head. And yet, here she was, no more or less struck down by the wrath of the Almighty than she had been the night before. But the day was still young . . .

"I may regret this," she had said to Emilio. And now that regret had come.

She had let herself be seduced by the man who was now sleeping far too comfortably and peacefully on the other side of the massive bed. She looked at his sleeping face, dimly visible in the gloomy light of the cloudy day that crept through the curtains and into the room. But even that weak glow was more than enough to reveal too much.

She buried her face in the sheets, hoping to smother a feeling that seemed to be building up to become either tears or screaming. Either way, she wasn't going to have Emilio waking up to the sounds of shouting from the woman he had been so intimate with the night before. Even if he was the man who had ruined her, he had also become, through death, love, and other irrevocable acts, the most important person in her entire life. It wouldn't do to upset him.

Spinning herself the other way, Sarah spent a few unproductive minutes attempting to will herself back to sleep. After all, if *she* could be the one to be woken up by *him*, it would all certainly be far less awkward. She could let him take the blame for all this. After all, when was it ever truly the woman's fault in these situations? And yet, she'd not really tried to stop him, had she?

What would her friends say? What would her father have said? Only Jenny was left to have an opinion.

Maybe God somehow punished her for her acts prematurely, ruining her life because he knew that she would eventually come to this. Was that even possible?

Sarah had never been much for the intricacies of theosophical debate. She had attended church for most of her life, but the Stanton family seemed more than content to simply sit in the pews and listen to whatever issue the pastor was attempting to unravel.

Now she thought back, trying to remember if she'd ever heard anything about the possibility of predetermined suffering.

No matter what the divine truth might have been, there was no undoing it. And at least now that they *had* done it, they could do it again . . .

Sarah shook her head firmly, trying to rid her mind of these new and even more seductive thoughts.

When the simple shaking didn't seem to work, she threw back the sheets and pulled herself upright. The cold air raised goose pimples across her skin, reminding her that she was entirely unclothed.

"Hello, Sarah," Tom said, his painted eyes staring at her from just beyond the foot of the bed.

Sarah, already scandalized, let out a stifled scream and then reflexively grabbed the sheets, covering herself before she realized that not only did Tom not have eyes to see her, he probably had as little prurient interest in her naked body as he did in a screwdriver, or a hammer, or a wrench . . . or something else that would have entirely no representational relationship to any part of the human anatomy whatsoever—if she could have thought of it.

Gathering her composure, Sarah glared at the mechanical man for a moment. Tom did not move, even when she angrily, and silently, tried to shoo him away with the back of her hand, hoping that he would at least have the common decency to leave the room until she was decent.

Instead, he spoke again. "We need to . . . talk." His voice strummed out his words with his usual even tone. Unlike the well-mannered machine he had once been, the new Tom was seemingly completely unaware of decorum, and was steadfastly ignoring Sarah's attempts to get him to leave before he woke the man sleeping next to her.

Hadn't her life already become complicated and corrupted enough without having Emilio waking up to see Tom in their bedroom? Especially now that she was . . . that they were . . .

Well, what were they now? *That* would be an important question to bring up with Emilio when he was awake—which wouldn't be now, she hoped.

"Shhh!" she hissed back at the mechanical man, realizing that if she didn't make at least *some* noise Tom would continue to talk.

"I apologize for startling you," Tom replied in a diminished glissando. Emilio twitched in response, but appeared to be content to remain unconscious—at least for the moment.

Still, it would be best if she could get the mechanical man out of her bedroom.

Sarah looked around frantically for something handy to wear. Distracted in the heat of the moment, it seemed that she had left nothing that could act as clothing within reach of the bed.

Finally Sarah saw one of the faded oriental robes that she had adopted. It was sitting on an oak chair a few feet away, doing a passable imitation of old upholstery.

As she moved toward the edge of the bed, intent on retrieving her garment, Sarah was reminded yet again that she was still quite naked underneath the bedclothes. And underneath (or perhaps because of) the shame, the wanton voice in her head reminded her that being naked was actually giving her a bit of a thrill.

Sarah tried to shut down the sly voice, but it seemed that now that this more sensual side of her had been awoken, it—like her—was not going to go back to sleep so easily.

Not that Sarah had managed to live nineteen years without any interest in the idea of sex, but she had always considered Sally Norbitt as the would-be libertine. The girl had been so utterly obsessed by the idea of what it would be like to "be" with a man that Sarah often wondered if she would be able to wait until marriage to find out.

She was sure that if Sally had been here now, the girl would pepper Sarah with lewd and uncomfortable questions.

Or perhaps, by now, her friend was engaged herself, stealing kisses with her husband-to-be, and looking forward to the wedding night, when Sally would finally lose her chastity and find the answers to all her questions.

But Sarah would never know for sure. After last night, she had finally fallen so far that the world she had known would forever be denied to her.

Being honest with herself, her father's relationship with the Paragons had always meant that the Stanton family was eternally on probation with New York's proper society. And although they *were* wealthy, money could only get you so far.

With both parents dead, even if she wasn't being hounded by a maniacal villain, returning to her old life would have meant being quickly married off to a man of lesser standing. She shivered at the thought of the shriveled up old ne'er-do-well she might have been matched up with. With her luck, she would have ended her days married to Helmut Grüsser.

But for better or worse, that life, and her old friends, were all closed to her now. Instead Sarah was here, trapped under the bedclothes, terrified to reveal herself to a mechanical man. It was as laughable as it was childish.

Throwing caution—and covers—to the wind, Sarah rolled herself out into the cool morning air. She felt goose bumps rising across her skin as she raced for the robe. As she scooped it up and used it to cover herself, she saw that Tom's head had turned toward her. Even though she knew he couldn't actually *see* her, she felt the surprisingly warm sensation of a blush rising up in her cheeks.

Her "slippers"—a threadbare pair of sheepskin-lined men's boots—lay nearby. She stepped into them and walked toward the exit with a practiced clumsy trot, leaving both Tom and Emilio behind.

While Emilio remained asleep, it took Tom only a few seconds to follow her out into the hall. Still stomping toward the front door, she heard him before she saw him, his piano wire flesh giving off a faint musical hum with every step he took. When she heard the thick rug that acted as her doorway thump closed against the wall behind him, she turned around and gave the mechanical man a stern look. "Just what did you think you were doing?"

"I came into your . . . room to . . . talk with you."

"And how long were you watching me before that?" She pointed an accusing finger at him, and could see that she was shaking with anger, and perhaps shame. The feeling was even more powerful now than she had imagined it would be when she was hiding in the bed.

"I cannot . . . see you."

"Don't give me that nonsense," she said, poking the extended finger at his chest. "See, hear, whatever it is you do, you're not supposed to be sneaking around in a lady's bedroom when she's sleeping."

"Again I . . . apologize." There was another pause. Longer than she had come to expect from him. "You were with . . . Emilio."

Sarah's eyes widened. Was this an accusation? Jealousy?

But when she thought about what to say next, she realized she had no idea what would be an appropriate response. She was still trying to come to grips with what had happened the night before, and now she found herself being interrogated about her relationships by a man made of metal. "That is entirely none of your business."

"I . . . apologize," he repeated. "It seems that I . . . cannot do anything . . . right today."

Sarah sighed. She considered Tom her friend, but whether this was a "new" Tom or not, she was beginning to realize just how little time she had actually spent with the metal man outside of the presence of Sir Dennis.

Being alone with him now, she was beginning to appreciate that he was like a child in many ways: easily confused by people, while curious about human emotions much the way that Adam must have been before he swallowed the apple. "No, Tom," she said, swallowing the tattered remnants of her pride, "I should apologize. I know you're not trying to hurt me."

"I only . . . wish for you to be . . . happy . . . Sarah."

She smiled at the thought of Tom having wishes. "I am happy, I think. Only, it's a very complicated world for a woman."

"And for a . . . machine man as well."

She laughed, and then felt a sudden jolt of surprise. "Was that a *joke*, Tom?"

He nodded. "Now that I have learned that I can . . . create things, I have been trying to make . . . humor. I think that it can . . . relax people."

Maybe Sarah had underestimated him. "That would rather depend on the joke, I think."

"It worked for . . . you."

"But it won't always," Sarah said, remembering how often her father's occasional off-color remarks had made her mother put on a grim smile that was hardly genuine happiness.

"I will keep that in . . . mind," he said. The subtleties of human interaction were still a curiosity to him. Although, as far as Sarah knew, they were beyond the reach of *any* man or machine.

"Now, Tom," she said, grabbing one of his metal hands in hers, "since I am awake, dressed, and outside of my bedroom, what is it that I can do for you?"

"I have . . . created something that I would very much like to . . . show you."

"What is it?"

"Follow me." Tom walked through the parlor and directly toward the front door. Sarah frowned when she realized she'd be walking across dirt yard in nothing more than a tattered robe and a pair of oversized boots. She had only managed to get dressed for a chat in the hallway, and now her already-inappropriate outfit was suddenly being pressed into service for an outing.

Not only were the shoes difficult to maneuver in, she had hoped to keep the boots clean enough to remain "inside shoes." The boots were sturdy enough to keep the soles of her feet from being penetrated by the occasional nuts and bolts that managed to appear everywhere in the house. "Where are we going, Tom?"

"Not far," he said, swinging open the front door, and letting her through. The breeze sent the wind up into her robe, reminding her again how utterly underdressed she was.

It took only a few steps before she determined that they were heading to a small wooden building a few yards out from the house. It had been built as a temporary workshop where Emilio could work on restoring the machinery that had been rescued from the theater before pressing it into service.

Sarah had actually suggested that they separate the primary workshop from the house entirely, sealing them off from the scents of oil and smoke that often wafted in from Emilio's current studio.

"I hope that you will not be . . . upset with me."

Sarah didn't like the sound of that. "I think that's going to rather depend on what you've done."

As they reached the shop steps, Sarah saw that things had come along much farther than she realized. Sitting in the back was the large boiler that Emilio was constructing to provide steam power to his tools. The tank stood upright, seemingly only waiting to be finished and painted. The wood platform that it sat on was also new, and there was an overwhelming scent of pine and fresh paint.

The space was so different from Darby's cave underneath the Hall of Paragons, and yet its purpose was the same. Sarah wondered just how much trouble Emilio could get into with his own laboratory—especially with Tom now here to help him.

The mechanical man pulled a tarp off a nearby workbench. What she saw sitting on it made her heart flitter. "This is for . . . you . . . Sarah." It was a gun.

The design of the weapon was similar to the one that her father wore, and had clearly been constructed with a memory of that weapon as its intention.

But the weapon was similar to the gun that she had once carried, as well: sticking out from the bottom of the gun was a metal sphere that had been screwed into the handle, clearly designed to hold fortified steam.

"You've replaced it . . ." Sarah's words trailed off as she picked up the gun from the table and held it in her hand. Feeling the comfort of it against her palm, she knew this was a newer version of the pneumatic weapon that Tom had given her the day the Darby mansion burned to the ground.

She had managed to use that weapon only a few times before it had run out of steam (and almost gotten her killed), but it had also allowed her to steal Tom's heart away from Eschaton, and saved her and Emilio from being skewered by the Bomb Lance on the ferry. And she had to admit, holding the weapon in her hand made her feel more like the Adventuress than she had in months.

The new model of the gun was slightly lighter than the previous one had been, while still somehow feeling more solid as well.

The gun's design was different also. It looked far more like a flintlock than a Colt revolver, and instead of using a cylinder to set the weapon's strength (as the previous gun had) there was a small dial by the grip that she could roll back and forth easily with her thumb. As she turned it, the small circle of brass switched positions with a satisfying click.

There was also a number clearly marked on each position, allowing her to tell just how strong a blast the weapon was capable of—something else her previous weapon had lacked.

As unladylike as the urge might be, she felt like hugging the weapon to her. She hugged Tom instead, her arms pressing into the metal strings that wrapped around his body. "Thank you so much, Tom! I can't believe you created this for me! Why would you ever think I might be unhappy about that?"

Just as Tom was about to reply, Sarah heard a distant shout from somewhere outside. At first she imagined it was someone arriving to drop off some scrap to the junkyard. Hopefully Emilio would be awake by now, and would take care of it.

The voice yelled again, and she realized that it sounded quite distressed.

"Sarah . . ." Tom said. "I think someone needs our help." The yelling was louder now, and Sarah realized that whoever it was, he was shouting out her name.

Sticking her head out the door, she saw a fat man crawling across the field. His clothes were drenched and burned, and his fingers were pulling against some kind of collar that seemed to be cutting into his neck. "Sarah! Gut God it is you! You are alive."

She took a few cautious steps before recognition hit her like a hammer blow. "Grüsser!" she shouted, and sprinted toward him, one of her boots flying free as she ran.

As she crossed the field there was a sound like a shriek from the sky. "No! You must run . . ." the man said, and then collapsed onto the dirt.

As she looked up something flew by Sarah's head. It was a large black spot, moving far too fast for her to make any sense of it. "A bird?" she muttered, and then a moment later the workshop she had just been standing in exploded behind her.

The force of the blast picked her up and tossed Sarah through the air before she crashed to the ground. Sarah landed hard against the cold earth, the force of her impact slapping the air from her lungs. As she sat there, trying to regain her breath, chunks of wood and metal rained down around her, the debris from what had been the shed only moments ago.

Despite the terror of the situation, Sarah could feel a familiar thrill coursing through her veins. The first time she had ever truly experienced it, that morning on the bridge, the sensation had seemed alien and terrifying.

The surge of energy that travelled from head to toe was invigorating; a sensation of power and possibility that only arrived when Sarah was fighting for her life.

It told her to get up, it told her to prepare to fight, and it told her to *win*! And as she listened to the sound of it in her head, she realized that it spoke in almost the same tones as the voice of temptation that had let Emilio pull her into bed the night before.

By the time the fragments of the shed had finished raining down around her, she was sitting up. She turned to look at the place where the building had been. All that remained was a shattered shell, containing nothing but rising smoke and flame.

Getting to her feet, Sarah staggered back toward the building, discovering that her lost boot had also survived destruction. She slipped her foot back into it, and walked closer.

"Tom!" she shouted desperately, but there was no response. The thumping in her heart increased as she looked around for any remains of the metal man—something that might let her know his fate. But the smoke was too thick, and she began to cough as she got too close, her eyes stinging from the acrid smoke.

"Grüsser!" If she couldn't find the Automaton she'd need to at least discover if the Prussian had survived the attack.

Walking a few yards, she discovered the Submersible lying on his back. It was impossible to tell if he was dead or alive, but at least it seemed that all his limbs and his head still remained in their proper places.

Sarah ran to him and knelt down by his side. "Grüsser, are you all right?" She gave the portly man a shove, and he let out an oddly reassuring groan.

His clothes were soaking wet, as if he had simply risen up out of the river itself before he had arrived here. And perhaps he had: he was the Submersible, after all. His appearance had come only moments before the bomb that landed in the shed. And there was something attached to his back; a large box of some sort that seemed almost to reach out like a spider, with rings that encircled his waist and arms, with a thick pole that rose out of it, connected to a ring surrounding his throat.

She peered directly down into Grüsser's face, marveling at the fact that even though he was still clearly heavy, the man appeared to be oddly gaunt, the folds of his chin less full then they had been the last time she had seen him. "Sarah!" he croaked out, a pained smile forming on his chubby features. "You're alive."

She nodded. "Of course I am, and it's good to see you alive, as well." It was very surprising to hear herself saying those words, and shocking to realize that they were true!

He pulled himself up, a disturbing wheezing sound coming from his throat. "Le Voyageur is here . . . we must run!"

Seeing that the Paragon had survived had raised a thousand questions, but hearing the Frenchman's name had thrown them all out of her head except for a single one: "But then, why are you here?"

"He has my ship. I've escaped, but . . ."

"Wait here," Sarah said, "I'll get help." She stood and turned toward the house, intent on finding Emilio.

"There's no time," she heard the Prussian shout to her.

She had taken only a few steps toward the main house when the same tearing sound that had preceded the last attack once again split the air.

Preparing for what would shortly follow, Sarah dropped to her knees, her hands covering her head.

The second shell landed a few yards away, crashing straight into the house. Despite her attempts to muffle the sound, the blast was deafening. For an instant the walls of the main house seemed to almost bulge as they tried to hold in the force of the blast, then they peeled apart, releasing a devastating blossom of orange fire with bright yellow tips, and black smoke at its center.

As the deadly flower moved closer, Sarah closed her eyes. She was prepared for death, but didn't have any desire to see it reach her. Then, she felt something hard pressing against her shoulders and suddenly she seemed to be floating through the air. Was this what it felt like to float up to heaven? It seemed different than she had imagined it.

When she opened her eyes the dream was shattered. She was tumbling, not climbing. The world turned from blue to brown over and over again, her vision filtered through strands of silver wires that seemed to have wrapped around her, like some kind of fine metal fabric. "Tom!" she shouted a moment before the two of them impacted earth, the wind knocked out of her as she bounced hard against the mechanical man's metal frame.

They continued to roll, and Sarah no longer felt invulnerable, but fragile instead. The image of herself as a tiny bird in a metal cage fluttered through her head as they finally rolled to a stop.

For a moment she simply sat there, unable to move from the Automaton's wired embrace. "Tom!" she yelled more urgently, making it more of a scream than a shout. "Let me go!"

She felt something release, and she tumbled onto the ground. Considering the state of the robe as she stood up, she doubted that her dignity had survived intact, but there were bigger issues than her dignity to be considered.

She looked around for Grüsser. He had landed only few yards away, his clothes smoldering from the flames. Sarah ran and knelt down next to him. She wondered if the Frenchman had intentionally been targeting him. Or if *she* was the one the old man had been trying to destroy, and the Prussian had simply been in the way.

She looked back to the burning house. Although it had fared better than the shed had, the flames were already consuming what remained of the building. The fire was working its way up reams of material that covered the walls, sending a twisting column of smoke up into the sky.

She felt a twinge of longing as she realized that somewhere inside the conflagration her costume was being burned up in the fire, not to mention the bed where she had so recently lost her innocence.

"Emilio!" she said with a sudden panic. The last time she had seen him he had still been sleeping.

Sarah saw that the laboratory was still intact, although a shocking amount of smoke was pouring out from the windows and underneath the roof.

She tried to move toward it, but the smoke was thick. Then she heard a pounding sound from somewhere inside the wall of the train car.

The heat was intense, and she could feel the sweat pouring out from her skin as she got close, as if it were being squeezed from her.

She tried to grab the handle, but it was too hot to hold.

Instead, a pair of welcome metal hands wrapped themselves around the steel. "It seems that you and I are bad . . . luck when it comes to the . . . integrity of . . . buildings."

She felt less surprise than she thought she might at Tom's safe return. "This is not the time for humor, Tom. I need you to save Emilio." She vaguely remembered Darby telling her that surviving explosions would be exactly the sort of thing that you needed to invent a mechanical man *for*.

Tom seized the edge of the train-car door and shoved it open with terrifying ease, the iron lock screeching for an instant, before twisting away and popping it off into the air as if it were constructed from nothing more than tin.

As the door slid back a cloud of smoke billowed out from the lab. Sarah found herself stumbling backwards even as she saw Tom dive in.

She found herself being pushed back farther and farther by the flames and the smoke, and after finally finding what seemed to be a safe distance, more long seconds dragged past as she waited for someone to emerge.

It was only an instant after Sarah was convinced that both man and machine had succumbed to the flames that Emilio came stumbling out.

His head was covered by a leather mask with long rubber hoses dangling from either side. He was moving backwards, dragging a large wooden case behind him, his gloved hands pulling it by a steel handle that had been bolted to its side.

A moment after, Tom reappeared. He joined Emilio and simply grabbed the box, hoisting it into the air and running out into the yard.

Emilio ran directly toward Sarah, pulling off his mask as he got near. "Viola?" Emilio shouted as he got closer. "Have you seen her?"

Sarah shook her head, and felt a twinge of guilt. She hadn't thought of the girl after the first shell struck.

She hadn't seen Emilio's sister since she had confronted her attempting to seduce Tom. But surely she wasn't still inside the house? The idea that Viola would have to pay *again* after having been so badly hurt in the last fight seemed almost beyond imagining.

Almost in defiance of her thought, something inside the building ignited with a throaty "woomf." It was a sound that Sarah remembered from when the Darby house had been destroyed. She ducked down, expecting to once again be pelted with shrapnel, but this time the building gave way upward instead of outward, releasing a tremendous fireball up into the air as the roof disintegrated.

Emilio let out a terrible scream. For an instant Sarah worried that he might have been hurt, but as she saw tears in his eyes she realized that it was a yell of frustration and anger. He had just lost not only everything that he had worked for, but the only family he had left in the world.

Sarah ran to him and grabbed his arm. "Don't worry, Emilio. I'm sure she's safe." The words sounded hollow as she spoke them, but the idea of giving up hope seemed so much worse.

"Yes, Sarah." Emilio nodded, but the tears in his eyes, and the defeated tone of his voice, were in complete disagreement with his words. Worse yet, his expression and posture made it clear that he believed they were already defeated.

Sarah could feel his depression threatening to roll over her like a wave. The girl might be dead or alive, but Sarah realized she wasn't about to sacrifice her own life, or that of the man she loved, to find out. She grabbed the arm of his jacket and pulled him forward. "Come on, Emilio, we need to go before he fires again."

"Not to worry . . ." Grüsser's grim voice shocked her, and Sarah jumped slightly before she turned to see the Prussian standing behind them. His white hair and outlandish beard had both been singed by the heat of the fire, but he seemed otherwise unharmed. "My ship hast only *zwei* guns, und I don't zink the Frenchman can reload zem without my help."

The mechanical man walked toward them and Grüsser's eyes grew wide. "Ach, das ist der Automat! Is that really you, Tom?"

"Mostly," the machine replied, and gave a quick shake to the hand that had been offered to him.

"I vunder if der Automaton might help me to remove zis." Grüsser pointed awkwardly to the ornate device attached to his back. "Der vasser has expanded it a bit, but I think in short time it will strangle me again."

"What is it?" Sarah asked.

Grüsser made a most unpleasant face at that question. "An unending nightmare that made me der Eschaton's prisoner."

Tom reached out and placed his hand against the ornate box on the back of the device. "What does it . . . do?" he said, even as metal fingers tapped against the veneer of case, exploring its purpose. The inlaid wood had already been damaged by its trip through the water, and Tom peeled it away.

"He called it der Chronal Suit. It chokes me to death, slowly—every day."

"I see," Tom said, nodding. After rubbing the surface for few more moments, he grabbed the device with both hands. For a moment it seemed as if all he was doing was holding it, and then the box began to crumple underneath the metal fingers.

"*Danke*, Tom, I . . ." The box began to tick loudly, and Grüsser's eyes went wide. Sarah could see that the collar around the Prussian's neck had suddenly dug hard into his flesh. His hands clutched at his throat, but the device was already too tight for him to get any purchase, or even allow enough air to escape for him to make a sound.

"Hold . . . still," Tom said, his voice sounding even more calm and emotionless than usual.

"Tom, you're choking him!" Sarah was shouting, although she was unable to think how she might actually be able to save the poor man if Tom couldn't.

"Just a . . . moment please . . . Sarah," Tom said. She could see him driving his fingers further into the device, almost prying apart the steel at the seams. Tiny rivets pinged and popped as the pressure tore them apart. "I believe I can . . . disable the mechanism."

With a little more effort the metal began to open, revealing a tiny gap. Once it had reached half an inch in width, Tom lifted up his right hand and held his fingers over the crack. After a moment the wires that had covered his fingers began to expand out in long loops that twisted their way inside.

Grüsser sagged forward, pulling the broken box away from the wires. Sarah raised a hand up to her mouth in shock: the poor man was clearly dying. But before the Prussian could fall any farther, Tom's left hand shot out and grabbed him, hoisting him upward by his arms—shifting the man's body forward until the box on his back was again just underneath the Automaton's fingers, the wires twitching once again. "Just a few more . . . moments Herr . . . Grüsser."

Sarah felt as if she should say something, either offering advice to Tom, or comforting the Paragon. But if Grüsser was in pain he was in no position to say so.

She wondered if the old Tom would have been as willing to let Grüsser suffer, even if his intent was to save him. She decided that either way it was a question that she didn't really want to know the answer to. Still, if Tom couldn't save him, then they could at least let the poor man die in peace.

The Prussian lifted up his head, and Sarah let out an involuntary yelp as she saw his eyes practically bulging out of his head, and a purple tongue sticking out from his lips.

Just as she thought the man was about to expire, there was a metallic "ping" and Tom jerked his hand violently upward, pulling out not only the wires, but a series of gears that had been tangled into them like insects in a metallic spider's web. As each one was pulled out of the box the machine let off another loud pinging sound.

But it was only after the twelfth gear was pulled free that the collar popped open. For a moment there was nothing, and then Grüsser let out a gasp that was easily the loudest Sarah had ever heard—as if the man were trying to swallow all the air in the world.

Tom lowered the Prussian slowly to the ground, leaving the still-gasping Paragon on his hands and knees.

"*Danke,*" Grüsser rasped out between coughs. "I am . . . finally free . . . of zis . . . cursed thing." He tugged at the metal straps binding his body and pulled the frame free, leaving him dressed only in a soiled shirt that she realized he must have been wearing ever since the device had been attached to him. "*Danke,* Tom."

"Now," said Emilio, with a raw edge in his voice, "if you could only find a way to save my sister."

Tom turned to face the water. "You will be pleased to . . . hear that . . . Viola was not in the . . . house."

Emilio shook his head and stomped toward the Automaton. "You'd better be sure of that, metal man."

"She left last . . . night."

Sarah turned to look out in the direction that Tom was facing, and saw that something was heading directly toward them from the river.

"Why would she do that?"

"Because she was . . . angry with me," Tom said.

Emilio made what was almost a growling noise in response, and Sarah grimaced as she realized that once again the Italian girl had managed to throw everyone into conflict—this time without even being there.

"And did she tell you where did she go?" Emilio asked.

"No," the mechanical man replied.

Sarah had some thoughts, but now was not the time to express them. "Grüsser, isn't that your ship?" she asked as she pointed at the object cutting through the river.

"*Ja*," the Prussian replied. "So zen, perhaps ve should run."

The boat was clearly headed toward the beach, although Sarah couldn't imagine what damage it could do to them without its weapons.

She expected it to stop at the land's edge, but instead it continued up from the river, the deck rising up until the vehicle revealed that it was no longer simply an aquatic device.

Underneath were two sets of locomotive wheels, but they had been fitted with a geared belt that allowed it to crawl up on the land without tracks underneath.

The design was utterly ingenious, and she instantly wondered why no one had thought of it before.

She could make out the hunched form of the mad Frenchman riding on top of it. Sarah had known this moment was coming, but she'd hoped they would have been more prepared when it came. Now they had once again been reduced to desperation.

The sound of the Frenchman's voice spread across the yard. "SARAH STANTON, YOU HAVE WHAT WOWD ESCHATON WANTS, YOU WIWW NOW GIVE IT TO ME!" She recognized the odd sound as from the amplifier that the Iron-Clad had once employed.

Le Voyageur's usual ridiculous speech was even more outlandish when amplified, but his intent remained utterly clear, and he was backing up his demands by targeting them with what appeared to be a very large brass gun, attached to the main deck of the ship.

When he pulled the trigger, a series of explosions ripped across the yard, ending with another round of destruction that collapsed the burning remains of the house. As it fell over, a column of smoke and embers climbed up into the sky.

"What is *that*?" Emilio said, grabbing the Prussian by his soiled shirt. "I thought you said he had no weapons!"

"I am sorry! I zought ze gun vas not functional, but it is clear zat der vere some . . ."

Sarah considered running, but she knew it would be a foolhardy decision. As the vehicle rumbled closer it was clear that if the Frenchman had wanted them dead he would already have killed them with the first volley. They were at his mercy. "Tom, go ahead and give the man what he wants," she said.

The mechanical man gave her a barely perceptible nod and dropped into a run. With only a few yards now separating them from the amphibious ship, it took only a few bounds before the wires wrapped around the Automaton's body had given him the bounce that he needed to fly through the air and land straight on the ship's deck.

As the Automaton hurtled toward the platform where the Frenchman stood, she thought she could actually see a smile on the old man's face. It puzzled her only for an instant, and then le Voyageur lifted up another weapon. He had been expecting this!

The device was a metal rod, covered at regular intervals with white ceramic rings. Before she could even wonder what kind of weapon it was, the rod spat forth a massive volley of lightning that caught the Automaton in midair, the electricity drawn almost hungrily to the mechanical man's metal frame.

Tom crashed hard onto the deck, his body limp as it tangled itself around the barrel of the gun.

Sarah felt like screaming once again, but she was getting tired of yelling in frustration. "Tom's taken out the gun. Let's get him!"

The three of them ran toward the vehicle, Sarah by far the slowest as she was once again hobbled by her boots. She willed herself to move faster, and as she did, she promised herself that she would never again allow her habits to become as slovenly as they had inside the junkyard house.

She had never believed her mother when she had told Sarah that good grooming was something to be relied on, not discarded, during times of crisis. She believed her now.

Emilio had almost reached the metal rungs on the side of the ship when it rumbled, belched out a cloud of black smoke, and began to rapidly slide into the river. The Italian's shout of "No!" echoed her own thoughts almost perfectly, but despite their desperation none of them were fast enough to reach the ship before it slid back into the water, and began to head down the river.

There was a crackle and a loud, ringing tone as the amplifier returned to life. "ZANK YOU SO MUCH FOW YOUW COWOPEWATION, MISS STANTON. I HAD HOPED TO END ZIS DAY BY KIWWING YOU, BUT I WIWW TAKE MY PWIZE AS CONSOWATION, AND IF YOU SUWVIVE, I WIWW SEE YOU ON ZE OTHER SIDE OF HUMANITY."

Sarah walked toward the shore and stared after the boat. It was far better than staring at the burning remains of the junkyard behind them. As the Submersible's ship chugged down the river, she wondered how they had managed to have been so close.

Emilio turned to Sarah. "So, what do we do now?"

"Ve have lost mein ship," Grüsser said, stating the obvious once again. "Und now they have der mechanical man as well."

"We have nothing," Emilio said, falling cross-legged onto the sand, his shoulders sagging with a level of despair that Sarah had never seen before.

Sarah nodded. They had lost a lot, including Tom. But Sarah had more. "We're going," she said grimly.

"Where?"

"Home," Sarah replied, her resolve stiffening as she realized it was well past time for this. "Back to the Stanton mansion."

She looked down at herself and frowned at her dirty, tattered robe. "But first I'm going to need to find some clothes."

Chapter 15
A Final Judgment

"You killed my father, you killed Sir Dennis—now it's my turn." Nathaniel wrapped his hands around Eschaton's head and reached for the heat inside of him. The power had been coming to him more and more easily, but now—just when he needed it the most—he felt it beginning to fall away.

Reaching deep inside, Nathaniel found more energy and rekindled the fire in his hands. The irony of it was too wonderful to ignore: he was finally going to destroy the man who had ruined his life using the very powers that had been given to him by Lord Eschaton.

For just a single instant, he felt guilty about his actions. Burning a man to death wasn't something a true Paragon would do. It was the act of a villain. But what he held between his hands was a true monster. Whatever he had been before, Eschaton had, through his machinations and intentions, sacrificed his own humanity and turned Nathaniel into a transparent abomination. He would burn Eschaton first, then he would find a way to bring the entire Hall tumbling down on top of him as a tomb.

Just as his heat finally grew back to its full power, Nathaniel felt several impacts against his flesh. The sensation of it was more shocking than painful, and he looked down to discover a series of metal knives sticking out of his skin. They had only penetrated slightly, the tip of each one sending out a web of tiny splinters where it had punctured his flesh.

A moment later the pain arrived, and the tip of each blade sent out a sensation like a wounded tooth, igniting his nerves on fire.

The shock of the sudden sensation made Nathaniel let go of the gray man, and the body slumped to the floor. His hands free and the heat already draining away from his fingers, he reached up and quickly took the blades out.

Almost the instant after he pulled the knives free, he saw the silver under his skin swirl around the damaged flesh, and he felt the pain diminishing.

There were definitely advantages to being the Mercurial Man, although nothing that made it worth having been transformed into a monster.

Dropping the knives to the floor, he looked up to see who had thrown them. The man standing in front of him was tall and thin, with a pencil mustache that only accented his wolfish, dangerous look. He didn't look familiar, but he was clearly one of Eschaton's stooges. "Who are *you*?"

"My name is Jack Knife." Yet another villain with a ridiculous name. But he had to remind himself that this was the world he had chosen to live in.

"And you're one of the Children?"

The man nodded in return.

He was feeling better every second, now. "Well Jack Knife, I'd run if I were you, because once I've burnt out Eschaton's brains I'm going to kill you next." For what it was worth, it wasn't a personal threat. His plan was to kill every one of the sorry muttonheads who had thrown their lot in with the gray man. The world would be better off without them, and with all of Eschaton's Children gone, perhaps there was hope that he could somehow return to a normal life.

Nathaniel took a threatening step forward before he realized that he needed to make absolutely sure Eschaton was dead before he dealt with anyone else.

But he was unprepared for what Jack Knife shouted out next. "Shell! Stop him!"

The remains of Hughes wheeled out of the darkness toward him. It was hard to take the misshapen monstrosity seriously as it trundled along on its wobbling wheels. The metal hands contracted into fists. Nathaniel felt the fire in his hands begin to grow—this wasn't even going to be a fair fight.

"You're a pathet—"

The blow came from nowhere. Whether it had been sheer speed or simply Nathaniel's misplaced bravado that had left him open for the attack, it was impossible to say. Either way, the power of the punch was literally mind numbing, and Nathaniel saw the world splinter as his left eye shattered from the force of the blow.

He felt himself falling backwards, and for an instant he wondered if his entire body might simply shatter like glass when it landed against the hard floor. But before he could find out, a second blow lifted him up again, landing like a hammer blow against his chin. This time he could hear the sound of its impact shuddering through him, and through the haze of confusion he wondered if his jaw had been completely pulverized by the blow.

Acting on pure instinct, Nathaniel stumbled backwards. The desperate maneuver paid off, and he watched with relief as Hughes's steel-clad hands punched into the empty air where his face had been only a moment before. A vague memory passed through the Mercurial Man's addled brains: hadn't Hughes once been a boxer? Perhaps there was more of the man left inside this pathetic creature than he had given credit for.

Taking advantage of the confusion, Nathaniel lashed out at the metal man. He could feel his hands cracking as they struck the monster's steel skin.

The creature moaned and paused for an instant, its twisted face hanging in front of him. Nathaniel balled his hands into fists, but felt himself hesitating before he struck. His fingers were already numb, and if he broke them off what would happen? Just how much damage could his new body rebuild? It was one thing to be a glass monster, and another to be one with only stumps for arms.

Then he looked through the metal slits and caught a glimpse of Hughes's eyes. They were wide open, as if the man had been caught in a perpetual moment of terror. Were the creature's mute cries the remains of Hughes's once-formidable personality screaming for release?

Nathaniel looked down at his fists and saw they had filled with mercury. Perhaps that would allow him to attack without fear of damage. As he pulled his arms back to strike, the Shell's metal-clad hands closed around his throat. His hesitation had cost him his opportunity.

As he reached up to grab the Shell's wrists he suddenly remembered one of the lessons that Wickham had given him in the Oriental fighting arts. He hadn't enjoyed the lessons, but his step-father had told him that the Sleuth knew secrets that had saved *all* their lives at one time or another, and attendance was mandatory.

Putting his hands together, Nathaniel slipped them between the Shell's arms, then pushed them apart. Much to his surprise, and relief, the creature's grip broke as he had intended.

Desperate for a moment's reprieve, he struck out with both arms, hoping to shove the monster away from him. The desperate maneuver worked, but he found his own footing had been less sure than he had imagined, and suddenly Nathaniel realized that he was reeling in the other direction.

Before he could begin to regain his balance, he had landed hard against the remains of the smoke-filled iron cage. Nathaniel could feel the metal twist underneath him as he crashed into it, glass splintering against his own solid skin.

At the same moment his shattered left eye suddenly filled with silver, half blinding him. His body was using its diabolical magic to heal the damage, but the timing was terrible. A part of him wondered about the mechanism of his recovery. Did he have only so much mercury to go around? Then how had he managed to make his whole body glow just a few minutes before?

Turning his head, he saw through his other eye that the missed attack had also thrown the metal-covered man off its center. The Shell teetered on its wheels as it tried to find balance, and the moment it did, it threw itself toward him.

Nathaniel raised his shattered hands out in front of him, hoping to find a way to stop the metal-covered monster from ramming him. His desperate ploy worked better than he had expected, and he found his fingers wrapping themselves around the creature's metal head.

There was an instant of panic as he thought that he might be unable to follow through on his attack, the fire that had come to him so easily only a moment before suddenly retreating from his control. The metal man's head twisted in his grasp, and he could feel an odd clicking sensation coming from inside of it as it tried to break free.

The Shell's fingers wrapped themselves around Nathaniel's wrist. Nathaniel's hands, already half-filled with his silver, flared white, and once again heat began to pour out from his skin.

The effect on the Shell was instantaneous, and the man-machine twitched in his grasp, its hands clenching so hard against his skin that fissures were forming as it tried to break free.

Nathaniel pressed harder, realizing that as powerful as the monster might be, his own strength as a "purified human" had also been amplified.

As the heat from Nathaniel's hands penetrated deeper, the Shell let out a terrifying squeal, like the cry a lobster might make when boiled alive inside its shell.

The silver had gathered halfway up his arms now, and Nathaniel harnessed his limited control over his powers to make himself burn even hotter. If his intent was to kill, then he should go through with the act.

After a few seconds the pathetic screaming began to die away. "I'm sorry, Hughes, but this madness has gone more than far enough." He had once been a Paragon—the least he could do was execute the man humanely.

As he increased the heat Nathaniel felt a rumbling coming up from inside the Shell's body, and a moment later a section of the suit buckled and burst open, a gush of dark liquid spraying out.

Where it struck Nathanial's hands it bubbled and burned away. He found himself suddenly grateful that all he seemed to be able to smell anymore was smoke, as if the whole world was on fire.

He let go and the corpse of the creature crumpled to his feet. Inside of him he could feel the quicksilver shifting again, moving back to finish the job of healing his head and arms that he had called it away from completing.

Nathaniel shook his head slightly with disbelief. Monstrous or not, the corpse that lay in front of him had once been a Paragon. And as ruined as Hughes had become—first ravaged by disease, and then transformed into a monster—there had been a time when he had fought side by side with this man in the name of justice.

As a child, Nathaniel had looked up to the Iron-Clad. And once he had joined the Paragons he had considered the red-haired warrior a kindred spirit: both of them men wrapped in machinery.

He deserved a more respectable death than being burned alive inside his suit: twice, if he were to consider what had happened in the Darby mansion.

Despite Hughes's betrayal, in the end it was Eschaton and his Children that were truly to blame for the atrocities that had been committed here. And now, with the Shell out of his way, it was time to wreak terrible vengeance on the rest of them—starting with Eschaton.

As he turned, he saw that the man with the knives and Murphy were tugging on Eschaton's shoulders, slowly dragging him away. The silver in his left eye finally cleared, and Nathaniel raised his hands as he stepped forward.

Jack saw him first, and turned to run. Although the slim villain had come to his senses in time to realize that Nathaniel was about to make good on his threat, he clearly hadn't counted on the interference of Anubis.

The jackal's face was hidden again—he had somehow regained his mask, as well as some of his confidence. Stepping in, he grabbed Jack's arms and pulled them tight. "Run, Murphy," Jack said.

Nathaniel stepped forward as the Irishman reacted. Looking up to see the Mercurial Man bearing down on him, the Bomb Lance let go of Eschaton and tumbled backwards, landing hard on his rump. "Where do you think you're going, murderer?" Nathaniel's voice was a horrible rasp, which seemed appropriate.

"Damn ya, boy, this isn't a fair fight." The squat man scrabbled backwards up the ramp, moving surprisingly fast. When he'd put a little distance between them the man reached one of his pudgy hands up and inside of his jacket.

"Was it fair when you murdered Sir Dennis?" Nathaniel said, raising his hand up into the air. He had control over his fire now, but even with that, he was beginning to feel drawn, as if he were reaching the edge of his new abilities. His flame was burning brighter than ever, but whatever well of fuel he was drawing this ability from, it was about to run dry.

He reached deeper, and felt a strange new kind of pain. But even if it cost Nathaniel his life, this villain was going to burn—he and *all* the children would be consumed by fire. The time for mercy was past. "You pinned me to the top of the bridge!" He could feel the heat he was bringing forward. The Irishman's whiskers withered and smoked as they began to burn away.

There was fear in the Bomb Lance's eyes, but not as much as Nathaniel would have liked. And then the old man offered something far worse: bravado. "I did that, lad," he said with a chuckle that was in no way a laugh. "I nailed you to that stone like a bug."

Nathaniel moved closer to the object of his fury, ready to kill, and when Murphy revealed his gun there was no chance of escape.

Nathaniel should have simply reached out and burned him, but his instinct for survival had yet to catch up with his new body, and by the time he was ready to complete the attack the barb was already pointing directly at his face. The Irishman smiled as he pulled the trigger.

The harpoon struck Nathaniel square in the forehead, the force of it sending him reeling backwards. He could feel the barb burrowing into him, just as he could feel his mind splitting apart, shattering him into one hundred pieces, and then one thousand.

His splintered mind was now an army of himself, all calling him an idiot. He tumbled, unable to do anything to stop his fall. And yet he could still see, and every tiny mind was overwhelmed with the image of Murphy's twisted grin.

As he crashed into the ground, the barb in his head shifted and the world went dark. And yet, if he still had enough of a mind to recognize that he *couldn't* see, that was something. He still had enough of a mind to recognize that he still had one to lose. And as he gathered his thoughts together, he recognized that he still had enough of a mind to want a drink.

"Now it's *yer* time to die," he heard Murphy's distant voice say. And in the darkness of his thoughts Nathaniel saw the silver sparkles in his blood dancing around him.

There were thousands of them, like fairy lights from a children's story. Whatever this strange world was, it seemed peaceful and beautiful. There was nothing he could do now—no way to save himself. And if this was going to be the end of his life, this might be an acceptable way to pass; free from the pain of the world.

Finally, the tiny lights around him began to dim. Perhaps the mercury inside him had given him up, freeing him to leave consciousness for the final time.

Then came a tugging sensation. Pain flared up inside him as something pulled free.

Another tug. Then a third, fourth . . . Each one was more painful than the last. "Damn you, come out!" he heard a muffled voice say. The fifth time something snapped, and the harpoon that had shattered his mind was pulled free. The world fell back together, roaring in on a locomotive of consciousness that burst through the darkness and shattered the world into light again.

Nathaniel's eyesight returned, and he heaved air back into his lungs, the oxygen seeming to ignite in his throat. Through his broken vision he saw Anubis holding the Bomb Lance's metal harpoon in his hand. The tip of it was twisted and bent. "I thought I'd lost you," the jackal said.

Nathaniel wanted to tell the man that perhaps he should have let him go, but when he tried to speak, what came out of his mouth was pure gibberish. The words were guttural and garbled, like something a baby or a simpleton might say.

"Take a moment," Anubis told him. "Your whole head is silver."

Nathaniel used his second of respite to look around the room to see what had become of his attackers. The Children, it seemed, had abandoned their father. Now only Eschaton remained, and the gray man was still at their mercy, although his hands had started to move.

Anubis stood and looked around the room. He ran to one of the walls, and then reached up to pull down one of the lights that had been screwed into the granite. As it pulled free, a length of cord came with it. It shot out an impressive shower of sparks, and the remaining lights flickered.

Nathaniel could feel just how far he'd managed to overdraw his energy reserves. He was hungry for something, but he wasn't sure what it was. He felt drawn, and clearly he needed sustenance, whatever that might be. "Help me . . ." Nathaniel gasped, finally managing choke out a coherent sound.

"Just one second," Anubis said. He knelt down, but instead of helping him, he grabbed Eschaton and began to turn the gray man over. It was clearly taking a great deal of effort, but quickly enough he had managed to use the length of wire to tie the gray man's hands together behind his back. "Who knows if this will work . . ."

Nathaniel took inspiration, flipped himself over and pulled himself to his feet.

Finding his balance, he took a few unsure steps across the room toward Anubis and Eschaton. "I need a drink." He said it calmly. This was no longer a desire, it was simply a fact.

Anubis looked up at him, clearly annoyed. "Is that all you can think of?"

"My brain was shattered, so it's amazing I can think at all," he said, noticing that there was a threatening sound in his voice that he hadn't intended. "I don't think you understand quite how badly I *need* it."

"Well there isn't any liquor. You'll just have to wait."

Seeing Eschaton lying on the floor, Nathaniel remembered something. He bent down, doing so slowly enough to maintain his balance. He began to dig into Eschaton's clothes. As his hands groped through the gray man's jacket he looked again at his translucent skin. If it had been anyone but him, he had to admit, he would have found it something truly marvelous, in its own way.

And maybe it was time to accept his fate. He still wanted desperately to believe that he could be the man he was before, but it was clear (in every sense of the word) that he was as likely to return to his previous state as a cooked Christmas goose could return to the skies. Having been so utterly transformed he would need to begin to accept it. And if he could figure out some way to control it, it might even be useful.

"A-ha!" His hand had found the hard outline of the flask in Eschaton's vest, and he searched desperately to find the entrance to the pocket where it was contained. When he found it, it took only an instant to remove the silver object and twist open the cap.

Tilting back his head, he brought the bottle up to his mouth and let the liquid pour into him. Through the smoke, he could taste some of the alcohol, even if his sense of taste had been forever altered.

The last of the liquor settled into him and spread through. There was a moment of deep satisfaction as his hunger evaporated.

There was no way that he would have previously been able to consume that much alcohol in a single go before. He let go of the flask, and it bounced loudly as it struck the ground.

What Eschaton had theorized was true; alcohol no longer had the same effect as before his transformation. Instead of the spirits clouding his head, he felt stronger, and his body filled with a sense of satisfied warmth. Liquor was like food to him now! "That's good," he said, although there was some small part of him that missed the fog.

Anubis shook his head. "Eschaton is waking up. We need to figure out what to do with him before the Children get back."

"It's simple," Nathaniel said. "I want him dead." The words had come out of him almost without a thought, but as he said them he felt satisfied with his answer.

"I'm not ready to let you execute him just yet," the jackal told him. "Not in cold blood."

"Blood?" he said mockingly. "Whatever it is that's running through that man's veins, it isn't blood. Neither is what's flowing through me, for that matter.

"And besides, would you let him destroy the world to satisfy your misplaced sense of justice?" What was it that he had become, that he could feel so calm about the idea of taking another man's life?

He had burned the life out of the Shell while what remained of the man had screamed. Now he found himself wanting more.

"Do I have a say?" Eschaton said as he rose up. His voice was clearly weakened, but just by his return to consciousness he already seemed larger.

"You've already been judged and found guilty," Anubis told him. "What we're discussing now is your punishment."

There was a shout from the door. "They're thtill here!" He looked up to see the boy with the broken teeth staring down at them. "And tho ith Lord Ethcaton!"

"Children!" the gray man bellowed with renewed energy, "Come save your lord!"

At the sound of their master's call, men began pushing past the boy and filing into the room. Clearly whatever fear had driven them away no longer held them in its grip. Perhaps they thought Nathaniel had been weakened and was now less of a threat, but he was about to prove them wrong.

"I think the time for talking has passed." Nathaniel said. He stared directly at Eschaton and held up his hand. He let the fire flow into it, refueled by the alcohol he had consumed. "It's time for the execution."

As his arm began to glow, the Children in the front halted. More filed in behind them until there were at least a dozen men. Most of them wore brightly colored costumes, although the material was threadbare and the tailoring shoddy. He recognized a few of them, including the Bomb Lance, who was pushing a man in a wheelchair in front of him. The Irishman's sudden interest in the crippled was not impressive.

Anubis took a step forward, but was held back by the heat. "This isn't right, Nathaniel, and you know it."

Even without seeing the doubt on the man's face he knew what Anubis was feeling. Whatever Eschaton had become, he had clearly once been a man of superior stock. And Anubis, while he had proven himself to be far more than Nathaniel would have ever expected from anyone of a lower class, was not.

But there were reasons that society worked the way it did, with some men on top, and others below. And men without gentility and guidance, no matter how brave or noble their intentions, would always have reservations when it came to carrying out justice on their betters. Nathaniel did not. Or at least, not anymore. "Don't worry, Anubis, I'm quite sure."

Nathaniel let the heat rise up, and everything felt right as it spread throughout his body, almost as if he had finally become this new creature, the Mercurial Man.

Then he felt it slip out of his control, as if there was another person inside of him taking command. The fire within him began to grow, and the silver under his skin expanded down his arms.

Anubis backed farther away, as did the gang of Eschaton's Children. "What are you doing?" the jackal asked.

He looked down to see the ground smoking underneath his feet. "It's not me!" Nathaniel said, hearing the panic in his own voice. He closed his eyes and tried to will himself to halt the silver, but the fire inside of him now had a mind of its own.

When he looked down at Eschaton, he saw that despite the fact that his clothes were now smoking from the heat, the man was smiling as if this was what he had planned all along.

Nathaniel felt the impact of a bullet against his skin the moment before he heard the report of the gun. It was quickly followed by a second shot, and then a third, each one smacking into him hard. He could feel his flesh shattering under the impact.

Whatever had taken control inside of him, it had been disrupted by the damage. His attention broken, the flame flickered out and the light emanating from him began to wane. Perhaps his body couldn't both heal and maintain such a high degree of heat? If that was the case, it meant that the silver that travelled within him had a will of its own—one that was capable of acting despite his intentions. It was a disturbing thought.

It seemed that the shooting had stopped, at least for the moment. Nathaniel checked himself to see what damage had been done to him. There were spiderwebbed cracks across his chest where he had been shot, and the lead itself was clearly visible inside of him, but they seemed to have done him less harm than the Bomb Lance had with his harpoon.

Looking up, he saw that the Children who had entered the gallery with the intention of attacking him were now holding back, unsure whether Nathaniel might still be planning to burn them to death. The man in the wheelchair was holding up his gun and grinning at him. "I think I might have taken the wind out of your sails, son."

Nathaniel's anger made him shake. He would figure out how to reignite himself, and once he did, he would reach out and burn the man down.

The rasping sound of Eschaton's laughter made him turn back to look at the gray man. "You should have let me finish my research, Nathaniel. I might have been able to help you learn more about what you've become." He nodded and raised his eyebrows. "It's certainly interesting."

He stared hard at Eschaton, hoping that his anger might reignite his fire. "You need to die." There was no sense of his heat returning, but if he had to, he'd throttle the life out of the man.

Another bullet struck him, this time directly into the side of the head. He could feel the splinters it left.

Pulling himself back to his feet he turned to take another step toward his attackers.

"No," Anubis yelled at him. "We need to go!"

He looked up at the jackal and saw that he was holding up the wings that Darby had created for him—the suit that had allowed him to fly across the sky in a previous life. With his new body there wouldn't be any need to wear the protective garment with the wings.

"I'll be back for you, monster," he told Eschaton as he ran up to Anubis and heaved the pack up on his shoulders. The suit felt much lighter than it had when he was simply a man. It took only a moment to strap himself in.

"I'll always be ready for you, Mercurial Man. After all, I'm your creator."

He felt his anger rising, but this would be the wrong time to rediscover his flame. "All you've done is given me the tools that I need to destroy you!"

For a moment he was unsure whether or not the suit would still work, but when he turned the dial, the pack flared to life. It seemed that Eschaton was still more interested in studying Darby's work than destroying it.

"Grab onto the straps," Nathaniel told Anubis. When the Negro grabbed onto him, he felt a slight wave of revulsion, but he was no longer a man of any color. What right did he have to judge?

"Where are we going?" Anubis asked.

"Up," Nathaniel replied. The turbines engaged, and they lifted up into the air, slowly at first, and then gaining speed. They crashed through the stained-glass ceiling and into the night.

Chapter 16
Destiny, Delivered

J enny Farrows nodded solemnly as the stone-faced lawyers in their black suits delivered the bad news to the staff of the Stanton mansion.

To be honest, she could barely make heads or tails of what they were actually saying, but the intent was clear: her life as she had known it was now over. She had been expecting it for weeks, and their arrival had been almost a relief.

Jenny had never had much patience for lawyers, and although she tried to never judge people simply by their appearance, these men were clearly, *deliberately* attempting to be imposing. They wore long, almost painfully old-fashioned tailcoats, with tall black hats, and thick mutton chops.

They had arrived at nine o'clock exactly. Their timing had been so precise, in fact, that their knocking had almost been missed under the loud chimes of the old grandfather clock in the hall.

And once the door had been opened, they had pushed past Mr. O'Rourke and marched straight into Alexander Stanton's office. The old butler hadn't really been himself since his employer's death, and he sat sputtering while the lawyers slowly covered the old oak desk with piles of documents. When they took a crowbar to the locked drawers, Jenny had been forced to pull him away before he expired on the spot.

She had tried to fix O'Rourke a cup of strong tea, but he shooed her away, holding a handkerchief to his eyes while complaining about the dust. She left him in the corner, the butler finally looking every one of his far-too-many years.

The lawyers had been only the first of their visitors that day. Next came the movers, their thick leather shoes creaking across the floorboards of the house as they began to pack up the furniture.

Finally the staff was brought to the office and asked to sit in chairs that had been brought from all over the house. Jenny could only imagine how angry Alexander Stanton would have been to have his sanctum invaded by servants. The lawyers were blissfully unaware of their transgression as they droned on and on about severance and final payments.

Despite her lack of understanding, she had begun to cry almost immediately. One thing was made perfectly clear: the Stanton mansion was being emptied and everything inside of it was being sold off. Today would be their last day.

The younger lawyer—and *young* was a relative term—shuffled through his stack of envelopes before picking one and sliding out a sheaf of white pages. He waved them through the air as if the words they contained might fly off the page. "*This*," he said very loudly, " states that young Miss Stanton has been declared legally deceased."

He began to slip the document back into its folder and Jenny found herself wanting to scream. It was, after all, utterly untrue! She had, with her own eyes, seen Sarah Stanton alive and well only a few days ago! But the girl had sworn her to secrecy, and foolishly, Jenny had allowed Sarah to do it.

It was still more of the nonsense, secrets, and lies that had already devastated the Stanton family. At least now, with the house finally gone, there was little more grief that could be added to the never-ending tragedy. Although, Jenny supposed with a grimace, if Sarah were to die for real, she would be the only one who would bear the burden of knowing that she had died twice.

"As the family has no other heirs, the house will be auctioned off to the . . ." The lawyer stopped for a second as a loud, but muffled, shout came from outside the room. He waited a moment, cleared his throat with a loud "ahem," and started again. "As I said, with the death of . . ."

The commotion from the hallway was louder this time, and much closer. Jenny could make out words as well. "Well, I *am* here, and I would like you to get out of *my* house!"

Jenny jumped to her feet, "Sarah!"

"Now really," the lawyer said. "That's nonsense . . ." His words were interrupted by the shuffling of chairs as most of the other members of the house staff leapt to their feet and surged to the library doors.

Jenny had reached them first, and when she threw the door back what she saw instantly brought fresh tears to her eyes. Not only was Sarah Stanton standing in the main hallway—alive and well—but she had brought Emilio, the Italian boy, with her. Grüsser also stood by her side, looking none too well.

Sarah was clearly angry, her finger pointed at the oldest of the trio of lawyers, his crooked mouth hanging down at the shock at what must have been the doubly confusing reality of not only being chastised by a woman, but by one who was, by all accounts, deceased. "But . . . but you're dead," the old counselor sputtered, his shaking hand holding up the envelope that contained legal proof of her demise.

Sarah seemed unimpressed by the man's paper shield. "But as you can see, I am clearly alive. So, if you would be so kind as to have your burly gentlemen return what they've stolen from *my* house, I'll send round *my* attorney to deal with the rest of this nonsense at my earliest convenience."

"Miss Stanton!" Jenny said again.

Sarah turned to Jenny and beamed. "Jenny! I'm so glad to see you still here!" She came and gave her friend a hug. "I'm sorry I've been gone for so long, but I believe it's high time that we got this house back into shape."

For a moment Jenny and the rest of the household staff were left speechless. Unlike the others, however, the only miracle of Sarah Stanton's return was the fact that the girl had finally come to her senses. "But, Sarah, what are you *wearing*?"

The girl's clothes were a mess. She looked as if she had just broken free from an asylum, wearing nothing more than a plain black dress, her hair pulled up into a sad, straggling bun.

"It was the best I could get under the circumstance." For an instant Jenny was glad that Mr. O'Rourke had been unable to answer the door. If he had, he might not have let Sarah in.

When she let go of the girl, Jenny realized the rest of the staff were clearly in some form of shock at the resurrection of their mistress, no matter what she was wearing. Most of them were open-mouthed, and a few clearly had tears in their eyes, Mr. O'Rourke included.

Jenny let her matronly instincts take over, defusing the situation before it exploded into hysterics. "You heard Lady Stanton," she said sternly. "It's time to get back to work!"

The staff glanced over at her, but they were still clearly too entranced by the still-living form of Miss Stanton to fully react. Jenny smacked her hands together twice, unleashing the sharp sound that was her trademark amongst the staff. "Chop chop! There will be plenty of time for gawking later!"

The familiar noise seemed to have broken the spell. Eloise, the youngest scullery maid, looked at Sarah and smiled before she walked through the door. "It's good to have you back, ma'am." The girl paused for a moment before continuing, a blush rising to her cheeks and the hint of a tear in her eye. "And it's good you being alive and all, ma'am."

Sarah took the comment graciously. "Thank you, dear." Jenny couldn't help noticing that between the maid and the mistress of the house, it was the servant who looked far more presentable, but she forced herself to swallow her smile.

If she had let the girl know that she'd found the comment amusing, it would take weeks to undo the damage. "All right, Eloise, we are all happy to see that Miss Stanton has returned to us safe and alive, but it's time to get back to work." She waved her hand in the direction of the girl, who managed to move as if she were somehow being blown by the wind that came from Jenny's waving fingers. She waved it in the direction of the rest of the staff, blowing them all back toward their work like leaves in the wind. "Now the rest of you!"

For a moment there was confusion amongst the rest of the staff. The butlers, footmen, maids and cooks all seemed unsure exactly *what* it was that they were supposed to do next.

Jenny let out a sigh. It had clearly been far too long since there had been anyone in the house to *do* anything for. Jenny gave Sarah a long look, letting her know that she considered her responsible for this terrible state of affairs.

"My friends and I could use something to eat," Sarah said helpfully.

"And a bath, and some clothes!" Jenny added, shaking her head slightly at the thought of the mistress sitting at the head of the dinner table looking like an urchin.

Finding their purpose, everyone moved at once, expertly sliding past each other as they filed out of the office and into the hall.

In an instant they had fallen back into a pattern that had never seemed to quite come together since the day Alexander Stanton had died.

After only a few seconds the room was cleared of the household staff, besides Jenny. She remained behind with Sarah, Grüsser, Emilio—and the lawyers, who simply stood quietly in the corner.

Jenny was so thrilled by Sarah's return, she was still tempted to embrace her again, even if she had only arrived at the last possible moment before they had all been turned out of their home.

Deciding discretion was the better part of valor, Jenny instead nodded in the general direction of the heavily-bearded gentlemen. Even though their features were hidden by their whiskers, there was no denying that the look on their faces was *very* sour indeed.

Sarah returned her nod, and walked over to the lawyers. "Can I help you with anything further today, gentlemen? I'd think you'd have your hands full making sure that all the family belongings were being returned to their proper places."

One of the lawyers turned to her. He was tall and thin, and Jenny thought the man's pinched and glaring features along with the unkempt gray eyebrows sticking over the top of his spectacles made him look a great deal like an owl. "Well, Miss Stanton," he hooted.

"If that is indeed who you are . . ." another one of the lawyers intoned.

"You have picked a most inopportune moment to return," the owl lawyer said.

Sarah turned to the man who had questioned her identity. He was the youngest of the three, although that didn't make him actually "young." His beard was scraggly and long. He'd clearly grown it out to try and make himself look older.

Sarah seemed equally unafraid of all of them, no matter their age. "Were you actually trying to tell me that you don't think I'm Sarah Stanton? Certainly a room full of servants who recognize me should be enough proof that I am who I say I am."

The third lawyer was taller but rounder than the other two. "Unless," he intoned, "you've brought the entire household into your scheme."

"It's her," Emilio said innocently. "Who else would she be?"

"A more important question is," the round man said, "exactly who are *you?*"

Jenny watched Sarah's brow furrow. "This is ridiculous," Sarah said. "I want you to bring back my things now, and then I want you all to vacate my house, immediately."

"Dead or alive," the tallest lawyer intoned, "you're not in much of a position to demand anything."

"And whether or not you're here in fact," the round one chimed in, "you're still legally dead."

"But she's not *actually* dead," Jenny reminded them.

"That," the owlish man said, leaning forward so that he was peering at Jenny over the top of his spectacles, "is for the courts to decide."

"Ach!" Grüsser said. "I have had more zen enough ov zis nonsense!" He blustered forward. "Do you know who I am?"

The round lawyer answered him. "Yes. I believe you're Helmut Grüsser, the Submersible."

"Und am I legally dead?"

"No," the tall man replied, "but I do believe you're wanted for questioning in connection with the murder of Alexander Stanton."

"Vas?" He shouted out, his face suddenly turning so deeply red that Jenny half expected to see steam rising up from his ears. His hands had balled into fists, and Jenny could see that things were quickly heading from bad to worse. If they were going to rescue the household, they would need the help of someone else. "Sarah," she said stepping forward, "doesn't your family have a lawyer?"

Sarah nodded. "Quite right, Jenny. Mr. Cleeves will be calling on you gentlemen soon."

"We know him very well," the tall one said.

"He was the one who signed the paper declaring you deceased," the round one added.

"And I'm sure you'll get to know him much better now that I'm no longer dead." Sarah's voice was rising with each word, "So until then, could you please *leave?*"

The men, clearly startled to have been challenged by a woman, stared at each other quietly for a moment. Then, as if they had communicated in some unspoken language, the men began to simultaneously bundle up their papers. "All right, Miss Stanton," the owlish one said. "But we'll be expecting to hear from Mr. Cleeves in the next few days."

"Fine," Sarah said, "But if you've emptied my room . . ."

"No, Sarah," Jenny said, hoping that the girl was probably looking to find something decent to wear, no matter how badly out of season it might be. "Your things are still here."

"Well, that's some good news, at least." Sarah replied. "Now, Mr. O'Rourke, if you could be so kind as to see these gentlemen out . . ."

"Yes, ma'am." He nodded. "And it is good to have you back, ma'am."

Jenny's eyes widened with surprise. Had the old butler just given Sarah Stanton a compliment? It was almost unbelievable. But then again, a lot of things about the day were turning out to be stranger than she had imagined possible.

Sarah and the others waited in silence while the lawyers vacated the room. Even though she had won this battle, Jenny couldn't help but notice that Sarah wasn't smiling.

And as the office door shut, Sarah sighed and plopped herself down into the large leather chair behind her father's desk. The springs let out a slight groan as she leaned back in the seat. She let out a longer, weary sigh. "I knew I never should have come back."

As happy as she was to see Sarah back in the family house, her time away had clearly done nothing for her manners. "Then why did you?"

"They blew up my house!" Emilio said.

"You mean your junkyard? What happened?"

"It vas le Voyageur," Grüsser said.

"Who's that?" Jenny asked the Prussian. "And pardon my asking, but where did you come from? Last I heard, you were with King Jupiter."

And then another question suddenly and violently sprang into her mind. "And where is Viola?" And then another: "And what happened to Tom?"

"Enough!" Sarah said, sitting up in the groaning chair. "I know there's a lot to catch up on, Jenny, but we don't have very much time." Seeing her sitting in her father's seat, it was impossible for Jenny to ignore just how much like Alexander Stanton Sarah had become over the last few months.

"Well, I'm glad you came back when you did, or you would have found nothing but empty halls."

"Is very nice," Emilio said. The boy looked uncomfortable, unsure how he really felt about such a residence after the one he'd come from.

"Everyone needs a home," Jenny said.

"And I had one, in Brooklyn."

Jenny just shook her head, refusing to say again how she felt about Sarah living in a junkyard.

"And now that we are back," Sarah continued, "It won't be long before Eschaton knows we're here."

"Und by ze looks of der lawyers," Grüsser added, "Ich don't think zat he vill need to use any of his powers to stop us."

Jenny crossed her arms and stared at the motley crew. "I know that this is all terribly important, but perhaps you should all take a moment to compose yourselves before you go gallivanting after a villain who can throw bolts of electricity through the air."

Sarah nodded. "Quite right," she said, surprising Jenny with her agreement. "We need a plan."

"Sarah," Emilio said, "Maybe you need to sleep first?"

"I am tired, my dear," Sarah said to the Italian boy, adding even more questions to Jenny's list, "but I have a few things I need to check on first."

Jenny had hoped for more of a reunion before she was going to be forced to reveal all that had happened since the last time she had seen Sarah, but it seemed that the new mistress of the house was bound and determined to deny her any opportunity to take things slowly. "Sarah, before you open up the wall, there's something I should probably tell you first."

"I'm sure it can wait, Jenny," Sarah said. She grabbed the gas lamp and gave it a pull. There was a solid thunk as the mechanism that controlled the secret panel engaged, and the portrait of Alexander Stanton began to rise up into the ceiling, along with the wall behind it. "I know you must think it's terribly important, Jenny, but I'm sure that whatever it is, it can wait until after I've had a chance to check on—"

As the secret room was revealed, so was the form of a man. And as the wall finished rising, Sarah visibly recoiled.

"Who, or what, are you?" Sarah said, with the sort of challenge in her voice that she might use on a lawyer, or one of Eschaton's villains. Jenny was sure that Sarah was about to be as surprised as Jenny had been only a few days before.

"It's me, Sarah," the transparent man said to her.

"It's who?" Sarah asked, but Jenny could see that the realization was already dawning, even as she said it.

"Nathaniel!" Sarah threw herself at him without hesitation, wrapping her arms around the boy. "It's you! You're alive!" She squeezed the crystal boy tightly, then leaned back to once again take in his transparent form. "But whatever have they done to you?"

Chapter 17

The Impossibility of Flight

Abraham clutched the Mercurial Man as tightly as he could as they flew up into the night, but truth be told, it was more the straps than his own strength that kept him from being torn away and dropped onto the streets below.

The heat that Nathaniel generated was almost suffocating, but at least it wasn't burning him. He wondered what would happen to him if the boy did suddenly begin to heat up.

Would he let go, or simply be burned to death there in the sky? In his mind's eye he saw himself tumbling into the streets below. He realized that in his imagination he was still fully dressed as Anubis, covered from head to toe in his leather suit. But that had been taken from him; he had no secrets any longer.

And some part of him was glad for it. Hiding the color of his skin from the world hadn't felt right somehow. And yet, he couldn't deny the utility that his secret had brought him. He had, after all, never pretended to be something that he wasn't—he simply hadn't revealed himself to be anything at all. It had been the world that had assumed, decided, and turned him into whatever it wanted him to be.

Now the world knew who and what he really was. Anubis was gone, and Abraham dangled in the skies, wondering where he was going to go next. "Where are we headed?"

"East," Nathaniel said.

He wondered if the boy was enjoying getting to pretend to be his old self once again. "We need to land."

"You're right. I'm heavier than I used to be, and this suit wasn't designed to carry two people for very long. But where should we land?"

"Somewhere safe."

"Where's that?" Nathaniel said, a hint of anger in his voice.

The night of the battle in the theater, Sarah Stanton had invited Anubis to come visit her in a Brooklyn junkyard. It hadn't taken him long to find her, and although he had fully intended to visit her only with the mask on, there was something about the girl that had gotten him to reveal his true identity to her on his very first visit.

He had visited her secretly a number of times after that, riding out to the house on an old wagon owned by a junk collector by the name of Mr. Niles.

Sarah hadn't talked much about the Paragons (besides the Automaton), but she had mentioned Nathaniel more than once. "He's a selfish, petulant child at heart," she had told him, and she clearly felt she had been more than a little responsible for what had happened to him. "But there's something truly noble inside of him just the same."

He wondered what she would make of Nathaniel's current state. As far as he could tell, even this total transformation had yet to turn him into the nobler man that Sarah Stanton believed Nathaniel could become. But maybe he could turn that to his advantage, "I know where Sarah Stanton is!"

"What are you talking about?"

"Your step-sister, I've met her." He looked up into the man's transparent face. Glowing and silver, with his metal wings spread out behind him, it was hard not to look at him as some kind of angel—or demon. "I know where she's hiding."

He turned to look down at him, his eyes flashing with silver. "If you're lying to me . . ."

Abraham supposed that men and monsters were all simply trying to get by for one more day. "Then you can drop me in the river, or you can drop me right here. At least we'll be moving faster."

Nathaniel frowned at that. "Are you making a joke?"

Anubis nodded his head in the direction of the river. "She's in a junkyard just on the other side of the East River. If we go there now, we might be able to make it."

"I'm not sure how far this suit can fly with both of us," he said, and tilted them in the direction of the river.

Anubis found himself getting angry at the boy's attitude. Was he always like this? Despite Sarah's warnings, it was hard to believe that this whining brat had once been hailed as one of the world's greatest heroes. He had known that the Paragons were men of privilege, but he had never imagined . . . "If we make it," he growled, "we'll find you some bourbon."

"You're sure that's where Sarah is?"

"She was the last time I saw her." Anubis looked down. They were still flying above the city, but the rooftops looked closer to them now. "Why are we falling?"

He could feel Nathaniel's arms twitching as he clutched at the controls. "That's what I was worried about. I think we're already running out of fuel."

Anubis made a silent prayer to God. He was surprised to realize that there was some part of him that was almost looking forward to his failure. If he died, it would be over and he could leave all of this behind. He had become a hero to help the common man, not to fight with monsters.

And why was he even here, floating hundreds of feet above the Earth? Perhaps the Paragons were trying to protect *their* world, but it wasn't a world that Anubis was interested in redeeming.

Truth be told, if he had a true affinity with anyone's agenda, it was Eschaton's: he and the gray man were both anarchists of sorts, save for the fact that Eschaton saw no harm in killing any number of innocents to get his way. And after all the things he had seen, he was beginning to wonder if the only way to change the way of the world *was* to smash it to pieces.

The suit lurched, and they began to fall fast enough that it was clear that crossing the river had been far too ambitious a goal. "We need to land!" Abraham yelled out.

"I'm trying!" Nathaniel shouted. But despite his intention to save them, the stress of keeping them in the air seemed to be having a different effect on the Mercurial Man. Silver streaks were gathering together in his arms, turning the limbs silver. It would be only a matter of time before they began producing heat, leaving Abraham trapped between two unpleasant deaths.

Anubis could see the rooftops too clearly now. It would be only a matter of seconds before they would be close enough to crash into them. He needed the boy to concentrate, and he had decided that if he was going to die he'd rather it was by fire than by stone. "Sarah told me you'd fail us," Anubis said, letting the words wander between a whisper and growl.

"What?" Nathaniel replied.

"She said that you always found a way to give up, and that if I met you, I wasn't to expect too much from you."

"You're lying! She would never say that."

Anubis laughed. "You know I'm not. I don't know you well, Nathaniel, but it seems pretty obvious to me that you've failed everyone who's ever loved you or cared about you. At least Darby and the Industrialist were men who could take care of themselves, but Sarah was an innocent until you let her get involved in all of this."

"Shut your mouth!"

Anubis smiled, knowing that being mocked by a Negro would be twice as galling to the boy. "And when Sarah ran away, did you even look for her?"

"She chose to leave!"

"You didn't even try?"

"I thought she was dead!"

"You pretended she was dead so you wouldn't have to feel responsible for her!" As he laid out the case for Nathaniel's failures, he found that his mock resentment of the boy was becoming very real. "If you loved her you'd have gotten your sorry self together and saved her!"

"Don't make me hurt you," Nathaniel said, his words turning low and cold.

"Are you going to burn me to death?" Anubis pulled himself up by the straps so that he could look the boy in his transparent eyes. "If you're a hero—a Paragon—then act like one. If you can't even save me, and yourself, then you'll lose everything you've ever cared about, forever."

Nathaniel frowned, but Abraham could see that he had managed to reach a part of the boy that might be willing to try. "This may not work."

"Then when you reach the gates of heaven you can tell them that at least you tried."

More silver threads slipped up into his arm. And when they ignited it happened so quickly that the bright light blinded Anubis.

Nathaniel's plan seemed to work as intended, the heat coming off of him giving a burst of energy to the wings on his back. And as the suit lifted them back into the sky, Abraham though that Nathaniel might be a true Paragon after all.

The Mercurial Man's light was growing brighter and brighter. Wherever they went, the Children of Eschaton would be able to find them. At least he had managed to maintain control of his heat, and so far Anubis remained unburned.

Looking downwards, he could see the area nearby had been lit up as if by a flare. There was an inviting rooftop, only yards away. If they could reach it, he would let go and . . .

They smashed into the church roof with a hard thud, and suddenly the whole world tilted sideways with a terrifying lurch.

Anubis could feel the roof against his feet, but it seemed impossible to gain any purchase on the slanted tiles. But they were still moving forward, and he could see the steeple heading straight toward them.

Reacting on instinct, he let his hands fall out of the straps. Freed from Nathaniel, he felt himself falling for an instant, and then he smashed into something hard, the impact knocking the air out of his lungs. For a moment he wondered if he would be rescued by Nathaniel, but as he fell farther he realized that the boy, now no longer weighed down by his extra passenger, had flown high up into the air, while he had been dumped against the deeply sloped sides of the steeple. Caught without any support, he was left sliding down the side of the cupola, and once he reached the edge there would be nothing to stop him falling into the street below.

His hands grasped desperately for any nearby purchase, but the shingles seemed to disintegrate under his hands, and without the usual protection of his gloves he could feel the skin of his fingers being torn away.

It wasn't until he had already slid over the edge that his momentum finally stopped, leaving his legs dangling high above the streets below.

Abraham took a moment to catch his breath, gasping in lungfuls of the night air even though the rooftop was cutting into his chest and making it hard to inhale.

Turning his head, he could see Nathaniel heading up farther into the sky, a glowing star leaving behind a trail of fire. Then, whatever fuel remained in the suit sputtered out and Nathaniel dropped, still glowing as he fell to the streets below.

Anubis still had his own problems with gravity. Despite his efforts to drag himself up, the earth was pulling hard at him, intent on dragging him off the roof. His arms were already tired from hanging onto the suit, and he wondered if he still had the strength he needed to pull himself to safety.

Grunting with what felt like almost-infinite effort, Anubis swung his leg back up onto the edge of the cupola. Then, using his newfound purchase, he gave a few twists and turns and managed to get himself seated on the edge. He had taken only a moment to catch his breath before he felt the wood beneath him begin to sag and crack.

He tried to move, but it gave way an instant later. "Dammit," he yelled as his hands grasped the exposed wood, driving a splinter into his already-raw flesh.

His entire body was hanging down now, and his legs swung freely, dangling over the four-story drop. Only a few feet in front of his face was a stained-glass window. It depicted a shining cross hanging over a field of sheep and lions lying peacefully together.

Abraham cursed again as he realized his fingers were already beginning to lose their grip, the pain of the wooden sliver in his hand adding to his weakness. It seemed unfair that after surviving so many insults to his person, he would finally be broken by a simple fall.

"No!" he shouted, hoping that a primal yell might give his body the morale it needed, and grasping tighter than he had before, he kicked his legs forward. Pain shot down his arm, but he managed to use his momentum to smash his feet into the tinted glass.

The lead lining that held the window together was stronger than it first appeared, and although he had managed to bash a hole into it, it had simply grabbed hold of his foot rather than shattering into pieces.

His hand was screaming now, and no amount of will to survive would keep him suspended above the street once the strength in his arms was gone.

Somehow he managed to wrench his foot free, losing the cheap leather shoe that Eschaton had given him in the process.

As his leg dropped down, adding its weight to the rest of him, his grip slipped, and his right hand fell away. He grunted with shock as he found himself dangling by only one arm, the fingertips somehow managing to support the entirety of his body. The free hand throbbed with pain.

Miraculously he managed to pull himself up enough to grasp the beam with both hands once again, although now his left shoulder had added another voice to the chorus of pain his body was singing. At least it kept his mind off of his hand. Sweat rolled down his face as he stared at the broken window in front of him. He realized that his terror had evaporated. The only thing he still had left was desperation.

With the last of his strength Anubis swung himself backward, and then propelled himself forward as hard as he could, lifting his legs so that his toes pointed in front of him.

His hands came free as his feet crashed into the window, and for an instant he simply flew through the air, until his body managed to shatter the stained-glass image. He made a small apology to God as he passed through the disintegrating visage of peace and harmony and into the darkness beyond it.

Chapter 18
Steeling the Flesh

As the boy flew up through the skylight and into the night, Eschaton could no longer deny the damage that had been done to him. Something inside him was very, very wrong.

He managed to rise up to his knees, but then fell back to the ground.

The White Knight was the first to reach him, "Are you all right, lord?" He grabbed Eschaton's arm and started trying to yank him up to his feet.

Even when he was trying to help him, Eschaton found the man insufferable. But there was more at stake than just his pride, and even if Clements was only barely competent, it would have to be enough.

"I'm fine, you imbecile." Eschaton shrugged the man off, although he truly wasn't sure if he'd be able to rise without him. "Go after them, and take some of these other idiots with you," he continued, pointing at some men nearby, "What are your names, Children."

The men looked shocked that they had been called out. One man held up his boxing glove–clad hand. "I'm the Pugilist, and my friend here is the Riveter."

"You see, Clements, a fine pair of heroes."

"And how are we supposed to find 'em in the dark?" Murphy asked.

"*You're* not. I need you and Jack with me." Eschaton dragged himself up to the pews and collapsed into one of the seats. The wood groaned under his weight. "Besides, that suit of his leaves a trail of fire behind it."

"Don't you worry, Lord Eschaton, I'll find them." The White Knight pulled on his mask. "Come on, boys, this isn't over yet." At least the man had enthusiasm—it was, in fact, his best feature.

Looking around the smoking ruins of the room, Eschaton admitted to himself that the day had not gone as planned—not nearly. And although he had considered some contingencies in his plot to remake the world, it had never occurred to him that things might go as totally wrong as they had today. The events that had occurred over the course of the evening had shaken his convictions even more than his stamina.

His head still rang with the pain from the attack, although at least his flesh seemed undamaged from the heat. Still, it had been a close thing. He had almost been . . . broken. There was no other word for it.

And the tragedy of it was that the process itself was working. There was no doubt that he had transformed Nathaniel into something better. Perhaps not completely purified—not yet—but he was very close.

But at the same time, it was clear that purifying the bodies of men was not the same thing as purifying their souls. Eschaton had hoped that turning men into gods would have had an effect on their minds as well as their bodies. It needn't have been as profound as the awakening that had overcome him when he had gained his powers, but in order to work on their minds he needed something . . . an edge to grab onto. Nathaniel, it seemed, had a mind as smooth and transparent as his body.

As Eschaton began to review his options, Donny ran up beside him, a desperate gleam in his eyes. "What about the retht of uth, thir?" he spat out pathetically through his shattered teeth. "What are we thuppothed to do?"

He was an instant away from telling the boy he could go rot in hell for all he cared, when another thought came to him. Eschaton looked deeply into the boy's eyes. What he saw there was the same lost innocence that he had come to see on the faces of all men, only on this boy's face it was more honest than on the other human flotsam and jetsam.

For reasons beyond Lord Eschaton's comprehension, the endless hammering of the world made some men more devious while it pounded the guile out of others.

And although Donny was a vicious, dangerous man who delighted in causing pain to his fellow humans, he was still an innocent—somehow as unaware of his own capacity for destruction as he was anyone else's. "Do you want to be purified?" Eschaton asked him. "If you could, would you become like me?"

"Oh, yeth thir," Donny replied, his eyes shining. "I'd want that more than anything in the world."

He grabbed the boy's right arm with his left hand. His intention had been to be gentle, but now that he felt the soft flesh between his fingers Eschaton couldn't help but squeeze into it until he could feel the fragile bones underneath. The pain he was causing the boy was clear on Donny's face, and it seemed to be reducing his own agony. "And if you had it, what would you do with it?"

The boy was clearly torn between trying to free himself and attempting to answer the question. "Whatever you'd want me to, thir."

He knew that underneath his obedient exterior the boy was a vicious killer, and he was growing tired of being lied to. "That's not an answer. If I gave you strength and invulnerability, what would you do with it?"

"I'd, I'd . . ." Donny seemed desperate now, clearly thinking that somehow the right answer would make his torture stop. "Pleathe, thir . . ."

Somehow, even as he tried to lighten his touch, Eschaton knew that he was tightening his grip. "My *lord*," Eschaton said with a snarl. He had wanted to unlock the secret to his power, and now he was beginning to see that perhaps it was the suffering of others that gave him strength.

"Pleathe, my lord," Donny parroted back, clearly desperate. Tears were leaking from his eyes now, the confusion and pain blending into a form of desperation that Eschaton found both comforting and pitiable.

"Answer the question."

"I'd take whatever I wanted—whatever I wanted!" he screamed out. The combination of forced honesty and pained desperation made Donny's words blend together into almost incomprehensible gibberish, but Eschaton still understood.

He threw the boy to the ground.

Donny grabbed his arm and rubbed the red flesh. By tomorrow it would be badly bruised. "Wath that the wrong anthwer, my lord?"

Donny was no different than the others. He would turn on him the moment he gained genuine power. "The question is, is it the only answer?"

"I don't underthtand." The boy looked up at him with the eyes of a wounded puppy.

"Clearly not. But you will soon enough." He pulled himself out of the pew. Something had definitely given him renewed strength. "Now get out."

The boy scrambled away.

"Why'd you go off on the boy like that? He ain't done nothing to ya." He looked up to see Doctor Dynamite staring up at him from his wheelchair.

The man had been badly broken during his battle with the Automaton. That he hadn't died was a testament to the powers of modern medicine, but he would never walk again.

Eschaton had to admit that he was desperately curious to see what the smoke would do to his broken body. "I'm tired of having my actions questioned by children."

This time it was Jack Knife's broken accent that cut him off. "I think he's decided that a world full of Paragons might not be such a good idea after all."

Eschaton's first instinct was to reach out and slap the man for his impudence, but Jack Knife was a very different kettle of fish from Donny. While they might both have been children of the streets, it would be a very foolish mistake to underestimate Jack's intelligence. That his men were clearly probing for weakness meant that now was not the time to lash out in anger.

"You're half-right, Jack," Eschaton said. It was true that the pecking order could be a factor of luck, but over time things settled out one way or another for a reason. There could be little doubt why Jack was the leader, and Donny was the lackey. "But in a new world I had imagined that men would learn to be equals."

The crippled cowboy let out a sarcastic laugh. "Everyone's always *half*-right, but what makes you *equal* is whether or not you have the gumption to back it up."

Eschaton nodded, wondering just how much dynamite the Doctor still had hidden in his chair. For a moment he considered taking the chance of finding out. Instead he turned and faced the other man. "And what would you do with your power if I gave it to you, Jack?"

"Dunno. I don't have it yet." Jack said, staring him straight in the eye. "But once you've given it to me, you can be the first to find out."

"Is that a threat?"

"I thought you were going to make us all equals?" Doc Dynamite replied without missing a beat.

"You never believed in my vision of a more equitable world, anyway. Why are you all so worried about it now?"

Jack spoke next. "Maybe all men aren't bastards, but I think it only takes a whiff of power to make them *think* they are." The look on the man's razor sharp face was an unhappy one. "Personally I don't think a world of *more* powerful bastards would be a wonderful thing."

"That's because you both don't have the good sense ta *believe* in anything," Murphy interrupted in his brogue. "All men have a touch of the divine, and you want to make it real." Eschaton could see the devotion in the old man's eyes. "Don't listen to him, Eschaton," the Irishman said, "Ya can still make us all better."

"Religious nonsense," Jack said with a scowl. "I never seen God shoot a bullet or take one, but he still gets all the credit when it happens to somebody else."

For a moment Eschaton could smell the scent of his defeat in the air. It reeked of rotting flesh and burning wood. "What you're missing," he replied, "is that what happened here today may, on the balance of it, have been a good thing."

"Yeah," said Doc Dynamite with sarcasm. "It's always a good day when they burn down your house."

"Well, then," Eschaton replied, "You'll be pleased to hear that I have opened my eyes."

"And what are they seeing now?" Jack asked.

Eschaton let out a rumbling chuckle. "Well, my clever boy, I've seen that while I can use the fortified smoke to transform men into more powerful creatures, the strength alone will not give them the vision that they need to use it with good sense."

"I could have told you that months ago and saved you the trouble," Jack grumbled.

Eschaton narrowed his eyes. "And if I asked you months ago, if you would have turned traitor for Anubis, would you have told me that, too?"

Jack opened his mouth to reply, but only a sputtering "I, I didn't . . ." came out.

Now it was Doc Dynamite's turn to laugh. "What's the matter Jack?"

"I didn't turn traitor . . ." he sputtered.

Eschaton had to admit that catching him like that made him feel good, although it might not have been the most prudent use of his information.

"Don't worry," the gray man said, taking a step toward him. "I won't hold it against you. It was my fault for letting him join us in the first place." Once again he felt better for the attack.

Jack stared down at the floor. "You know I've been on your side since the start," he said in a tone just barely above a mumble. "But you always *knew* the jackal wasn't one of us, so why did you let him hang around?"

Eschaton surveyed the damaged Hall. Nathaniel's powers had done an effective job of burning down his pulpit. Parts of the structure were still glowing, the smoke being pulled up through the hole in the ceiling where the two men had escaped. "Why did I treat him like one of the Children, you mean?" Perhaps it was a fitting metaphor. "I thought he might open his eyes."

"Me too," Jack said as he followed him down the ramp. "Besides I like him, and I think you do, too."

"Normally, Jack, I wouldn't feel the need to explain myself," he said, walking down the ramp toward the unmoving metal husk in the middle of the floor, "but given the events of the day, perhaps I'll indulge you."

"Only if it pleases you, *my lord*," the thin man said. But it was hard to hold his cutting tone against him. Outside of occasional moments of shock and surprise, Eschaton wondered if Jack could be genuine even if he tried. His disdain for authority clearly reached down to his bones.

"I wanted to see if he could change," Eschaton told him.

"And instead he changed Jack," Doc Dynamite noted.

"Maybe you just don't know me that well," Jack snapped back.

"Or maybe you don't know yourself as well as you think," Murphy said, stomping toward the stage.

"Perhaps you could both stop bickering for a moment." Eschaton hobbled slightly as he reached the burned remains of the Shell. The twisted armor lay in a pile by the smashed glass cage, looking like a puppet that had suddenly lost its strings.

"This is a right mess we have here," Murphy said as he came up behind Eschaton. "But I can't say that I'm sorry ta see the monster gone."

"He gave us all a bit of the creeps," Jack said. "And he was starting to smell worse, if that's possible."

"And yet he should be mourned by all of us." After the birth of the Shell,

Eschaton had spent days poring over Darby's machinery, but there was little left to give him insight into the cause of the transformation. "He was loyal to the end, and Hughes helped me to discover secrets that I didn't even know existed.

"He won't be forgotten." Eschaton reached out a foot and prodded the dead thing's armor. "When this is done we'll build a statue in his honor."

"Why don't we just turn him into one?" Jack said with a snigger.

"The man was not only one of my Children, but he was also the only true Paragon." Eschaton raised his voice as he spoke. "The only one of them to see the potential in the future that I offered." The shining metal had been scorched by the heat, and stained where the fluids of the remnants of humanity it had once contained had been boiled away.

"It didn't end well for him though, did it?" There was clearly a genuine tone of regret in the Irishman's voice.

"It's not just how it ends, though, is it, Murphy? Eli also sacrificed his life, as did so many others who shall go unmourned."

Eschaton had always known there would be sacrifice. It was the destruction of the man he had been in that smoke-filled chamber so many years ago that had begun his journey to becoming what he was today. Terrence Harrington, the man he once was, was now as dead and buried as any of the others who had been sacrificed to the smoke.

He had believed that the power of that rebirth would be enough to open the eyes of any man, but Nathaniel had rejected his rejuvenation. "No matter," he whispered to himself, bending over toward the remains. If the new world demanded a leader, he would find a way to rise to the challenge.

He stretched out and touched the Shell's arm. The steel limb was lifeless but still warm in his grasp.

Then, with a shock, he realized that where his fingers touched the Shell's body there was something like a buzzing underneath his hand. For a moment he thought he might be imagining it, but looking down he could clearly see that the white energy underneath his skin was travelling down his arm, pooling together where it touched metal.

As he lifted his hand away, his flesh seemed to almost cling to the metal, as if it had somehow been joined to it. He could see the flashes of small sparks jumping between his fingers and the metal as he peeled it off. It made him feel strange, but somehow energized as well.

Eschaton stood up and rubbed his hands together, feeling the energy dissipate back across his body. "Jack, come here."

The thin man walked up next to him. "What can I do for you, my lord?"

"Touch that and tell me what you feel."

Jack was clearly nervous being so near to the Shell's body. "I'm a marksman by nature—more about distance than touching," he said, taking a step back.

"A coward, more like," the broken cowboy said with a chuckle.

"I'm not asking," Eschaton said, and shoved Jack forward. Murphy walked closer as well, obviously curious but not wanting to be pressed into actually being involved.

"All right then." Jack knelt down slowly, folding himself down until he looked like a poorly made chair. He grimaced as he reached out his hand, and then slowly pressed his finger against the metal arm.

"What do you feel?" Eschaton asked.

"It's warm."

"Anything else?"

Jack held his finger there for a moment. "No, lord. Just warm." He looked up and raised his eyebrows. "Can I stop now?"

Eschaton nodded, and Jack rose, wiping his finger against his pants like there might be something stuck to it.

"All right, all of you, stand back." Eschaton didn't need to ask twice. Both men took the opportunity to walk back up the ramp and find some small measure of cover behind the rows of pews. Doc Dynamite rolled away as well, still shy after his last encounter with one of Darby's creations.

Eschaton knew that he was once again playing with forces he didn't yet fully understand. Whatever process Darby had used on the Shell's body, it had taken place on a level he had yet to comprehend. "If only I had that damn heart," he muttered out loud.

Still, he wasn't without his own resources, and Eschaton wouldn't be cowed by a mechanical ghost. Raising his arm into the air, he began to concentrate energy into it, filling it up until it was pure white. The effort of it drained him, and the pain behind his eyes grew. Someone would need to suffer soon.

He brought the energized limb slowly down toward the Shell's broken body. By the time his fingers were a foot away, the energy was leaping off his skin and into the metal. It took all his strength to keep his hand from dropping, as if his limb were becoming heavier the closer it came to the strange steel. He almost yelped as a chunk of it leapt upward into his hand.

There was a sensation of overwhelming vertigo. He could feel the energy being drawn out of his body and into the steel.

Strangest of all, he could feel his muscles relax, drained of the tension that had been a constant part of his physiology from the moment he had first bathed in fortified smoke.

And in that moment everything was peaceful. But when Eschaton opened his eyes he saw that he had fallen to the floor. Jack and Murphy were standing over him, their eyes wide.

From somewhere nearby Eschaton heard a tapping sound. He jerked himself up and was surprised by what he saw when he looked down at his hands. While the flesh was still *gray*, it contained a tone of human pink he hadn't seen in years. He pressed his right thumb into the palm of his left hand and was astounded to see the flesh actually yield to the pressure.

The tapping started up again, and he jerked his head toward the source of the sound. "Incredible." What was making the noise was the jerking body of the Shell. Somehow, contact with the electricity produced by his body had reanimated it.

He heard Murphy's voice. "Are you all right, lord?"

The Irishman was wild-eyed, clearly almost as shocked to see Eschaton on the floor as he had been by the twitching metal corpse. Eschaton began to pull himself up, but it seemed that the metal had drawn more out of him than he realized. "Don't just stand there gawping! Help me up!"

Jack ran up, and each man grabbed an arm, lifting Eschaton back onto his feet. As he moved away the steel cadaver slowly returned to rest, the remains of the energy that powered its ghoulish exertions being drained away.

"What happened?" Jack asked him, taking a tentative step toward the now utterly inanimate shell.

"Darby did it," Eschaton said, the realization of what had just occurred falling into place in his head even as he spoke the name out loud.

"What do you mean?" Murphy asked. "I killed him."

"Touch it now," Eschaton said, giving Jack another shove.

"Not bloody likely," the thin man said, moving himself both out of Eschaton's reach and farther away from Hughes's corpse.

"I'll do it if you won't," Murphy said, stepping forward and reaching out. As he neared the metal arm, a spark leapt up from the steel to his hand. "Dammit," he said, yanking his hand back.

"Better you than me," Jack said with a laugh.

"Residue of the energy it pulled from me." Eschaton took a step closer and kneeled down, careful not to get too close.

"I don't understand," Murphy said. "Is it dead or not?"

"The man is dead." Eschaton nodded to himself. "Darby was no fool. While he may have banished me for my experiments, he was clearly unable to kill off his own curiosity about my discovery—the possibility of binding the power of fortified smoke to a living creature."

He dropped his head and laughed. Even though it had been necessary to kill the man, it was hard not to feel some sadness at his loss—especially now that he could see his flaws. "I was focused on finding ways to bind the power of smoke to human flesh so that I could create a better man." Eschaton knelt down and brought his hand close enough to the metal skin that he could feel it calling out to him again, attempting to drag the power out of his flesh. "But Darby went in the other direction."

He saw Jack taking a step closer, the light of dawning recognition in his eyes. "You mean that metal, don't you? What did he do?"

"He somehow fused the power of fortified steam directly into the steel," Eschaton said. The sheer rightness of Darby's work was overwhelming him now. He and the old man had both been on the same path, but once again it was Darby whose vision had more clarity.

"Tom's heart must be made of the same stuff." He'd taken his disaster and used it create a living heart for his mechanical man. "If only I'd gotten my hands on the Automaton man. Damn that girl."

"That machine is the devil's work."

"It is that, Murphy." The only option now was to take the gifts he had been given and move forward. "Darby wanted to fuse the Automaton's heart with this armor and make an entire man from fortified steel. Then he'd take control of the building."

Most of those mechanisms had been damaged or outright destroyed when the Shell had first tried to take control of the building. Hughes's damaged humanity had been insanely underprepared for the task.

"But what about me?" Eschaton let his hand fall on the steel skin once again. He could feel it feeding on him, hungrily grasping at the energy inside his body. This time, instead of tearing his hand away, he brought his mind to bear.

If he could gather his energy together, surely the opposite must be possible? He concentrated on letting the power draw back into his body, denying the hungry metal its meal. For a moment it almost seemed to be reaching into him, desperate to find the source of the spark that would give it vitality.

For a moment man and metal fought for control, and then, like a dog or horse that had been broken of its wild nature, the steel simply let go. Eschaton pulled his hand away and stared at his pink palm. He rubbed the skin over the stony surface of his arm, enjoying the sensation of soft flesh once again. As he lost himself in it, the flood of thoughts in his brain receded, and a smile appeared on his face. Fortified steel robbed him of power, but it could give him so much more. If his improved humans needed a leader, it would be one clad in shining skin.

A moment later the supple flesh began to transform back into a stonier form, taking with it the soft sensations of humanity. Not wanting to linger on his sacrifice, Eschaton's thoughts returned to the task in front of him.

He pointed to the cart that had been used to bring the Mercurial Man into the room. "Gentlemen, if you would be so kind as to strap this metal husk to that cart and take him down to my laboratory, there's a great deal of work to do before we can finally end this, and we don't have much time."

Chapter 19
Brothers and Sisters

At first, the heat pouring off of his body had given him the extra burst of energy that he had been looking for, but once he had lost Anubis the suit had over-compensated, shooting him high up into the sky. That had sent Nathaniel into a panic, and as he rose into the night sky he lost his ability to control the heat that was pouring off of him. It took only a moment for the fuel inside of the suit to erupt, exploding outward and igniting as it made contact with his flesh. It was a painless experience, but there was no doubt that the Turbine had made his last flight.

As gravity grabbed him and Nathaniel began to tumble from the sky, he fully expected that his glass body would shatter on impact with the paving stone. He wondered what it would feel like to have his thoughts be literally strewn across the ground.

The impact was terrible and jarring, and for a moment he could feel nothing at all. Then, as sensation began to return to him, he could feel long cracks running deep into his flesh. But despite the terrible fall, he had not been shattered. Instead of the road, he had landed in the foul mix of dirt and stinking muck that filled the yard behind one of the tenements.

Realizing his predicament, he once again gave thanks that his sense of smell had been taken away by his purification, and wondered again at the strange silver entity that now lived inside him. It seemed that even though he had been robbed of his humanity, something in him now was determined to keep him alive far past anything that any mere human would have been able to withstand.

By the time he pulled himself back to consciousness, a number of the wretched tenants had come down to stand on the back stoop and stare. One blond-haired child pointed at him and said, "Seraph!"

It was at that moment when he realized that Darby's wings were still attached to his back, and that he was, quite literally, burning. He was sure if he had been able to see himself, a creature of silver and fire covered in filth, he would have considered himself some kind of demon, but he was flattered that the child had chosen to put him on the side of God.

He sat up, slipping his arms out of the straps that had held the wings onto his back. He stood and looked at the remains of the contraption that had once let him soar through the sky. It was amusing that the child had considered him an angel only *after* he had fallen from heaven.

As broken as they were, it was hard to leave the wings behind. But there was no purpose to them any longer. He found himself pleased that there had been one last opportunity to take to the skies.

No one watching complained when he had grabbed a sheet from a clothesline on his way to the street. They were too awed by their celestial visitor.

As a sheet-covered figure on the streets of the city, he was more invisible than he would have been in his transparent skin. People in New York ignored what they didn't want to see, and as he stumbled through the streets he had no thought of where he would go. Finally he came upon the idea of going back to the Stanton mansion. If Sarah was truly alive, as Anubis had told him, he was certain that she would return to her home eventually. Meanwhile, he was fairly certain that Jenny Farrows would take him in, no matter what his condition.

He arrived by the servant's entrance, knowing that if anyone was going to recognize him in his altered state it would be the staff, but it couldn't be O'Rourke. The old butler simply wouldn't be patient enough to hear out his story of tragedy before either calling the police or attempting to do away with him. At the very least, he was sure that he would be facing a slammed door.

But he had been wrong about that. The old man had let him in without a word. Perhaps he was simply happy to discover that not all the members of the Stanton family were dead.

The butler had quickly alerted the maid, and she had been instantly sympathetic. He'd spent a day stashed in the basement, perilously close to stacks of highly flammable books and papers. Knowing what the consequences might be, he had turned the maid down when she had offered him a drink, and instead discovered that he could still eat food after a fashion, although watching his digestive process in the mirror had, in retrospect, been the most disturbing incident of his transformation so far.

After only a short period he had quickly become bored sitting around the Darby house. It had taken him only a little while to remember the hidden entrance into the walls, and even less time for him to begin exploring it once again.

He had been in the Industrialist's room when Sarah had arrived, going through the drawers and marveling at all the outfits that Alexander Stanton had created for his other persona.

Holding a costume again, Nathaniel had been fantasizing about what kind of costume he might wear if he was ever to become a hero again—thinking that perhaps he could become what that child had imagined him to be, wearing a pair of glass wings.

Nathaniel had been lost in thought when the wall opened, revealing Sarah and Grüsser on the other side.

The fat German had run when he saw him, and it had taken the rest of them to stop Nathaniel from attacking the traitor. He supposed it was a good thing that they had. Grüsser had, in the end, been loyal to Sarah, and he supposed that had to count for something.

Finding him in her father's closet had obviously been a shock, but she sent everyone else away, and they sat in the office. Sarah looked as if she had spent the last few months in an asylum or a nunnery.

But despite her lack of respectable clothing, or perhaps because of it, she seemed oddly suited to be sitting in her father's chair.

"How do you feel, Nathaniel?"

He looked away. "I'm fine, Sarah, really."

"It doesn't hurt?"

"No." He flexed his hands and watched the flesh at his joints flake and crack as he moved his fingers around. The silver inside him immediately moved to repair the damage. "It's more strange than painful."

"I'm truly sorry, Nathaniel."

He nodded. "I'm sorry, too."

Sarah canted her head to the side. It was a look she only gave when she was truly interested in something, or truly confused. "About what?"

"For the way I treated you that day in the Darby house."

"Don't be ridiculous. That was all a lifetime ago."

"Anubis told me that you'd met him. He said that you told him I always found a way to give up."

Sarah's eyes grew wide. "You met him?"

"We escaped from the Hall together. Did you know he's a Negro?"

"I do," Sarah said. "Where is he?"

"I don't know. We were flying, and then my wings stopped working. He was falling . . ."

"No," Sarah said. "Do you think he's dead?"

"I don't know. I fell from the sky as well. I could have been killed." He took a pause for a breath. "Maybe you think I should have been."

"Nathaniel, I never meant to—"

He cut her off, having heard all he needed to. Anubis hadn't been lying to him about any of it.

He supposed he should have known. For a moment he was angry at her, all of his feelings of betrayal coming back in a rush. But beyond all that he heard Alexander Stanton's final words. "He told me to protect you," he said.

"Who?"

"Your father. I was there when he died—I tried to save him, I wanted to, but I had been . . ." He couldn't tell her the whole truth. He had been drinking, and it cost Alexander Stanton his life. He couldn't forgive himself, why would he expect her to. "It was terrible. He died in my arms."

"Oh, Nathaniel." Sarah stood up and walked around the desk to him. For a moment he wondered what would happen if he started to cry. Would the silver inside of him leak out? Would he start to burn again?

He gathered himself together. "He told me something else, something he wanted to tell you."

"What was it?"

"Darby's will. The old man had wanted you to become a Paragon, in his will."

"That's . . ." Sarah laughed nervously, and then stopped herself. "Section

266

106. That's what it was." She looked away from him, and put her hand up to her chin and drew in a deep breath. "Why didn't he tell me?"

"He had it secretly removed." Nathaniel felt a pang of guilt. He could see that she felt betrayed. "He was only trying to protect you, Sarah."

She turned back to him, and now there were tears in her eyes. "You were *all* trying to protect me. And look how it turned out."

"You're alive, at least."

"And so many others are dead, and you're . . ." Sarah's words trailed off.

"What am I, Sarah?"

"I'm sorry, Nathaniel. For a while I thought that perhaps I could be a hero. I thought that the world needed me. But now you're here, and Grüsser."

"You can't rely on him, Sarah. I promise you that he'll fail when you need him most."

"He had some horrible device attached to his back. He was under Eschaton's control."

Nathaniel clenched his hands together and heard them crack as they splintered all over again. "I know all about it, but that's what it takes to be a hero."

Sarah leaned back against the desk, looking slightly deflated. "You all keep saying that, but who knows what we would do in that situation?" She shook her head. "Darby wanted me to be a Paragon, but the Paragons are gone now. Maybe none of us are that strong."

"Look at me, Sarah." She did, staring almost fearlessly into his face. He realized at that moment that he was still smitten with her. "It seems to me that while everything else has fallen, you've managed to climb up. I can't say I understand it. Being a hero isn't easy for anyone, but it's what you do in those moments when the world is falling apart that makes you special. That day, on the bridge, it was you, not me, who faced off against that madman."

When she raised her head, she was smiling. "I think that's the nicest thing you've ever said to me, Nathaniel Winthorp."

"I love you, Sarah." The words tumbled out in a confused jumble, but he made his way through all of them.

"I know you do, Nathaniel. I love you too, but not the way you want me to."

He nodded and turned away for a moment. "I know. Who could love this monstrous thing I've become?"

Sarah stepped forward and took his hand. "You and I would have been a terrible match no matter what you looked like. Not to mention that it would have been a scandal of epic proportions."

His heart sank, but not as far as he'd expected it to. "And you've found that Italian fellow."

"Emilio. Yes, I guess I rather have."

"And he's nice to you?"

She smiled. "He is nice. And an inventor."

"Like Darby?"

"Different, I think. I don't think anyone is going to be like Sir Dennis ever again."

"I miss the old man. I think he would have been able to put a stop to all of this." He stood up from his chair and sat on the desk next to her.

"That's what Eschaton thought, too. It's why he had him killed."

Nathaniel looked around the room at all the things that had belonged to Alexander Stanton. Sarah had lost both parents now—the same as him. This home was hers now, as were the responsibilities that came with it. "You need to stop Eschaton."

"Me? What am I supposed to do?"

"We're all that's left of the Paragons now. And if he has Tom . . . I know Eschaton wanted him very badly, he told me that himself. With the Automaton he must be very close to completing his plans."

She shook her head. "I can't do it alone, Nathaniel. I'll need your help."

He was stunned. "You'll need *my* . . ." She wanted to *lead* them? Being a Paragon was one thing, but the idea that she would lead this group when there was a perfectly serviceable man to take on that role . . .

He considered denying her. What use would a woman be in battle? But then, what use had Darby ever been in a fight? It was his mind, not his fists that had made him a great leader. And what good had he ever been really? "The last thing your father said to me before he died was 'Do more. Win.'"

She shook her head slowly, in wonder. "It certainly sounds like him."

Nathaniel frowned. "I'm not sure that we could win even if we still had all the Paragons. He's incredibly powerful now."

Sarah closed the gap between them. "My father could be very demanding at times. Just do your best, and we'll go from there." It was ridiculous to think that she might give him orders, but looking at her, seeing the set of her jaw and the determination in her eyes, he realized that she possessed something that he never would.

Nathaniel laughed. "My best could be better." He suddenly felt a burst of heat surging through him. "Sarah! Get away!" What had set him off? His anger? His resignation?

He stepped back from the desk, and looked around the room. The walls were loaded with books. If it came to it, he would run outside rather than see this house burn down like the Darby mansion.

"What is it, Nathaniel?"

"I'm not . . ." He held up his arms. They were rapidly filling with silver, and the panic that struck him seemed to be emanating from the very core of his body. "I'm not in control of what's happened to me."

She took another step toward him and reached out a hand. "Perhaps you just need someone to trust you."

He shook his head. The heat was already starting to pour off of him. He needed to get away. "Stay back, Sarah! I'll hurt you."

"No," she said firmly, "you won't." She took a step closer, and Nathaniel found himself jumping back.

"Now, take my hand."

"I can't!" He felt the old panic rising further. And underneath it all was the overwhelming urge for another drink. So many times he thought he had overcome his weaknesses only to rediscover them again and again. He had destroyed everything he ever cared about, except for Sarah. Now he was about to kill her as well.

"You can," Sarah said, but he could see that the heat was affecting her. He needed to run. "You can," she repeated, "you just can't do it alone. None of us can. And I need your help, and I need your power to stop Eschaton."

He closed his eyes, but he could still see the world, blurred and refracted through his transparent eyelids. The panic swirled, like the silver inside of him. Then he could feel her hand in his. She must have been terribly burned, but as her fingers gripped his, he could feel the heat draining away. "All right, Sarah. You win."

"We'll win, together," she replied, and when she brought her other arm around his shoulders and smiled, for an instant Nathaniel believed her.

Chapter 20

Declarations of Lust

As he placed the living metal against the girl's face, the Frenchman smiled with satisfaction. So much had happened in the short time since he had returned from his successful attempt to recover the mechanical man, and this would be the final triumph. "Thewe you go, my deaw. We are almost weady to begin."

She looked up at him and smiled, the flesh still twisting underneath the mask. "Am I beautiful?"

It was a ridiculous question for so many reasons, not least of which was that female beauty had never much interested the old man, even in his more . . . virile days. But he knew enough to know that women often demanded a more subtle touch than the usual hammer blows he tended to wield. "You awe gowegeous," he said, attempting to appease her. "But of couwse, we have so much mowe to do."

She nodded groggily and smiled. The influence of the opium he had given her was fully in effect. "Now, my deaw," le Voyageur said, picking up two vials and holding them out in front of her. "Siwver ow Gowd?" The metallic liquids inside swirled around, occasional bolts of light sparkling in each of them.

She squinted slightly and leaned forward, the mask shifting slightly on her face. Placing the vials back into their velvet-lined box, he reached out and gently pushed her back down against the metal table. "Relax, my deaw." He pulled one of the leather straps across her and into the buckle before readjusting the plate. If it slipped while she was in the chamber there was no telling what the results would be.

"What will they do to me?" the girl asked.

He shook his head. "Lord Eschaton said that you wiww take on the pewsonawity of the metaw you choose."

Although it was, scientifically speaking, nonsense, there was, he believed, also some truth to that description. Certainly every metal they had tried so far seemed to have a different effect, and his description appeared to have satisfied the girl. "Silver, then. Gold is for the wealthy and fools."

He began to strap her hands and feet into the restraints. There would no doubt be more pain than she would expect. "Automaton!" he yelled, looking up at the machine man. "Make sure the chamber is filled with steam."

The nearly completed rocket loomed over everything else in the laboratory now. It was at least three stories tall, the huge black engine hanging in its frame. They had managed, with great difficulty, to rescue the massive boiler from the ruins of the building where it had been constructed. It had been damaged in the collapse, but it showed little of it now.

An array of pipes and machinery sprouted out of the top and bottom of the massive metal tubes, leading down to the array of nozzles securely attached along the bottom of the frame. The cones alternated between large and small. The large ones were designed to give it enough lift to send it up into the sky. The smaller ones would make sure that the maximum amount of vapor was released into the air, in a mixture of smoke, steam, and metals that Eschaton had carefully determined to be able to transform the largest section of the population into something that would, they hoped, no longer be able to be called human.

"Tom!" the girl said, struggling feebly against her bonds. "I am sorry. I never wanted them to hurt you."

The old man scowled. What was it about this animated man that made people treat a pile of cogs and wheels with the same respect afforded to a living, breathing human?

The metal man was in a cage of his own now, his body firmly strapped into place with leather and wood. Le Voyageur's theory—that the mechanical man could be immobilized by a continuous application of electric current—had been proven true. After using it to disable the metal man during the attack on the junkyard, he had fine-tuned the process so that he could render the machine harmless, while still effectively producing the massive amounts of steam they would need to launch the apparatus up into the air.

"Lay back, Viowa. Tom can't talk anymowe." The current that immobilized him apparently kept him silent, as well.

If the experiment on the Italian girl proved successful, they would be able to launch the rocket at any time. Once the ship had reached the proper altitude, a burst of electricity would ignite the fuel inside and tear it apart, providing a spectacular finale for the rocket's ascendance across the skyline as the gas settled across New York, bringing with it a new era of mankind.

Le Voyageur was far too old to survive the purification process when the time came. His last whiff of the black gas had led him to several days' worth of sickness, and had almost cost him his life. Eschaton had offered him a chance to escape. "If you want to leave before the launch, I won't hold it against you."

The Frenchman had laughed at that, ending with his usual mocking cackle. "Your vision is too cweaw! I do not want to wun, having spent my wast days on this pwanet in the sewvice of such a dweam!"

Le Voyageur had worked with Eschaton before all this had begun, back when he had simply been Mr. Harrington, also known as the Clockwork Man.

The Frenchman had hired the young scientist to help with some of his more fanciful projects, and had demanded that they sit together and discuss their philosophies of machinery and construction before he would "allow" any of his designs to "fondowed" by the boy. Eschaton had still been sickly back then, before he had discovered his purification.

But despite his attempt to match their philosophies, he soon realized that Harrington's vision and skill were greater than his own. In hindsight it had been a simple case of jealousy, but the two men had a very public falling out, ultimately pitting their battle machines against each other in the streets of New York. Le Voyageur smiled at the memory of how quickly *that* had earned the attention of the Paragons.

Once Darby and the rest of his band of do-gooders had come after them, the two patched up their differences in order to escape—cementing a bond of friendship that the old man would take with him to the grave.

Turning his attention back to the girl, le Voyageur unscrewed the cap from the end of the silver vial, and fit a needle to the end of it. As he plunged the syringe into her arm, the girl let out a yelp. "What are you doing to me?"

"Kiwwing you." He rolled the cart toward the large brick chamber on the other side of the rocket. "But when you awe webown, you wiww become mowe powewful zan you evew imagined."

"I don't want power." Her words were already beginning to slur.

"Then what do you want?" he asked her. It was hard to believe she didn't want strength in one way or another. The only way for anyone to enforce their will on humanity was to have the power to threaten or dominate those who would impose their will on you. In a world of walking weapons, everyone would be free.

"Eschaton promised me *revenge*," she croaked out.

"Did he? Against who?" He rolled the creaking cart to a stop in front of the smoking room.

"Everyone."

Le Voyageur gave a slight cackle at that. It was certainly ambitious, to say the least. "You have a gweat deal of bittewness for one zo young. But I zink that youth aways wants to see the wowld faww so that they can stand taww."

"Sarah didn't. She wanted to *save* everyone . . ." He had added a large dose of morphine to the formula to dull the pain, and it was clearly taking hold of the girl now—her consciousness was beginning to fade.

He didn't need to understand the Italian girl's motivations to know she would ultimately discover that the results of the experiment were different than her expectations: transformation had a tendency to change the mind as well as the body.

But no matter. Le Voyageur had lived a very long time, and the one advantage of outliving all your friends was the wisdom that came from being the last man standing. During his long life he had come to discover that the dreamers who accomplished their dreams were transformed by them. Even his own body had been broken and twisted by the years spent working to create the machines he loved so much.

And while the gears and pistons that he spent his days crafting were most certainly not alive, that didn't mean that they weren't capable of taking a bite from their creator now and then. Even his damnable lisp had been the result of a flywheel accident that had only been a few centimeters away from tearing away his jaw entirely.

Perhaps it was that very unpredictability that gave the Automaton his charm.

Checking the gauges to make sure the mechanical man had followed his orders, he spun the wheel on the chamber door to begin venting the smoke out of the room. The next phase of the operation would be the most delicate, and the most dangerous.

He slipped on his rubber gloves and pulled the hood down over his head. A long hose led from the helmet to a pipe that carried in air directly from the outside. While none of the air in New York City could be considered "fresh," it was close enough for his purposes.

The fan rattled as it vented the gas inside, and after a short wait he opened the outer door of the brick chamber, releasing a thick cloud of the caustic fortified smoke into the room. From somewhere behind him he could hear muffled coughs as the girl inhaled the diluted fumes. It would be nothing compared to what was about to come.

Stepping into the chamber, he saw the light glinting off Eschaton's skin. "Are you conscious, my wowd?"

The voice that responded sounded different than the man he had placed into the room the night before. "Jean-Jean, is that you?"

"It is me, my fweiid." He grabbed the cart and pulled. Eschaton had been heavy before, and now he weighed almost twice as much. Still, after a few tugs he managed to get the table rolling. "Wet's have a wook at you."

He dragged the cart out into the laboratory. The light from the arc lamps glimmered off the living metal that now covered the man's once-gray body. Continuous application of smoke and steam had bonded the plates of Darby's living steel to Eschaton's flesh. The metal was covered with a light grit, but he had expected a thicker layer of soot. Perhaps it had been absorbed by the metal itself. "Cuwious," the old man mumbled.

The thick glass of his protective suit made it hard to see details, and le Voyageur desperately wanted to pull off the helmet and take a closer look, but even the smallest taste of the smoke might send him into a coughing fit. "West easy, my wowd."

The girl had turned her head to look at Eschaton. "Ith he not beautifuw, my deaw?"

"He's amazing!" The words came out in a long but understandable slur. "Will I become like him?"

"A wittle. Youw face wiww be made of metaw. You must wemembah to zank him for parting with some of his pwecious metaw so that you might become whowe once again."

"I will."

From somewhere behind him came the sound of screeching metal, and when he turned around to look he saw that Eschaton had torn out the restraints that had held him to the metal table during the transformation.

As the new Eschaton rose, it was clear that he now stood taller than he had been before. Le Voyageur's eyes widened as he saw a crackle of electricity shimmer across the metal body. "How do I look, Jean-Jean?"

The Frenchman smiled. "Most impwessive, my wowd."

Eschaton brought up his arm to stare at it. "It seems that the bonding process has gone even better than we imagined."

"If ownwy we couwd discovew ze secwets of Dawby's miwacuwous metaw."

"Given time, we will uncover all of his secrets, and so much more. I only wish you could be there to join me, Jean-Jean." Eschaton held out his arm, and let out what could only be described as a lightning bolt. The Frenchman could feel the heat, and the sheer force of the energy it contained made his hair stand on end. It was both terrifying and fantastic. He felt a warmth growing in his heart that hadn't been there in years. If this was to be his final voyage, it would also be his greatest!

"Now, there is one thing left to try." Eschaton walked across the room, the metal that covered his feet ringing with every step. He stopped under the shackled Automaton, hanging from the wall. "What do you think, Tom? It wouldn't have been possible to fuse this metal to myself without the steam you provided, and now I've used it to take the body that Darby had created for you."

Eschaton banged his hand against his chest, letting out a series of deep "thunks." "It is a miraculous gift that Darby planned on giving you, but I somehow think you still would have wasted it, making a mockery of life instead of celebrating it."

Tom, slowly, but with clear determination, shook his head at the metal-covered man. "I . . . would . . . not . . . become . . . you . . ."

Eschaton turned to le Voyageur. "I thought you said he could no longer talk."

"It seems zhat his detewmination is gweatew zan I imagined." Or he simply had underestimated the power of the machine.

Eschaton reached in through the wooden frame that held the mechanical man in place. The wire "flesh" that had wrapped the Automaton's metal limbs was now mostly torn away, leaving him a shining steel skeleton in a cage.

Le Voyageur had considered smashing the Automaton's face, robbing him of the machine's last pretense of humanity. But ultimately he found himself unable to do it. Despite his lack of belief in the metal man's soul, the Frenchman still preferred that a talking creature have a visage, no matter how fake it might be.

Eschaton's hand moved closer, and he let it hover over the Automaton's heart. Sparks jumped from his fingers. "The last time we met I had to tear you to pieces to get to what you carry in your chest. Now I could simply pluck your heart out from you."

"I . . . am . . . not . . . afraid."

Eschaton smiled. "No, I didn't think you would be. You don't have the sense." He pulled his hand back. "But rest easy for now. I'll deal with you soon enough."

"Don't hurt him." The girl's voice was slurred, but her tone was still demanding.

"Hush, Viowa," le Voyageur said. The last thing he needed now was to make Eschaton angry before he had been given a chance to understand his new powers.

Eschaton crossed the room and looked down at the girl on the table. Smiling, he brushed his hand across her head. "Look at you. You're already so beautiful, but once you've been purified, you may be fit to stand by my side." The caress clearly caused her pain, but she didn't cry out. "But you'll need to decide whose side you are on first."

"Tom is more than that . . ."

Eschaton placed his hands together. "You would give us your brother and Sarah, but somehow you still have concern over an animated engine. Is his charm with women based on something maternal, or are there more carnal instincts in play?"

The Frenchman stepped forward. "I have found, my wowd," he said, pondering the repercussions of Eschaton's words, "that when it comes to the weakew sex, it is aways a mixtuwe of both."

"Quite right as always, Jean-Jean." Le Voyageur smiled at that. There were times when the two of them could work together almost like a single person, each driving the other to greater vision and insight. "It took me many years to realize that the greatest difference between men and machines is that any time you attempt to expose the secrets of humanity by tearing it apart, you always raise more questions than you answer."

The giant looked back to the girl, and le Voyageur watched, fascinated, as Eschaton's metal skin shimmered with gray and silver. "I won't destroy him yet, Viola, if that's what's worrying you. You'll see him again." He took a deep breath and caressed her head with his hand. "But I will transform him, just as I'm going to transform you. We must all prepare for the new world in our own way, just as I am going to prepare you."

She nodded slowly through her haze, but the Frenchman wondered if it was out of understanding, or simply fear. Her body would be starting to die under the stress of the metal coursing through her veins. "It's time fow you to begin youw journey, my deaw."

Eschaton gave le Voyageur a slight nod. "Don't be afraid, Viola. It may be painful, but I think you'll be pleased with the results."

Le Voyageur picked up another syringe and jabbed it deep into her flesh. The screaming began an instant later as the second, larger dose of liquid metal began the process of remaking her from the inside.

He didn't need to imagine the fear of encroaching death that must be consuming her now as the poison attacked her organs. Age had already given him the privilege of that sensation on a daily basis.

As she struggled and squealed, the Frenchman wheeled the red-haired woman into the chamber. He didn't imagine her crimson locks would survive the transformation, but there was no way to be sure until she came out again. "Now my deaw, you wiww feew some pain. But if you can, imagine what you want to become, and pewhaps youw dweams wiww come twue."

He centered the cart in the room and walked out again, using the wheel on the door to seal the chamber. Grabbing the lever by the entrance, he released the fortified smoke into the room. Even through the brick walls and his mask he could hear her shrieking, louder and louder, until finally it faded away, the sounds choked out by the black gas that filled her lungs.

After checking the rubber seals of the door to make sure that none of the gas was leaking out, he pulled off the mask and took a deep breath. The air was clean enough. "Wemembew, Tom," he yelled out loudly, "without you pwoducing the steam, it is vewy wikewy zat she wiww die fwom ze smoke."

Tom gave no verbal reply to le Voyageur's orders, but the clicking sound of Tom's heart began to increase, responding to the threat.

Lord Eschaton surmised that the steam acted as a medium for the smoke, allowing it to more completely, and more powerfully, penetrate the body. It also seemed to mitigate some of the more caustic effects of the smoke alone. It had proven true with Nathaniel, and in Eschaton's case it had been the steam that had allowed them to further augment his own body, years after he had originally been exposed. If only they had been able to give Eli some of the steam, perhaps his death could have been avoided.

Le Voyageur made a few final checks of the equipment, reading the dials that had been placed into the wall. "She wiww, I zink, be one of youw gweatest cweations, my Wowd Eschaton."

Eschaton was still staring at his newly metallic flesh. "Perhaps . . . But I wonder if, with the discovery of this new metal, we may have gone a step beyond what we even knew was possible."

"What do you mean?"

The silver giant walked across the room. The white bolts that had once lived under his skin seemed to almost leap from his flesh now, turning it a glowing silver.

He stopped in front of a tall wooden rack.

Sitting atop it was a long scepter. It had initially been designed as one of the Frenchman's "paratonnerre contraire" machines. This particular device had been designed to channel Eschaton's living electrical energy, but the original prototypes had proven less then efficient.

Le Voyageur had shaped the top of it to resemble a large Omega symbol, sharpening the exterior edge so that it could be wielded as a blade if anyone came too close. Metal wires sprung from the shaft, with a series of clay isolators near the top that would allow Eschaton's living energy to be concentrated and channeled at its targets.

"I pwomised I wouwd make it wewk," the Frenchman said apologetically, "but I'm afwaid with aww ze othew zings I've had to do, it is not yet compwete."

The cloth-wrapped wires hanging from the end flopped around limply as Eschaton picked up the spear and raised it into the air. "Not to worry, my friend, you've done excellent work!" Arcs of power seemed to swirl around his hand, reaching out from the silver surface of his skin and connecting with the exposed ends of the wires. "Now let me finish it for you."

As the electric arcs touched the wires, they came to life, wriggling and dancing like charmed snakes. Le Voyageur watched wide-eyed as the wires lashed themselves around the copper rivets. "As you can see, my rebirth has given me new abilities."

Eschaton's skin was shimmering now, and he turned toward Tom. "What do you think of that, my mechanical friend? Perhaps I have now surpassed even your amazing powers!"

Lifting the device above his head, Eschaton released a large bolt of electricity that leapt out from the tip and crackled through the air. The living lightning, looking for a place to go, reached out to touch the rocket's frame. Once it contacted the metal it arced down its sides, sending out a shower of sparks.

Le Voyageur felt a stab of panic in his heart. The ship was loaded with fuel and almost ready for flight. If it were to ignite now, in this enclosed space, it would be catastrophic.

His fear was so great that for an instant the Frenchman thought he had felt the earth trembling beneath his feet. He held his breath, bracing for his inevitable destruction.

The old man relaxed as the last of the lingering energy dissipated. He would, if everything went to plan, be taking his final journey soon, but he wanted to savor every moment he could between now and then. "Please, my wowd, be cawefuw. Ze wocket, she is vowetiwe."

Eschaton turned to him, a strange look on his face. "I think, Jean-Jean, that you can call me *King* from now on."

The old man took an involuntary step backward. "What?"

"I had some time to think inside of the chamber, and I've decided that the time has come for me to take on a new title—one that better defines my role in the new world." Once again he raised up his spear and let the power arc out from him. The bolts spread out in all directions, although they seemed to be conspicuously avoiding the rocket. "I am King Omega now!"

Then the earth rumbled again. It was far more intense this time.

Across the room there was a thundering snap as a long crack appeared in the stone walls. "*Sacwe Dieu!*" the Frenchman cried out. There wasn't much that made him afraid, but one of the reasons that he enjoyed being able to so quickly travel across the surface of the Earth was so that he could stay out of its clutches. "Is this youw doing, Eschaton?" The last thing he wanted was to find himself entombed.

"No. Nor do I think it is another of Darby's ghoulish plans from beyond the grave," the silver-skinned giant replied.

The rumbling slowed and dust rained down from the ceiling. The motes of earth sizzled slightly as they fell onto Eschaton's skin.

The Frenchman settled himself in a chair. His heart was racing in his chest. "Zen what is it?"

Eschaton scowled, then spat on the ground. "It's them."

"Who?"

"Those god-damned heroes!" he shouted. "Who else would arrive just in time to spoil my ultimate moment of rebirth and triumph?" Eschaton placed his spear back onto the rack and walked over to one of the dynamo control panels near the wall.

"It's what they do! It's what they always do!" he continued. He approached a tall cabinet constructed to restrict and channel the flow of electricity. "That girl, her father, even Darby—reaching out from the grave!" Arcs of electricity leapt out from Eschaton's skin toward the panel. The rows of incandescent lights that had been strung along the wall just behind it began to glow brightly.

"What awe you doing, my wowd?"

"King!" Eschaton roared. "I'm King Omega now!" Something inside the cabinet shifted as if there was some kind of beast trapped inside. Then the front panel buckled, spilling out the wires and gears that lived in it. They leapt toward Eschaton as if magnetized.

"This isn't *their* world anymore, it's *mine*! They just don't realize it yet." The disgorged elements were wrapping themselves around him, sending out laddering arcs as they covered his skin.

"Jean-Jean, prepare the rocket." The spidering arcs of lightning grew brighter, and le Voyageur realized that Eschaton was actually using the electricity to cut the steel from the machinery around him. The freed metal seemed to almost float onto the silver giant's body.

The process didn't take long, and when he was done Eschaton had covered himself completely with an armor constructed of plates of steel, with thick wire woven underneath. The man's head was fully exposed, but sitting on his back was a dynamo unlike the Frenchman had ever seen, constructed from brass and large glass isolators that poked out of him like the spines of a porcupine. "What have you done?" he asked.

Eschaton laughed. "With this metal flesh, I can now do what the mechanical man does: rebuild machinery with the power of my mind alone! I can turn my vision into reality with nothing more than a thought, and I can think of things his mechanical mind could never dream of!"

The Frenchman felt doubt stabbing deeply across his chest. It had always seemed so practical to be playing with the smoke, working to transform men into gods. But now that one of them stood before him, it was terrifying to behold.

"We need to launch it now, before these fools can do any more to stop me."

"Yes, my wowd."

Lightning arced around him, trapping him for an instant in a cage of energy. "King Omega now, my friend," he said with a serious tone. "Remember that."

"Yes, my King." It had been less than a century since France had taken down its monarchy in a bloody revolt. And even if the terror that followed had occurred shortly *before* his birth, it had only been a decade since the last Napoleon had finally been deposed. The last thing he wanted to leave as his legacy was another king. Especially one that had the true powers of a god.

But he had come too far to turn back now. Jean-Jean grabbed a lever near the rocket and pulled it down. The platform that the craft sat on gave out a groan, and then began to slide across the floor. The metal craft shook slightly as it gained speed, but didn't appear to be in danger of toppling.

Eschaton said, "I won't need your heart for long, metal man. Soon I will build my own!"

He stumbled across the room and reached into the machine where they had kept the Omega Element. The metal sarcophagus had originally been created by Darby—a device used to create fortified smoke. They had rebuilt it, turning it to their own ends as a source of the smoke that they needed to fill their rocket.

Eschaton thrust his hand deep into the device, and the metal seemed to shimmer and glow. Le Voyageur could hear the delicate machinery inside being shattered. Whatever power he had used to build the armor was obviously at work here. Pieces clattered to the floor, joining the cacophony of technology that was already covering him.

Finally Eschaton let out a large grumble and held his hand up triumphantly so that the old man could see the key he held.

The Frenchman stared, eyes wide. "What awe you doing, Escha . . . Omega?"

Eschaton gazed at the small chunk of shimmering metal as if he had never seen it before. It seemed to be reacting with his flesh. His fingers, where he touched the metal, were turning black. "First, I must apologize, Jean-Jean. I know this isn't what you expected or wanted, but if my plan is going to come to fruition, we must wait a little while longer before we can share the world equally amongst the purified."

"Zose sound wike the wowds of a tywant, not the man who towd me he wanted to change ze wowld."

Eschaton nodded. "I know it must seem that way to you now, my friend, but I've learned a great deal in the last few days. I promise you that the world we dreamed of will still come to pass, but to get there we must go much further than we had originally imagined." The silver-gray man stuck out his tongue. The appendage was gray and shining, like some kind of dangerous tentacle.

As he gingerly laid the key on it, Eschaton's tongue turned black. Eschaton rolled it back into his mouth, seemingly unconcerned by the danger of ingesting such a strange object.

For a moment le Voyageur felt like crying. They had called him a madman all his life, but nothing he had ever done compared to the idiocy that he was seeing now. "What have you done?"

"Taken a desperate measure for a desperate time," Eschaton said with a smile, and swallowed the metal object with an audible gulp.

"You see, Jean-Jean," he began, and then the smile disappeared from his face.

"My wowd?" The Frenchman saw a series of fine black lines beginning to crawl up Eschaton's silver skin.

"I'll be fine, just give me a moment to, *ungh*," he said through gritted teeth. "I'll be fine," he repeated, but le Voyageur wasn't so sure.

The blackness in his skin continued to grow, and it took only a minute before the darkness had replaced the metal entirely. Eschaton had been transformed from a man of metal into a shadow, every muscle tightly contracted within the armor he had built around himself.

There was an endless moment of quiet, and then all of Eschaton's muscles released at once, and he simply slumped to the floor. Le Voyageur ran toward him, fearing the worst. As he came close, the black figure raised his head and let out a scream. The terrible sound was carried on a stream of black smoke.

Recognizing the fortified smoke for what it was, the Frenchman stumbled backwards, searching desperately for his helmet. He spotted his protective hood on a table, and hobbled over to it. Forced to take a breath, he was glad to find that whatever was happening with Eschaton, the man had yet to poison the air.

Slipping the hood over his head, he turned to see a blue glow filling the room as the dynamos on the far wall began to spin up and hum with power.

Eschaton still lay on the floor, but the glass tubes on his back were glowing now, as large arcs from the machines leapt across the room to the back of the armor that covered his black body. The crackling sounds increased as more and more of the machines sent out their power.

The electricity arced across the metal he wore, dancing across a costume of steel and ceramic that seemed to be bonded to his skin.

He rose slowly to his feet, and then lifted his spear above his head. "The

284

time has come for us to complete our plan, Jean-Jean." Behind him, the remaining dynamos went dark, one after another, as they overloaded from the energy Eschaton drew from them. His skin slowly regained its metallic properties until he was silver once again. "It is time for us to meet our enemies head on!"

The rocket had finished its transit, and now stood on the lift, waiting for its journey out from underground. Eschaton stood next to it on the platform. Despite his size, the machine's frame still dwarfed him. "Yes, my wowd."

"I can't hear you, my friend. Take off the helmet. There's nothing to be afraid of."

The Frenchman was unsure, but he pulled off his mask anyway, setting it down on the table. "Yes, my King."

Chapter 21

Shaking the Foundations

The carriage was dark, but not completely sealed off from daylight. If there was any doubt in Emilio's mind about how foolish their plan actually was, it was made even stronger as the four of them rumbled over the cobblestones in their costumes.

The last time he had seen the Hall of Paragons, Emilo had come to the building with the ridiculous hope of joining the organization, with the prototype for his spinning shield in a cloth bag. The line to enter the building had been surprisingly long, with he and the other would-be heroes all shivering in the cold of a damp April morning.

He remembered thinking how ridiculous and outlandish the men dressed in their costumes had seemed. Emilio had promised himself that he would never be one of them—or at least never be one of them *again*. After all, his il Acrobato suit would have put them all to shame. It had been constructed from circus clothing, and although the basic color had been black, he had worn an orange and green tunic, with similarly colored leggings.

In the end, the bright colors had been a bad choice for a variety of reasons, but mostly due to an inability to hide effectively while being chased across the rooftops.

It was while waiting in that line of would-be heroes that he made a promise to himself: he would never again be a costumed hero. Instead, he would let his inventions be his costume, just as Darby had done. And he had broken that promise only a few days later when he had put on the Steamhammer outfit to battle against the Automaton after he had inhabited the body of Vincent's mechanical creation, the Pneumatic Man. He had mostly forgotten the events of that day until now.

And here he was, back at the Hall, wearing the costume he had sworn he would never wear—this time at Sarah's insistence, with Nathaniel helping to strap him into the outfit, using his transparent hands with surprising confidence and familiarity.

But rather than riding in as heroes, they were skulking in a darkened carriage like robbers. The so-called Society of Steam was, before even announcing its presence, acting like a bunch of common thieves.

As he had been put into the costume, Emilio considered how quickly he had come to inhabit so many different personalities. He certainly would never again be the Acrobat. Although there were skills that would last him the rest of his life, he was long out of practice as an aerialist. From time to time he would awaken with a sensation of twisting and falling, his hands slipping from the bars of the trapeze, falling to his death, rescued only by his return to consciousness. It was a nightmare he'd had since his childhood in the circus, and the dreams of dying had only grown when he had become il Acrobato. Ridding himself of those miserable dreams was one of the many benefits that had come with hanging up the costume, but he had done it too late to save his family, and they had never left him completely.

The shield-wielding Flywheel, his second identity, had been born out of necessity, although when the spinning device had become his only salvation he had also been forced to become far more hands-on than he had ever been as the stealthy Acrobat. With the shield in his hand he had been forced to crash into danger instead of cartwheeling away.

His shield had performed heroically during its short time in his hands, and although he didn't think of himself as a coward, he still missed the protection that it had offered him. Unfortunately there hadn't been time to construct an improved version of the device for his new identity, although if they survived this encounter he would most definitely consider it. Perhaps he would even change his name. But for now he was once again the Steamhammer.

Certainly wearing mechanized chisels at the end of his arms was something that would have never occurred to him if it hadn't been forced on him. But having felt what it was like to wield them, it was hard for him to deny the seductive allure of their power.

Emilio had first taken on Vincent's legacy to protect Sarah from the

Pneumatic Colossus. But it had only been in retrospect that he had learned what it meant to take on a dead man's persona. Even now he felt the spirit of Vincent with him under the mask he wore.

But if it was wearing a mask that made him brave, where did the coward go while his other guise inhabited him? More troubling still, how would those experiences change the nature of Emilio Armando when his real face was revealed? His head was spinning slightly from just thinking about all the ways he had been changed by the people he had chosen to become.

The carriage came to a halt, and a voice whispered to them loudly from outside. "We're here, madam!" The man driving them was Jenny's husband. Sarah had been resistant at first, but her friend had insisted that he would get them there safely and quietly. The maid hadn't been wrong.

The door opened, revealing a short distance from the side of the street to an alley beyond. Sarah had insisted that it would be their best avenue to sneak into the Hall unnoticed.

The four of them filtered out, the carriage rising noticeably as Grüsser stepped out onto the street.

Sarah had sworn that even in costume they would be able to slip into the alley unnoticed. Emilio had refused to believe it was possible, but there was no denying it now.

The carriage pulled away as they ran down the side of the building. Nathaniel was quiet for a moment, then slapped his hand against the solid granite wall of the Hall of Paragons. "You haven't been inside, but this was my prison for almost a month." Although it was impossible to fully comprehend the emotions that were flickering across the face of a transparent man, Emilio thought he could see a painful memory surfacing. "I watched Alexander Stanton die in here, and Eschaton has turned it into an abomination of everything good and decent that the Paragons once stood for."

Emilio found himself hearing his sister's voice for a moment, her mocking tones questioning exactly what those "good and decent" things were that the men who had sat inside this building for all those years had done. Now it was more than likely his sister was inside those walls of her own free will—accepted when he had been turned away.

"I'm sorry, Nathaniel," Emilio said. He didn't know the boy well, but he felt that he should make an effort to connect with someone who had been such an important part of Sarah's life.

"Don't *pity* me," he said, showing a trace of the old anger that Sarah had warned him about. "I'm not looking for it, and I don't want it."

Emilio almost apologized again, this time for his previous apology, and then stopped himself. Instead he raised up the two chisels that sprung out from the arms of the suit. He had replaced the broken originals with new ones, and he had modified them slightly. One was still pointed, designed to crack and pulverize. The other had a wide flat end, like a thick shovel. He had built it to maximize the vibrations, hopefully to throw any attacking enemies off their feet—quite possibly along with himself. "Then it is time to do this."

"I'm worried about Sarah," Nathaniel said. He placed the helmet over Emilio's head with the easy confidence of someone who had rushed into battle in a costume a thousand times before.

"I *always* worried about her," Emilio replied. "But I've also learned that it doesn't mean you're ever going to make a difference in what she chooses."

"Perhaps," Nathaniel said, patting the Italian on the back, "that's why she ended up with you instead of me."

"That's *one* of the reasons." The sound of Sarah's voice was slightly muffled by the mask, but he could hear the mix of exasperation and just a touch of anger. It was a tone she reserved for giving someone just one more chance before she unleashed her full fury.

Nathaniel held up his hands. "I'm sorry if I offended you."

Sarah laughed. "An apology from Nathaniel Winthorp? We haven't even begun to fight and today is already a miraculous day."

Emilio felt himself wanting to come to the boy's defense, but even if Nathaniel was only her step-brother, he knew enough about brothers and sisters to stay out of their way. He decided it might serve them better to entirely change the direction of the conversation instead. "Perhaps we could see your costume, Sarah?"

So far he had only seen the long coat she had been wearing to cover what the women of Stanton house had put together for her. He knew that it was loosely based on her father's costume, and had, in fact, been constructed from pieces of his original outfit, but he couldn't begin to imagine what it might be.

"Don't be so eager, Emilio." But even hidden away under her coat, the costume seemed to be having an effect on her. She stood tall and proud, her hair once again returned to its proper blonde color, although it seemed to have been impossible to effectively clear away all the red; and a tinge of copper still danced in it. "Before we get started, do we all know our part in the plan?"

Nathaniel nodded. "Just don't get too confident, Sarah. Eschaton is a clever, dangerous man."

Sarah raised her eyebrows. "Last time we met I knocked him on his behind, and this time I have a better gun."

"He isn't that man anymore." Nathaniel held up his transparent arm. "He may have begun to unravel the secrets of the universe, but I'm inclined to believe that his mind is going with it."

Emilio didn't like the sound of that. It was one thing to face an evil genius, and quite another to be confronting a madman. "We need to find my sister."

Sarah nodded. "I haven't forgotten about Viola. *If* she's in there, we'll find her, but first we need to get inside."

He nodded in agreement, but he had little doubt that Viola had ended up inside these walls. There were few places she would have gone without telling him, and unlike Sarah and the more genteel women that she was accustomed to, Viola was capable of heading out into the city without getting lost or hurt. "All right, Sarah, but we save her, no matter what."

What he hadn't said out loud was that the more he thought about it, the more he realized that his sister joining Eschaton was inevitable. Although he had wanted to believe she was a hero in her heart, he also knew that the villain's plan to destroy the world made his goals the same as hers.

Sarah didn't move, or even blink—or at least not so far as he could see through the helmet he wore. If he'd had more time he would have removed the glass eye covers entirely. Perhaps that's why Vincent had taken out the second layer of glass by the time he had put the costume on in the theater. With the old showman dead and buried, it was far too late to find out. "First we find Tom. Once we have him back, we'll be able to fight more effectively."

"If he's still alive," Nathaniel added.

"That's quite an enlightened attitude, Nathaniel," Sarah said with a smile. "I thought you believed a machine couldn't be a living thing."

"I haven't changed my mind on that account," he told her, "but I can tell the difference between a broken steam engine and a working one, and we need him."

Sarah stared at Nathaniel quietly for a moment. "Hopefully Tom will be able to convince you. Now wait a few minutes, and then you can begin."

"Where am I supposed to start?" Emilio asked. It was one thing to have an ambitious plan, and quite another to put it into action.

"Right there," Sarah said, pointing at a large white crack in the marble. It had clearly been patched multiple times with concrete, and it looked as if it would soon need it again. "That is where the original Steamhammer tried to bring down the Hall of Paragons before my father stopped him. But this time," she said, whipping open her coat and pulling out her gun, "you'll have the power of the Industrialist on your side."

"Are you taking your father's name, Sarah?" Nathaniel asked with an incredulous look on his face.

"Hardly." She finished undoing the thick black buttons on her overcoat, a gesture that Emilio hoped Nathaniel wasn't finding as alluring as he was. She pulled off her hood and dropped the coat to the ground in a single grand gesture.

"You can call me Columbia now." Sarah took a quick turn, showing off the entire outfit. Emilio gasped in spite of himself. The new costume did indeed incorporate the patriotic theme from her father's original Industrialist costume, but now it had been taken to an almost absurd extreme.

The leather jacket was still mostly the same, but underneath it was a billowing dress of taffeta that had been designed to suggest the form of the United States flag in full wave.

And wrapped around her head was a red and white striped headband that might have been pulled completely from her father's original top hat. But most shocking of all were the two guns holstered on her waist: one was the pneumatic weapon that Tom had given to her. The other was her father's weapon, the bullet feed that powered it leading up to the canister of fortified steam on her back.

"Well, gentlemen," she said as she finished her twirl, "What do you think?"

"It's good . . ." Emilio said, finding himself at even more of a loss for words than usual.

"It is good," Nathaniel confirmed, and then let slip a small chuckle.

Emilio was shocked to find that he had let out a small laugh, as well— one that he hoped would be concealed by the suit. But it seemed that was not to be, and the transparent man responded to his slight laugh by letting out a larger guffaw.

Somehow that sound made Emilio laugh even harder, and it took only a few moments before the two men found themselves gasping and leaning against each other as the laughter rolled out of them.

Emilio tried desperately to control it, but the dagger-filled look that he was being given by Sarah only confirmed his fears that she was taking this entirely the wrong way. "I'm sorry, Sarah," he managed to choke out between fits of laughter.

"Fine, then," she said. "You two *children* can have your laugh at my expense, but this is deadly serious business. If nothing else, I was hoping you could at least support me."

Nathaniel was the first to calm down, and he spoke as Emilio pulled off his helmet to get a breath of air. "I'm not mocking you, Sarah, truly I'm not."

She squinted, eyeing him with a sincere lack of trust that made Emilio glad that he wasn't the one who had spoken up first. "Then what is it that you've found so amusing?"

Emilio broke in. "It's a very," he choked down a chortle, "very strange world that we've found ourselves in, I think."

Nathaniel nodded in response, clearly less in control of his laughter than Emilio was. "After all this," he choked out. "To see *you* in *that*."

Sarah frowned. The explanation clearly wasn't making her feel any better. "All right, you two can make your excuses later. For now, I need you to get to work."

Emilio nodded and stepped forward. Sarah almost turned away, but for whatever reason she hesitated, and he took the moment to plant a kiss directly on her lips. "I love you, Sarah Stanton," he said in a half whisper. "Whatever happens, be safe. I want you to come back to me."

He stared directly into her eyes. His declaration of emotion seemed to give her a bit more confidence. "I love you too, Emilio." She leaned forward and he gave her another kiss—one far more passionate. He closed his eyes, and was glad that he couldn't see Nathaniel's face.

As she pulled away Sarah smiled at him for a moment, then let the emotion pass. She pulled a wire-wrapped key out of her pocket and walked halfway down the alley, toward a metal door with a hole in the center of it.

As she approached the entrance, she pulled the gun out of its holster with her right hand.

Emilio had made some changes to the weapon, but like everything Darby had created, the work in the gun's design spoke to a level of insight and skill that seemed beyond reason. It would have been one thing to simply read about such marvels. There was not an inventor in the world who didn't live in awe of the machines that Dennis Darby had created. But Emilio hadn't just touched the master's work—he'd talked to it.

Emilio watched intently as Sarah slipped the key into the door and held it there. There was a loud "thunk" and the door consumed it. A few seconds later, the door popped open. "No turning back," Sarah said, pulling the pneumatic gun out of its holster, and slipping into the blackness.

Emilio was thunderstruck. "She is amazing."

"She is, at that. You're a lucky man."

Emilio laughed and held up the metal arms. "Luck will be us staying alive."

"True enough," Nathaniel said. "Now how do we start up this ridiculous contraption you're wearing?"

"The switches that are down there," he said, nodding at the device at his back. "Turn them all on."

Nathaniel did as he was told, and Emilio could feel the device coming to life as the water inside it began to swirl. He had only begun his modifications on it when the attack on the junkyard had come, and although he had finished his work in the workshop at the Stanton mansion there had been no time (or way) for him to test the device before putting it on.

It was certainly nowhere near as complex—or as full of mystery—as Darby's devices seemed to be, but even so there was a chance that the changes he had made could cause the chisels he was wearing to malfunction with catastrophic consequences.

Most troubling was a specific bit of strange machinery that Emilio didn't fully understand. He referred to it as "The Harmonic Neutrality," and it was, as far as he could tell, the part of the device that allowed it to send tremendous shockwaves outward without tearing apart the person inside. If he had damaged it—or thrown it off-balance—the suit's tremendous energy would be thrown back at him.

"So, where do we begin?" Nathaniel said, smacking his glassy palms together. "It's time we showed the Children some manners."

Emilio smiled. Whenever he had read about the exploits of the Paragons, they had always been peppered with tremendous amounts of pithy bon mots directed at their enemies. Up until now he had always assumed that these were literary embellishments designed for the readers, but it seemed this was really how a gentlemen adventurer spoke. Hearing it with his own ears gave him a thrill and filled him with pride. "Let's make them shake with fear!"

"That's the spirit!" Nathaniel said. "We'll make a hero of you yet!"

Emilio took a few steps toward the corner of the building and pressed the chisels against the cracks. "This is for you, Vincent," he shouted, and then depressed the switches at his fingertips.

The eye-covers snapped shut, and an instant later the shaking began. The effect was immediate and devastating. The concrete turned to powder almost instantly, sending out a blinding rush of dust, and Emilio was finally glad for the extra layer of protection the suit had placed over his eyes.

Unable to see or hear, he had only his sense of touch to guide him as he drove his arms deeper and deeper into the marble. Feeling the earth parting at his touch gave him a sense of something that went beyond simple pride. It was a moment of almost God-like power. He had become a mythic being— a character out of legend! Emilio Armando would be the man who brought down the Hall of Paragons!

He pressed down with his thumb, injecting a small puff of fortified smoke into the water tank on his back. The machine reacted as though it were an angry mule, bucking and jerking. For a moment he was convinced that he had misjudged his modifications, and the suit might tear him apart, but before he decided to pull his fingers off the triggers it settled into its next level of power. The vibrating seemed to calm down again, and he could feel the ground giving way even faster than before.

Driving the chisels downward, Emilio dug deeper into the foundations of the building. He could feel the ground sinking away underneath him. It was as if the earth beneath his feet had suddenly transformed into a gas, and he was sinking into the very bowels of the planet.

Even surrounded by the dust he could see that the sunlight was disappearing. Before he fell completely into darkness, Emilio lifted his fingers from the activators and the chisels slowed down. The eye guards snapped back, and he looked out to survey his handiwork.

Sarah's plan had been for him to simply crack a hole into the side of the Hall. It would announce the arrival of the Society of Steam, giving him and Nathaniel the unenviable task of dealing with the first wave of defenders while Sarah snuck in. But as the dust cleared, it was obvious that the Steamhammer had gone a great deal farther than that.

Emilio found himself at the bottom of a pit ten feet deep. The corner of the Hall above him was gone entirely, and what remained of the building was not only shattered and cracked, but a large chunk of the granite floor hung precipitously over him, held up by nothing more than wishful thinking and some very good engineering on the part of the building's designers.

He heard Nathaniel's voice calling down from above. "Well done, sir! No one can question your enthusiasm."

"I don't think I can get out!" Emilio said, waving his chisels above his head.

"At this point your best bet may be to just keep drilling straight through to China!" It was followed by a large guffaw. The sound seemed entirely incongruous with its transparent source, although he was happy that the Mercurial Man was still in good spirits.

"What should we do?"

"I can get into the building now. I think I should go and help Sarah."

Emilio realized that in his power-mad foolishness he had not only become trapped, but had also rendered himself unfit to provide aid to the woman he loved. Up above, he saw Nathaniel leap across the hole he had made, landing inside the building. The transparent man looked back down at him, the sun shining through his skin. "Will you be okay?"

"I figure it out." A spray of dust rained down on him from above. "Go help her!"

Nathaniel nodded, then disappeared. Emilio wondered if he had done the right thing.

Looking around, he saw that the foundations of the building were fully exposed now. The wall in front of him was patched and broken. Vincent had told him that the original Steamhammer had managed to break into Darby's lab. This must have been where . . .

"*Naturalmente!*" If Vincent had used the suit to enter the building after he had been buried there, he could do the same thing.

After waiting a moment to make sure that Nathaniel had gotten completely clear, he pressed the chisels up against the side of the building, and pressed down on the activators once again.

The eye covers dropped into place, and the rumbling started up again. He pressed harder into it, until suddenly there was no pressure at all. He managed to avoid tumbling into the abyss he had just opened by only a hair's breadth, but the ground under his feet betrayed him anyway, his legs sliding out from under him as the loose earth drained away, dragging him into the darkness that he had opened under the foundation of the building.

As he fell, Emilio was struck with an almost-amusing thought: he had, like any human who dreamed themselves to have the power of a god, simply opened a path to the underworld.

Chapter 22

A Confrontation of Opposites

As Anubis crashed through the church window he had no idea what to expect on the other side. After his recent luck, he fully expected to be taking the same drop on this side of the window that he had just avoided on the other.

At least his body wouldn't be subject to the same indignities inside a church that it would be on a New York City street.

But his fall was mercifully short, and he travelled only a yard or so through the air before landing hard on the top of an oak desk. The impact knocked the breath out of him and pens, papers, and a bottle of ink all went flying in different directions as his momentum slid him across the surface and onto the ground.

The air had been knocked out of him, and Anubis lay there for a moment, catching his breath, stunned by both his fall and the fact that he had managed to simultaneously reach the ground and stay alive. He felt pain shooting down his leg from knee to ankle from kicking in the window. He flexed his toes to make sure that they still worked, and then slowly dragged himself upright.

As high up as he was, he could still hear the shouting from the street below. "Where are you, Negro?" He'd heard those voices before, back when he was a boy, and they were never good news. "You might as well come out. We'll go easier on you!"

This particular accent was not only familiar; it sent a shock of fear dancing up Anubis's spine. The White Knight had left him badly beaten after their last encounter, but it had only been his flesh that had betrayed him in the fight. The fear he felt from the sound of Clements's voice was the kind that clung to a man's soul. "C'mon, Anubis. You know we won't kill you. I saw you fall off of the quicksilver man, and I need to bring you back to Lord Eschaton."

Perhaps, if he just lay low, they'd go away. "Knight! Over here!" shouted one of the other men. If they had stumbled onto some of the debris from his crash it was only a matter of time . . .

Pulling himself up to his feet, Anubis stumbled toward the entrance. There had to be more than one way out. Maybe he could slip free before they found him.

The door to the office creaked loudly as he opened it. Not loud enough to be heard by the men below, perhaps, but certainly enough to alert anyone inside. Still, he had little time to be stealthy now, and he headed toward the stairs as quickly as he could, urged on by the shouts of the Children outside as they began to piece together what had happened to him.

Anubis found himself limping as he scrambled down the staircase, but his foot was in surprisingly good condition considering the blood streaming down it. His preoccupation with his physical condition had him almost crash straight into a man with a cleric's collar who stood on the landing. "Can I help you, my son?"

"Father," he said breathlessly, "they're after me." He tried to bring his voice down to the bass rumble of Anubis, but without the mask there was really no point. The man already knew the color of his skin.

"It's Reverend. Reverend Charles." The cleric's shirt was hastily tucked into a pair of riveted jeans. "And who are 'they,' exactly?"

There was a pistol in the man's left hand, and it was pointed at him. "Bad men, Reverend. They mean to kill me."

"In my time I've found that men who call other men bad aren't usually so good themselves." The Reverend stepped back to take a long look at Anubis. "But I'm more interested in how you managed to end up on my stairs without coming in the front door first. I'd also like to know what the hell you're wearing."

Abraham considered patience to be one of his strengths, but in this case it was already beginning to run out. "That's a very long story, and one I'd love to tell you if I had the time." The banging on the church doors was so loud and hard that it sounded like someone was slamming their body against them. "I can only promise you that once they have their hands on me, they plan to do me grave bodily harm."

The reverend seemed to be unconcerned by the attack against his church. He narrowed his eyes. "And what have you done that they would wish such ill upon you?"

It was a good bet that trying to proclaim innocence was not an answer that would satisfy the cleric, but he was running out of time. If God *had* answered his prayers by sending him this man, he was responding in a very strange way. "I used to run with them, not too long ago." There was another round of banging. "But now I'm running in the other direction."

The man chuckled at that, lowered his gun, and stepped out of the way. "There's a door in the back, through the kitchen. If you can make it that far, you should be able to escape." Another crash came from the outside, louder this time. "Go."

"Thank you, Reverend."

"It's not the color of a man's skin, but what's underneath that counts." He caught Abraham's eye as he passed him by. "I hope I'm right about you."

Anubis nodded and ran down the stairs. He wondered if the man would have been so eager to let him go if he'd been wearing the full Anubis costume. Perhaps this was the one time where showing his true face had gotten him out of trouble instead of getting him further into it.

The steps took him down directly into the reverend's living quarters, and the door he had mentioned was only a few yards away.

Anubis ran toward it, and was two steps out into the back alley when he heard a tremendous splintering crash from behind.

The Children had broken in, and for an instant Anubis considered staying to fight. The reverend was armed, but there was no telling what Jack Knife and his men would do to the old man. It was possible they would simply leave him alone and go on about their business, but Clements didn't seem the type to have much respect for a man of God.

Still, Anubis was beaten and bruised—hardly in any condition to take on rampaging racist brutes. He took a few more stumbling steps into the alley and heard the shouting begin.

"This is a house of God!" he heard the reverend yell, his voice projecting the wrath of the Almighty. "You will leave this place in peace!"

Despite his effective delivery, the men he was attempting to influence were not the type to be easily swayed by an appeal to higher powers. Eschaton had genuine abilities, and he was on earth in the here and now. The gray man's wrath would certainly be more terrible than any punishment that heaven would be delivering anytime soon. He couldn't hear exactly what the Southerner was saying, but the guttural laughter of the men was chilling and mean.

"Stay back! Damn you, heathens!" If the reverend had intended it as a warning, it wasn't a very good one. A second later Anubis heard the sound of the shotgun's discharge. At least the man had been smart enough to only shoot off one barrel.

Before he could think, Anubis found himself heading back up the stairs and into the kitchen. As he passed by the sink he grabbed a wooden rolling pin off of the drying rack. As weapons went it was hardly the most elegant, or the most stylish, but at the very least it was reliable, and close enough to his missing staff that he was hopeful he might get some use out of it.

The main church was just beyond the living room, and as he opened the door to the sanctuary Anubis could see four men surrounding the reverend. Two of them were dressed in costume.

"You killed the Pugilist!" The man was dressed in thick leather, and was reaching into a bag at his side with a pair of iron tongs.

Whoever it was on the floor was unmoving, his hands bound up inside a pair of large metal boxing gloves. From the wounds on his chest he had been the recipient of the reverend's buckshot.

"It was God who brought him down. I was only his instrument!" The reverend's voice was thunder and fury, and Anubis was impressed to see that although the Children of Eschaton might not be believers, at least the White Knight had the good sense to take a step back when presented with such a powerful voice behind a loaded shotgun barrel.

The man with the tongs drew a glowing plug of metal out of his bag. "This is my instrument, priest."

The shotgun barked out a reply of fire and brimstone that knocked the villain to the ground. "It's Reverend."

"Well, Reverend," the White Knight said, advancing toward him. "It's just you and me now, and it looks like you're all outta shots."

"But not out of friends," Anubis said. He ran forward, swinging the rolling pin in front of him.

The White Knight brought up his hands in time to deflect the blow before it could smash into his head, but he shouted out in pain as the heavy chunk of wood crashed into his arms and shoved him backwards, throwing him off-balance. "There you are. We've been looking all over for you." As Clements pulled off his mask he seemed to be growing taller. "Now I'm finally going to kill you, Negro!"

Anubis was astonished by the speed and ferocity with which the villain leapt toward him. Despite his weakness and injuries, the attack was clearly superhuman. Anubis was thrown to the floor, the rolling pin spinning from his hands. Before he could react the man's thick hands were around his neck. The man definitely *had* grown bigger. This was clearly part of the powers that Eschaton had given him.

Anubis knew he should have run away and never looked back, and yet in the end it was his kindnesses that defined him. They were what made him a hero.

Once again the blackness closed in on him, but this time there was no respite. The roaring grew to fill his ears. He had tried to be good, he had even tried to be just, but in the end it was nothing compared to the overwhelming power of human cruelty that was the true legacy of mankind.

As his thoughts finally disintegrated into darkness, Anubis heard a crack that he was sure must be his neck giving way to the unbearable pressure that had been put to his throat. Then a burning rumbled up his chest to become a desperate, sputtering cough.

Air flooded into his lungs as his vision swam back into focus. The first thing he saw was the pasty pink of Jordan Clements's face as he moaned next to him. There was a gash in the side of his head, blood already welling up from the wound.

Anubis tried to talk, but the only sound he could make was a pitiable, guttural cry.

"Time to get up, son," the reverend said as he reached for his hand. "You were certainly right about them: they were very bad men." He let the reverend help him to his feet. "I'd still love to hear the story of how you managed to make them so damn angry."

Anubis exhaled. He saw the White Knight starting to move despite his brutal wound. There was no way the reverend could know that the man on the floor was no longer simply human. He knew what Clements was capable of, and the White Knight clearly had more control over his abilities than the last time he'd fought him. Looking around the room, he saw the rolling pin on the floor. He stumbled toward it just as the White Knight roared up to his feet.

"You're going to pay," Clements bellowed. "You're *both* going to pay."

"Dear God, protect me!" the preacher said, backing away from him.

"That's right, Reverend, you call on your precious savior. But I'm something new under the sun, and I don't think he's ready for me."

He took a step forward, and Anubis could feel the ground shudder from his step. "The Negro will have to wait his turn while I send you off to heaven." The White Knight's baggy clothing was filling with the villain's expanding bulk as the man continued to grow.

Wrapping his hand around the handle of the rolling pin, Anubis stood up. He coughed, and then shouted, "Come on, you white monster. If you want to kill me, now's the time."

What turned to face him was no longer human, but simply a leering smile in the middle of a vast field of dough. The face had grown unevenly, and the grin revealed teeth separated by wide gaps along the gums. "All right, boy, if that's the way you want it, you go meet God first."

Clements plodded toward Anubis. "I know you think you have something in mind. But whatever desperate plan you think is going to save you, it won't help."

As he got closer, Anubis reared back with his rolling pin and looked up. The White Knight towered over him now, arms raised, each hand big enough to crush his entire head.

Anubis realized that even if he attacked, his swing wouldn't reach up past the White Knight's chest. Once again it seemed that he hadn't had the good sense to simply run away. He made a small prayer to God for forgiveness, and held his ground.

"I still can't believe that Eschaton thought you could be purified." Clements said. "I've always known that no matter how much you try, you can't wash the black off of a nig . . ."

The sound of the shotgun was deafening as it loosed both barrels. For an instant it seemed that even the Remington might not be enough to stop the monster.

Clements just stood there, looking stunned. Then he let out a gurgling sigh as his eyes rolled back into his head. He teetered forward slightly before his legs gave way, and the huge man crashed to the floor, revealing that the back of his head was mostly gone.

Anubis let out a sigh. "Thank you, Reverend."

"You came back to help me."

Anubis nodded. "I'm stubborn that way. But some people wouldn't have looked past the color of my skin."

The reverend laughed and cracked open the breach on the barrel. "What a man looks like on the outside has never been no never mind to me. I was an abolitionist before the war, and I snuck plenty of men up into the North."

The preacher reached down into one of the pews, pulling out a few more shells from underneath a hymnal. Now it was Anubis's turn to laugh. "I don't suppose the congregation minds you hiding your ammunition down with the prayer books."

He slipped in the second shell, then snapped the Remington closed with a practiced hand. "Not so many people share my enlightened views, so it isn't very often we fill them enough for anyone to notice. Besides, I'm the only one in the church allowed to carry a shotgun—on Sunday, anyway."

Anubis nodded and looked around. He'd lost Nathaniel, and his costume, but he'd somehow survived once again.

He reached down and picked up the White Knight's hood.

"Looks like one a those gentlemen adventurers the papers are always going on about," the reverend said.

"A pretender and a villain."

The reverend eyed him up and down. "And I suppose you dress up in a costume, as well."

Anubis looked down at the ragged outfit he was wearing. He had some older pieces, and at least he still had his chestplate. "Hard to deny it."

"What do you call yourself?"

"Anubis."

"Not exactly a Christian name—or," he said, wagging a finger at the golden ankh on his chest, "a Christian symbol."

Faced with the priest's condemnation he felt duly chided. "That's why it's supposed to be a *secret* identity."

"So, what's next?"

He pulled the mask down over his face, trying to ignore the scent of the dead man that clung to it. As sweaty as Clements had been, it seemed he'd at least bothered to bathe, and there was a faint scent of lavender behind the sour odor. "How does it look?"

"If you follow me you can have a look for yourself." Anubis did as the Reverend asked. They left the sanctuary and headed back into the living area.

Once inside the living room, the holy man lit a chimney lamp and held it up in front of a mirror. "What do you think?"

Seeing himself wearing the stolen face of his enemy, he felt as if he had been reborn. The white of the mask would be a good match for his Egyptian skirt.

"Anubis. Something to do with the underworld, right?"

Abraham nodded. "He weighed the hearts of dead men, and determined if they were fit to go on to the underworld."

"Seems a bit dark for a man wearing a white mask. I'm in the redemption business, myself, and when a man rises up after being saved, I always say it's time to take on a new name." He rubbed his chin. "Usually I tell people they should keep it a secret, but in your case, I—"

"How about Ra?" Abraham said. It had come out of nowhere, but it seemed absolutely right. "That's the sun god."

The reverend made a show of thinking about it, and then nodded. "It's not the son of God, but for a pagan deity, it just might do."

Abraham was already thinking he liked it. He'd have to make a few changes to the costume. First and foremost, he'd need a new mask. Ra was a bird-headed god, but at least he could still carry a staff. He didn't want to give that up. But being the light-bringer certainly seemed like a better job than being the judge.

"Now, son, I've got three dead bodies on my floor, and I'm going to need a hand cleaning up the mess before my worshippers get here in the morning."

Chapter 23
No Joy in Revenge

Somewhere deep inside his body, Nathaniel felt something like a twinge of guilt as he ran into the Hall of Paragons. He had left Sarah's suitor standing at the bottom of a very deep hole, and despite strong feelings of jealousy and anger, he had begun to have a grudging respect for the man who had stolen Sarah's heart. And he suspected that the Italian had taken more than that from her. Possibly her honor, as well . . .

All the same, there was very little either of them could do from inside a pit, and Emilio had been adamant that Nathaniel go and provide the distraction that would protect Sarah.

Still, someone should have warned Emilio. Any new hero, when given a power they didn't fully understand, had a tendency to fall prey to unfortunate circumstances. His own first attempts at flying in the suit Darby had created for him had been full of near misses, and his death-defying stunts had been far more about desperation than grace or planning.

But the true reason for his guilt was that despite the realization that he would never have her, he still wanted to prove to Sarah that he was worthy of her love. No matter how ruined or ridiculous it was, it was impossible to ignore that he wanted her to believe in him. He had thought his transformation might have made him inhuman enough that he was beyond petty jealousies, but his return to the Stanton household had shown him that no amount of "purification" could make him immune to the pain in his heart—even if he wasn't sure that he actually still had anything like a heart beating in his chest anymore.

As he ran across the front foyer, the ground shook under his feet again. "What the hell is Emilio doing?" he muttered to himself. The fresco of the ceiling above him had already been damaged by the birth of the Shell, and defaced by the Children of Eschaton, but with the Steamhammer's attack the few remaining pieces were giving way—collapsing in large chunks, battering Nathaniel with the dusty remains of the idealized Paragons.

There was a time when that would have struck him as ironic, but as he brushed the plaster off of his transparent skin he realized that the time of those old heroes was now so lost that he could no longer feel much sorrow at their passing. Of all the men who had once stood proudly in these halls and called themselves Paragons, only he and Grüsser were left, and he was hardly the man he used to be.

Across the room a number of men poured into the Hall. Some of them he vaguely recognized from the trial, the others wore the distinctive jackets that marked them as Jack Knife's Blades. "If you're looking to find out what all the trouble is about," Nathaniel said, reaching down to his side, "you've found it."

He lifted up an iron flask wrapped in asbestos, and pulled free with his teeth the cork that stoppered it. Even through his smoke-ruined senses he could smell the whisky inside. Opening his mouth wide, he poured the brown spirit straight down his throat. The effect of the strong liquor on his system was almost instantaneous.

In the days since he had first come into his new powers, the delay from the time he consumed the alcohol until he felt the liquor course through his body and light his nerves on fire was becoming less and less. This was genuine irony, at least: the very same liquid he had once used to dull his senses now inflamed them.

The last few days in the mansion, Nathaniel had spent his time beginning to learn to "speak" with the quicksilver that lived inside his skin. While it still seemed to act on its own, he had at least managed to get it to pay attention to him from time to time. As the Children rushed toward him, he called the silver up into his arms and ignited it. The flare of heat surged out of him with an almost physical force, and the men threw their hands up over their faces and stumbled backwards, their hair shriveling from the heat. The ones in front crashed into the ones behind, and they all landed in a heap on the floor.

For an instant Nathaniel felt tempted to finish the job, and burn the Children to death. He held up his arms, fully intending to do the deed, and was only stopped by a sudden memory of the fate of his parents. "I'm no villain," he told himself, lowering his arms. "Not like him."

But not completely unlike the Crucible either, he realized. More irony to be heaped onto what seemed to be an ever-growing pile. As he walked through the doorway, another group of Children ran toward him. He raised his temperature and watched the men peel away as the light flared out of him.

"Where is Eschaton?" he yelled after them as he strode down the long granite corridor. Since no one was willing to answer him, Nathaniel moved toward the conference room. He found himself eager to confront the gray giant again. This time, free from the interference of Anubis, perhaps he could finish the job.

The plan had been for him to engage with Eschaton (or at least to threaten to), creating a distraction while Sarah snuck quietly through the building, rescuing Tom and Viola. Grüsser would use his knowledge of the secrets of the Hall to create further distractions.

The moment he saw Sarah standing in the corridor, Nathaniel saw just how badly that plan had failed. He had arrived just in the nick of time—she was facing off against the Bomb Lance and a number of Blades. The damned Irishman had his barb leveled at the girl's chest.

"Dammit lass," the Bomb Lance said, "how is it that I can never be rid of you?" In the confined space of the hallway there was little chance that he could miss.

Nathaniel rushed forward as fast as he could, praying that he could tackle the villain from behind before Sarah was hurt. He had felt the sharp end of the Irishman's barbs more than once, and he was determined that she would never suffer the way he did.

"This will be the last time," Sarah said. For an instant Nathaniel was pleased with his transparent form for providing him with the stealth to sneak up on the Irishman before any of the Children could stop him.

What he had failed to account for was the fact that Sarah, seeing only the danger, and not her transparent rescuer, would pull the trigger on her weapon, sending a blast of wind rushing down the corridor in his direction.

The Bomb Lance fired in response to Sarah's attack, but even the slim harpoon couldn't avoid being swept up in the vortex her gun created. It engulfed Murphy and Jack first, spinning the two villains up into the air.

Nathaniel's brain told him to stop, but he couldn't react quickly enough. Then the wind swept him up as well, dashing his body up against the ceiling, then back down onto the ground.

The electric lights on the walls had mostly gone dark, the fragile bulbs smashed in the wind. Nathaniel could sympathize, his own body feeling shattered.

"Where are ya, ya damn harpy?" Clearly the Bomb Lance had managed to rally himself more quickly than the other Children. Nathaniel couldn't see him in the dim light, but the Irishman was yelling loudly. "I'll pierce you like a pincushion!"

"I have a gun as well, sir," Sarah replied. Nathaniel cringed, finding her too easily in the gloom. He wanted to shout out to her, but the painfully familiar hiss of the Bomb Lance's gun meant that the Irishman had seen her as well. Nathaniel swallowed hard as he waited to hear her cry out, fatally pierced by the man's barb.

Despite her bravado, determination, and family heritage, Sarah had never been trained for combat. In the end, the difference between life and death was a matter of knowing when to avoid your instincts. After all, it was never the thing you noticed that became the end of you.

Nathaniel lit up his arm, filling the hallway with a dazzling brilliance that would hopefully be blinding. Staring through his own phosphorous light, he looked around and saw nothing. Neither the Bomb Lance nor Sarah. Instead, there were only the open doors that led into the meeting room—the place where he had seen Alexander Stanton die; the room he and Anubis had escaped only a few days before.

Nathaniel hesitated just for an instant. He heard Sarah shouting out his name from down the bend in the corridor.

He followed her call, stopping short when he reached the turn. The lights were still working in this section and he had Sarah's back this time, but she was in no less danger now, and this time there was far less that he could do.

She and the Bomb Lance were now aiming their weapons directly at one another, which was an improvement. But sitting a few yards behind him, slumped in his wheelchair, was Doc Dynamite, a revolver in his hand and an unlit stick of dynamite on his chest, waiting to be ignited and flung in their direction.

"Let her go!" Nathaniel yelled at the Irishman.

"I'm not holding her, ya daft boy," the Irishman yelled back.

Nathaniel frowned. He knew their plan was doomed to failure, he just hadn't expected it to fall apart quite so quickly.

He took a step forward, and then jerked back from the crack of a bullet against his shoulder. "That's far enough," the Texan said, waving his still-smoking gun.

If the Texan was so confident with his aim, why hadn't he just shot Sarah and been done with it? Nathaniel took another step.

The second bullet struck him directly in the head, but the force of the blow simply knocked him backwards instead of shattering his mind as it had previously. He could feel the silver liquid protecting him, as if there was a second living creature inside him, learning and responding to what was going on around him. "If you harm a hair on her head. . ."

"You shouldn't be so worried about her," the Irishman said. "You're one of the Children now. It's time for you to admit it."

"I'm still a Paragon." He said it proudly and took another step forward.

"Stop, Nathaniel," Sarah said. He almost cringed when he realized that she had actually turned to look at him. If they had wanted her dead, she would have been dead. Perhaps Eschaton still needed something from her?

"You'll be the last one," the Texan said.

"You think we won't kill her if we have to?" The Bomb Lance asked, waving his barb around. "I almost had ya twice, girlie, it'll be a pleasure to finally finish ya off." But he hadn't shot her yet.

"It's me," Nathaniel muttered to himself. The only thing holding them back from killing Sarah was him. He was something more than human now, and they were smart enough to realize that if they killed Sarah he'd cook them both.

"I've had enough of this standoff," Doc Dynamite said. Despite the broken state of his body, the villain's arm windmilled around with a practiced ease that was almost terrifyingly calm. As the arm came up, something flared in the man's hand. The man had struck a parlor match against the wooden edge of the chair.

The tiny flame had barely ignited before it was pressed against the fuse of the explosive that lay against the Doctor's chest.

Even though he had watched the entire event, it still took Nathaniel a moment to comprehend what he had just seen. By that time, the Texan's arm was swinging toward him, the fuse sparkling as it burned.

Nathaniel would have sworn that the lit stick had already been sailing toward him before Grüsser grabbed the Texan's arm, but he caught the Doctor just before he could throw.

The fat German stood directly behind Doc Dynamite, and his sudden interruption of the swing had jolted the stick out of the Doctor's hand. It landed on the blanket across his lap.

"Run, Sarah!" Nathaniel said loudly, and she turned toward him. He considered running as well, but he had a far better chance of surviving then Sarah did, and if she reached him, he could shield her with his body.

He stared into Grüsser's eyes. He had never liked the Prussian much, and he had never understood why they had let him become a part of the team. He had turned traitor to Eschaton to literally save his own neck.

But in that instant, Nathaniel was proud of the man, and he was sure that the other Paragons would have been as well.

No matter what he had thought of him in the past, he had proved himself now.

"Thank you!" he began to say, but Sarah had already reached him. He grabbed her as she ran by, shielding her from the explosion, and then a second unexpected pulse of powerful heat that came as all the sticks hidden in the Texan's duster ignited simultaneously.

The heat was intense, but didn't burn him. He could feel his flesh almost drinking the energy in, somehow absorbing the fire, and hopefully protecting Sarah from being scorched. There was nothing to be done about the force of the explosion, however, and he and Sarah were tossed helplessly down the corridor. Somewhere along the way, Sarah was torn away from him and thrown into the darkness.

As the roaring died down, Nathaniel once again found himself in the dark. Standing up, he ignited his hand, but the smoke and dust from the explosion still swirled around him. As he moved, the world was brown, with some of the particles bursting into tiny flares as they came into contact with his hand.

He looked around, waving his arm back and forth until he found Sarah. She was utterly unconscious, and Nathaniel hoisted her onto his shoulder with surprising ease. He seemed to be continuing to evolve in ways that would confound Charles Darwin. Perhaps he would write the old man and tell him about what had happened to him, if he survived.

Marching back down the hallway toward the exit, he found his way through one of the side corridors and then into what appeared to be an accounting office. The rows and rows of pigeon holes in the walls had once been neatly stacked with papers—all the day-to-day affairs of the Society of Paragons, when it had been more than just a cover for the activities of Eschaton and his villains.

Now it was a ransacked mess, the papers scattered and strewn across the floor by the same barbarians who were supposedly going to remake humanity and restart the future. Nathaniel supposed that men who were expecting the end of the universe had little time for planning out their finances.

The lights reacted to the door closing, giving out a pop and a hiss. They flickered into brilliance as Nathaniel eased Sarah down and sat in the chair next to her.

These lights were unlike any he'd ever seen before. Recessed into the ceiling, they were long tubes that flickered to life with a strange hum. Instead of the warm yellow glow he had come to expect, they gave off a disconcerting cool blue light. Nathaniel imagined they must have been one of Darby's side projects. The old man had always claimed that Edison's bulbs were a failure by their very nature, and that there were far better ways to create illumination then by simply burning things, no matter how long they lasted. "Nature abhors a vacuum, but loves a noble gas!"

"How are you doing, Sarah?" He still hated how different his voice sounded, but no one else seemed to notice.

"You saved me, somehow . . . from the fire."

Nathaniel nodded. "Not sure if I could do it again if you asked me, though."

She sighed. "But, Grüsser is gone . . ."

"Yes," he replied grimly.

"I'm sorry about that."

"All the Paragons are gone now."

"What about Tom?" she asked.

"Whether he's man or machine, he's no more the same Automaton you once knew, than I'm still the Turbine." He looked at Sarah in the blue light, trying to determine if she was more hurt than she was letting on. She had been scorched and knocked about in the explosion, and her hat was gone, but beyond a few bumps and bruises, it seemed she had sustained no real damage.

"But we got the cowboy as well," she said.

He decided to let her change the subject. "That's one for our side."

Sarah nodded. "But what about the Bomb Lance?"

"I didn't see him."

"How could God protect him after all the terrible things he's done?" She stared directly at him, but from a quick glance down at his hands and legs it was clear that this light rendered him even more translucent than normal.

"Your father told me that you need to have your enemy's head on a pike before you can stop looking over your shoulder."

"That does sound like my father," she said with a small smile.

Nathaniel put his hand on her shoulder. "I miss him. He was a great man."

She shook her head slightly. "I'd like to think that he understood. But what he did after Darby died . . ."

"And it didn't make any difference. Look at you! I think he would have been proud of Columbia."

Sarah looked up at him and smiled. He couldn't remember having ever seen her give him that look since they were children. "Thank you, Nathaniel." Even in the blue light, it looked like sunshine. "You know, I think that despite what it did to your complexion, your transformation has made you a better man."

Nathaniel felt a fleeting instant of anger before another part of him realized that she might have been right. "I'm not sure Eschaton would be happy to hear that."

He randomly grabbed one of the papers from the floor. It concerned

Darby's death, and the date at the top read January 11th, 1880. Only six months, but it had been a different world then.

"We still need to find Tom." Sarah began tying a handkerchief around her head, and pulling it back so that her hair would remain out of her eyes. Nathaniel was always stunned by the ability that women had to take the most casual actions and accomplish them in a way that made them heart-rendingly beautiful. "Tom?" she asked again. "We need to go find him."

"Emilio may be down there already," Nathaniel replied. "Under the building."

"What?" Sarah asked.

"He'll be all right, I think. He just dug down too far." It seemed that nothing he was saying was actually helping the situation. "I told him to dig down to the basement."

Sarah rolled her eyes. "What if Eschaton's down there?"

"What if he's up here?" Nathaniel felt a touch of his old anger rising up. "We're trapped in a building full of enemies, all of whom are looking to kill us, or worse. What do *we* do next?"

Sarah rubbed her hand over the kerchief that covered her hair. "We show them just how powerful you are," she said.

Nathaniel frowned. He didn't like their odds. It had been a fool's errand to begin with, but they'd lost the minimal element of surprise, along with the only other member of their party who had any genuine fighting skills. "We need to leave, Sarah."

"Without Emilio? Are we going to abandon him?" Her smile was gone, replaced by anger. "Do you want him to end up like *you*?" she said, her voice rising to a shout.

Nathaniel felt stung. "A better man?" It had sounded clever in his head, but the words sounded petty, even to him.

He let the fire trail up his arm, and touched his hand to the floor. The papers ignited to his touch, curling up as they burned. "Let's go."

He opened the door, revealing a figure dressed mostly in black except for a white hood and skirt. A mask over his face gave him the faintest resemblance to a bird.

"I found you," the voice rumbled.

Chapter 24
Sibling Rivalry

Viola wasn't sure how long she'd been sitting in darkness, and to be honest, she didn't care. At first the drugs that the old Frenchman had given her had done their work, but as the opium had worn off the burning sensation had grown more and more powerful until it had become overwhelming and all-consuming. Strapped to the table, unable to move, she had found herself praying for unconsciousness or death to release her from her suffering.

Neither had come, and eventually that scorching pain had become her entire existence. What made it worse was the occasional cool breeze that seemed to sweep across her, providing a tiny moment of relief before another terrible wave of burning agony.

In those occasional moments of thought that came between the suffering, she wondered if she was already dead, and had entered into the eternal torment of hell that her mother promised would be the eventual fate of all wild and uncontrollable girls such as herself.

But a part of her doubted she had left the mortal world behind. No version of hell Viola had ever heard of came with a rattling fan and a rhythmic hissing. She knew that somewhere nearby the Automaton's heart was beating and guiding her transformation. It was the fortified steam that came directly from Tom's heart that was washing over her.

Somewhere above her a hatch opened, and light flooded into the room. The fan rattled as it slowed, and then began spinning in the opposite direction, pushing fresh air in. Unlike the burning of the smoke, this felt like a thousand needles piercing her skin.

She began to cough, pushing the remaining gas from her lungs. Suddenly desperate to escape, she tried to sit up, only to find herself jerking against her restraints. "Let me out!" she shouted. "Somebody help me!"

She was glad when she heard a muffled, unintelligible voice, followed by the squeal of rubber and metal as the door was thrown open. "Viola? *Sei tu?*"

For a moment she couldn't believe the words she was hearing. It simply seemed too impossible that he might be here. "Emilio?" she asked. The word was slurred slightly, but she was unable to tell if it was the lingering effects of the smoke, or the fact that her face was still covered by a mask. "Get me out of this," she yelled at him in Italian.

"Viola! You're okay!" He ran toward her, hands fumbling against the straps and opening the buckles.

"Brother, how can you be here?"

"Sarah brought me," he said as he finally released one of the restraints. "We came to rescue you."

She frowned, or half-frowned, at least. "How did you even know I was here?" Viola put a hand up to her face. The patch of living steel was still in place, and it had indeed attached itself to her skin. She could feel where it had bonded to her flesh in some miraculous transformation. But something had clearly gone wrong: Eschaton had promised her that if his process worked the metal would become like her own skin, supple and alive. Instead what she felt was something dead and hard pulling against the bones of her cheeks.

"When you disappeared after the attack we thought that you must have . . ." He cut himself off. "We thought you must have been taken."

Emilio's hand brushed her face, but she could feel only the barest trace of his fingers against her flesh. "They have done something terrible to you."

She laughed despite herself, and pulled her legs off of the table. "Did they?"

He nodded. "They put some kind of metal into your face."

Had he said *into*? At least the mask was part of her now. "How do I look?" she asked almost desperately. "Is it worse or better than it was before?"

She could see by her brother's expression that he had been surprised by the question. "I can't," he stammered, "I can't tell in the darkness."

"Then get me out of here." She stumbled slightly as she got to her feet, and Emilio put his arm around her to give her some support. Her instinct was to pull away, but she was too weak to do so. Instead she sank into him and let him carry her out into the main room, her feet barely managing to keep up as he dragged her along.

"How long was I in there?" she asked as he helped her to sink down onto one of the work stools.

"I have no idea," he replied. "I only arrived a few minutes ago."

"And how did you do that?" she asked him, the reality of his being here once again overwhelming her with its sheer impossibility. Having her hapless brother be her rescuer was no more likely than an ant finding its way to the center of a beehive unhindered and un-stung.

Emilio held up his arms in response. Bent back from the wrists were two long metal shafts, hinged so they lay along the arms, and locked into place so that he could use his hands freely. The costume was changed and updated, but she recognized it as the costume he had taken from Vincent. "I dug."

"What were you thinking?"

"I was trying to rescue my sister."

She looked around to see if there was any sign of Eschaton, but he, the rocket, and the old madman had all disappeared. "Rescue me from what? You thought Eschaton had kidnapped me? That he had taken your worthless sister with the intention to somehow bribe your lover into giving him the metal man?" As she mentioned Tom's name, she looked up and saw that the Automaton was still hanging on the wall above them, frozen by le Voyageur's electricity.

Emilio followed her eyes up, and then his own widened. "Tom! What have they done to you?" He spoke the words in English. How quickly his grasp of the language had improved once there had been a woman to motivate him.

Men, despite their complex plans to cover the world in logic and machinery, were ultimately creatures of simple desire. What continued to astound Viola was the lengths they were willing to go to, in order to deny that basic truth.

She had protected her brother for a long time, kept him hidden even after he had lost his wife and child to the authorities, but he was bound and determined to let his lust rule his heart and call it love.

"What's wrong with him? Have they stolen his heart?" Emilio began to reach up toward the metal man. "Why won't he speak?"

"Don't!" Viola grabbed her brother's hand and pulled it back down. "He's been electrified."

"What do you mean?"

Viola pointed out the thick, pitch-covered cable that ran out from where the Automaton had been wrapped in a large sheet of canvas.

Emilio followed the wire across the room to a device that looked something like a large, shiny beetle. The dynamo was smaller than the others, but it still gave off a menacing, insect-like hum, spitting out sparks every few seconds as it provided the power needed to keep Tom from moving.

She followed behind him, and noticed with concern where a number of the nearby machines looked as if they had been consumed, leaving only bits of scorched scrap metal on the ground.

Her brother reached out toward the large switch on the front of the box. She considered attacking him before he could free the Automaton. Once the Automaton was freed, even her brother's pitiable denial would no longer be enough to protect her from the truth. Tom would tell the entire truth, no matter what the consequences.

She plucked up a large metal pipe from the floor. The metal felt cool in her hand. If she did this, she would have to kill him. Emilio would never forgive her for such a betrayal.

But as he pulled the lever she found herself frozen, unable to carry out any action against him. For an instant she wondered if perhaps something external kept her from attacking him. She willed herself to bring her hand down, but something inside of her had frozen her arm as surely as the electricity had immobilized Tom. Despite her belief that she wanted to do it, Viola couldn't bring herself to move against her brother.

The moment passed, and Emilio reached out and threw the switch. The machinery let out a groaning whine as the dynamo inside began to spin down.

Viola lowered her hand, and they both turned at once to see what effect removing the current would have on the Automaton.

As the last bolts of power drained through the wires, Tom's body jerked in response, his flailing arms reminding Viola of a broken doll being violently shaken by a disturbed child. The links of chain that held his body to the wall rattled, the sound echoing through the huge, empty cavern.

Viola took a step back, terrified by the strangeness of it all. Up until now she had been convinced that on some level Tom was fundamentally a man. But as he twitched and jerked in front of her, the Automaton seemed alien and unreal.

The body fell limp. The tarp that had been covering the lower half of his body fell away. Viola could see now how badly the lower half of him had been mangled, his legs pulled completely apart—pinned to the wall by huge iron spikes. His lower torso hung between them, limp and dead, a long tube running out from his chest to channel the fortified steam his heart had been producing.

"Tom!" Emilio yelled, but if the metal man had heard his name, he wasn't responding to it. "Tom! We need you! Sarah needs you."

At the mention of Sarah's name, Viola almost turned and ran. She felt her shame as a blush across her face, stopping only where the metal mask now covered her skin.

But the same hesitation that had stopped her from striking down her brother grabbed her again, holding her in place. She could feel her fate hurtling toward her, but even if it was a locomotive that was coming, she wanted to embrace it.

A low groan began to rise up. It emanated from Tom's body, amplified by the walls. With his strings ripped away, Tom's voice was no longer a harmonious strum of music, but a buzzing cacophony that rose up from the chains that bound him and the very walls themselves. It seemed random at first, like angry bees. As it grew in intensity Viola realized that the sound was calling out her name—and it was angry.

But even still, she found herself frozen in place. It wasn't until she heard a single word from her brother that she could move. "Run," Emilio told her, and she finally did.

As she took her first steps, she reflected that her brother wasn't half as foolish as she had imagined him to be. Despite his desire to believe that his sister had been dragged here against her will as part of an elaborate plan, he had known the truth—that she had come here deliberately. Viola Armando had taken a side against her brother, Sarah, and Tom.

Viola made it to the stairwell against the far wall before she felt something closing around her neck, jerking her to a stop. A strange sound came from her throat as she involuntarily gasped out the last bit of air in her lungs.

She grabbed onto the chain that was both choking her and lifting her up into the air.

As the ground pulled away from her feet, she could feel her body flooding with panic. But even as that physical sensation of fear continued to spread throughout her body, there was a sense of calmness in her thoughts. Viola realized that this moment was one that she had been waiting for all her life.

The world spun and twisted as the chain, somehow animated, reeled her back across the room. She could feel it humming with whatever energy Tom was using to bring it to life, and it took only a few moments for it to bring her face-to-face with the Automaton.

"WHY?" he asked her. The voice was thundering and deep, and yet she could still hear the intelligence behind it.

From somewhere beneath her she heard her brother's voice rising up. "You're choking her, she can't talk."

Viola felt herself being lowered to the ground, but the Automaton's face followed her as she fell, the painted eyes unblinking and accusing. Her brother came into view in the corner of her vision.

Finally the metal grip relaxed slightly, turning from a choking grasp to simply a collar around her neck. She gasped for air, but even as her body desperately fought for breath, her mind remained calm.

Tom's face swayed closer to her. Alfonso had done excellent work. The expression was neutral, but somehow she could sense anger behind it. "Why?" Tom asked again.

She gritted her teeth, and then shouted at him, surprising even herself. "Look at me! Look at what you've done to me!"

The head shook slowly from left to right. "I cannot see, Viola. I can only . . . feel."

She laughed at him. "You play games like a man . . ."

"I—"

She cut him off before he could make his excuse. "You *know* what you did. I never asked to be a part of this."

Tom's head turned slightly, giving it that air of curiosity that seemed to be the one emotion the Automaton had truly mastered. "No one asks to . . . exist. We are the sum of our . . . choices."

Viola shook her head. "I was forced to take a side, this is the side I'll take." She wondered what Emilio would think, hearing her words. But he had chosen badly before . . .

"What do you . . . want?" The words were somehow softer.

"I want to be left alone, but that's not going to happen while the world is full of people who think they know better."

The floating face nodded. "And you would let . . . Eschaton destroy the rest of the . . . world, and kill the people you . . . love?"

Viola couldn't feel the tear rolling down her face until it slid past her unfinished metal skin. "I suppose."

"What if I . . . killed you? Would the end of your . . . existence make you . . . happy?"

She smiled. "I wouldn't know. But we can try."

"Viola! No!" Emilio's selflessness struck her as sweet, but also foolish. She could see Tom's other arm wrapping around him, binding her brother.

"Let him go," she said, and then realized how foolish *she* sounded, ordering him to do anything. She was appealing to a humanity that the mechanical man simply didn't have.

"Where is . . . Sarah!" Tom boomed back at her.

That girl. If she died, what kind of monster would Tom become? "I don't know." She wondered if Eschaton had ever considered that for all his bravado, this machine represented far more of a threat to the future of humanity than he ever could. If the Automaton ever realized that his enemy wasn't any particular human, but humanity itself . . .

"Upstairs!" Emilio yelled out, his voice almost smothered by the metal tentacle wrapped around him. "She's up there, trying to find you!"

The metal arms unwrapped from them both. Grasping the spikes that held him into the wall, Tom tore them from the rock, and lowered himself to the floor.

His body began to twist, taking on a strangely inhuman form. Viola wondered if Tom had decided that he no longer wished to be human, but the strange configuration only lasted for an instant before it resolved into a more natural shape.

He was still recognizable as the Automaton, but he looked more angry and aggressive than he had been before. Chains replaced the strings that had been wrapped around his body. He was more massive and threatening now, but to Viola he seemed more tragic and vulnerable than he had been before. Emilio hung his head. She couldn't tell if he was angry or ashamed.

"It is . . ." Tom said, his voice turning from a growl to a roar, "time for all this to . . . end."

"We need to go. Eschaton has taken the rocket up to the courtyard. I think he plans on launching it soon."

"Tom," Emilio said, looking up at the roof. "It's time."

The machine man nodded. "Viola, you need to . . . leave as well."

She felt a cold shock run through her. She expected to feel the chains wrap around her neck, choking the life from her until the world went dark.

"Go where?" she said quietly.

"Away," Tom replied firmly. "Anywhere that I . . . will never . . . see you again."

The tone was so flat and unemotional that unscrambling the meaning was almost like a puzzle. She turned to her brother. "Emilio . . ."

He was staring down at his feet, unwilling to look her in the eye. "You should go, Viola. He's giving you another chance."

She took a step closer to him. "Emilio," she repeated, "is this what you want?"

"It's what you said *you* wanted," he replied through gritted teeth. "It's what you *chose*."

She could feel the burning sensation of tears forming, but only in the eye that was uncovered by her metal flesh. "I didn't mean to . . ." but the lie died on her lips before she could finish speaking it. It had been her decision that had put them onto opposite sides.

"Don't worry too much," he said, tilting his head upwards slightly. "There's a good chance that none of us will live through this."

"Before you . . . go," Tom said, "I have a . . . question." He turned his painted mask toward Viola. "You were my . . . friend. Emilio's . . . sister. Why did you . . . give yourself to Eschaton?"

She laughed. "When humans are broken they can't just repair themselves. I wanted to become better than I was. I wanted to be like you."

For a long, quiet moment Tom's face stared at her, as inscrutable and implacable as always. It neither wavered nor blinked. "I don't . . . repair myself," Tom rumbled. "I grow."

His head turned away, and the Automaton began to rise up, his body elongating and stretching toward the ceiling. Emilio, cradled in chains, rose with him.

Viola took a step back, and then another. Then she turned and ran. This time when she reached the stairs, there was nothing to stop her.

Chapter 25
Purification

Eschaton grabbed the handle and squeezed, freeing the lever. As he threw it forward he felt the platform beneath his feet shake as machinery hidden deep underground rumbled to life.

For almost a minute nothing moved as the elaborate system that Darby had constructed built up pressure. It was only when it had become powerful enough to overcome the massive weight of the rocket that the platform began to rise, lifting slowly away from the floor of the laboratory and into the air.

The rocket wobbled only slightly, but the Frenchman's reaction was much more pronounced. Eschaton could see that the old man was clearly not convinced that the device was safely secured. "Don't worry so much, Jean-Jean. We are reaching the end of a long journey. We'll be fine."

"I am so gwad of youw confidence." Le Voyageur shook his head. "But wife does not werk zat way. We must stwuggle to ze vewy end, and even zen it is only an instant aftew ouw death zat ze werk we have spent ouw entiwe wife to achieve is undone."

Eschaton smiled, thinking of how all Darby's carefully laid plans had rapidly fallen to pieces after his passing. "I thought it would make you happy to see your efforts coming to fruition."

The Frenchman rolled his eyes. "You aways wewe and ideawist, Wowd . . . King Omega."

It was good hearing the Frenchman using his proper name. Ultimately, in the new world, it would only be the title that would matter. It was the beginning of a new world, but in his own thoughts Eschaton was still waiting to be reborn. Once the rocket launched, *then* he would truly be a new man.

It was possible that his own reign would be short. Surely one of the survivors of the smoke would become powerful enough to destroy him and take power. It was not the legacy that he had originally wished for, but it was preferable to having his egalitarian paradise ruled by idealists and pacifists like the Mercurial Man. There would be no place for that kind of weakness in the world to come.

Holding up one of his metal-covered arms, Eschaton flexed his hand. With every movement a small spark of electricity travelled across his skin. There was an irony in the fact that he now wore Darby's legacy as his own flesh. It was surely one that would have been lost on the old man.

The suit he had crafted for himself had come as a sudden inspiration—one that he could credit to the Automaton. Having taken the Omega Element directly into him, he needed a way to store the living energy that he produced. Every second he had more and more power at his command . . .

"King Omega!" the Frenchman yelled. "Open the couwtyawd hatch!"

Omega grabbed the second lever of the three in front of him and gave it a tug. Up above them the ceiling cracked open, allowing a beam of sunlight to filter down from above and split the darkness.

He had hoped for rain the day of the launch, figuring the water might act as a catalyst for the smoke, but perhaps a blue sky would mean that the gas could travel farther. There was no way to know for sure until they tried. And once this experiment worked there would be other cities, and more rockets.

As the gap continued to widen and the platform climbed closer to it, Eschaton could hear shouting from the courtyard above. A few moments later, a man slipped through the hole. His shout lasted only for an instant, before he crashed down into the framework of the rocket and hung silently.

"*Sacwe Dieu!*" the Frenchman shouted, and reached out to touch the ship, as if his ancient arms might steady it somehow.

The body slipped off and landed on the platform with a thud only a few feet away. It was dressed in a worn tweed coat, and for a moment Eschaton wondered if the thin figure was Jack, but kicking the body over with his foot revealed that the broken figure had only been one of his Blades.

As the nose of the rocket rose into the courtyard the cries of battle could be heard more clearly. Eschaton looked over to the Frenchman. "It seems that one of your prophecies of doom has come true."

"I nevew expect wife to give me anything mowe zen it has so faw."

Eschaton nodded. "But there's always hope."

As his eyes rose up over the edge of the ground he could see that the battle was in full swing. He was entirely unsurprised to discover that Sarah Stanton was one of the attacking "heroes," although it was a surprise to see her dressed in a leather jacket similar to her father's, along with a billowing red, white, and blue skirt.

He was amused to see that she held two guns, one in either hand, and as one weapon burped out a wave of wind that knocked over four of Jack's thugs like bowling skittles, the other fired bullets with a puff of smoke.

The girl had more than likely been the cause of the man who fell through the ceiling, the wind from the gun blowing the boy helplessly into the hole and down to his death. "I thought you didn't like killing men," he yelled out at her.

Sarah turned to look at him. Her face hardened into a grimace, and she took a shot at him. The bullet ricocheted harmlessly off of his skin.

She held up the other gun and fired a blast of wind at him. Having been thrown off his feet by the tiny weapon's gale the last time they had faced each other, he leaned forward, and managed to remain standing.

The Frenchman had hidden himself behind one of the thick fins of the rocket. He muttered *"Mon Dieu"* to himself over and over again as the massive machine rocked slightly in the breeze.

Having weathered the onslaught, Eschaton stepped forward. He lifted up his spear and felt the living energy inside of him expand into it. He sent a searing light across the Omega-shaped blade, to hurl a bolt of living energy directly at the girl.

But before he could finish, a new sensation ran up the entire back side of his body. At first it felt as if his flesh was burning, but he realized it was only his metal suit conducting waves of heat down into his flesh. Then he realized that he could feel the surface of the armor as if it was his own skin.

As he turned to face the source of his pain, Eschaton realized he had been wrong about the light. What Eschaton had assumed to be sunlight was nothing of the sort. It had been the Mercurial Man exercising his miraculous abilities.

Facing his greatest creation glowing with energy and power should have been a moment of ultimate satisfaction. There was no doubt that the transformation of the boy had been his greatest biological triumph. Eschaton had assumed that with the successful creation of a purified man he would prove his philosophical truths as well, but *that* had turned out to be a failure. The boy's stubborn refusal to accept that he had become a god among men had shaken Eschaton to his very core, and forced him to take drastic action.

"Eschaton," Nathaniel yelled out. "We're here to stop you and your mad plans."

When he had begun this plan, it had been his belief that a world full of purified humans would be a paradise and that all men—once shown their potential—would realize that no amount of sacrifice would be too much to rescue humanity from it's pathetic state.

"My name," Eschaton pointed his spear at Nathaniel, letting his power and consciousness flow into it, "is King Omega!" He unleashed a ferocious torrent of electricity at the boy.

Nathaniel, for all his power, appeared uniquely vulnerable to King Omega's electrical attack. The living energy struck him hard, his transparent body writhing in agony. Eschaton concentrated, drawing on the stored energy in his suit to increase the power of his attack, and the boy fell writhing to the ground. He wished that he could have destroyed him utterly, wiping away the shame of his failure, but it seemed that there were limits to the Mercurial Man's vulnerability.

From somewhere nearby he heard a woman's voice shouting with rage, and he turned to see that Sarah had engaged with one of his Children. The man had named himself Piston Pete, and Eschaton doubted it would take her long to best a "hero" who had done nothing more than create a set of metal gloves he wore over the tops of his hands. As the man charged Sarah, she quickly and efficiently fired a single shot from her father's gun into the man's leg. The almost casual efficiency of her attack made Eschaton regret that he hadn't been able to use her instead of her step-brother for his experiments. He imagined she would take to her power far more quickly than Nathaniel had.

The Stanton girl was fighting side by side with a second man, his face covered in a white hood, with a white leather mask over the top of that. It made him look like an angry owl. It took Eschaton only an instant to realize that it was Anubis dressed in a new costume.

Almost as if she could sense his attention, Sarah turned and stormed toward him, guns in either hand, while Anubis held the Children at bay with his staff.

Eschaton considered hurling a bolt of electricity at him, but he could feel that the spear needed a moment to rebuild its power.

"What have you done with Tom?" she asked him.

"He's safe." Although, if he had known that she would be coming to the machine man's rescue, he might have finished dismembering him before coming to the surface. The Paragons and their progeny had an annoying habit of bringing the metal man back to life.

And all he had ever really needed was the creature's heart, although there had been some satisfaction to bringing suffering to Darby's creation. But now that he held the key inside of his body there was little need even for that.

He felt the power grow inside the weapon, and he lifted up his spear to deal with Sarah. Some part of him still wanted to spare her, and in the instant of hesitation Nathaniel once again came to her rescue. This time the boy was too close to stop, and Eschaton suddenly found himself grappling with the white hot fury of his own creation.

The heat and ferocity caused Eschaton to drop his spear, but he still had more than enough energy to send bolt after bolt into Nathaniel.

He could also feel Nathaniel's heat pouring into him, climbing up his arms and into his body. But there was more going on here than simply the clash of elemental forces. He wondered if he might be outmatched, the youth of his opponent giving him more of the pure power that he needed. And the boy glowed so brightly that Eschaton was practically blinded, his squinting eyes unable to close out the dazzling brilliance.

There were other complications, as well. Without the spear it was difficult to channel the power of the dynamos on his back. Omega let the energy pour out of him. The lightning arcing from his hands quickly overpowered the heat . . . or was it blending with it in some way? For a moment he could barely tell where his own power began and the Mercurial Man's ended. It was a strange sensation . . .

He heard Nathaniel shout as ever more electricity poured into him. For a moment his hands still held fast, and Omega wondered if the boy was even capable of letting go.

Feeling a sense of desperation, and a slight moment of panic, Omega drew deeper, pulling not only the power from the reserves on his back, but also as deeply as he could from his own well of strength.

"I'm here for ya, my lord," said a familiar Irish voice. Then the Mercurial Man shuddered, his voice rising up to a scream. Eschaton saw the harpoons sticking out of Nathaniel's back.

After the second harpoon pierced him, sending splinters across his flesh, Nathaniel released his grip and staggered backwards.

The arcs of energy from Omega's hands were jumping between them now, scoring the boy's flesh. For a moment Nathaniel simply stood writhing in pain, the metal barbs in his back beginning to droop and melt away from the heat. Eschaton held out his hand, concentrated, then sent a blast of energy that dropped the boy to his knees.

As the living electricity left him, Omega could feel his final reserves running out. He could restore all his energy in time, but the day was not yet won. He needed to conserve his power, due to the boy's inability to recognize his defeat.

Omega ran toward Nathaniel. "Fall, damn you!" he shouted as he kicked the boy in the face. "Fall down!" he yelled again and delivered a second blow, this time with his fist. He could feel Nathaniel's jaw shattering beneath the punch, and the Mercurial Man finally fell backwards to the ground. "Good boy," he said, and gave him another, harder kick, sending Nathaniel's clear flesh tumbling across the ground like broken glass.

Two more kicks to the head and the Mercurial Man's glowing skin dimmed, leaving him transparent once again.

Nathaniel had landed on his back, but the melted metal of the harpoon barbs propped him up as if he were sitting on some torturous chair. Inside the boy's clear body a sliver of silver still swirled through him, racing to repair areas that had been burned and broken. It rose up into his head and pooled into his jaw. Somehow the liquid seemed to know where he was injured. "Not dead yet, are we, boy?" He hesitated and looked around. The Bomb Lance was reloading barbs into his frame.

But it was unnecessary. Without Nathaniel to scare away the Children, the battle was quickly turning against the would-be Paragons that remained. The two of them were surrounded by Blades, and this time Jack was there to lead his men. As Sarah brought her pneumatic gun to bear, a blade stuck fast in her hand. She let out a yelp and dropped the weapon. The blade hadn't gone deep, but it had done its job.

"Sorry, girl," said Jack stepping closer. "We've had quite enough of your gusty gun for today." He grabbed her and pulled her away from her companion.

The white-masked man growled out a response. "Damn you, Jack."

Omega nodded at him. "That really is you, isn't it, Anubis? I'd have thought you'd have known better than to come back here."

"My name is Ra now."

Omega laughed and bent over to pick up his spear. "Of course it is." Holding it up, he shot an arc across the courtyard. When the electricity touched Abraham, he dropped like a stone.

"What do we do with her?" Jack asked.

"Let her go," Omega replied. The thin man smiled and gave her a hard shove. Another bolt of energy dropped her to the ground.

"Now tie them up." Omega walked back over to Nathaniel, who was lying on the ground. "I have a plan for them."

He lifted his spear over the Mercurial Man. "But you are done." It was impressive to see just how much repair the metal that flowed through the boy's veins had already done. It was a shame that he had been forced to do this. "I'm sorry, my boy. I'd hoped that you would realize the value of the gift that you'd been given, before it was too late."

He had not realized that Nathaniel was awake, and when he turned to look at him, Omega imagined he could see the sadness in his transparent eyes. "Did you think I'd thank you for this?" he asked. His voice was trembling with pain. "You're nothing but a freak, Eschaton, and now you've made me one, too."

The silver giant shook his head. He had been so sure that the act of purification would grant enlightenment, and it saddened him to realize that most of humanity simply wasn't ready to accept the possibilities. In the new world he would teach the survivors, but he had no more time to waste with failures. "Let's rectify my mistake."

Eschaton crossed his hands and flipped the spear over. It crackled with energy as he held it above Nathaniel's chest, the resentment and anger he felt for the boy's betrayal charging it with power.

"Do it, then," Nathaniel said.

The spear crackled loudly as he thrust it down hard into the boy's chest. The glassy flesh resisted at first, but finally gave way as he wedged the pointed end back and forth, driving the blade deeper and deeper into the Mercurial Man's body and cracking him apart.

As he expected, the silver liquid under Nathaniel's skin began to swirl around the wound. When most of it had gathered at the tip of the spear, Eschaton ignited the device with electrical energy.

The Mercurial Man began to glow for the last time. This time, the light came from the living electricity as it cascaded through Nathaniel's body. Omega poured the energy into him for as long as he could, only stopping when he had nothing left to give.

As the light faded, what remained of the Mercurial Man's body was now shattered and scorched, the silver inside of him burned away, replaced with black and brown.

He pulled the spear free and took a step back. The battle was almost over. It was time to move forward.

"All right, Jean-Jean," Eschaton said, turning toward the Frenchman who still hid behind the fins of the rocket. "It's time to finish this."

Chapter 26

The End of the World

As Sarah awoke, she began to regain control of her senses. Somehow she was hanging high above the ground, and felt pain in all her limbs.

A quick look down told her all she needed to know: she had been chained directly onto the metal frame of Eschaton's rocket. The tight metal links were biting deeply and painfully into her legs, and she was thankful that her father's leather jacket was cushioning her from the pain the metal would have caused her upper body.

As her eyes adjusted, Sarah looked down across the courtyard to see that it was now half-filled with milling villains. These were the remains of Eschaton's so-called Children. Most of them were strangers, but a few of the men were familiar to her now. She recognized one of them as Donny, the gap-toothed boy who had threatened her that night at the theater before Tom had returned to life and saved her.

Glancing up, Sarah could see the clouds sweeping across the sky, pushed by a warm summer wind. Rays of sunlight broke through the gray, lighting up the day. They reflected off Nathaniel's clear skin down below. His prone form still lay on the ground where Eschaton had pierced him with his deadly spear. "I'm sorry, Nathaniel."

"He may end up being the lucky one," growled a voice to the side of her. Sarah turned to see the white-masked face of Ra. They had let him keep his secret identity, although they had stripped her of her own mask.

"Abraham! Are you all right?"

He laughed, and then coughed, his chestplate clearly not protecting him from the chains as effectively as her jacket was. "I suppose it was foolish to think that we ever could have stopped him."

Sarah frowned. "But we had to try. And I'm glad you joined us in the end."

"I've learned that I'm not quite as good at keeping my word as I thought I was . . ." Abraham had revealed himself as Ra after scaring the living daylights out of her in the accounting room. He had come to visit her numerous times at the junkyard, but never in costume. And now, here he was again—reborn as a new hero, only to be trapped by the same villains who had destroyed his previous identity.

Omega—Eschaton—walked toward the rocket. "Children of Eschaton! Gather around me! Our time has come!"

As the men came together, she realized that there were more than a hundred of them now. Two dozen or so were Jack's Blades, and they clumped together in a group of tweed-jacketed ruffians. The Society of Steam had gone from four to two in the space of an afternoon. She hoped that Emilio had at least escaped, but she doubted that he would be able to get free from the basement.

Bomb Lance stood, as he almost always did, right at Eschaton's side. The man had more lives than a cat, and fewer morals. If she was going to die soon—and it seemed very likely that she was—it would be one of her greatest regrets that she hadn't removed that murderous villain from the world before she departed from it herself.

The rest of the Children seemed to primarily be a motley group of would-be heroes. Looking at them, dressed up in their ridiculous costumes, it was hard not to feel a bit sorry for them all. They clearly wanted to be like the Paragons so very much that they were willing to join a madman and destroy the world simply for a chance.

"My Children," Eschaton said, raising his weapon into the air, "we are about to change everything!" For a moment she thought she saw the silver man falter, but he righted himself so quickly that she was almost convinced that it had been her mind playing a trick on her. Though, perhaps defeating them had taken more out of the villain than he was letting on.

Almost as if in response to her doubt, the dynamos on Eschaton's back glowed, and suddenly a wave of energy burst forth, igniting the spear, and bolts shot into the air. She found herself gasping as the Children stepped back.

He pointed a glowing silver hand directly up at her and Ra. "My enemies have fallen, my plan is complete, and now there is only one thing left to do: it is time to ignite the rocket and bring about the true Eschaton!"

A cheer went up from the men, but it seemed that the events of the day had sapped at least some of their enthusiasm. She could only imagine that many of them were fearful that they wouldn't survive the process of purification.

"So why doesn't he get on with it?" she heard Abraham asking her.

Sarah opened her mouth to reply, but instead it hung open in surprise. She had noticed two men entering into the courtyard. One of them, wearing an insect-headed mask with long metal arms, was instantly familiar to her. As he looked up at her and waved, she prayed that she was the only one who noticed the dashing fool who had come to her rescue.

The other figure was dressed in rags, and moved with a strange, almost disturbing stride. Sarah closed her mouth and willed herself to show no emotional response—to give nothing away to the crowd of villains below.

"In this new world," Eschaton shouted out, "we will all be equal men. But I have discovered that even among equals there must still be one who leads."

Sarah was barely keeping track of the nonsense Eschaton was spouting. She had heard more than enough of his dark philosophy from Nathaniel.

She only hoped that his ridiculous speech would allow them to escape before they were hurled into the sky. She clamped down hard on her jaw as a long-forgotten quote from Darby rose up into her thoughts. "Heroes never actually win, you know," he had told her one day after relating to her a story of the Paragons that he had deemed fit for a thirteen-year-old girl. "In the end, it's the villains who defeat themselves."

"With your help, I will be that leader." Eschaton was getting more excited with every breath, motivated by his own words. "I will take us into our new paradise and reveal the glory of this new world!" The sparks were flying faster and faster now, and the large metal and glass objects on his back were beginning to glow. If Emilio was going to save her, the moment would need to be soon. "I will be your king!"

The ground beneath them began to rumble, throwing everyone off-balance. Sarah felt a sickening moment of vertigo as the rocket behind her swayed.

From her vantage point, Sarah could see everything—and she could see that someone else had noticed Emilio. The thin dandy had already pulled a small knife and was preparing to skewer her Italian. If she had any illusions about whether or not she loved Emilio, they disappeared in that moment.

Sarah shouted out his name, unable to stop herself. She realized that she had also just alerted a hundred villains to the presence of a single man, and all Emilio did was turn to look at her, still unaware of the danger that was rapidly approaching.

Then he disappeared under a billowing cloud of white steam. It moved more quickly than she had ever seen steam move before, covering the courtyard like a flood and rising up almost to her feet.

The gas undulated and billowed, and deep inside it she could see blue bolts of lightning flashes. The glow revealed the shadows of the men who had been trapped within it. There were also shouts and screams, but no voices she could recognize.

"We need to get down from here now," Abraham said.

"I'd be game, if you have a plan." Sarah flexed against her bonds, but the chains were clearly not going to give way. Even if she could have snapped solid iron, falling down into the roiling soup at her feet seemed unpleasant to say the least. And once they were in it, they would be at the mercy of what was happening below.

Then, almost ashamed that she hadn't realized it before, Sarah understood. "Tom!" Sarah yelled, "Tom! Let us free!"

"Are you sure it's him?" Ra grumbled in response.

"Tom has no vision. He only uses hearing."

"That's good thinking," he replied. Sarah had to admit that it was nice to hear that *someone* considered her thoughts worthwhile, without the underlying intimation that women of intelligence were only a small step above annoying shrews.

During his visits to the junkyard, Abraham had said surprisingly little to Sarah, preferring to spend the time quietly reflecting on the water, or helping Emilio with occasional projects—although the Italian had no idea that Abraham was anything more than a friendly ex-servant, much the way Jenny had been.

But they had discussed her idea for a new team of heroes. He had been somewhat dismissive of the idea, and yet here they were, ready to die at each other's side. "Thank you, Ra, but the Automaton hasn't actually come to our rescue yet."

As if in response to her doubt (and perhaps because of it), a strange arm made from chains and wire rose up from out of the fog and grasped the chains that bound them.

The Automaton used their restraints to pull himself up. The mechanical man's weight pulled their restraints tighter, and Sarah let out a choked yelp. The white steam streamed off of Tom as he pulled himself toward them.

"Tom!" she gasped. He had changed again. Although the face and frame remained, the body was no longer the delicate structure it had been. It was now covered with thick chains and metal. He looked less like a clockwork angel, and more like a mechanical demon.

"Hello . . . Sarah." Chains leapt out from his body and looped themselves over the frame of the rocket. "You should not have . . . come."

The metal that bound her gave way, and she felt herself drop for an instant. This time when the restraints held her, she could feel Tom's intelligence animating them. "We came to save you."

"We needed to save the world," Abraham added.

"I suppose that you . . . could not help . . . yourselves." Tom lowered her and Ra into the cloud of steam beneath their feet. Sarah noticed that it had already begun to dissipate.

"Have you stopped Eschaton?" Sarah asked, wondering what might be waiting for them down below.

As if in answer to her question, Sarah heard the sound of roaring wind, and she was slammed backwards into the frame of the rocket. The chains that had been cradling her vanished, and she plunged downward into the whiteness, landing inelegantly against the wooden planks of the launching stand.

Eschaton stood in front of her, his spear held high in one hand, Sarah's gun in the other. His metallic skin had an oddly pinkish hue, as if some of his humanity were peeking though.

The gust of wind from the pneumatic gun had cleared the steam from the air, revealing the Automaton. Eschaton raised up his spear to strike.

Sarah thought she might have been screaming as the bolts struck Tom, but the sound was drowned out by the sizzles and zaps as the living electricity flew through the air. Yet somehow Eschaton's laughter could still be heard above it.

The Automaton began to twitch and dance in the exact same way as when le Voyageur had attacked him at the junkyard, his body rising high into the air as the chains that now formed his legs tightened.

Sarah felt a pair of rough hands at her back, then the weight of another body against hers. The sensation was familiar, momentum rolling her out of the way as Tom's flailing body crashed down, chains trailing behind him.

As she came to a stop she once again heard Ra's voice in her ear, his hands still wrapped around her. "That's the second time I've done that."

There was a flutter in her heart, just for an instant, as a stray thought fluttered through her head on the more intimate possibilities of grappling with other men. Still, she would be covered with bruises, and in a fight there was little contact that came without pain, whatever the fantasy might be. "And I'm as grateful the second time as the first," she told him through gasping breath. "Maybe we'll live long enough that you'll get to do it again."

"Doubtful, Sarah Stanton," said a thundering voice from above her.

"Lord Eschaton," she replied with a scowl, struggling to sit up. "The murderer of so many people whom I've loved."

He smiled down at her. "They all shared the same bad habit of getting in my way."

A mocking laugh escaped from Sarah's lips. "In the way of this mad plan? In the way of your need to destroy the world so that you can play God?"

The smile died on Eschaton's face. "You're an ignorant child, spouting Darby's . . ."

"Don't you even *dare* to say his name!" She rose up, and took a moment to reseat herself inside her corset. "He may have been a bit pompous, but he knew better than to think that he could remake the world in his image."

"You think so? I worked with him, I gave him the fruits of my genius, and he took them all for himself."

"And *now* look at you." Sarah could feel the spirit of her father rising up in her. "It wasn't Darby's anger and jealousy that turned you into a monster.

And it's *your* hurt pride that won't be satisfied until every man, woman, and child in New York has been sacrificed to try and staunch that infected wound. But even that won't be enough. Nothing ever could be."

She pointed a finger directly up at Eschaton's face. An electric arc leapt out from his skin, burning the tip of it, but she refused to pull it back. "It would be horrifying, if it weren't all so pathetic."

For an instant Lord Eschaton said nothing, then his metal-covered hand descended toward her. "Perhaps you have a point, but I don't agree. I think, instead, that today I will send *all* my enemies to the grave." She expected him to crush her there and then, but instead he shoved her out of the way, grabbing Tom's body. He heaved it into the air, grunting slightly as he lifted it up.

He turned back to look at her, his grim smile once again painted across his face. "And I'm going to let you witness me kill the rest of them before you die at my hand."

Sarah watched in horror as Eschaton poured his living electricity into the Automaton. At first the metal man twitched and jumped, just as he had before. "Stop!" she shouted, but if Eschaton heard her, he made no reaction. "Stop, damn you . . ." she repeated, but Eschaton simply laughed.

Sarah tried to rise up, but she felt something sharp pressing into her back. "Stay down, girlie," she heard the Bomb Lance say. "Stay down and let the men finish their work."

"One day I'm going to kill you, Murphy," Ra said. He had been so quiet that she had almost forgotten he was there.

"Maybe," he said with a hint of his rasping chuckle, "but let's see if you survive today first."

She turned to look back at Tom, hoping that he might have one more secret left. But it seemed that Eschaton was simply too powerful for him. Just as he had done to Nathaniel, Eschaton's energy was overwhelming Tom's body. First the chains dropped to the ground, then the metal limbs slowly ceased their thrashing, like a poorly crushed insect finally succumbing to death.

Sarah could feel the tears coming to her eyes, her blood boiling from shame and rage. She had given so much of herself to save Tom, to bring him back into the world so that he could live and grow, and it had all been in the service of nothing.

Deciding that he had finished, Eschaton heaved the Automaton through the air. The metal body flew across the courtyard, chains trailing behind it. The metal skeleton landed with a clanking crash on top of Nathaniel's lifeless body.

"Stand up, both of you," Eschaton said, pointing his spear down at her and Abraham.

The barb pressing against Sarah's back receded and Sarah rose to her feet. She felt bruised and battered from her fall, but she supposed it wouldn't matter for very much longer.

She had lost every weapon. Finally there was nothing between her and the madman whom she had sworn to destroy, and she had nothing left.

This close, it was impossible to ignore just how much of a monster Eschaton had become. He towered over them, impossibly altered by whatever alchemy he had performed on himself. He seemed more like a moving wax-work than a living human. "Did you want to beg for your life?" he asked them both.

"Would it make a difference?" Ra replied.

Eschaton shook his head. "I tried to give you both a noble death, riding into the heavens on top of my rocket," he said, lifting his fingers toward the sky, "but you spurned the opportunity."

Sarah brushed herself off. "I'd rather die staring you in the eyes, Lord Eschaton."

"That'll be a better way ta go than your father did," Murphy said to her. "He died like a child crawling through the dirt."

Sarah felt her anger rising up, making her desperate enough to act, but Eschaton spoke first. "Enough, Murphy. She fought well, but she has lost, and she knows that now." The man who had destroyed her world looked into her eyes. "You think you know me, Sarah Stanton, but you don't. You think that I am nothing more than a madman. Considering the men who raised you, you can be forgiven for your confusion."

Sarah pursed her lips together. The fear had drained out of her, and all that was left was pulsing fury. Eschaton tilted his head slightly toward the Bomb Lance. "Murphy, if you would do the honors, it's time to send our former companion to meet his dark god."

"I am Ra now, and he *will* take vengeance."

"But *you* won't," said the Irishman from behind her. "So long, Negro. I always kinda liked ya. Sorry ta see you go." She heard the frame moving behind her as the Irishman took aim.

But before the inevitable sound of the harpoon firing, Sarah felt a familiar rumble as the ground underneath their feet began to shake. The quake had the signature of the Steamhammer, but it was more powerful than she had ever felt before. The pulsing vibrations threw everyone off their balance, even the silver giant.

For a moment Sarah considered making one last futile attempt to attack the madman in front of her, or perhaps she could strangle the Bomb Lance before he could use his steel barbs on her. But it was seeing Eschaton's eyes widening in disbelief that compelled her to instead turn and see what could cause the almighty Eschaton to react with such shock.

What came rising up from a thick cloud of steam in front of her was almost beyond belief. Its proportions were basically human, but just a little odd, as if all of its limbs had been stretched apart. The skin was white, like a clear pearl. Underneath it she could see the outlines of the steel armatures that Emilio had created, but in the center of its chest, underneath the clear skin, was a clockwork heart—Tom's heart. With its every pump she could see clouds of steam circulating through the body. The creature's skin was turning white, and sending off waves of heat, but not to the degree that Sarah felt as if it might burn her.

Eschaton stumbled backwards, something about the creature striking him with fear.

As the man-machine took another step toward them, Sarah recognized that it looked like Nathaniel. "Sarah . . ." it said, releasing a cloud of steam from its mouth. "We're here to save you."

The voice boomed. The words were not only spoken, but also came vibrating up from the ground and straight into her body.

She looked into the man-machine's glowing eyes. "Nathaniel?" she asked.

"Gabriel," it replied. "Tom and I are . . . together now." Sarah noticed that its pause was utterly unlike the Automaton's stammer, and it had Nathaniel's eternally dour tone. "It's very . . . strange."

The Bomb Lance lifted up his arm and fired a harpoon in a single motion. The barb smashed straight into Gabriel's shoulder, spinning him around and throwing him to the ground. "You're quite a monster," Murphy said, aiming his second harpoon toward the creature's head, "but we'll soon have you sorted."

Sarah turned rage into action, lashing out with her gloved fist and smashing the Irishman across the jaw before he could fire again. Her father's metal-lined glove made a satisfying smack as it struck the man's face. She wondered how many other villains had been taken by surprise by a pair of Stanton hands inside these very gauntlets.

To her surprise the act of violence had only stirred the fires of rage higher, and reaching into the frame, she spun the dazed Irishman around in a full circle. She raised up the Irishman's limp arm, and pointed it towards Lord Eschaton. Lifting the harpoon until it more or less faced the madman's head, she wrapped her fingers around the Bomb Lance's hand and pulled the trigger. If someone had described the moment to her, she would have considered it a desperate act, but as the harpoon flew free she could almost feel the spirits of the men who had been murdered in the madman's plot guiding the weapon home.

Her moment of satisfaction was followed by a sharp sensation of pain as one of the harness wires sliced through the cloth of her shirt and cut into her flesh. But the gurgling scream that Eschaton made as the barb punctured his exposed neck made it worthwhile.

Sarah hissed, and pulled her arm out of the frame. Free from the device, she shoved the Bomb Lance away from her, sending the Irishman stumbling back toward Gabriel. She hoped they would know what to do with him.

Living electricity danced across the metal shaft where it had penetrated Eschaton's throat, along with a white fluid that pulsed out from the wound.

"I thought you said you were invincible," Sarah said, holding the cut on her arm as she stepped closer, trying not to think about her own leaking flesh. She could see the pink of Eschaton's skin where it peeked out from underneath the armor. "The steam has returned your humanity."

"It's made me *weak*, but only for a moment." Eschaton growled and gurgled as he dragged the barb out through the back of his neck, and then let it clatter to the ground.

The villain coughed, then spat out a mouthful of white liquid before he spoke again. "I'll destroy you for this." The words were tinged with anger, but Sarah just shook her head and began to walk around behind him.

Up until now Eschaton had seemed unstoppable, and perhaps he had been. It was only now that she saw him weakened that Sarah realized just *how* ridiculous it was to have *ever* considered fighting him at the peak of his power.

But she had hurt him, and she wouldn't give him another opportunity. He tried to follow her, stumbling in a circle, as she bent down to pick up the Bomb Lance's harpoon that Eschaton had pulled from his neck. Sarah looked for some words to say, something that felt just and right. She almost smiled when it came to her. "I swear to fight for honor, integrity, truth, and righteousness," she said, speaking each word slowly and deliberately.

The attack had slowed the giant down and left him dazed. Sarah continued to speak the oath: "I will use the secrets and powers of the Paragons," she said, lifting the weapon over her head, the pain only sharpening her resolve, "to protect those who cannot protect themselves."

Sarah was behind Eschaton when she drove the bar through vents in the back of his armor. "*Die, villain!*" She screamed as she thrust the barb upwards, driving it deep into Eschaton's chest. She twisted the harpoon as she shoved it farther in.

Eschaton only let out a grunt as the metal pushed through his body and struck the interior of his chestplate. The white blood was warm on her hands, tingling with his power. And when she let go, the giant dropped to his knees. The armor Eschaton wore, so recently alive with energy, began to drop to the ground in chunks, each piece landing with a clank.

His white flesh turned grayer with every passing second. The metal on his skin faded away, as if it were pouring out with his blood.

"You've lost," Sarah said, looking into the villain's face.

He focused on her and then smiled. "Not nearly as much as you have."

Turning away, she looked to see what had become of the Irishman, hoping that Gabriel had taken his revenge. Sarah was disappointed to see just a glimpse of the Bomb Lance's tweed-covered backside as he slipped out one of the courtyard doors. He hadn't been the only one. It seemed that most of Eschaton's Children had also used the confusion as a chance to escape.

The one man she did see standing there was Emilio. He snapped back the metal arms and ran toward her. "Sarah!"

She grabbed him and gave him a kiss. It was less chaste than she had intended, but it made him smile.

"I saved you!" He gave her another kiss, and his lips opened as she pushed herself harder into him, anger, excitement, and fear all combining into a single wave of passion greater than she had ever felt before.

The Frenchman's voice cut through the moment. "Now, King Omega! Launch ze rocket and we wiww stiww win ze futuwe!" Le Voyageur stood on the rocket's stage, Eschaton's metal spear in his hands. He shoved it deep into the framework of the rocket.

Eschaton rose to his feet and smiled. "Even in death . . ." he managed to gurgle out, "I will change the world." Eschaton took his final shuddering breath, and filled the air with light and fury as bolts of living energy rippled up his body.

The crackling electricity leapt the short distance, channeling itself directly through the spear's metal shaft and into the rocket. As the power coursed through him, the Frenchman started to shake and sputter. Then, with a crack of what sounded like thunder, the sparking energy picked up the old man like a rag doll and flung him through the air.

Le Voyageur's final journey was a short one. He crashed down in the courtyard with a sickening thud, and then lay there unmoving. The old man's neck was twisted at an unnatural angle against the cold concrete.

Sarah stared with shock at the Frenchman. She was still prepared for him to move and attack one more time, or simply pick himself up, brush himself off, and make some kind of rude remark. But as a pool of dark liquid began to gather around his wiry white hair, it was clear that he would never speak again.

Eschaton still stood, his body unmoving, his arms raised into the air. Then he tilted forward and toppled to the ground. He bounced once, his left arm breaking away at the elbow, before he fell back against the ground and shattered into large stony pieces against the concrete.

Standing behind him was Ra, his hands still outstretched from having given Eschaton a shove. "You're done, monster."

Sarah took a step toward her fallen enemy, but Emilio still held her hand in his, and he was clearly intent on not letting her go just yet. He gave her arm a tug, and she turned to look at him. "What's the matter?"

He nodded slightly, and Sarah turned her gaze to follow his. Emilio was looking back up at the stage. "The rocket." Steam had begun to leak out from the large nozzle on the bottom of it, and from somewhere deep inside there was a terrible hissing noise, growing louder every second.

Ra was the first to speak. "I think we'd better run."

"And where are we going to go?" Sarah asked. "We need to stop it!" If the wretched machine actually did manage to launch, all of New York would be covered in Eschaton's deadly black smoke.

"No, Sarah, not you. I do." She turned around to see the glowing creature that had once been Tom and Nathaniel standing above her. His skin was a cloudy white, and the calm voice, along with the angelic smile he wore, almost had her smiling back before she realized what he had just suggested.

"Not you! We'll fix you! You have to stay with me!"

It laughed at her. "I'm not broken . . . anymore. And what would I be staying for, if it meant I would . . ." she heard the pause in his voice. His pauses had always sounded confused, but this one seemed contemplative, "lose you."

The sadness and confusion felt like those days after her mother had died, her father trying to explain that her mother was in a better world. That she had gone to a place so far beyond her comprehension that it might as well have been magic. She could feel the heat in her face as tears worked their way into her eyes. "Tom, Nathaniel—please! Don't go!"

"I love you, Sarah Stanton. I don't think I ever truly knew what that meant before."

She reached out to touch him, stroking the face of this strange angel. She let her fingers trail down to his heart, and she could feel it pumping underneath his chest. "I always loved you both."

With a smile the creature turned and leapt onto the stage with a single bound. A second step lifted it up into the air as it climbed up the frame of the rocket.

Then the last Paragon disappeared in a hiss and a cloud of billowing steam that rushed out from the rocket's mighty engines, lifting the ship up from the launching stage, up into the summer sky.

Chapter 27

A Short Evolution

He could remember what it was like to die. Even as he had been stabbed and shocked, he had been terrified of death. He had wanted it to end, but when the end came he had fought it. It had been painful and he had been helpless but—and this was surprising—not angry.

And when the end had finally come, the world just stopped—like the hands of a broken watch that hung next to a moment that was never going to come.

He could remember what it was like to break, over and over again. Torn to pieces, beaten, and shocked, until finally his heart stopped.

It had been so easy to be reborn when all he'd ever had to do was become something new. He had memories but never thoughts, desires but no emotions. He could know, but not feel.

Who and whatever he had been, had all been destroyed by the same man, and yet the murderer was also their father. His arrogance had lain the foundation that brought them together. Now they were more than they had ever been alone.

The metal of Tom's heart had reacted to Nathaniel's seared flesh. His body (their body now) had been shattered and broken, but wasn't truly dead. It had simply been diminished by the loss of the part of himself that had kept him alive and whole.

Tom had been dead before, of course. Lost inside his own heart, unable to communicate with the outside world. Reduced to his bare essentials and most minimal sensations.

He could remember it all . . . Travelling in the suitcase, Sarah's words. It had all resonated inside of him, all been captured somewhere in the metal: a vibration, a sound.

And when his heart had fallen on Nathaniel, when the clear flesh had touched him, he knew what to do. It was the only thing that made sense: Tom made steam.

He could only create a tiny puff, but it was enough. The crystal flesh had woken up only for an instant, but *that* was enough. It gave Tom the ability to beat again, and the skin had reacted again, giving energy back to the mechanical heart.

It hadn't happened instantly, and it hadn't been easy. But as skin and steel began to work together, their thoughts had returned, and then began to fuse.

That had been the most difficult part. Even if all that remained of Nathaniel's humanity were dreams and lies, he clung to them with the same desperate desire that he had given them his entire life. And Tom had never truly had thoughts before. For him there was only reason and knowledge.

And so their first moments together had been pure anguish, full of fear and death. Tom had found that his true wish was to escape and go back to what he had been before, instead of becoming part of something that hated him, and hated change, so very much.

As metal and flesh fused, they tore off their old head, a useless lump with no real meaning. And when he opened his eyes (he had eyes!) and saw the light of the world for the first time, he forgave himself.

His heart beat stronger now. Steam pumped through this strange body, and the flesh began to heal. Inside of him, metal shifted and his form changed. Tom had rebuilt himself so many times, it was easy to do it again. Nathaniel had abused his body so many times, and this was much better than that.

They needed a name, and it came to them. "Gabriel," they said together, and it was almost one voice.

They were reborn into one being. But neither of them had forgiven the man who killed them. They hadn't forgotten that there was someone they loved, and that she was in danger.

When they stood up, the remains of Tom's mechanical body had been scattered around them. What would Darby have thought of all this? They imagined that the old man would have been shocked, and probably upset by this abomination of flesh and metal they had become. They thought of the rebirths of Hughes and of Eschaton that had come from Darby's living steel, and smiled at the irony.

They needed to merge. For Tom, it would be easy to let himself go and sink down into being someone, or some*thing* else. After changing himself so many times, the opportunity to finally and truly transform seemed almost like a blessing.

But what would they become?

From somewhere in Tom's vast memory rose up Sir Dennis's last words: "When dark times come, it is men of honor who must lead us back to the light of reason."

"But I am not an honorable man," Gabriel whispered to himself.

"No. But you can be . . . the light."

The ride was dizzying as the ship flew higher, expending the fuel rapidly. But it was intended to be a short trip. It would be only a matter of seconds before the ship would turn and begin trailing fortified smoke across the New York skyline.

Gabriel reached into the body of the ship, his flesh splintering as the metal frame exploded out from underneath his skin, the limb expanding until it reached the metal box that contained the rocket's steering mechanics.

The steel hand torn open the iron cover. His fingers merged with le Voyageur's contraption, and as it responded he could feel his consciousness slipping into it, and he became part of it. He didn't control the machine as much as lent his intelligence to it. He had merged with it, and it would forever be a part of him.

Gabriel felt a twinge of sadness that Tom had never been given the chance to fulfill the destiny Darby had lain out for him. If he had merged with the Hall and become the Paragon, it would have been glorious.

But there was no time for regret. The machine beneath him had revealed its purpose: having touched the sky, now it wanted only to give birth. The smoke in its belly was a pregnant future. Then it would die, tearing itself apart. It yearned to open the vents along its side.

Gabriel held it back, forcing it to hold on just a little longer. Tearing his own flesh once again, he plunged his other arm into the engine, opened his heart, and let the fortified steam race out of him.

The nozzles roared loudly, and the rocket flew up higher, gaining speed and height until the sky above them began to fade from blue to black, the air growing thin, the sounds of the world disappearing from even his sensitive ears.

As the ship turned over in the sky, Gabriel saw the outline of the world below. The earth was vast and beautiful. How was it that he could see everything, but no one could see him?

Only a few people would ever know the sacrifices that the Paragons had made to protect them. "It's your world now, Sarah. Take care of it."

The rumbling grew stronger, and he tried to hold Eschaton's rocket from its destiny for one more moment, giving him one more moment to savor the view beneath him.

And then the ship, no longer willing to wait, exploded.

Chapter 28
For the People!

As she walked to the podium to give her speech, Sarah felt more than just the usual churn of nervousness that Emilio had told her anyone standing in front of three hundred people might feel. Part of it was, perhaps, that the stage was the very same platform that Eschaton's deadly rocket had launched from, although they had painted it.

The courtyard was packed and the day was hot, even for July. Sarah could feel herself sweating in the costume, her hair tucked back under her hat. They had made her a version of the Columbia costume that was far more demure than the "battle attire" she had been wearing when she fought Eschaton on this very spot only a month ago. She was sure that tomorrow's papers would still be filled with commentary about just how "unladylike" it was for any woman to be wearing such an outfit.

She had endured a great deal of that kind of rhetoric over the last month as the truth behind the destruction of the Paragons and the Hall itself had come to light.

They had edited the truth more than slightly. There was no discussion of Hughes's betrayal, or Eschaton's beginnings as an assistant to Sir Dennis Darby.

And in death, the madman had become the villain he had always wanted to be: a devious trickster whose persona as King Jupiter had fooled even the most eagle-eyed members of the city's government.

Large rewards had been posted for the capture of the Children of Eschaton, and even now the public was on the lookout for the Bomb Lance, Jack Knife, and the other survivors of the apocalypse.

They had also wiped Vincent Smith's slate clean, letting him rest in peace as the provider of the Steamhammer costume to Emilio.

Even Sarah's own history had been softened for public consumption. No mention was made of the junkyard. Instead she had spent that time imprisoned deep underneath the Hall of Paragons alongside her heroic step-brother.

Keeping track of all the lies and half-truths made her head spin, but no one seemed too concerned with the details. They were far more intent on judging these "costumed ruffians" who had taken over the Paragons, no matter how noble their actions or heroic their intent. But despite being considered hooligans and misfits, Sarah intended that the Society of Steam would be here to stay.

Stepping up to the amplification tube, she cleared her throat. It was a small sound, but the machine made it loud enough to echo off the walls. She was sure that the press would consider it improper for a lady to be using it, further shredding the tattered remains of her reputation as a woman of society.

Truth be told, she didn't much like the device, but it was preferable to yelling, and it was certainly better than arguing with her husband-to-be about it.

Emilio had invented it, based on the remains of Darby's speaking machine that he'd built into the hall. Although he didn't have Sir Dennis's gift for sheer invention, he had a particular genius when it came to electrics, and he had spent much of the last month laying as much wire as he could into the walls of the Hall as it was being rebuilt. He had even dragged Thomas Edison up from the wilds of New Jersey to discuss the potential uses. Sadly both the Italian and the inventor seemed to find the other's methods more than a bit disagreeable, and both men were glad to see the back of each other after a strained afternoon.

"Ladies and Gentlemen," she began, the amplified words immediately quieting the mumbling crowd. "I am Sarah Stanton, leader of the Society of Steam, and I would like to thank you all so very much for attending our inaugural event." The amplified voice sounded strange to her ears, although everyone she had spoken to swore that it sounded exactly like her. "I apologize for bringing you out on such a horribly hot day, but considering the alternatives for ourselves, and for this city, I am just glad we could all meet here, safe, and together."

Light applause rippled through the crowd, the journalists steadfastly abstaining from any show of support beyond the most perfunctory clapping. Sarah supposed that was to be expected—they had already made their distaste for her and this "band of unruly thugs, misfits, and lower-class ruffians" all too apparent, although it would have been nice to hear at least a little more genuine enthusiasm from the crowd. On some level, perhaps, it was enough of a blessing that they weren't all about to be lynched.

"I know," she continued, "that the revelations of the events behind the destruction of the beloved Paragons have come as a shock to this city, and indeed the world. We will mourn the losses of the great men who fell to protect us from villainy, my father among them."

The burials for the Paragons had been a citywide affair, with a huge memorial stone of their likenesses placed over a mausoleum built for them in Central Park. She wasn't sure how much her father would have liked the idea of spending eternity next to them instead of her mother, but being a part of the Paragons was something her father had chosen to do, and obligations were, she had discovered, even harder to change once someone had died.

Sarah hoped that with her speech they might begin to move forward, but there was no guarantee. "But I continue to believe that from the sacrifice of these great men, something greater will be born—something that will give direction to those who are lost, hope to the downtrodden and abused, and strength to the weak."

For this next part she had first turned to Abraham for help. He claimed he had no genuine writing skills of his own. Instead he'd introduced her to Reverend Charles. The man had saved Abraham's life, and helped to lay down the White Knight.

After some long discussions about the appropriateness of a hero wielding a shotgun, his alter ego, "the Revivalist," was now part of the team. The man was as fearless with a crossbow or a Remington, and while he wasn't so thrilled about Sarah's Catholic fiancé, he seemed excited about being part of the team.

"I know that many of you would rather the Paragons were standing here today instead of me. And on that I agree with you. But we cannot bring back the dead."

Her father's fortune had turned out to be larger than she had imagined, but she soon discovered that in the case of Peter Wickham's untimely death, all of Sir Dennis's patents and other discoveries went to her, as well. The lawyers, as terrible as they had seemed when they were allied against her, had managed to use that information to make a convincing case that the entire Hall was also part of the family inheritance, and although the city was still putting up a fight to claim it for themselves, for now it was hers to do with as she pleased—and she was pleased to make it a home for the Society of Steam.

"We have lost so many good men: Peter Wickham, William Hughes, Helmut Grüsser, Nathaniel Winthorp, the Automaton, and Sir Dennis Darby." She let the names of the fallen heroes echo away as she took a deep breath and cleared away any hint of tears. It was a skill that she had become far too good at. "And my father, Alexander Stanton, who I hope would be proud of me, even if he wouldn't agree with me."

She missed them all—perhaps not all equally, but she felt the loss as deeply. And part of her sadness came from the realization that over time she would miss them less. Trying to sort the affairs of the Stanton household while simultaneously rebuilding the Hall had meant that the last month was the busiest of her entire life. The moments that hadn't been filled with work had been spent uncovering the intimate secrets of impending matrimony. Sally Norbitt had even come around to gossip and ask her entirely inappropriate (and much appreciated) questions about her new "Latin Paramour." It seemed that marriage had only sharpened that girl's interest in other people's business.

"But rising from the ashes comes a new generation of heroes, just as committed and brave. I know that many of you think that we are too common, foreign, or colorful to replace the great men who once filled these halls."

"Or too feminine!" a voice rang out from the crowd.

Sarah frowned. "And yes," she said, pushing down the urge to find and punish the man who had made that comment, "perhaps that as well." She was still the only woman, and although she had once imagined that Viola might have joined them on this stage, it was clear that she would never be a hero.

Emilio refused to tell Sarah exactly what had occurred when he confronted his sister in Darby's laboratory. His only comment was that they would never see her again. Sarah had tried to press him on it, but it was clearly a subject that he would say no more about.

"But I have fought beside these brave heroes, and they would gladly give their lives to protect yours. While these may not be the heroes that all of you wished for, we are the men *and women*, who have taken on the mantel, and are willing to do the job.

"Ladies and Gentlemen, I am proud to introduce to you, New York City's newest team of heroes: The Society of Steam."

In her mind's eye she could still hear the thunderous applause that she had dreamt of since she had first discovered her father's secrets in his hidden closet.

And while it might not have been as loud as she hoped, at least this audience was applauding. She knew that they hadn't been accepted yet. No one would compare them to the Roman gods of old.

The other members of the team filed in behind her: Steamhammer, Ra, the Revivalist. It was a small group, but there would be more. She had already begun to interview new members, although no one had passed muster yet.

She wondered if Sir Dennis would have been proud of what she had built. It wasn't the old man's dream, but that had died with him. And, although she would never say it publicly, ultimately Eschaton was partly Darby's creation—monsters creating monsters.

For now, the world was free of living machines and men who could throw lightning bolts. And in the meanwhile, the planet was safe, and so was a single glowing key that would allow the members of the Society access to fortified steam.

As the applause faded away, Sarah stepped forward for questions. She hadn't expected the speech to convince anyone of anything. Her father had said that it was always easier to crack skulls than to change minds, and the events of the last month had proven it in ways she could have never imagined before she had taken over the Hall.

Suddenly, from the back she heard a shout. The murmur of the crowd rose up before she could make out the words, but as the boy ran up, he repeated his cry. "The Bomb Lance, ma'am! He and some others are robbing a bank in broad daylight."

She had wondered what had happened to the old Irishman. Perhaps this time they would make him pay for his crimes! Sarah smiled and turned to the men behind her. "You heard them, gentlemen. For the people!"

Ra lifted up his alabaster staff. "For the people!" he shouted back to her.

The rest of them joined his cry, and they ran off the stage toward the battle, together.

Chapter 29

The Society of Smoke

Jack carefully peeled the tip of his knife underneath the tip of his fingernail, cleaning away another speck of imaginary dirt. "Donny, I'm bored."

"Yeth, thir."

"I'm bored of picking pockets and stealing bread."

"Yeth, thir."

Jack tipped back his barrel and sighed. Besides a few petty crimes, they'd been doing little but bracing themselves for an attack by the police, or the band of heroic fools calling themselves "The Society of Steam."

Tired of grooming, he threw the knife at the barrel in front of him. It knocked the previous blade out of place, sending it falling to the ground with a clatter.

He'd been at it for weeks now, carving a decent-sized hole into the barrel. Anyone stupid or unaware enough to sit on his target of choice would quickly discover that he wasn't giving any warnings to anyone who got in the way, although so far he'd done no more than slice a few pants legs and draw a little blood.

Most of his blades were scratched and dull, and Jack himself felt like an unsharpened edge, having spent far too many days with Donny and the other Blades.

He'd always appreciated their hideaway, but now that he was trapped in it, all he wanted to do was get out.

But there were posters of Jack Knife everywhere. They weren't a bad likeness—perhaps even a bit flattering. But having his face plastered on half the lampposts in the city meant that if he dared to step outside the maze wearing his favorite jacket, he would more than likely found himself wearing irons before he'd gone a single city block.

At first he'd considered the end of Eschaton and his mad plans a bit of a relief. Simply hearing about the boy and the metal man fused together into a single monster had given him nightmares for weeks. He could only imagine the full extent of horrors there would have been if Eschaton had managed to bring about the world he had been intent on building.

He was also, against all wisdom and common sense, proud to see that the man who had once called himself Anubis was now part of the Society of Steam. Seeing him succeed as Ra, despite their differences, gave a man hope, even if he had no real idea what he was supposed to do with it once he had it.

But he was tired of waiting, and as mad as Eschaton's plans had been, for all their flaws, the Children of Eschaton had been a brotherhood. It had been good to feel that there was someone watching your back.

"Well, look what we have here," said a voice in a familiar Irish brogue. "The skinny Brit is a woodcarver now! I never thought I'd see ya come to this."

Jack swept up and around. The man was still Murphy, but if you didn't already know his face he seemed like a different man. He'd been cleaned up: his beard was trimmed, his tattered clothes replaced by a fine suit. He leaned against a cherrywood cane. "Well look at you, all fine and dandy, ya damn Irishman," Jack said.

The Bomb Lance nodded, raising a hand to the rim of his bowler hat and tipping it forward. "Thank ya kindly. It's rare for me to get a compliment."

"It's still bloody miraculous you even survived."

"I told you, Jack, it's the planners who pay the price. We murderers always get away with it in the end."

A few of the Blades had already begun to gather around, as eager as Jack for anything that might bring some interest to a dull day. Donny held out his hand, a smile on his gap-toothed face. "Mithter Murphy! It'th tho good to thee you!"

"You too, lad!" They clapped arms around each other and slapped backs like old friends.

"What bringth you here, thir?"

"Well, Donny, it's funny you should ask." Murphy looked over at Jack with a stare of importance. "I have a new boss now."

"And who's that?" Jack asked.

"Someone who'd like to bring a bit of mayhem back to this old city of ours."

Donny's smile grew wider. "That soundth amazing. We've been terribly bored thince Mr. Ethcaton died."

Murphy winked at the boy. "I can only imagine."

Jack shook his head. "New boss? *I* haven't heard anything about him. Is it someone I should know?"

"Oh, I think you're going to like *her*. She calls herself the Harlot."

"A woman?" Jack said with surprise. Wasn't it bad enough that it had been a woman who had defeated Eschaton? "And she's sent you out to do her dirty work for her? Is that right?"

Jack felt something sharp prick him in the back. For an instant he thought he might have been skewered, but although the blade had broken the skin, whoever it was hadn't gone a touch deeper than was needed to draw a drop of blood. "No," said a woman's voice in his ear. It was clearly Italian and slightly seductive. "This Harlot is capable of doing her own dirty work, especially where men like *you* are concerned."

Jack felt the pressure leave his skin, and he turned around to see this new villain. She was impressive at first glance, dressed from head to toe in white crinoline and black lace. A string of wire-and-cloth roses formed a circlet around her head that held up a dark veil covering her face. He couldn't see her clearly enough to tell whether she was beautiful or ugly underneath, but there was something hidden there. "A masked woman? Why don't you show yourself?"

She laughed and lifted a fan. It clanked slightly as she opened it, and he could see that the razor-tipped edges were red with his blood. "We all have secrets, Jack. Some of us more than others."

Jack felt anger rising in him. "And what plan do you have for us? Do you want to change the world, as well?"

"Nothing so bold. All I want to do today is rob a bank. Maybe get your men some better clothes." She laughed and snapped the fan closed. The blood spattered against the cobblestones. "Changing the world can wait for a bit."

Jack stared into her veil, trying to read the mystery. He'd already barely survived one madman's scheme. For some reason, and despite what she said, he had a feeling that whatever this woman had in mind would be far worse. "Hell hath no fury like a woman scorned."

"Everyone scorns the Harlot." She gave a little laugh and took a twirl.

"Well," he said, hopping down from the barrel, "I could use a new jacket. Someone just poked a hole in this one . . ."

Chapter 30

A Message from Above

"*Life is short,*" Darby had once said to him. "*And yet it is the nature of man to make it move faster all the time!*" Gabriel smiled at the memory. He had travelled over the length and the breadth of the planet thousands of times now. Sunrises and sunsets occurred over and over again with surprising rapidity.

There was no air up here, and no ether. There was nothing but the dark and the light, and the Earth far below as he spun around it over and over again. The sunlight would glow inside of him, making him warm and alive. The darkness froze the steam in his veins, sending him back to sleep.

And below him all those people! All those *lives!* Darby had been right. It was obvious now. But the old man had also been impatient. He had wanted to do in a single lifetime what should have taken many. He had tried to fix the world, and instead spawned a creature bent on destroying it.

Gabriel wouldn't die up here. His steam was slowly running out, but he would simply sleep in the cold and quiet. The part of him that was machine would survive until mankind was ready.

One day they would break the shackles of the planet that held them. They would rise up on a column of smoke and steam to find him waiting.

And he would be there for them, ready to help them remake the world.

Acknowledgments

It's been five years since I first began my journey with these characters, and the story of my own life over the two years since the first book came out has seemed almost as epic, although blissfully devoid of supervillains. But even without a superpowered nemesis, nothing in my life has been as constantly challenging as finally telling the origin of the Society of Steam.

And for those of you who are tempted to write a trilogy as your first series, remember that it won't be until the third book that you're supposed to be writing an ending.

You can't take any epic journey without great companions, and having recently discovered that gratitude is an antidote to fear, I'm going to unleash a big dose of thanks to those who made this last book possible:

Lou Anders, who made it all possible.

The Pyr graduating class of 2012: Clay & Susan Griffith, Sam Sykes, Jon Sprunk, Lisa Kay Michalski, Meghan Quinn.

Gabrielle Harbowy, for knowing me well enough to smother 4,000 words in their sleep and make a stronger book for it.

Jenny Cullum, who has willingly taken on the job of officially saving my ass on a daily basis.

My bestest friend, Ken Levine, who will probably never read this book, but helped me with it anyway.

Ted Naifeh, who is always generous and patient as long as he can compare everything to Batman.

Ken Vollmer, who read the whole damn thing when it wasn't ready to read, and then told me what parts needed fixing.

Ashley Murphree, who taught me that life is a river, and we fish gotz to swim right meow.

Rosanna Scimeca, who is way too talented, so she went to New York.

Joan Bowlen, who broke my heart precisely along its fault lines, and then stuck around for the aftermath.

Chris Bennett, who is always willing to chat.

Peter Zimmerman, who continues to help me discover the joy of new music. Also Fleetwood Mac, for some reason.

Douglas Rushkoff, who has always enjoyed my non-Euclidian view of the universe and has always told me to just write.

Nicholas Stohlman, who is not only a ridiculously talented artist, but is willing to share.

Shanna Germain, who manages to bring class and poise to anything and everything she touches.

Jonathon Swerdloff, who advises me on matters of the heart and agrees with me on almost nothing else.

Laurenn McCubbin, who never calls me first, but who I know still loves me.

Doctor Barbara Killian, who isn't afraid to put her medical skills to work in strange places.

Bruce Scanlon, who will be reaching enlightenment any day now, and Kathy Guidi who is closer than she thinks.

If I missed you, and you deserved to be in here, I apologize.

And thanks to everyone who has followed me this far. I hope you enjoyed the grand finale.

Andrew Mayer
San Francisco, October 2012

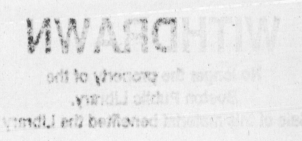

About the Author

ANDREW P. MAYER currently lives high atop Potrero Hill in San Francisco, California, where he often stares out across the city and wonders just how it is that he ended up back here.

When he isn't dreaming up new worlds of his own, he works as a digital media strategist, helping people to create and re-create their virtual realities.

He has also recently started to play his ukulele again. People of the planet Earth, beware!